Also by L.V. Gaudet

From Indigo Sea Press

The McAllister Farm

indigoseapress.com

Where The Bodies Are

By

L.V. Gaudet

Stiletto Books
Published by Indigo Sea Press
Winston-Salem

I hope you enjoy this book

L.V. Gaudet

Can you handle a little darkness?

Stiletto Books
Indigo Sea Press
302 Ricks Drive
Winston-Salem, NC 27103

First Stiletto Books edition published
January, 2016
Stiletto Books, Moon Sailor and all production design are trademarks of Indigo Sea Press, used under license.

For information regarding bulk purchases of this book, digital purchase and special discounts, please contact the publisher at indigoseapress.com

Cover design by Stacy Castanedo

Manufactured in the United States of America
ISBN 978-1-63066-345-2

Dedication and Acknowledgments

This story was years in the making, being completely re-written into something very different from the original idea. Perhaps the worst part of writing and editing this book was finding myself driven by my own compulsion, a compulsion to dig deeper into the story behind this one, making me put this book aside to delve into the darkness that lies within it. Or maybe that wasn't such a bad thing.

With that urge I wrote The McAllister Farm, a prequel to this story that goes deeper into the history of the story behind the killer and started writing White Van, an entirely different story within this killer's world.

I would like to thank my family for putting up with me, particularly my kids who have given me that special kind of crazy that makes a better writer. Many of my stranger ideas have come from them. And especially Steve, who is always coming to my rescue when my whole world falls apart from technical and, yes, user problems, repairing and replacing my laptop and recovering my files when I've thought I lost all my writing files.

I would also like to thank Pat Bertam, who encouraged me shortly after we met online to put my fears aside and publicly call myself a writer; and Mike Simpson at Indigo Sea Press for giving me this chance and publishing my first novel. As well, the online writing community for their support and help over the years and the real life people who very recently helped me with the nearly impossible job of writing the synopsis for *Where the Bodies Are*.

Part One: Jane Doe

1

Flies buzzed noisily around the over-filled garbage bins in the narrow alley. Bags of garbage were heaped against them as if the gluttonous bins had puked them out.

A small brown and black filth-matted mongrel trotted up the alley.

He paused briefly to sniff disinterestedly at the cool flesh of the dainty hand poking out beneath the bags of garbage next to the bins in the dirt-strewn lane.

Looking up at the darkening sky with sad brown eyes, he shivered and whined pitifully as a deep rumble rolled threateningly through the heavens.

With a shake of his coat the dog scampered off down the narrow alley as the first heavy drops began to fall.

Sunlight slanted through the thin slats of the hospital blinds, splashing across the pale face of the woman lying unconscious in the narrow bed. Her hair spilled across the white pillow in stark contrast with the antiseptic whiteness of the room. The harsh glare of the overhead lights made her look even more pale and drawn.

The machines beside the bed monitored life signs with soft beeps. The never ending noise of the hospital made the stillness of the room seem strange.

Footsteps entered the room, whispering lightly across the floor.

A competent masculine hand reached out, firmly gripping one limp wrist and lifting it gently from the bed.

Holding the slender appendage between two fingers, Doctor Greenburg studied his watch, checking the patient's pulse.

Carefully replacing the arm, he turned to the nurse who had just entered the room and came to stand beside him.

"Have you checked her file? Has there been any word from the police on her identity?" he asked.

Dr. Greenburg was a short balding man wearing an immaculately clean lab coat. The fine lines at the corners of his eyes and grey running through what little hair he had added to his distinguished authoritative look.

"No," the small mousey middle-aged nurse reported. "An officer was just here checking up on her. He said they haven't matched her description to anyone yet."

The nurse, Molly, fidgeted with her clipboard. Doctor Greenburg always made her nervous with his crisp businesslike manner and neatness bordering, she thought, on psychosis.

"I just can't understand it," confessed the doctor. "She's been here a month now and no one seems to have noticed her missing."

This troubled Doctor Greenburg deeply. The young woman could be his daughter. She shared with his daughter the kind of similarity so many young women of the same age seem to have with each other.

He brushed some non-existent dirt from his lab coat and strode toward the door, pausing briefly before going out into the hall.

Turning to the nurse he asked, "You're new here aren't you? What's your name?"

"Molly."

"Molly, have me paged as soon as you hear anything." He paused thoughtfully. "Or if her condition changes, although at this point I don't think it will."

"Yes Doctor."

He strode out of the room and down the hall.

With a sad look at the woman in the bed, Molly started checking the intravenous tubes and monitors. She stopped to scratch busily on the patient's chart after checking each thing.

She felt sorry for this mysterious patient.

"It's just not fair," she said to herself. "She's so pretty, so young; she just looks so innocent and helpless laying there." She shook her head in sad disbelief.

"I feel the same way," a man's voice interrupted her reverie.

Molly jumped, looking startled at this unexpected intrusion into her private thoughts.

She turned to the doorway to find an orderly standing there.

"I-I didn't realize you were there," she stammered, her heart pounding furiously with a mixture of emotions.

She felt both embarrassment at being caught talking to herself and the tightness of fear from the sudden intrusion that startled her.

The orderly was new to the hospital, even newer than her.

"In fact," Molly thought to herself, "didn't he start around the same time the Jane Doe came in?"

Something about him unnerved her, and not in a good way. A thin sense of danger that seemed a part of this man tickled at her nerves, making her feel off.

It wasn't the bad boy danger that excited many a young woman's pulse with a thrill of excitement and need to possess, to face the danger and tame the bad boy. No, this was the tingling of danger that turned your veins to ice and froze your mind in an instant of fight or flight panic.

Straightening, he stalked into the room, looking the nurse up and down, weighing her, assessing her character and more.

A sharp thrill of excitement involuntarily shivered up her spine as his eyes travelled her, her heart fluttering at the brief thought that a handsome man like this could actually even consider dowdy little Molly worthy of a look over even as her nerves screamed "Danger!"

"Is it true about her?" he asked in a conspiratorial whisper. "It's all over the hospital." He indicated the patient in the bed with a casual movement of his head.

A little flustered and a blush rising up her cheeks, Molly found herself answering although she knew she shouldn't. The tightness in the pit of her stomach made her feel no choice but to answer his questions.

"Yes," Molly said softly. "It was a miracle she was even alive at all when they found her." She paused, uncertainty clouding her eyes. But then she met his gaze again and continued as if with no will of her own.

"She's barely stable now and still being kept in a drug induced coma. No one thought the poor thing would last this long."

"So she still might die?"

"Yes, she probably will." The nurse looked at him searchingly, unsure for what.

"And no one has called the hospital looking for her yet?"

A grimace spoiled his face, making him look cruel. Was it of disgust or pleasure? She couldn't tell which.

"No," she replied. "The hospital contacted the police, but no one seems to have reported her missing."

She looked briefly at the woman in the bed, then turned back to him and said in a low whisper, "she isn't likely to ever wake up to tell us who she is either, even when the doctor does let her out of the drug induced coma."

Molly didn't know why she said this. She just felt like it was something she really should say to the orderly. Although at this point they could not be certain what affect the woman's head injuries would have on her, Molly felt a certainty deep inside that she would wake up and be just fine. She also felt it would be bad to tell the orderly this.

Molly often got these feelings. She even thought of herself as being a little bit psychic.

"So, no one knows who she is or where she came from," the orderly stated more to himself than to the nurse, pulling Molly back to the moment. He then turned and sauntered out of the room looking almost satisfied, like the cat that just ate the bird.

Feeling uneasy, Molly watched him go.

She turned back to fussing with the patient.

"And apparently," she mumbled to herself, "no one cares to find her."

2

An ancient rusting brown Oldsmobile, an anomaly on today's roads filled mostly with newer cars, rolled to a stop in front of the building which contained the police station, law courts, and city hall.

The car's mottled color was more the result of a terminal case of rust than from its brown paint.

Its springs and joints creaked and squealed as it rocked to a standstill at the curb in front of the building's entrance. The engine coughed and stuttered sickly when the ignition was shut off. A faint ticking as the overheated engine quickly began to cool came from under the hood like a chronic cough.

The driver's door hinges screeched in protest when it was thrust open.

A large man grunted as he pulled his morbidly obese frame out of the car. His rumpled clothes, greying uncombed hair, and untrimmed moustache gave him an unkempt look more suiting to a vagabond than a police detective.

The car door shrieked as he slammed it closed and ambled towards the building, ignoring the no parking sign standing tall next to the car.

Breathing heavily and puffing air through his shaggy moustache, Detective Jim McNelly stomped up the stairs and into the building.

It was the sort of older civic building you would expect to find in a smaller city that was more of a town.

The city was small enough that fitting all these civic offices into the same building was simply a cost effective measure, but large enough for a single police station to not be enough.

Inside the doors was a small crowded foyer. Straight ahead lay the city hall offices, and to the right lay a hallway leading to the law court offices. To the left, past a steady stream of people, a couple rank vagabonds, and a boy selling shoe shines at a small single chair stand that belonged in an era long gone by, was a dirty but wide stairway leading to the police station on the second floor.

This was a somewhat ill-considered arrangement. Having the police station on the main floor and saving the officers from the peril of wrestling unwilling guests up a flight of stairs would have made much more sense, but the mayor and his cronies were not about to start doing stairs when they could ensconce themselves on the main floor by right of position.

The normally empty foyer was filled with people, most of them talking animatedly or looking around eagerly for someone to talk animatedly with.

A constable hung around near the bottom of the stairs, stopping people and asking their business before letting them ascend to the police station above.

McNelly groaned inwardly, his eyes flashing with anger.

News of this case must have leaked. And, like any small city, the news spread like wildfire through the gossip mills.

No doubt by now most of the city has heard some twisted version of what little is known, well spiced with rumour and speculation.

The mammoth detective bullied his way through the throng, mounting the stairs like a tired behemoth, his breath wheezing in and out with an unhealthy heavy effort.

"Hey, you can't park there," the constable called up to him. The front of the building was supposed to be for cruisers with detainees.

McNelly waved a hand dismissively, not bothering to look back as he continued his climb.

Breaching the second floor, he entered a large room fronted by a long desk for complainants.

The police station buzzed with activity. This was not unusual for a small city with only one police station, but the activity had a more frantic edge to it than normal.

The discovery of a woman's body and then the leak to the media about the first woman, a living survivor, suggesting the possibility of a serial killer stalking their city, had put the whole department on edge.

A red-beaked man stood behind the desk grudgingly helping a nattering old lady fill out a form. She brandished her cane wildly as she fervently gesticulated her story. The officer's bored putty-like face looked as though he had one foot in the grave already from an excessive love of alcohol.

A young man dressed in tattered leather, hair dyed black and spiked, jeans adorned with chains, bad tattoos and piercings standing next to her cringed and edged a little further away with each wide swing of her cane.

Desks crowded the room haphazardly, most occupied. A carnival of clattering keyboards, whispering of shuffled papers, scratching pens, whining, crying, swearing and complaining bounced from wall to wall; amplified by the lousy acoustics of the room. Many of the officers were busy taking statements from victims or suspects.

A large round clock hanging high on the wall silently ticked the seconds away, marching through time in a steady cadence, reminding all that time stopped for no one.

Angling his way past the complainants and through the entryway in the counter, Detective McNelly entered the hubbub of the section beyond. His furious gaze cutting a path through the commotion, McNelly stormed through the central office towards the door of a rear office.

The tension in the room visibly increased as heads turned to watch the volatile detective move through their midst, a breath of relief passing silently in his wake.

The rear office was a much smaller room, containing only three desks closely bunched and a row of four filing cabinets crammed into one corner. The only wall decorations were a worn map and two corkboards, one overflowing with photographs, mostly children and young women, all missing. The other board was currently empty.

The window on the far wall looked down into the street below and the illegally parked ugly brown Oldsmobile.

The desk nearest the window was occupied.

McNelly trudged to it and stood over a pretty thirty plus woman sitting there working busily on her computer.

She tensed with his proximity, obviously annoyed by him. The computer beeped angrily when she typed in a wrong code, her fingers misdirected because of his presence.

McNelly was frustrated, a dark mood hanging over him. He

hated this case. He hated all his cases, the pain and suffering that led to them landing on his desk, events he thought he should have somehow stopped before they could ever happen. He stared at the woman's back, his frustration making him lash out at anything within easy reach.

"Damn it Beth, don't you know how to use that thing yet?" he growled, towering over her to watch the computer screen.

"Get off my back and I wouldn't be having any problems," she snapped, her ruby red lips forming an angry tight line. Her long nails, painted to match her lipstick, tapped smartly as they hit the keys. Her eyes showed early age lines from squinting too much at a computer screen.

Beth was getting frustrated too, from both her lack of success with this case and McNelly's mood since they got the case.

NO RECORD appeared on the screen for the last of too many times.

"Another dead end," she said flatly.

McNelly moaned, running a pudgy calloused hand through already untidy brown hair.

"That's all you've given me so far, is one dead end after another." McNelly swore fervently. He was talking more to the case than to Beth.

He stalked off to pace the small room.

He thought as he paced, his mind working as ponderously as his body, grasping details and rearranging them like a puzzle built in too many dimensions for the average mind to grasp.

"If you think you can do any better Jim then be my guest," Beth said, pushing herself from the chair.

Beth's comment brought McNelly back from his musings. He hadn't really heard what she said because his mind had been somewhere else.

"I can only work with what you give me, and with the room to think!" Beth emphasized this last.

She stood there, arms crossed angrily, glaring at him.

"Damn, she looks gorgeous when she's pissed," McNelly thought. Of course he would never repeat these thoughts for anyone's ears, especially Beth's.

He felt a light burning of shame for having taken his frustration out on Beth. It wasn't her fault this case was completely leadless. She was the best there was at her job, digging through the invisible mountains of computer crap to find that one missing needle in the haystack that might be relevant to a case.

Grunting acknowledgement of defeat, he gruffly apologized.

"Sorry Beth. I didn't mean to be so rough. You're doing a great job."

She looked at him reproachfully.

"Really, I mean it," he insisted.

"Then get out and let me do my job." She sat back down and resumed her work. No one else in the department would have dared talk to McNelly this way.

"Okay, okay," he raised his hands in front of him, palms outward, as if to ward off an attack.

Resignedly he turned to leave, pausing in the doorway, his large frame filling it.

"If you come up with anything on the Jane Doe in the hospital, I want to know immediately. Then call the hospital and get them off my back if you got an ID." He ran the thick fingers of his right hand through his hair, looking quite haggard.

He felt haggard. Every time he got a case like this it kept him up night after sleepless night until the case was solved. He'd spend long hours cruising the darkened streets in his ancient Oldsmobile and haunting twenty-four hour coffee shops, mindlessly guzzling black coffee and gnawing on anything from donuts to jerky of indeterminate age discovered in a dusty jar on the counter of a hole-in-the-wall drug store where he stopped in to get something to sooth the burning acid of chronic heartburn and his ulcer. His mind would compulsively turn over every scrap of information on the case, over and over, obsessed with it, unable to settle into the quiet hum of blank thought necessary for him to sleep.

"In the meantime I'll be contacting the press," McNelly continued. "It's already hit the papers anyway, damned leak. Maybe with more coverage someone will come forward and identify the Jane Doe."

9

"You do that," Beth said dismissively, without looking at him or pausing in her work. She smirked behind his back as he waddled away, a small victory smile.

3

Smoke curled lazily from the cigarette bobbing beneath the shaggy moustache over Jim McNelly's mouth. His fat stubby fingers gripped it and tapped the ashes onto the dirty floor.

Behind him a no smoking sign hung on the wall, looking old and yellowed from age and the grime of many cigarettes.

The lighting in the bar was dim, though not dim enough to hide the shabbiness of the place. This was a neighborhood most people fortunate enough to not live in would not dare to visit willingly, and the local bar fit right in with the neighborhood.

Gulping his beer, he licked the foam off his moustache as he studied the man sitting across from him at the small scarred table.

The man was Lawrence Hawkworth, a reporter with less than moral morals and a penchant for getting himself into all the wrong situations, but with an uncanny ability at uncovering the dirty truth about almost anything.

McNelly didn't like the reporter. The man was completely unlike himself. He was the dirtiest, most unscrupulous reporter in the city, and was not only his secret weapon but also his best friend.

Yeah, he didn't like the man, but he loved him like a brother. The sort of brother that annoyed the hell out of you, but when push comes to shove you'd drop everything to have his back.

McNelly smirked inwardly, his mind roaming over some of their past exploits. They had a past, and what a past it was, this most unlikely pair of friends. He knew the feeling was mutual. Hawkworth disliked him as much as he did the tall scrawny man, yet he knew he could trust the man with his life and his confidence.

The rail thin reporter scratched busily at his notepad, stopped, and pushed the pencil behind his ear. He somewhat resembled a buzzard.

"So, let me read this back to you."

Pausing, he looked over what he had just written.

"White female, about twenty to twenty-five years old, five

foot, five inches, brown hair, almost a dirty blond, blue eyes." Lawrence looked up expectantly.

"Yeah, that's right," McNelly nodded.

Rock music beat quietly in the background.

Leaning forward, his reporter instincts buzzing, Lawrence's voice dropped to a conspiratorial whisper.

"Rumour has it she was found dumped in with the trash in an alley."

Blinking his surprise at this information that had been kept a closely guarded secret, the fat detective's jowls wobbled as his mouth snapped shut.

Hawkworth was both a trusted source of information and a reliable method of releasing certain information, but it still bothered him that the man always seemed to already know information that had not been released.

This could jeopardize their efforts to sort the nuts from the perpetrator if it got out.

"Who else knows?" McNelly wondered silently.

"Yeah, by a store owner," McNelly said. "He went out back to empty some trash and almost dumped it right on top of her. Chinese herbal place it was."

Ignoring this attempt by the detective to fish for just how much he knew, and Lawrence knew it was no Chinese herbal shop, the reporter's eyes shone excitedly with the confirmation his information was correct.

"She's dead?" Hawkworth eagerly declared. It was more a statement than a question. He knew the woman lay unconscious in a hospital bed. He was just toying with McNelly now.

"Almost. She's being kept in a drug induced coma while her body mends through the worst of it, and it's not looking good."

McNelly eyed Lawrence warily. The man was a tricky sparring partner when it came to hiding and divulging information.

"What happened to her?" Hawkworth asked, a spark of concern showing through his buzzard-like expression.

Fidgeting and seeming slightly embarrassed, a quality that just didn't fit on this large brute of a man, the detective replied in a low voice.

"Brutally beaten and left for dead," McNelly said.

The reporter sat back in his chair, a dazed expression on his face. He reached for his glass and downed the amber liquid in one gulp, grimacing as the bourbon burned as it coursed down his throat. He hated bourbon. He hated the smell of it, the taste of it, and how it burned the throat. That's why he drank it. The displeasure of the drink reminded him that distasteful things should be reviled, not enjoyed the way he enjoyed them in his job.

"Could mean trouble for her when he finds out she's alive." Hawkworth seemed concerned.

"Yeah, we'll have to keep a close watch on her hospital room. It may not be just her family that comes looking for her." McNelly gave the reporter a meaningful look.

"Especially if he thinks she can identify him," Hawkworth observed.

"Yeah," McNelly agreed.

"I'd like to interview the doctor and the shopkeeper for the story," Hawkworth said.

"No." McNelly gave the reporter a warning look.

"Why not?"

"That's our job and we want as little information getting out on this as possible."

McNelly blinked through the smoke and dim light to the bartender, caught his eye, and nodded to indicate his order for another round. He looked back to the man sitting across the table, trying to be menacing.

"You stay away from them Hawkworth, or I may just find something to charge you with," he threatened, knowing that this would only encourage the reporter to dig around on this case.

Quite frankly, they were up against a brick wall in a dead end ally on this case with nowhere to go. They were going to need any help they could get on this one, just so long as the reporter didn't step over the line and report anything without checking in first.

Hawkworth could typically be trusted in this regard, although he liked to tease the opposite. Actually, detective McNelly scared the crap out of him despite their long-standing

13

friendship. Regardless, Hawkworth wouldn't dare release any information that might jeopardize a case this important. He could be unscrupulous at times, but he did have a conscience.

"Like what?" Hawkworth asked innocently with feigned indignation, knowing full well that his investigative tactics left the detective a long list of possible charges if he knew even a fraction of what he's done. And he knew the detective knew more than he would have liked.

The waitress brought another round to the table.

"Obstruction of justice, interference with an officer performing his duties, sticking your bloody vulture-beaked where is doesn't belong ..."

"I get it, I get it," Hawkworth interrupted impatiently. They have danced this same dance many times at this same worn table.

"Good, keep it that way." The fat detective downed his beer in one gulp.

Pushing himself up from the table, he butted out his cigarette and stared down at the other man.

"Not a word gets printed without checking with me, right?" It wasn't really a question.

Hawkworth nodded.

"One more thing," McNelly added.

Hawkworth waited, knowing what was coming.

"You know I could lose my badge for this, for giving you this information."

Hawkworth nodded again. Nothing more needed to be said. They had danced this same dance many times and they both knew well that both knew the score.

McNelly nodded back, turned away, and concentrated on not staggering as he stumbled his way out of the bar and into the blistering daylight beyond the dimly lit room, blinded by the drastic change in light.

The reporter bobbed his head in a bird-like fashion as he turned over the facts in his mind. His excitement grew in leaps as he dwelt on the detective's insistence that he leave these people alone. He smiled a sharp unpleasant grimace, but his expression quickly turned deadpan, then sad, and then angry as he thought about what this monster had done.

4

Smoke curled lazily from the cigarette lying on the rim of an overflowing ashtray, tracing intricate patterns in the still office air like a belly dancer from the netherworld. Grasping it loosely in his fat stubby fingers, Jim McNelly tapped the long ash off the end, missing the ashtray. The gray cylinder of ash disintegrated into a pile of powder when it hit the desktop.

Of course the building was a no-smoking building, they all are. McNelly apparently didn't notice or didn't care.

He was alone in the office.

"Yeah, sure," he said into the phone. He paused, listening, slouching back lazily in the chair. Taking a hard pull on the cigarette, he held in the smoke, clearly enjoying it.

His face turned hard.

Sitting up abruptly, he let the smoke out so quickly he almost choked on it.

"No," he demanded into the phone. "That's not good enough." He slammed his fist onto the desk with a loud thunk.

"This can't wait! I need some answers and I need them now!" He listened.

"No!" he barked, "Now!" McNelly slammed the receiver onto its cradle.

His face burned with anger, and his mind boiled with the details of the conversation.

"Not good enough, not fucking good enough," McNelly muttered to himself.

There was something he was missing, something important. He could feel it, as if it hung invisibly right in front of him and all he had to do was reach out and grab it, if he could just see it.

"Calm down," a man laughed from the doorway. "Hey, I thought this was a no-smoking building."

McNelly tensed with anger, swivelling violently in his chair to confront this joker. His glare broke instantly into a grin.

It was the orderly from the hospital, now dressed in street clothes.

The orderly, in fact, is a detective with McNelly's team and is working undercover to watch the Jane Doe in the hospital in case the perpetrator showed up there to come after her. The perp often does for one reason or another. The violence of the attack suggested it was personal, giving them more reason to expect the woman's attacker to show up.

"Michael, how's the hospital gig going?" Although he wouldn't call him a friend, McNelly liked Michael Underwood. He was the sort of guy you instinctively liked the moment you met him, the sort you could see yourself doing things with regardless what sort of things you were into doing. He was the kind of guy who would be just as at ease at a baseball game or guys poker night as at Aunt Martha's quilting group.

Still standing in the doorway, Michael smirked.

"Cleaning puke and bedpans is a real shit, but dealing with these junkies with degrees sure as hell beats the scum on the streets I usually deal with."

"How's our fair lady holding up?"

"If you call lying around like a vegetable progress, then she's doing great."

Michael blinked slowly, deliberately, and took a deep breath before he continued.

"She's found herself a mother hen, though."

The fat detective raised one bushy eyebrow in question.

"A nurse, she started there a few months before all this began."

"Is she getting in the way?" McNelly asked.

"Mother hens are usually trouble despite, or maybe because of, their best intentions," McNelly thought. He didn't like trouble.

"She will," Michael laughed, "I think she's suspicious of me, like I might be the monster that did this to that poor girl, or might try to date her daughter or something."

Jim chuckled as he lit another cigarette.

"Great, just great," he grumbled through a cloud of smoke. "This is just what we need." He smoothed down his moustache in irritation, thinking, distractedly rolling scraps of information around in his head.

"We have a lot to talk about," Michael said, closing the door before coming to sit in the chair across the desk from his boss.

16

5

Molly looked up nervously from the nurse's desk she stood behind, searching the empty hallway around her.

She shivered.

Shifting her weight uneasily, she tried to calm herself.

"What's the matter with you, Molly?" she berated herself. "Why are you acting like this? Feeling so scared? You've done night shifts before."

Unable to rid herself of this disquieting sensation of being watched, studied by unseen eyes, she jumped in fear and almost ran when the elevator nearby pinged to announce its arrival.

The doors slid open, releasing the babble of voices. The car was full for this late hour; staff returning from a break.

A nurse exited the elevator before its doors slid shut on the rest of the passengers. She went away down a hall with the unhurried fast gait of a nurse on a mission.

Catching a blur of movement out of the corner of her eye, Molly whirled around to see the orderly from earlier disappearing around a corner down the hall.

Her eyes widened in wonder and a little excitement tinged fear.

"He's been watching me," she gasped quietly. "Why has he been watching me?" Her mind raced, her chest tightening with the thought that maybe he was attracted to her, and sunk as she quickly dismissed that silly notion. A man like that didn't get attracted to a plain-Jane frump like her.

It was a relief too. Something about him scared her. Molly couldn't put her finger on it. It was just an uneasy feeling, like you get when you think something is out of place but can't figure out what it is.

Her face settled into a determined but strained look as the realization hit her. She paled noticeably.

"It's her," she exclaimed. "It's her he's watching. He's only been watching me because he has to get past me to get to her."

Horrified, she looked back up the empty hallway where he disappeared.

"What does he want with that poor girl? Is he the monster that attacked her? What is he going to do to me for being in the way?"

"Don't be so silly Molly," she admonished herself. "Of course he isn't that man. He just works here and everyone is concerned about Jane Doe."

Standing there, swaying slightly, she closed her eyes and turned back to the long nurse's desk, facing the elevators.

Molly realized now why she'd felt so uneasy and jumpy all evening. She had been getting a bad feeling about something without knowing what.

Taking a deep calming breath, she opened her eyes and took a step back, startled.

Standing in front of the elevator door, looking around curiously, stood a tall rail thin man, vaguely resembling a buzzard.

He rubbed his long beaky nose and turned to look at her. He gave her a toothy smile that more resembled a wolf's grin with his too big teeth in his scrawny face.

He approached with a purposeful step.

"Hi there," he announced, "I'm Lawrence Hawkworth." He stood leaning on the desk, surreptitiously glancing at the papers and charts lying on the desktop.

Fidgeting and trying to collect herself, Molly looked inquiringly up at the man. A distant part of her mind wondered why she hadn't heard the ping of the elevator.

"May I help you sir?" she asked in her best no-nonsense nurse voice.

"I am looking for Jane Doe," he stated abruptly.

"Visiting hours are from noon to eight p.m.," she said coldly. "You'll have to come back tomorrow."

Hawkworth quickly changed tracks. Telling the woman he was a reporter clearly would not help him here.

He stared back at her, feigning surprise.

"But ... but, she's my sister," he stammered.

"Hmph," she looked him up and down with a nursely snort.

There was certainly no resemblance at all between this ugly man and the pretty young woman lying comatose in a room nearby.

"And I'm her sister," she glared. "Leave or I'll call security."

Ok, so the nurse isn't going to buy the concerned brother tactic, Lawrence thought. Truth after all? Maybe. Perhaps with a touch of embellishment.

"Ok, you got me," he deferred, holding his hands in front of him as though to ward off her wrath. "She's not my sister."

She looked at him reproachfully, hands on hips, saying nothing.

"Lawrence Hawkworth of the InterCity Voice," he declared confidently, extending his impossibly long arm to her, fingers spread like long bony spider legs, a gesture indicating she should reach out and grab his hand in a friendly handshake.

Looking at his hand, the thought repulsed Molly in some indefinable way. She ignored his outstretched hand.

"I don't read that paper," she said dismissively, obviously intended to show that the name and title meant nothing to her.

"What do you want?" she asked sternly.

"I just want to ask you some questions about Jane Doe, the woman who was attacked and left for dead."

"She's in a coma and you can't see her."

She came out from behind the desk, positioning herself between the reporter and the room where the girl in question lay.

"That's all I can tell you."

Molly motioned towards the elevator.

"Now leave before I call security."

"Hey, I'm just trying to get some facts for my article," Hawkworth wheedled. "Surely you can tell me something."

He gave her his best hopeful pleading look which, unfortunately, looked more sinister than needy.

"Come on," he begged. "I only want to help the poor girl."

He sighed.

"No one has claimed her have they?"

He saddened his expression.

"No one seems to even know she's missing, do they?" he continued.

He tried to look her in the eyes, but she avoided eye contact.

"She must have someone somewhere," he pleaded. "Family, friends…"

Molly's misgivings almost wavered.

19

She looked at the reporter sternly, trying not to show how distraught she really felt, and shook her head slowly.

"What condition is she in?" he asked. "What are her injuries? Has anybody claimed her yet? Is she improving? Waking up?"

Molly reached for the phone on the desk to call security.

Lawrence caught her hand on the receiver, covering it with his long fingers.

She trembled, nearly jumping back in panic.

Looking around for help, she realized for the first time that the hallway was still deserted. She was alone with this strange man. Even seeing the orderly who keeps hanging around that poor girl's room would be a relief right now.

They stared each other down, the tension and her fear increasing.

Both Molly and the reporter flinched and turned in surprise at the commanding male voice that interrupted them.

"May I help you?" a man demanded. "Or are you just here to harass our nurses?"

"Dr. Greenburg," Molly gasped.

The reporter smiled confidently at the doctor.

"Hi there, as I was saying to your lovely nurse here," he gestured toward the somewhat frumpy and still jumpy Molly, "I'm Lawrence Hawkworth with the InterCity Voice."

"And I suppose you're going to tell me that you have a family member or friend staying with us," the doctor remarked sarcastically.

"Well, I ..." the tall man started.

"He claims to be the brother of our mystery woman in room 214B," the nurse cut in sharply.

Her expression changed quickly, realizing her mistake in revealing the girl's room number to this odd bird of a man, and worse, right in front of the doctor.

Doctor Greenburg raised both eyebrows questioningly.

"Well, actually," the reporter began again, "I'm trying to find out more about the Jane Doe for my article for the paper."

"She's not doing any interviews at the moment, so please leave," the doctor ordered.

Standing around the corner, Detective Michael Underwood adjusted his orderly's uniform again.

"Damn uniform is too small," he complained in a quiet whisper to himself. "Can't they at least get me clothes that fit?" The shoulder seams dug in uncomfortably along with seams in other places. The uniform felt constrictive and twisted no matter how much he pulled and tugged to fix it.

He glanced at his watch again before sneaking another look at the trio standing in front of the nurses' desk by the elevators.

"Can't they just kick him out already?" he grumbled impatiently. "That doctor has been trying to make Hawkworth leave for ten minutes now."

The mousy looking nurse stood with her legs spread in a determined stance as she glared wrathfully at the ugly tall man.

The short doctor stubbornly shook his head "no", the ceiling lights glaring off his bald forehead while his hands roamed his lab coat impulsively in search of offensive lint that wasn't there.

The reporter continued smiling like a cunning wolf; his arms gesticulating wildly as he excitedly explained the merits of getting the story about Jane Doe in the newspaper.

Michael didn't want the reporter to see him and risk the man blowing his cover with a slip of the tongue or a sign of recognition on his face.

Michael turned his watchful gaze away from the trio to stare gently at the closed door to room 214B.

6

The little brass bell hanging over the door jingled merrily as Lawrence pushed open the door to the little gift shop.

The frail looking elderly shopkeeper smiled a greeting at the tall gawky man coming into his store.

He smiled back, nodding in reply to the older man's welcome.

On pretence of inspecting the shelves of ornaments, stuffed toys, and various trinkets, Lawrence wandered slowly through the store, waiting for the two other customers to leave.

When they finally left he approached the elderly shopkeeper standing behind the counter.

"May I help you?" the shopkeeper asked, giving Hawkworth a friendly smile.

Hawkworth studied him briefly and decided on the direct approach.

"Hello there," he extended his hand. "I'm Lawrence Hawkworth with the InterCity Voice. I'd like to ask you a few questions about the woman you found in the alley behind your store."

Flustered, the shopkeeper timidly reached his arm out, allowing the tall man to wrap a large paw around his small bony hand, covering it effectively like a mutated cocoon. He looked down at his hand a moment then up at the tall man.

The old man suddenly felt even more infirm and frail, little more than a wraith that would blow away in a puff of smoke at any moment. His face reddened, he could feel the flush blossoming out to include his neck and ears, tinting them scarlet.

"Are you the one who found her?" the reporter asked, although he already knew the answer.

"Y-yes."

Lawrence retrieved a small writing pad from his pocket, flipped it open, and then pulled a pencil from behind his ear.

Licking the tip, he put it to the paper and looked at the shopkeeper expectantly over the circular rim of his wireframe glasses.

"Your name?" he asked.

"Uh, Harry Lacerte."

"Ok Harry, let's start with the basics. What were you doing when you found the body?"

"Uh, taking out the trash."

Hungrily, Lawrence got to the heart of the matter.

"Describe it for me please," a look of concern clouded his face.

It was important the interviewee think he is sincerely concerned for his well-being.

"If you can, that is. Tell me as much as you feel you can handle."

"I can't," Harry shook his head sadly. His stomach turned to acid at the thought of that terrible moment.

"The police told me not to talk to anyone about it." Harry felt nervous. You always did what the police said, and they told him not to talk to anyone.

Lawrence tsked in disappointment.

"But you must talk," he urged. "Right now, as we speak, that poor girl is laying all alone in a hospital bed with nobody. Nobody even knows she's there. No family, no friends. They must be so worried for her, not knowing where she is and all. This article may be her family's only chance at finding out she's in that hospital bed. What if she has a cat? Who's feeding the cat? Do her loved ones even know she's missing? That poor girl is depending on us, on you." As he spoke, Lawrence's gestures complemented his words, bringing more urgency to them, a well-rehearsed act.

Harry's flush deepened. He ached for this girl's pain and suffering, her loneliness. His frail body trembled with distress.

Harry responded in a thin voice.

"This is all just too much," he shook his head sadly. "I won't be able to deal with any customers after this."

Stepping out from behind the counter, he went to the door and locked it. Turning the "Open" sign over to show passersby the words "Sorry, we're closed ... please call again", he turned back to the tall gawky man.

"Let's go sit in the back room," he suggested. Leading the

way, he offered Lawrence a coffee (being an avid teetotaller he had no liquor in his store, though at this moment he was questioning the merit of this abstinence).

He began his narrative as they sat across from each other in his little office with cups of steaming coffee.

"The day I found that poor girl, I thought she was dead you know, when I found her. This is what happened ..."

"And thank you very much," the elderly shopkeeper smiled brightly at the middle-aged man standing across the counter from him.

Closing the cash register drawer with a quiet sound, he escorted his last customer for the day to the door.

"Have a nice evening," he waved to the departing man with one frail arm as he closed and locked the door.

Turning over the Open sign to show the store was closed, he began his cleanup chores for the day.

He was glad the day was over. He loved his little shop, its customers, and the care it needed, but he tired so early these days.

In the storage room at the back of the shop Harry turned off all the shop's lights, leaving only a token security light illuminating the back room. The light shone just enough through the doorway and into the front store area to outline the shelves of neatly arranged goods and any unwanted intruders.

Picking up the bag of garbage, Harry left by the back door leading to the alley behind the shop, locking the door behind him.

He whistled spiritedly to himself as he walked up the alley to the garbage bins. There was a group of bins piled high with garbage and more bags and boxes standing sentry on the ground against them.

He made sure he selected a stable spot on the unstable mountain of bags and other refuse for his garbage.

Out of the corner of his eye Harry spotted a hand, the arm visible halfway up to the forearm, sticking out of the rubbish pile at his feet. The dainty hand was dirty, streaked and splotched with some sort of red-brown paint, and dangling in a shallow

24

puddle of dirty rainwater. It had been raining on and off all day.

Looking down at the hand for a moment, he merely registered that someone had thrown out an old mannequin and thought nothing more of it.

He was adding his garbage to the pile, shifting one foot forward for balance as he leaned over the garbage bin to place his bags on top of the mound.

His foot bumped the mannequin's arm.

It moved slightly with the impact, but it moved soundlessly, felt soft not hard. It did not scrape against the concrete like a plastic mannequin hand should.

Harry pulled back from the pile, trash bag still in hand.

Bending forward a little, he studied the hand more closely. He pushed it with his foot, listening for the scraping sound, feeling for the hard plastic. It moved soundlessly, felt soft but firm, not hard.

Startled, he took a hurried step backwards, almost dropping his trash bag.

Gathering his courage, he knelt down to examine his find more closely. He reached forward with his left hand and discovered, to his surprise, that he was still holding the trash bag. Tossing it aside, he tentatively poked at the arm. It was firm, giving only slightly, yet felt soft, like flesh. He placed his hand on it. The flesh was cold. Too cold to be alive, he was sure, but still soft.

The words "fresh kill" leapt unbidden into his mind.

Shaking his head to rid it of this morbid thought he pulled some of the garbage away, digging it out.

The rest of the arm appeared, obviously a young woman's arm. The top of the head appeared, then a face. It was a badly bruised and swollen face, unrecognizable through all the crusted dried blood. Rivulets of blood had dried as they seeped from her cracked lips and bloodied nose, like streams frozen to ice, caught in a sudden chill that stopped its flow mid-gurgle.

Harry staggered backwards, almost falling over. His pale face looked like a terrified ghostly phantom in the darkening gloom.

The shadows were long and getting deeper as dusk chased

away the sunlight, preparing for the blackness of night.

Unable to quit, he attacked the pile of debris, trembling, drooling slightly, his eyes crazed. Digging frantically, he threw garbage into the air.

The rest of her body appeared, dishevelled and beaten.

Gagging, he turned and ran in a stumbling shuffle back to the store's rear entrance. He fumbled the keys from his pocket, dropping them with a merry clink on the pavement. Trembling, he tried three times before his fingers could coordinate enough to pick them up.

His mind began playing tricks on him, imagining he heard the soft sound of shoes scraping on the ground behind him, heavy breathing approaching, and a menacing presence just out of sight. His head swivelled, looking around fearfully. Not seeing anything, he turned back to the locked door, frantically trying to open it.

The wavering key could not find its way into the lock. It glanced off the side, hit the top, and finally bounced out of his hand to the pavement at his feet.

This time it took him only two tries before his palsied fingers finally grasped it firmly enough to bring the key back to the lock. It hit home on the first try. He almost pulled the key out of the lock before he realized that he finally did it.

Wiping his brow with a quivering hand, he turned the key. It wouldn't budge. Sweat trickled down his face despite the cool breeze wafting down the alley.

He tried again, harder. It wouldn't move.

He slapped his forehead, realizing what he was doing wrong in his panicked state. He groaned miserably.

"Wrong way," he hissed.

He turned the key the other way. With a dull thud the tumbler fell over, releasing the door lock.

He gasped a breath of relief, not realizing he had been holding it.

Harry ran into the store, chased by the scrape-rustle of papers blowing along the pavement, sounding more like skeletal fingers reaching out to pull him back into the growing darkness.

He slammed the door closed behind him, his fingers

fumbling with the lock.

He almost tripped and fell running for his little office, slamming and locking that door behind him too.

Picking up the phone, he was trembling so hard he dropped it with an earth-shattering clatter. Scooping it up, he dialled the police station's number directly, a number he had memorized long ago from keeping shop in a not so nice neighborhood.

"Hello, police, how may I help you?" a thin slightly metallic voice asked him.

"Unnngh," he croaked into the phone, the words choked off by the intense fear and shock constricting his throat.

"Hello?"

"Unngh—uh—I—Uh."

"Is this a prank?" The voice sounded irritated.

"W-woman—I—uh—dead."

"Who is this?" the officer demanded.

"Uh, H-Harry," he managed to squeak out.

"What is this about?"

"I—uh, a w-woman," he choked out, "dead ... d-dead. In the alley." He nearly fainted with the effort of forcing the words out.

"Where are you calling from?" the officer asked, sounding more brisk and businesslike now.

"M-my—my store."

"And then the police came and blocked off the alley," the elderly man finished his narrative.

"And you called the ambulance?" the reporter asked.

"No. The police, they must have."

"They didn't suspect you, did they?" The concern intentionally showed through Lawrence's eager expression. Of course they didn't, but this was part of the act.

"They said I'm not a suspect," Harry chuckled sadly, humourlessly. "But at first they questioned me like I was Hannibal the Cannibal."

They talked long into the night.

After leaving the little shop, Hawkworth went around the building instead of across the street to his car.

He had to walk almost the whole block before he found an opening to the alley behind the strip of stores.

Once in the ally Hawkworth backtracked, counting the doors as he went until he was certain he found the right spot.

There, in the alley not far from the rear exit of what he was sure was the right shop, were the garbage bins.

The bins were large and empty now, their contents having been removed following the discovery of the young woman left tossed out with the trash. That is, unless they were taken away bin and all for inspection and replaced with others.

It was dark, darker than it would have been when the shopkeeper was closing up shop.

Hawkworth stopped and just stood there, between the shop door and the trash bins.

He pictured the man coming from the door, letting the door close behind him, clicking as it locked automatically.

He watched as the man who wasn't there ambled over towards the trash bins, garbage bag weighting him down. He pictured the overfilled bins, trash heaped on the ground around them, loose garbage fluttering in the breeze.

In his mind the wind picked up. It was cool. Clouds covered the sky. It had been raining off and on since the day before. He knew this because he'd looked it up.

Knowing little details like the weather could put the whole story into a new perspective during the investigation period.

He imagined the old shopkeeper approaching the piled garbage, selecting just the right spot to add his own bags to the debris pile, and his shocked reaction to finding the woman who appeared to be dead.

He watched the shopkeeper scramble back to his shop's back door, frantic and tormented.

The moment the door closed behind the retreating elderly man the alley changed.

Hawkworth now imagined the events that must have happened some time earlier.

The sky darkened, the alley becoming very dark. The sky overhead filled with dark storm clouds, chasing away what little light might have been offered by the moon and the stars.

He imagined it would have to be late, very late, a time when no one would likely come along.

The alley was deserted, the garbage piled high, and the shadows hiding whatever might be huddled there in pools of utter blackness.

The alley had a sinister feel to it that sent a shiver down his spine.

The sound of tires splashing through a puddle came from somewhere not far away and a dark car turned the corner, entering the alley with its headlights off, driving slowly down the narrow road behind the shops.

No, he corrected himself, driving at night without headlights would attract attention.

The car turned the corner into the alley, its headlights splashing the grimy alley with light like twin flashlight beams. The car drove slowly down the alley, stopping by the garbage bins piled with refuse.

The lights clicked off soundlessly.

The car he saw was dark, it looked black, but that meant nothing and he decided to call it black. Having the very rare form of color blindness, Monachromacy, color was meaningless to him. For him the world was all shades of grey. But living in a world that defined everything by color, he had learned to think in colors too, as though all those shades of sameness had some meaning. Naming shades of grey that could be any color had become as automatic as putting that next foot forward.

A man got out of the car. He was shrouded in darkness, his identity as much a mystery as is that of the man who abandoned the young woman for dead.

The man looked around, reassuring himself that no one was around, before moving to the back of the car and opening the trunk.

Lawrence tried to imagine what the man must be feeling, the nervousness of getting caught as he dumped the body.

Another quick glance before the man pulled the woman's body from the trunk, her limbs falling loosely, swinging slightly, and walked to the piled garbage, her weight doing little to affect his walk.

Did the man just drop her carelessly?

No, he didn't think so, not when the man took such care covering the woman up under the debris.

The man kicked at the trash bags piled on the ground, knocking some away to leave a flattish area like a bed.

The man stooped down, gently laying the woman on top of the pile of trash, taking care to arrange her legs and arms.

The man gently touched the woman's cheek, feeling the cool flesh that gave ever so softly to his touch.

The man didn't react to this, the idea certain in Lawrence's mind that the man did not expect rigor mortis yet, the stiffening of the muscles and flesh that sets in some time after death.

The man covered the woman with trash bags, leaving her face for last.

Shrugging against the chill, rain threatening to spill again from the clouds above as the wind brought the cold scent of the rain to come, the man gave one last glance at the trash pile before getting back into his car and driving slowly forward, clicking the lights back on just before exiting the alley at the other end.

The car faded away, leaving the alley empty.

Lawrence just stood there in the darkness, thinking, imagining, trying to get a feel for the dumping site, the trauma to Jane Doe, and the shopkeeper's distress.

He pushed his mind, trying to get a feel for what the perpetrator might have been feeling and thinking, what might be motivating the man, and he is certain it is a man. These were crimes of a nature that was not natural to female killers. This was a crime of passion without a doubt, committed with extreme rage and violence. The question is: does the victim know her attacker? Most likely she did, but he couldn't assume that. Could it be an estranged husband? Ex-boyfriend? An associate who wanted but couldn't have her? Was this an act of jealousy? Revenge for being spurned?

All this will help him get a feel for the story, to put himself inside the story.

At last Hawkworth started wandering around the alley, looking at everything, absorbing everything his eyes saw, the smells, the feel of the air, studying every detail of the alley. His search is not without purpose and goes beyond putting himself into the feel of the events that happened here. He also hopes to spot anything that might be a clue the cops missed. It wouldn't be the first time. It could be something as simple as a conveniently located fire escape or an object that at first glance seems it's supposed to be there but feels out of place, or just the lighting or location that has a certain feel about it.

This is what made him such a good reporter, and it is also why McNelly relies on Hawkworth for certain cases where the police find themselves stumped. Hawkworth has a knack for picking up on things even the most detailed forensic investigators sometimes overlook as being entirely within the ordinary.

He has an uncanny ability to pick up hunches that proved to be correct that any cop would envy.

Lawrence paused to inspect the odd thing more closely. A door across the alley from the shopkeeper's, a small boarded up window, a discarded candy bar wrapper laying half crumpled on the ground that surely was dropped after the lane was cleared.

He was coming up empty.

He couldn't even seem to get a feel of the perpetrator's mind the way he usually did.

"Maybe I'm looking at this wrong," he thought.

7

The soft ping of the elevator door echoed hollowly down the empty hospital corridor. The doors slid open with a quiet whoosh.

Adjusting his glasses, Lawrence Hawkworth, reporter extraordinaire of the InterCity Voice, stepped from the otherwise empty elevator with a long confident stride and an ego filled with self-righteousness.

He lived by the belief that looking like you belong often gets you through when you are caught in the act by someone who does not know you don't belong.

He glanced around quickly, surveying the corridor in each direction.

Not a sign of life. Good.

Cautiously, he approached the nurses' desk and looked over it. The night nurse was off making her rounds.

"Two-fourteen b, two-fourteen b," he chanted over and over silently in his mind.

Studying the numbers on the rooms close by, he saw to his pleasure that he didn't have far to go.

"Fantastic," he whispered happily as he slinked to the second door down from the nurses' desk.

Entering the room cautiously, he slipped inside and carefully closed the door with an almost soundless click.

He held his breath.

The room was dim, with a single low light glowing softly on the wall immediately over the head of the bed. The utter silence and lifelessness of the sterile room made it feel to him as though he were standing in an ancient tomb about to confront a desiccated corpse, rather than the sterile modern hospital room it was.

Hospitals made him very uncomfortable.

Pulling a camera out of the bag slung over his shoulder, he reached for the light switch on the wall inside the small room. He changed his mind just as his fingers brushed the switch, pulling them away without flipping it up.

The light might show beneath the closed door, despite the brightness of the hallway outside.

He quickly grabbed a spare hospital gown that was sitting on a shelf, rolled it up and lined it along the floor against the crack beneath the door to block the flash of light that will blink briefly.

Groping his way through the dim room to the bed, he snapped a shot in the direction of the pillow to get his aim. He snapped off a few more, stopping abruptly.

Breathing shallowly, as quietly as he could, he listened intently. Was that a noise he heard? Or is he so jumpy that he's imagining things?

There was a soft shuffling noise outside the closed door, a footstep.

Hurriedly, he thrust the camera into his bag, not taking the time to turn it off.

The doorknob turned.

He whirled around to face the door, briefly debating whether he could make it to hide in the too small closet for the patient's personal effects.

The door was thrust open quickly, throwing a long rectangle of light across the floor to the foot of the bed.

The room brightened enough to see clearly.

A man in puke green hospital scrubs stood on the threshold, backlit by the bright glare of the fluorescent ceiling lights in the corridor, casting his face into shadows.

The shadows made the man unrecognizable, filling the room with foreboding.

A thrill of fear coursed through Lawrence.

"What the hell are you doing here?" Michael whispered angrily.

"I'm Lawr—" he was cut off mid word by the other man's fierce whispered snarl.

"I know who you are." The man stepped away from the doorway into the light of the hall, motioning the tall gawky man to follow.

Guiltily, shoulders slumped; Lawrence shuffled forward, his head hanging shamefully like a naughty little boy.

Out in the hall, he looked regretfully at the shorter man, an orderly he judged by the uniform. The ill-fitting shirt showed his muscular chest through the tight fabric. He was a not bad looking man, medium height to tall by most people's standards, and obviously strong. This was not a man he wanted to mess with.

The man had a familiarity about him, one that didn't feel like he'd seen him at the hospital. No, he knew this man from someplace else.

He also had a danger about him, something indefinable. Lawrence just couldn't seem to place where he knew the orderly from, though his mind was usually very keen when it came to these things.

"Hope he doesn't get rough with me," he thought. "This guy could do some serious damage."

"What the hell are you doing sneaking around the hospital in the middle of the night?" the orderly demanded venomously, still whispering.

"I-I just," Lawrence began.

"You stay away from here," Michael cut in coldly. "Don't let me catch you snooping around this hospital again. And don't you worry, I'll be here watching for you." He poked the taller man in the chest painfully hard for emphasis. His eyes blazed cold hard anger.

"Day or night, I'll be watching."

Lawrence swallowed the bile rising in his throat.

"And stay away from her," Michael added with deadly finality. "If I even hear of you asking about her again I'll make you wish you'd never even heard of that damn paper you work for." He glared Stilettos.

Lawrence turned quickly and hop-stepped to the elevator, trying with great effort not to run. He pushed the button three or four times, anxious to get out of there.

When the doors finally glided open, he hurried in and started jabbing at the close door button, staring back at the angry orderly who stood sentry until after the doors whispered closed between them.

In the private confines of the descending elevator Lawrence gasped for air, his heart hammering mercilessly in his chest. He clung to the wall, feeling faint.

Lawrence was, in fact, quite the coward. Sure, he's broken plenty of laws in the pursuit of the story. And he's had his share of run-ins with people on the darker side of human nature and gotten into many dangerous situations. But, when something frightened Lawrence, it terrified him out of his wits.

His mind raced, automatically sorting and compart-mentalizing every detail of the encounter right down to the smell of the orderly's breath.

The encounter had unnerved him in ways he couldn't quite grasp. It was more than the sneaking about in the night and getting caught. Something was niggling at his mind. Some detail, something he missed or didn't miss but isn't yet aware of. Was it something in the room? Something about the girl?

Somehow, though, his mind kept getting pulled back to that orderly.

The orderly definitely would be worth looking into.

When the elevator reached the main floor he rushed out and ran through the lobby past the startled security guard, disappearing into the night outside.

Part Two:
Losing Grip

8

Tires crunched on the decorative gravel lining the edges of the driveway as the dark blue car turned off the quiet residential street into the driveway of a tidy little house, the sun glinting off the metallic surface as the car rolled to a stop.

The house looked quiet and dark. There was no other car in the driveway or on the road in front of the house. The house seemed empty at the moment.

The man's hand resting on the steering wheel started drumming fingers in time to music coming from the car's speakers. He started singing with the song in a quiet guttural off-key tone. The gentleness of the voice belied the violence trapped inside the man.

He smiled knowingly.

Staring at the reflection in the rear view mirror, he watched the scene a few houses up the street intently, where two young girls and a small dog were playing in front of a house, her house.

He had seen the woman weeks before and followed her to this house. Now he was waiting to get another look at her. He had been here many times since that first day.

He was methodical, careful. He didn't act without first studying the scene and investigating the players.

It wouldn't be long now, and he would act. He would take the woman.

As he waited and watched his thoughts wandered and the movement of the children caught his attention. He watched them in the mirror's reflection, his eyes reflecting back in the mirror, cold and strangely empty.

Watching the two girls play drew other thoughts unbidden from the dark recesses of his mind. Memories he'd laid to rest many years ago. They were dark memories, terrible and frightening. Memories he just wanted to shove in a dark closet and lock the door to shut them away forever. They made the smile fall off his face, a darker look crossing his eyes.

Balancing unsteadily on one foot, the little girl bent forward at the waist, her knee barely bending while the leg she kicked out behind her flailed high in the air and bent at a sharp angle. She stretched her arm out, reaching with visible effort for the little pebble at her feet. Her flared skirt billowed slightly in the breeze; the colourful flowered fabric looked like a bouquet of cartoon flowers dancing in the wind. Her unruly mop of soft brown hair fell delicately over her pretty little face.

Her tiny fingers brushed the ground as they clasped possessively around the grey speckled rock, worn smooth from much handling. It was her favourite rock.

She stood on one of ten squares in a hopscotch pattern drawn crudely in chalk on the sidewalk leading up to the front door of the house.

She teetered precariously, almost falling as she straightened up too fast.

She froze.

At least as frozen as a gelatine statue in a wind storm could be, but she imagined herself holding absolutely still.

Wind-milling her arms and kicking her leg at the air behind her, she scrunched her face into a grimace of effort, eventually regaining her balance.

The man didn't see the little girl. In her place, he saw his sister who she had an uncanny resemblance to. That is, a resemblance to the girl of so many years ago at that same age, before the accident.

A wave of nostalgia washed through his mind, drowning out conscious thought. He became transfixed on this little girl. His sister? No, of course not, she's dead, he had to remind himself.

The more he watched her, the harder it became to remember if this was his sister or not. But no, of course she isn't.

His sister would be just a few years younger than him, had she still been alive. He was a grown man, this a little girl.

The distinction grew fuzzier, harder to see. This wasn't the first time he sat here watching the little girl. Each time he came to study the woman he became mesmerized by the little girl.

Each visit he grew more confused, the distinction between this little girl and his long dead sister more blurred; his confusion stronger.

He longed to have his sister back; he needed her and missed her even after all these years.

He suddenly felt so alone, and so filled with the empty pangs of a guilt that can never be satisfied.

He continued to watch, humming quietly to himself, seeing not the little girl playing, but the ghost of his baby sister.

He rolled down his windows to hear the children's voices better.

Mandy hopped one-legged to square number three, dropping her stone onto the next square before hopping her way to the end of the hopscotch drawing.

Sandra, everyone calls her Sandy, had been standing to the side watching, hands on her hips, and trying to look older and indulgent of her younger sister. She thought she was being kind by bothering to play with Mandy.

Six year old Mandy skipped over to her older sister, looking up at her proudly.

"I did it?" I did it, Sandy! See, I told ya' I could do it!" she gushed.

Sandy grinned down at her little sister.

"I knew you could do it too."

She raced to the beginning of the hopscotch, calling over her shoulder.

"It's my turn now."

Skippy, a tiny black and white bundle of long shaggy fur with a punched in pug-like nose, hopped on his hind legs as Sandy started hopping down the sidewalk.

He yapped furiously as he jumped up at the older girl just as she was straitening up from picking up her stone, knocking her off balance.

She stumbled forward, dropping the stone, and falling to her knees, one hand on the pavement.

"Skippy!" she admonished. "You made me fall!"

He rushed to her, jumping up and eagerly licking her face,

38

his whole bum wagging furiously with his tail.

Pushing him away, she got to her feet and prepared to finish her turn.

"Butterfingers!" the younger girl squealed with delight.

"Dropsies," she quickly called back.

"You have to miss a turn now," Mandy happily chanted in a sing song voice. "You said if you drop the stone or touch the ground you have'ta miss a turn."

"I said dropsies, so it doesn't count that I dropped it," she retaliated.

"But I said butterfingers first," Mandy insisted. "You said if I say butterfingers before you say dropsies, then your dropsies doesn't count."

"Ok already, I'll skip my turn," she gave in grudgingly; annoyed with her sister for remembering the rules she had quickly rattled off at the beginning of the game.

The man shook his head with an indulgent smile.

"Cassie," he thought, "that is so like you. You always caught me when I cheated and stood your ground. Nothing got past you and you never let me get away with anything."

His eyes narrowed, memories flooding through his mind, dark memories taking him years back into the past.

He grimaced with the physical pain of it, clutching the steering wheel so hard his knuckles turned white and jolting in his seat as though he had just suffered a sudden and terrible physical blow. His face twisted in pain and tears formed at the corners of his eyes. His breaths became ragged and heavy.

He was lost in the past, reliving events that happened so long ago, unable to come back to the present.

It was dark and shadowy, slats of light coming through rough plank walls. It stunk of ancient manure and stale hay. He was in a barn.

He pressed himself harder against the rough planks making up the stall wall, desperately wishing he could disappear.

The smell of blood touched him. It filled his nose until he gagged on it and vomited into the musky stale hay. The blood. So much. So much blood.

"NOOOOO!!!!!!" he screamed.

He looked around frantically. Where was the blood?

Gulping for air he realized it was a nightmare, all a terrible nightmare. There was no blood. He was sitting in a car and his sister still played with her friend up the street.

He looked around sheepishly, a flush of embarrassment now tinting his face. The world continued calmly as before. Relief flushed through him. He hadn't screamed out loud.

He rubbed the tears from his eyes, trying to blink the redness away.

He watched his sister happily playing.

His face paled. It was a nightmare, but it was more than that. He'd seen her die. He'd seen her die for real. He knew it without a doubt.

Panic gripped him. Confusion.

Yes, she was going to die, had already died. He had seen it. He was there. But she was right there in front of him right now. There was still a chance to save her. He had to save her.

He acted. His body went through the motions on autopilot while his mind was trapped in another world years in the past.

Putting the car in gear, the man slowly rolled it backwards out of the driveway. Aiming it up the street where the girls are, the car crept forward.

When he came to watch today he had planned on watching and then just driving on by, just like the other times. But without even knowing what he was doing, he pulled up and stopped in front of the girls' house.

"Hey, little girl," he called out invitingly through the open curbside passenger window.

"What are you doing?" a small distant part of his mind screamed. "Just keep driving, keep driving!"

He didn't keep driving.

Boldly, the younger of the two walked up to the car and leaned on the open window of the passenger side.

"What do you want mister?" she asked.

"No Mandy!" her sister called out, standing a safe distance away. "He's a stranger! Mom says never talk to strangers!"

"It's ok," the man said, his voice gentle. "I'm a friend of one of your neighbors. I just need some directions."

"See, it's ok," the younger girl said triumphantly, proud of being right for once.

"Stop! What are you doing? You're going to get yourself in trouble!" That distant shred of sanity tucked deep in his mind reeled, tried to warn him. But he went on, mechanically, not in control of his actions, begging himself to stop even while his conscious mind played out a scene he'd fantasized a million times over as a boy—saving his little sister from a certain and brutal death.

"Look, why don't you just get in and show me how to get there? Then I'll drop you back off here when I know my way. It's not far, really close by, I promise," the man suggested logically.

"Okay," Mandy said. She turned and called to her sister, "You coming for the ride Sandy?"

"Mandy!" Sandy commanded sternly, fists at her sides and giving a stomp of her foot for emphasis. "Don't get in that car! He's a stranger!"

But it was too late. The man had already opened the car door, even as that little sane voice in his mind screamed at him to stop, shut the door, it's not her, it's not your sister, just shove the little girl out and shut the fucking door and drive the fuck away!

The little girl was already climbing in.

Sensing trouble, the small dog started growling and yipping wildly, its bark a frantic squeak.

The older girl screamed as loud as she could.

"Mommy! Mommy! Mandy's getting into a strangers car!"

Hearing the furious screeching yip of the dog, the girls' mother, Carole, had already started coming out of the house to investigate and quiet the dog before he annoyed the neighbors.

Seeing her younger daughter climbing into the strange car she cried out.

"Oh, God! No!"

Carole paused for a second or two that seemed an eternity, standing frozen on the doorstep. Her eyes widened and filled with terror. Her heart became a dead lump in her chest, heavy, weighted down with dread. Her jaw dropped open. The world beyond that open car door vanished.

Mechanically, she stumbled down the steps, sprawling on the pavement at the bottom as her legs fumbled woodenly, skinning a knee.

Coming to her senses, Carole gave her head a shake and quickly stood up.

She was already racing towards the car as her older daughter screamed her first "Mommy!"

What Sandy said after that was lost in a haze of panic.

Carole reached the car and grabbed the door, gripping it with all her strength just as the man grabbed the door handle to close the car door on her innocent little baby.

She felt helplessly weak. It wouldn't be enough, she'd fail, and her baby would be lost to whatever depravity this monster was after. She'd failed as a mother, failed to protect her baby.

These thoughts rushed through her mind in seconds.

She thrust herself between the door and the car interior, reaching for the little girl in the front seat, the door slamming painfully against her body as the man pulled on the door, stopped short by her body blocking it from closing.

In the front seat of the car, Mandy stared at her mom, wide eyed and tears welling because of the terrified look on her mother's face, frightened that she did something very bad and would be spending a long afternoon on time out in her room.

Mandy was scared she was in trouble, but she was also scared because she'd never ever seen her mom look scared like that before. That terrified her more than being in trouble ever could, no matter how much trouble.

Swearing, the man reached over the now frightened little girl with his other arm, trying to push the woman out of the way and close the car door.

Taking his foot off the brake with the effort, the car crept forward.

With nobody controlling it, the car began to glide towards the other side of the road.

Thrown off balance, Carole landed hard on her buttocks, maintaining her hold on the door handle, fighting to keep him from closing it.

He hit the gas and the car lurched forward, wrenching her arm painfully.

The little girl in the car screamed. "Mommy! Don't hurt my Mommy!"

Sandy stood there shaking, unable to move. Huge tears rolled down her cheeks.

With a large snarl for such a small dog, the little black and white bundle of fur and teeth sprinted after the car, his little legs pumping furiously and his fur bristling. His breath rasped past his bared sharp little teeth with the effort of chasing the car.

Skippy caught up just as the car began to accelerate.

Launching himself through the still open door and into the car, he bounced over the little girl, aiming straight at the man holding tightly onto the struggling girl.

The man cried out in pain as Skippy sank his sharp little teeth into his hand, making him let go of the child.

His foot involuntarily pushed out, pressing against the gas pedal, causing the car to lurch forward, gaining speed more quickly.

"You little fuck!" he swore as he turned his attention on the dog.

Dragging on the pavement as the car accelerated, Carole held onto the open passenger door for dear life, reached in and grabbed at her daughter.

With his attention distracted by the dog the man loosened his grip on the girl.

Pulling the terrified child roughly, Carole yanked the girl out of the car and onto the street.

Mandy cried out in pain and shock as she hit the pavement hard, scraping and bumping on the pavement.

Unable to hold on any longer and relieved to have her daughter safely out of the car, Carole let go of the door.

Banging hard against the side of the car as she rolled and skid along the pavement, she narrowly missed having her arm and leg run over by the rear tire. Her head bounced off the road with a sound that seemed to explode inside her skull as she rolled.

Blood running down her face, arm, and legs where the skin

was badly scraped, she lay sprawled on the roadside barely taking in the sight before her. She moaned from the pain and the effort of trying to remain conscious. Her head swooned with dizziness.

Sandy stood frozen in place, her legs and crotch soaked from peeing herself, a puddle pooled on the pavement beneath her.

Mandy lay in a foetal position in the road, holding herself and crying, oblivious to everything around her.

The car's engine roared as it was flooded with gas, the vehicle leaping forward like a startled stallion bolting away.

A high yelping screech echoed down the street as the tires spun then suddenly gripped the pavement.

Inside the car, the man grabbed the squirming dog by the scruff of the neck with one hand and thrust him outside the open driver's side window, holding the squirming bundle of fury dangling over the road.

Skippy yelped from both shock and the painful grip. Not liking this one bit, the dog kicked and squirmed, flailing in the man's fist, crying in a high yipping while frantically twisting his head and trying to nip the hand holding him.

Seeing a car approaching from the opposite direction, driving too fast for this residential street, a cruel smile creased the man's lips.

Watching the rear view mirror he surveyed the trio behind him, willing them to look, to watch his small act of vengeance.

Hearing the yelping dog, realization hit both children as one.

Their beloved pet was still inside the stranger's car.

Sandy turned and watched the car with a look of horror.

Mandy sat up in the road and put her hands out as if to catch their beloved friend.

Following the children's horrified gazes, still lying bruised and broken on the road, their mother saw the dog dangling and kicking from the man's outstretched hand.

The struggling dog was trying desperately, without success, to bite and shred the man's hand and arm.

"No. Please don't," Carole whimpered. "Not in front of the girls." Her voice trailed off.

She lay there helpless, unable to stand, and unable to stop

44

what she knew was coming.

The girls cried out in unison, shrill and spine chilling. "Skippyyyyyyy!!!"

Rolling over onto her stomach, Carole pulled her arms under herself and tried to push, to get up and go to her girls.

Her arms shook violently with the effort. Sweat dripped into her scrapes and cuts, making her grimace.

She started to rise, then dropped back to the pavement, exhausted and defeated as her arms gave out.

Tears shimmered in her eyes as she cried quietly to herself. "No, no, no."

With a satisfied look of triumph, the man gunned the engine, the car leaping forward at greatly increased speed, just before he flung the small dog in front of the fast approaching car.

The driver of the other car just stared at him as if he couldn't decide if this were really happening or not.

Snapping out of it, he reacted too late.

Tires screeched as the shocked driver tried to stop.

There was a dull thud as the small body hit the windshield, cutting off the little dog's last yelp just as it began.

The dog stuck there briefly, as though pasted to the glass. Then, spinning slowly, the bundle of fur glided down the windshield to the hood.

Swerving out of control, the car spun and slammed into a parked car with a sickening crunch, the driver flung hard against the steering wheel and up over it, his head cracking hard against the windshield with a loud thud. His seatbelt hung uselessly beside the seat, unbuckled.

There was a faint cracking sound at the moment of impact, and a spider web of lines formed on the windshield.

The air bags exploded out and puffed up with air just a moment too late.

He'd meant to get those checked.

The driver's eyes fluttered briefly and rolled up into his head.

The little dog slid off the hood of the car, hitting the pavement with a dull wet smack, leaving a trail of blood smeared down the hood.

"Serves 'em right," the man in the dark blue car growled. "She was mine, damn it. Mine!"

A small voice in his head whispered, she's not your sister, she's not yours.

He turned his attention back to the road with some difficulty, suddenly shaken.

The car disappeared around a corner, the children's shrill screams filling the air behind it.

Silence briefly descended on the street like the calm before a storm.

Up and down the block curtains fluttered as curious neighbors snuck a peek at what was happening in the street.

The wail of sirens, barely discernible in the distance, gradually drew nearer.

Entranced by the terrible events, a crowd of neighbors and passersby began to form. They hovered, fascinated yet afraid to approach the scene of this brutality that has forever changed their peaceful little street.

In the house next door to where the two young girls live, a proud but homely looking woman slowly replaced the phone receiver in its cradle.

Her eyes blazed with fury as she thought about the police officer on the phone.

"That imbecilic son of a bitch," she muttered, remembering how he had treated her like she was some crackpot. "Throwing what must have been a misunderstanding between a neighbor and her boyfriend into unrealistic proportions, that's what he thought," she grumbled.

She'd hung up on the officer and called the ambulance herself.

While she was calling the police, she had missed the sight of the dog being thrown into another car's windshield, causing an accident. She was arguing so furiously with the officer on the phone that she hadn't even registered the crunching of metal impacting on metal or the screech of tires braking hard. That, at least, would have caught his attention.

She stood there trembling from anger, a calmly determined yet angry look on her face. She straitened noticeably and walked outside to offer any assistance she could.

All at once the scene broke into chaos.

An ambulance came careening around a corner, throwing splashes of red across the houses. The siren died as the vehicle came to an abrupt halt.

More neighbors emerged from their homes to satisfy their morbid curiosity, drawn by the plaintive wailing of the ambulance siren.

A few approaching cars stopped, blocking the street in their drivers' morbid excitement to see what happened.

Sandy, acting quite grown up for a ten year old, went first to check her little sister who was still letting out hiccupping sobs that made her whole body shudder.

After reassuring herself there were no major injuries, she helped her sister to her feet and led her limping to where their mother lay at the roadside.

By now, Mrs. Doherty, the neighbor who attempted to summon the police, was crossing her yard after hanging up from calling the ambulance.

The girls were crying over their mother's injuries as the older woman approached them.

Grasping defiantly onto consciousness, Carole tried to calm and reassure her two daughters.

In shock, the two girls clung to each other as they drifted to where Skippy lay motionless on the road.

Sickened with fear, yet strangely fascinated, they studied the inert form.

Sandy reached out one tentative hand to touch him as she knelt down beside the dog.

Seeing the paramedics unload a stretcher from the ambulance, Mandy ran to them and looked up at each man expectantly.

"Are you here to help Skippy?" she asked naively. "He's my dog. He's hurt really bad."

Seeing the pain in the little girl's huge round eyes, the older of the two shook his head sadly.

"Sorry sweetheart, we're a people ambulance. We don't look after dogs." Reddening guiltily, he turned away and rushed over to the woman sprawled at the roadside.

Tears filled the little girl's eyes and spilled over, rolling down her face.

The second paramedic crouched in front of her. Taking her tiny hand in one large paw, he gently rubbed away her tears with the other.

"Some more people will be coming to help soon. I'm sure one of them will have dog training," he explained badly as he quickly checked her cuts and scrapes.

Turning around to reach for his medical kit, he spotted the smashed car only because of the crowd gathering around it.

"Shit!" he exclaimed. "What the hell happened here?" He gawked incredulously. "No one said anything about another car."

He was still a rookie on the job, and until now had seen nothing more gruesome than the occasional heart attack and stroke.

Calling out to his partner, he pointed to the car then raced to the ambulance's cab to radio for help.

His partner, who was working over the woman lying on the ground, and the neighbor Mrs. Doherty, looked up in unison when he called. They looked curiously in the direction he indicated.

"Oh, my God!" Mrs. Doherty put a hand to her mouth and stared in shocked disbelief.

Whistling quietly in surprise, the medic rose slowly to his feet.

"This is more than just a domestic," he commented aloud to himself.

Seeing his partner racing back to the ambulance, his professionalism returned and he knelt again to work on the woman.

Silently, as though nothing unusual has happened, a squad car pulled up alongside the ambulance.

Looking at the lights flashing on the ambulance, the older of the two uniformed officers casually reached forward and flicked the switch to turn on their own lights, adding to the pulsing flashes thrown off by the other vehicle.

Getting out of the car, the two officers came around the

ambulance and stopped dead in their tracks when the scene materialized in front of them.

One by one, the sounds invaded the haze of surprise surrounding them; children crying, the morbid chatter of excited onlookers, and the distant wail of an approaching siren.

Quickly snapping out of it, Sergeant Kilowski reached for his radio to call for backup.

His young partner staggered forward a few steps, stating dully, "this is no domestic dispute. Where's the couple having a fight?"

He stopped when a reassuring hand gripped his shoulder.

"Not a good call for your first day on the job," Sergeant Kilowski agreed. Giving the younger man a brief moment to collect himself, he urged, "let's get to work."

No matter how many times you encountered a scene like this on the job, Kilowski thought, you still always feel that first moment of surprised body numbing shock, even if only for a heartbeat or two.

A second ambulance arrived and the attendants took over administering to the man in the damaged car. The paramedic already there went to assist his partner who was preparing to load Carole into their ambulance.

The police officers were already working on moving the crowd back away from the scene to give the paramedics room to work.

A second squad car came wailing up the street, slowing to barely a crawl and beeping its horn at the cars and people blocking the way as the paramedics shifted Carole onto the stretcher.

The two girls rushed over as the stretcher was raised to full height on its wheeled stand.

Grabbing the rail on the side of the stretcher to steady herself, Mandy stood on tiptoes to see her mother better.

Sandy grabbed her mother's hand and held it firmly, cupping her other hand over their joined hands.

"Momma? Mommy, are you going to the hospital now?"

"Yes sweetheart, but I'm all right." It came out a hoarse whisper. She could barely raise her head from the waves of

L.V. Gaudet

dizziness spinning the world like a wildly out of control top.

"Can we go with you? We want to come too."

Butting in, Mrs. Doherty put a hand on each girl's shoulder, trying to draw them away from their mother.

"Of course you can't go with your mother," she proclaimed, pulling at the girls. "You're too little."

"No!" Mandy screamed as she pulled away from the elderly woman's grip. "Mommy! I want to be with Mommy!" She burst into tears.

Reaching an arm past the stretcher railing, Carole put a comforting hand on her youngest daughter's head.

"It's okay," she soothed. "Everything will be just fine."

The little girl's chin quivered as she looked up at her mother. She sobbed, sending a shudder through her tiny frame.

"You're such a big girl now Mandy. Show Mommy how you can be such a big girl."

Mandy slowly shook her head back and forth, silently mouthing the word, "no." She neither felt like nor wanted to be a big girl right now.

Cupping her daughter's chin in her hand, she continued. "Stay with your sister and Mrs. Doherty. I'll see you later." She mouthed a thank you to Mrs. Doherty for looking after the girls.

The ambulance attendants had finished locking everything into place and were waiting for her to finish reassuring her daughters.

Giving up, the girls followed the attendants as they wheeled their precious cargo away, wandering off by the time the attendants got halfway to the ambulance.

The distant wail of sirens from more approaching police cars could be heard just before the ambulance drowned them out with its own keening wail and pulled out, rushing down the street.

Watching the ambulance carrying their mother drive away, Mandy turned to her older sister as they walked back to where Skippy still lay motionless on the ground in an already drying pool of blood.

She knelt down, reaching one small hand out to tentatively touch the dog's blood-matted hair.

"Why didn't they take Skippy to the hospital too?"

50

Distraught, Mandy waited for her older sister to make her understand, to make everything all right.

"They don't take dogs to the hospital," Sandy explained, kneeling beside her little sister and staring down at the broken little dog.

"But why not?"

Coming up behind them, Mrs. Doherty stood between them and gently touched each girl's shoulder.

"Come girls, let's get into the car so we can go and see your mom at the hospital." She tried gently but firmly to draw them away from the dog lying in the street.

Pulling out of her grip, Mandy stepped back and stared up at her defiantly.

"No!" the little girl demanded. "Skippy has to go to the hospital too!"

Overhearing this, Sergeant Kilowski came over to them. Kneeling in front of the little girl, he gently placed a restraining hand on each arm.

"I have medical training in dogs," he lied reassuringly.

Giving the girl a light squeeze, he let go and moved to crouch over the dog. Performing a brief inspection, he looked up at her, shaking his head slowly.

A kind elderly neighbor who had come to watch offered his jacket and Kilowski carefully laid it over the dog, covering him completely.

"That means he's dead, doesn't it," Mandy said blankly. "I saw it on TV."

"Yes, I'm sorry, he's dead."

"Thank you for looking after my dog," Mandy sniffed.

All resistance gone now, the girls let their neighbor lead them away and usher them into her car.

9

The dark blue car sat parked in an alley. The male figure inside was slumped over the steering wheel, violent tremors wracking his body.

At last he sat up, staring at himself in the rear view mirror.

The eyes in the mirror were red and rimmed even redder. They were haunted by terrible visions and unbearable knowledge.

Tears flowed freely, unstoppable.

He sobbed a deep shuddering sob. He shook his head in disgust and self-loathing, his mind reeling.

He had come back to his senses just as the first police car drove past him with lights and sirens blaring, startled back by the lights and noise.

Brought suddenly crashing back to reality, he had quickly turned into the first semi private place he spotted and put the car into park, finding himself in a dirty alley. It looked and felt as deserted and desolate as he felt.

Before he had even put the car into park his mind began fogging over the recent events he so desperately wanted to erase, pushing the world around him to a distant place where he'd be safe from it.

He sat there, stunned, feeling numb and detached the way a heavy fog makes the world seem far away and unreal.

Faint ghosts of his actions moments before tickled at his memory.

The memories of his sister's accident so many years ago, vague and full of missing pieces, huddled in the dark corners of his mind, giving him teasing glimpses that he didn't want to see.

He couldn't quite remember what happened on that tranquil neighborhood street. The memory was just right there, tantalizing and dreadful, a gossamer veil he could just barely brush with his fingertips. Drawn by the need to see as much as by the revulsion and need to escape it, the man wanted to pull the memory up but didn't dare. He tried to push it away instead.

The scene, the fantasy he'd replayed in his mind over and

over a million times as a child until he'd finally pushed it away and blocked it out, now teased and tormented him, flashing glimpses at him in a blinding fashion, confusing the past with the present.

More confusing were brief flashes of scenes on that street.

The happy smiling face of a little girl looking up at him with eyes full of trust.

The terror filled eyes of a woman in a face twisted with determination.

An approaching car.

The pleading look of a child standing on the sidewalk.

The beautiful trusting eyes of a little girl turning to a liquid look of fear.

A little bundle of teeth and hair.

"What did I do?"

He looked down at his hands. He held out his hand, staring at it in wonder.

The flesh was punctured, blood still dripping from the wound.

He felt a wave of sickness wash over him, reeling with a strength-sapping stomach-churning, dizziness.

"What did I do?" His voice trembled.

A black void now lived where the memories of the moments between watching the house and being awakened by the wail of a police car should have been.

It was impenetrable.

He'd blacked out, lost time and memories. Just like that time he'd gotten stupidly drunk as a younger man.

Only this time he wasn't suffering from the after effects of alcohol poisoning.

He had no memory of what he had done, but he knew. My God, he knew. And even God would not wash this sin away, would he?

He had tried to kidnap that little girl, that innocent little girl who he would never think of hurting.

He leaned out the open car window and vomited. His whole body convulsed with it, vomiting until there was nothing left to vomit out but his self-disgust.

He would gladly vomit that out too if he could. But no, he needed that self-loathing, that putrid disgust. It reminded him of who he was. What he was. He deserved to suffer. He could kill himself, or turn himself in. But that would be an act of kindness that he didn't think he deserved.

His stomach continued to clench painfully, heaving long past when he was certain he must have puked his empty stomach out to join its contents on the dirty pavement, his whole body shuddering with each painful spasm.

Part Three:
Suffer the Righteous &
Pamela Makes Three

10

The woman's hips swayed as she sauntered out of the shop, her bag swinging as she turned at the door to look back at the friendly shopkeeper in his early fifties.

"Bye Sam," she called out happily with a delicate wave of her hand.

Walking up the street, she turned into the door of the car parking garage for her apartment building located next door to the little grocery store. Skipping lightly down the stairs, her heels clicked smartly as she crossed from the stairwell into the darker recesses of the garage, leaving the hollow echo of her footsteps on the stairs behind.

A shadowed figure in a dark blue car watched the young woman leave the little grocery store and walk up to the next building, his eyes were all that is visible in the deep shadows inside the car. They were cold, agitated looking. Sweat dripped into them although it wasn't hot enough to cause excessive perspiration.

A curly brown cloud of hair like dark taffy framed her face. The breeze billowed her burgundy coat around her slim legs.

Once she was out of sight he inched the car forward and drove on.

Tall and suave in his tailored business suit, Roger burst through the heavy fire door into the stairwell leading to the parking garage below his apartment building. The stairs clanged noisily beneath his feet, echoing up the narrow stairwell as the tall, lanky man ran down the last two flights of stairs to the level his car was parked on.

L.V. Gaudet

"Damn, I'm going to be late for that meeting," he swore, glancing again at his Rolex.

He couldn't stop the boyish grin that claimed his face, though, at the thought of why he's late.

Seeing Pamela standing there, her long slim legs extending below the baggy dress shirt, his shirt, which was all she wore. The swell of her breasts was only hinted at.

His gaze trailed from her tiny feet and delicate ankles, up the gentle curve of her beautiful legs, dwelling on the slight curve of buttocks peaking teasingly below the curved hem of the shirt, a flash of sumptuous cheek showing now and then when she leaned forward, reaching for something as she prepared something to eat.

That's as far as his eyes had gotten before the impulse took hold of his senses.

Dropping his briefcase and suit jacket to the floor in a heap, he grabbed her, swinging her up into his arms as she giggled and struggled playfully.

He carried her to the bedroom.

Bursting through the door of the car parking garage beneath the apartment block, Roger collided with a bulky shorter man who was slightly above average height, but still shorter than him.

Muttering an oath under his breath followed by a curt "s'cuze me," he barely took in the man's filthy kaki jacket covered with stains, worn jeans, and badly weathered sneakers.

The man's greasy brown hair hung limply as he glared hatefully with bloodshot yellowed eyes at this man with the impeccable suit and well-polished shoes.

Roger tried to avoid eye contact, uncomfortable with the man's proximity, by his very existence even. But the man's glare caught him as an unwilling captive, making eye contact he didn't want.

Something in his eyes froze Roger's heart for a moment. The man's eyes held a cavernous depth that seemed overflowing with all the vileness of anger, hatred, fear, and the desperation of a man who is utterly lost to himself.

"Watch where ya goin' nex' time," the man growled in a drunken slur, his breath fowl with stale whiskey and old vomit.

56

The man himself smelled of sour alcohol, unwashed body and old urine.

After roughly bumping into him, on purpose Roger suspected, this unpleasant vagabond staggered off into the darkened recesses of the garage and vanished into the shadows.

Shrugging off the incident and his unease, Roger hurried off towards his BMW.

Walking around to the driver's side, he spotted the glint of the ceiling lights flashing off something shiny lying on the concrete in the shadows by his front tire.

Worried that it may be a sharp object that might puncture his tire, his hand stopped mid-way reaching for the car door handle.

Taking the few steps to the front bumper, he crouched to investigate. Placing one hand on the fender for balance, he crouched slightly, leaning over to take a look.

He stared for a brief moment in disbelief, although it felt like a very long time.

A horrified look slowly fell over Roger's face as the realization of what he was staring at sunk in.

Falling over backwards, he scurried crab-like away.

He weakly pushed himself up and ran for the stairs, windmilling his arms crazily as he almost fell over again.

It took him a few tries before he finally managed to pull the door open without losing his grip on the handle.

He ran blindly, able to see only the vision of what lay on the dirty pavement in front of his front bumper; the glint of the dainty gold bracelet caressing the delicate wrist, shining vulgarly in the glare of the overhead bulb.

Glassy eyes stared blindly after him, mocking. The trail of blood dripping from her mouth, long dried and flaking, and that final glimpse down at the pale flesh, bruised and bloody.

In the shadowed recesses of the garage a pair of headlights clicked on, washing the concrete and cars ahead of them with light. The engine chugged to life and the vehicle crept forward. The overhead lights glinted metallically off the dark machine, its color and shape lost in the poor lighting as it passed unseen beyond the furthest row of vehicles.

The vehicle turned and turned again and mounted the ramp,

coasting out to be swallowed by the dazzling sunlight.

Pamela was standing at the kitchen sink washing dishes when she heard the door in the other room burst open and crash loudly against the wall.

Smiling sweetly to herself, she picked up a tea towel to dry her hands and started walking out of the kitchen.

"Did you forget something? Or couldn't you face the day without a little more?" she called out playfully as she strolled into the living room.

She gasped and her body went rigid. She dropped the towel.

Bringing her hand to her mouth, Pamela stared in astonishment at the figure standing framed in the doorway.

Roger stood there swaying unsteadily, his smoothly pressed suit now rumpled and smeared with dirt, his carefully polished shoes scuffed. His tanned face was ghostly pale.

Bringing a trembling hand up, he ran his fingers reflexively through his dishevelled hair before bringing it down to wipe his haggard looking face, as though to wipe away the gruesome sight still flashing before his eyes. Wild and manic, his eyes darted nervously around the room as his parched tongue tried to wet dry lips.

"Roger? What happened?" Pamela exclaimed, rushing to his side. She took his weight on her small frame as he nearly collapsed into her arms.

Helping him to the sofa, she began trembling violently herself from the shock of seeing him in such a state.

She sunk to the seat beside him.

"C-c-call the police," he managed between the shudders wracking his body.

"What? Why?" she whispered.

"C-car garage," he gasped. "Th-there's a w-w-woman there, she's d-dead," he stammered before lapsing into the dazed silence of shock.

Stunned, Pamela got shakily to her feet and walked unsteadily to the phone. With a frightened glance at Roger, she picked up the receiver, looked down, and began to dial.

The keening wail of a siren, coupled with a blaring horn, went from distantly quiet to loud as it approached.

Two young boys, barely in their teens, cowered in a doorway, panicking in their haste to hide the joint they were smoking.

Relief showed clearly on their faces and they giggled nervously as they stared after the ambulance that raced past them and on up the street.

11

Footsteps and voices echoed hollowly in the busy parking garage. The wail of sirens and the slamming of car doors outside echoed in over the din of the crowd gathered by the entrance. Flashbulbs popped with nearly silent clicks like a miniature lightning storm as a throng of reporters tried to push past the patrolmen barely succeeding in controlling the crowd of excitement seekers.

The overhead lights inside the garage glared down crudely at the policemen, coupled with the bright crime scene lights set up to aid in the search for evidence.

Despite this, the garage managed to be gloomy and full of conspiratorial shadows.

Even the hub of activity surrounding the slain woman's corpse couldn't entirely mask the tomblike silence that hung over the place like a shroud.

Upstairs in the witness's apartment, Detective Jim McNelly stood slouching at the window, propping one curtain slightly open with a stubby, tobacco stained finger.

He stared distastefully at the scene in the street below.

Cars blocked the road, their horns honking and drivers rubbernecking in hopes of seeing something exciting. Throngs of people, curious bystanders who somehow seem to sniff out a tragedy and come scurrying out of the woodwork like vermin, pressed in on the police holding them back like spectators at an underground fight ring.

"It never changes," McNelly muttered under his breath to himself.

They pressed forward eagerly as the first of the procession came into sight from the bowels of the apartment building's parking garage. Excitement coursed through the crowd, sending an electric thrill racing, edging them ever closer, if possible, to the barricades. Their morbid curiosity awakened into a lustful hunger to see more, they watched eagerly, frantically snapping photos and recording video snippets with cell phones, as the stretcher bound corpse was wheeled out to the waiting ambulance.

Amid the pressing and jostling crowd one lone man stood stock still and taller than the rest, his attention held away from the stretcher like a lord among a throng of rag tag tragedy hungry peasants surrounding the gallows. His long nose, a vulture's beak, pointed to the sky above.

The sun glinted off his wireframe glasses as he studied the windows above, eagle eyed, and thinking.

Someone up there knows something. Someone saw something. He grinned hungrily. Somewhere in one of those apartments is the person who found the body. Somewhere someone who saw something might be too nervous to come forward, or not even know they held a valuable key.

Lawrence Hawkworth, reporter for the InterCity Voice, appeared to be staring directly at the window where, hidden by the closed curtains and glare of the sun off the glass, Detective Jim McNelly studied him and his brethren in return.

Like starvation-crazed vultures, the media swarmed forward, circling, eagerly trying to snatch a tender tidbit of news from the hungry maws of their pack-mates.

Lawrence slinked away, looking for an unguarded entrance into the apartment building.

Jim McNelly turned away from the window in disgust and waddled back to the couch to butt out his cigarette in the ashtray on the small round table beside the chair.

Pamela looked up at the portly detective expectantly from where she sat with Roger, her eyes shining with tears that threatened to spill over.

She winced when a shudder ran through Roger's body, causing him to tighten his already painful grip on her hand.

She quietly bared the pain without trying to pull away.

"I believe we have all the information we need from you right now," the detective began, thinking only of how badly he wanted a drink right about now to wash away the nasty taste in his mouth, and perhaps some jerky of indeterminate age or pickled orbs whose original identity is questionable.

"If we need anything further, one of my men will contact you," Detective McNelly stated unnecessarily.

He turned to the door, ready to leave, the other officers in the apartment following his lead.

McNelly thought about the sight of that young woman downstairs in the parking garage, her hair spilling gently to the dirty floor, her dead eyes staring up at him accusingly.

"You could have prevented this," they said to him.

He paused with his hand on the doorknob.

Roger almost bumped into him.

Roger had gotten up unsteadily and followed the officers to the door on shaky legs.

The other officers filed out past McNelly, waiting in the hallway. He was the detective in charge of this investigation. They were all waiting to follow his lead, waiting for wherever he may send them.

Looking past Roger, McNelly studied Pamela intently, making her nervous. Her slender body, childishly delicate features, and fine brown hair. He judged her height to be about, what, five feet three inches? Just like the others.

Everything was just like Jane Doe and the woman downstairs. The similarity to others who were reported missing over the years, but whose remains haven't been found, was less.

Those were his secret, not revealed to anyone, guarded against the news hounds learning about them and causing a panic or spoiling any possible clues. There were too many of them, the missing, for any similarities or differences to be coincidence. Every fibre of his being screamed with it.

"Would you like some milk to go with that cereal?" his mind flashed facetiously at him, taunting him with his inability to find and stop the perpetrator who he was certain was a serial killer.

McNelly blamed himself for each and every victim. His gut roiled and burned, acid creeping up his oesophagus, making him wince at the pain this caused his ulcer.

He opened his mouth to say something. He wanted to warn Pamela, to tell her that she could be next. He thought better of it and closed his mouth without uttering a word. After all, he didn't want to scare her too much.

He felt protective over her, like a father wanting to protect his daughter from ever knowing that evil exists in the world. He felt like this about all the victims.

Opening the door, McNelly turned and looked back at her once more.

"Be careful," he said to her.

"I will," she replied.

The door clicked quietly shut behind him and he joined the other officers waiting in the hall. His entourage followed him down to the parking garage.

As Roger turned away from the door, he heard two of the officers in the hall discussing the similarity between Pamela and the woman found in the car parking garage downstairs.

He blanched as he pictured Pamela being that girl lying in the garage.

Bursting through the door from the stairwell into the garage, feet clomping loudly down the stairs, Detective McNelly stormed like a sloppy giant back into the confused hubbub surrounding the murder scene below.

The officers following him down the stairs came through the door moments later, most racing to keep up.

It looked like there was a lot of confusion but little actual work being done.

He looked around moodily. In this business you spent a lot of time doing little but watching the scene.

12

A few blocks away from the apartment block that rose above the parking garage that just gave up its grisly secret, a dirty man wearing a stained kaki jacket stumbled out of a liquor store, holding his treasure wrapped in a brown paper bag protectively against his chest.

He squeezed the paper around the bottle's neck, twisting it tighter as though trying to throttle the significance of the venom within out of existence.

His hands trembled from more than just the burning need to sake his thirst. He had just witnessed a vision of a new demon that has come to inhabit the mortal world and prey on the unsuspecting flesh of the innocent.

His eyes burned with their need to forget in the sweet nectar of alcohol. They burned with an emptiness too, a void filled with desperation and righteous sorrow.

Seeing the deserted yard of a warehouse that is now closed permanently, he changed direction and made for it on unsteady legs.

"I need a quiet place," he mumbled to himself.

He looked up at the sky. The light in the sky was quickly dimming as dusk drew a heavy blanket across the world.

He crossed the nearly deserted street.

"Forget, forget, forget," he chanted quietly in a drunken slur, holding the bottle of cheap whiskey like a protective talisman warding off demons, except that all his demons were in his mind, although he could not see that. He firmly believed that some also walked the earth in solid form.

Maybe he's right.

"You can't stare those ones off with a cross and a prayer," he reminded himself, talking about the ones trapped within him.

He staggered into the deserted parking lot beside the darkened warehouse.

"Demons," he whispered fearfully. "They're everywhere."

He cracked open the bottle, unscrewing the twist off cap, and took a swig.

"Couldn't take it anymore, the demons. Fighting them, fighting, always fighting them. Couldn't protect my lambs, my poor poor little lambs."

He bumped into the side of the warehouse and followed the wall.

It was well shadowed here, as though night had already fallen in the space behind the warehouse.

"I am the Shepherd and they are my Lambs. But I couldn't protect them. The wolves, the demons, they kept getting my precious little lambs. Making young girls pregnant. Fathers, husbands, deserting the sanctity of the marriage. Mothers, wives, behaving promiscuously. Drugs, the drugs claiming so many young victims. The demons are what got them. The demons took their souls, turned them evil, and used them to commit evil. They stole with those empty vessels. Stole and robbed and hurt people."

He leaned way back, taking a long pull on the bottle, almost falling over backwards.

"I am the good shepherd; the good shepherd lays down His life for the sheep ... even as the Father knows Me and I know the Father, and I lay down My life for the sheep," he quoted from the Testament.

He followed the wall around the corner, looking for a quiet place to drink and forget.

"That poor, poor lamb," he slurred, again seeing the man dumping the bruised and battered body of a young woman out of his car in that parking garage beneath the apartment building.

"It is a powerful demon indeed who comes in the flesh to do his master's bidding."

A car engine roared behind him like a hole cracking open in the pavement down to the bowels of the earth.

He whirled, gaping in astonishment through a fog of liquor.

The headlights washed him in their burning glow, swallowing him, blinding him like the fires of hell.

And that's exactly what the ex-priest thought was bearing down on him. The very gates of Hell had opened to this world, drawing him into the bowels of the netherworld.

He was even certain he could see the wickedly grinning visage of Satan himself, or perhaps one of his generals, one of

65

the fallen angels come to cruelly take him to Hell and punish him for eternity for failing to protect his flock.

A suiting punishment, he thought.

But the thought terrified him. It terrified him so much that he pissed himself as his horrified gaze was trapped in the eyes of the demon beyond the blinding light.

His nose twitched, he was so certain he could smell the stench of brimstone and sulphur, sure he could hear the crackle and feel the heat of the hellfire.

Then he saw it.

It wasn't Satan, but a demon in human form.

It was the very same face he had seen dumping the poor young woman's body in the garage.

"You," he gasped.

"I KNOW YOU!" the ex-priest roared over the sound of the revving engine.

The tires squealed like the eager cries of hellish minions erupting into this world, hungry for chaos. Plumes of foul smoke filled the air as the heat of the tires tearing at the pavement burned the rubber off.

It took the drunken priest a few heartbeats to realize the beast wasn't moving.

Screaming a torrent of psalms, proverbs, and prayers, desperately trying to invoke the wrath of the Father to destroy this satanic beast who has taken possession of this poor soul's body, he stared at the man in the car.

He turned and ran.

The car lurched forward. It looked black in this light, the running lights twin red orbs staring at him from hell, the bright headlights swallowing everything their light touched, the engine screaming, the driver grinning wickedly.

It caught up to the ex-priest, keeping pace at his heels for a moment.

With a triumphant cry, the driver tramped the gas pedal to the floor, the car eagerly leaping ahead.

The car quickly caught the running man, knocking him down, driving over him like an over-zealous metallic dragon consuming its prey.

The last thing the former priest saw was the sun burning bright as it hung low in the dimming sky, bathed in the reddish glow of oncoming sunset, imagining it to be the hell fires he's destined to endure eternally for failing and then deserting his flock.

"You were in the wrong place at the wrong time, Father," the man whispered to the corpse lying broken and bloodied on the cracked pavement behind him.

"You shouldn't have seen."

Part Four: Deadly Sandcastles

13

Blackness. Whispers. Vaguely, far away, a faint reassuring coolness.

"Is that my arm? I think so, but I can't see it or move it. I'm not sure I even feel it."

Then again ... nothing.

The IV drips lazily and the monitor beeps quietly, unheard. The antiseptic smell permeates the air, un-smelled.

The nurse gently rolls the patient over in the process of changing the sheets, unfelt.

"Poor girl," tu-tutted Molly. She fidgeted as she marked off her chart.

"Jane Doe, doesn't anybody miss you?"

"Hey there Molly," a man called to her good spiritedly from the doorway.

She jumped, immediately recognizing the orderly's voice. An instant feeling of nervous edginess washed over her.

Waving timidly to the man who had paused in his task of pushing a cart up the hall, she quickly turned her back to him.

The thought came unbidden in the back of her mind, that place where things register on a barely conscious level, mostly unnoticed.

"Odd," she thought to herself in the back of her mind. "He seems unusually agitated, like something is really bothering him."

In the forefront of her mind, one thing stood loud and clear.

"Please go away, please go away," she chanted silently to herself.

The wheels on the cart squealed quietly, ominously she thought, as he continued down the hall.

Holding her breath until she could no longer hear the cart, relief washed away the uneasiness, although not completely.

Molly whispered to herself.

"What's his interest in you, you poor thing?"

She looked sadly at the unconscious woman.

"He asks about you and hangs around your door, but denies having any interest."

She looked up at the wall thoughtfully for a moment, tapping her pen against her thin lips.

"No one here even knows anything about him. He only started here shortly after you were brought in. Or was it the same day? And he definitely isn't a very good orderly."

Molly patted Jane Doe reassuringly on the hand.

She turned suddenly, surprised by a crash followed immediately by a sharp cry and a loud gasp from the hallway.

Molly stepped out to see what was happening.

Not far down the hall broken glass littered the floor.

A nearby nurse was already on the scene, carefully looking over the orderly's hand as it dripped blood into the glass shards.

14

"One two three, you're it!"

"Olly-olly oxenfree!"

"I'm the king of the castle, and you're the dirty rascal!"

"Tag, you're it!"

"But I'm always it! I don't want to be it anymore!"

"Last one to the sandbox is a rotten egg!"

The joyful squeals and scattered arguments of children playing filled the playground as they rushed from the school doors into the fresh air outside, chasing each other and starting their games even as they burst free from their prison, pouring out across the playground, only to be shattered suddenly by a terror filled scream.

Kids running, jumping, playing. They all stop, group by group and one by one, like a wave crashing through the playground as the sound washed over them. The odd kid looked out of place for not having noticed and continuing their game after all others froze. These too soon broke stride, looking around in confusion with the uneasiness of survivors who came just moments too late to meet a tragic end or witness the accident.

Finally total silence fell on the playground except for a single forgotten ball bouncing hollowly on the pavement by the school, the hollow sound lessening as its bounce died.

They all stood there looking around to see where the scream came from, finally turning as their attention was drawn to curiously watch the small group at the sandbox, mesmerized.

The only sounds now as the ball dribbled to silence is muffled hiccupping sobs and the quiet murmuring of frightened children.

Drawn to the sandbox by some inexplicable morbid curiosity, the children of the playground ran, shuffled, and walked closer, surrounding the group at the sandbox in a tight circle, leaving a few feet of distance to maintain that they are separate from the four at the box.

They stood there like sentinels at first. Looking but not

believing; four guardians looking down at the gruesome object in the sandbox. Fingers poked up out of the pea gravel filling the box.

"It's a doll," said one boy.

"Naw, too big. It's a mannequin," said another boy knowledgeably.

"Eew, don't touch it!" cried Susan.

Kneeling in the sand, Timmy reached towards the fingers poking up through the surface of the sand. He grasped them and pulled slowly.

The fingers came out, followed by a hand. The pea gravel fell fluidly from the stiff arm as it lifted slightly, revealing itself and part of the body curled into a ball.

It was a woman's body marked by bruises and gaping cuts filled with the gritty sand.

"Oh, gross!" Susan sobbed into her hands as she turned away and moved a few steps away to sit on the grass, too sick to stand any longer.

She looked up, looking around in shock to see if the world had gone back to normal yet.

It hadn't.

Her three friends still stood at the edge of the sandbox.

The rest of the school still stood silently watching, spellbound.

She saw Mrs. Crawshank, the teacher on duty, walking purposely towards them from across the schoolyard with a stern look on her face.

"No! No, don't!" gasped Susan as Timmy, who was never afraid of anything, not even scraping a dead frog off the road with a stick, began scooping sand away from the body in the sandbox.

"I'm looking for a face," he said quietly. "Then we'll know it's just a doll."

Using his arms like a bulldozer, slowly drawing the sand towards him, it washed over his legs like tiny tidal waves. The yellow grains running through his fingers in little streamlets back into the pale ocean that is the sandbox.

15

There is a flicker of movement under Jane Doe's eyelids from the twitch of her eyes. Her mind jumps to life. "Who am I? Where am I? What..." and it is lost again in pleasant reassuring nothingness.

The intravenous dripped silently, nothing more than a saline solution and pain medicine now, the doctor having stopped the medication that kept the woman unconscious in a coma-like state.

16

Jim McNelly's fat fingers tightened on the InterCity Voice, his hands shaking and face reddening in anger. The article was on the body discovered in the school playground. His eyes blazed with fury as though he willed the paper to burst into flames before them.

"Too far," he growled. "He's gone too far this time. Damn, we haven't even finished questioning the family and he's already got it in the paper. He must have identified the victim even before we did."

Angrily, he folded the paper over and tossed it down.

Michael Underwood came into the office.

He took one look at McNelly's angry expression and turned to do an about face and leave.

"Underwood," McNelly barked as Michael started to turn around.

"Damn," Michael thought.

"Have a seat," McNelly said, pointing at the chair in front of his desk.

"Where's Beth?" Michael asked.

"Trying to track down anything she can on the victim from the parking garage," McNelly said. "We still haven't been able to identify her."

McNelly noticed that Michael seemed to get immediately agitated at the mention of the victim from the parking garage.

"Dental records?" Michael asked.

"We put the description out, but until we have some possible victims to compare, they're useless," McNelly said, "nothing yet."

"She didn't match any local missing persons?" Michael asked.

"No," McNelly said. "It doesn't look like she's local."

McNelly puffed out his upper lip, making his scraggly moustache look briefly like a caterpillar.

Michael was really bothered by the discovery of this body. Who is she and why was she left there in that particular spot of all places?

73

L.V. Gaudet

They were completely without witnesses or suspects.

"That other case," McNelly said, "the young woman found in the school playground, I think it's the same guy."

Michael looked at McNelly, his eyes flashing a little alarm. This one troubled him too, very much. A lot more than the other one did.

"It does make sense," Michael said. "Both bodies were dumped where they were sure to be found quickly. These bodies have to be getting dumped like that for a reason."

He was talking more to himself than to McNelly, thinking out loud.

"The first body made a media splash, but it must have not been enough. I-," he stopped himself, thinking quickly. "He wanted more media attention than it got. He needed a bigger bang."

"Well, he got it," McNelly said. "Whatever the perp is up to, I have a feeling it won't stop until whatever he's after is satisfied."

McNelly looked at Michael, noting how agitated the younger man was.

"These cases are really hitting him hard," he thought. "Hope he doesn't end up like me, soured with a gut-rot the size of a baseball."

McNelly's heartburn flared in response, as if agreeing.

McNelly was haunted by these two young victims just like he was haunted by all of them. Letting them haunt you didn't help you do your job or sleep at night.

"You heard that the reports came back on these two vics?" McNelly asked.

"Yeah," Michael said. "But, I haven't had a chance to read them yet. All I got was the skinny from some rookie over the phone."

"The teacher, the one found in the playground, was fresh. She went missing after school the day before. The other one, the one in the garage, was older. Not decomposing yet so the body isn't that old, but she's been buried and dug up."

Michael shuddered.

Dug up! His mind whirled with the possibilities that opened.

It still made no sense to him though.

"The only witnesses from the school yard are the ones that found the body, pretty much the whole school. No witnesses to the abduction, though, and no reports of any unusual people or cars in the area."

"It's an elementary school," Michael said. "The streets are filled with unusual people and cars twice a day."

"Nothing that seemed odd to anyone canvassed in the area," McNelly said.

"Nothing more on the other one, the garage girl? No witnesses yet?" Michael asked.

McNelly let out a frustrated puff of air.

"We might have had one witness," he said.

Michael perked up, his look guarded.

"But the witness was taken care of," McNelly finished.

"Taken care of?" Michael asked. "What do you mean?"

McNelly met his gaze.

"The perp must have seen him, known the man saw something. Looks like the bugger was chased and ran down in the yard of an abandoned building nearby," McNelly said.

Michael didn't bother trying to hide his surprise.

"Ran down?" he said. "Who's our witness?"

"A vagabond," McNelly said. "You probably read about it in the paper. Some drunken homeless man, used to be a priest."

"A priest!" Michael was even more surprised. Not that it was a priest, but that a priest would end up a homeless drunk.

"The priest himself has his own past. Killed some of his own followers, but got off on an insanity plea. He thought God was talking to him."

He couldn't help snickering at the irony, although he did not find it funny.

"Could be one of his victim's people caught up with him," Michael suggested.

"Could be, but I don't think so," McNelly said. "Whoever it was, though, was very angry."

"How so?" Michael asked.

"They ran him over repeatedly."

Michael looked at his watch.

"I gotta go," he said. "I start shift at the hospital soon."

"Happy bedpan cleaning," McNelly smirked, watching Michael leave.

17

The man sat in a car parked on the side of a street. He'd spotted the picture on the front page of the newspaper stuffed in the door of a newspaper vending box and pulled over to grab a paper from the box.

The newspaper crumpled as his hands tightened into fists, tearing the paper where it caught between his fingers.

He trembled with excitement.

He stared breathlessly at the photograph of the young woman sleeping in the hospital bed.

In his mind he sees the face of his young sister transformed into what it might look like had she been alive today. It was the face of a young woman, round and delicate and framed by soft hair with eyes that should be laughingly staring out at him.

The eyes were troubled instead.

A frown creased his forehead at the unhappy eyes.

"It's ok," he whispered, "I'll protect you. I'll keep you safe."

He didn't really know what he needed to keep her safe from, but he didn't question it either.

The photo in the paper wasn't perfect. He could see the minor little details that didn't quite match. He blamed the poor quality of the picture for that.

"I'm coming for you," he whispered then tossed the paper out the car window.

He pulled out from the curb, disappearing into the traffic down the street.

The paper ruffled in the breeze, the pages separating, fluttering. Some rolled down the street, others took flight.

One page lifted slightly, quivering, bringing an unearthly life to the blurred photograph of a pale and battered woman lying asleep in a hospital bed.

The headline announced: MYSTERY WOMAN! Jane Doe Found in Back Alley Still Unidentified!

The paper briefly settled on the ground before levitating again on the breeze and rolling down the street like a broken tumbleweed until a car mercilessly ran over it.

L.V. Gaudet

Part Five:
Finders Keepers, Shoppers Weepers

18

In the darkened hospital room Jane Doe moaned, a grimace of pain creasing her forehead as she thrashed around in the bed.

Tears slid out between her closed eyelids.

Sitting next to the bed, Michael reached for her, grasping her hand and holding it firmly, trying to give the unconscious woman comfort.

Michael watched her hopefully, with a pained expression, wishing he could take her nightmares away.

He was dressed in his orderly uniform, supposed to be on shift at the hospital. He had snuck into Jane Doe's room when no one was looking, just wanting to check on her.

He was going to just take a quick look then leave. He did this at the start of the other shifts too.

But this time was different.

She looked so frightened even in her sleep that he felt the need to comfort her, to help her feel safe by his presence.

He leaned back in the chair he had pulled close, his arm stretched out to hold her hand in comfort, watching her twitch with her dreams.

Terrified, Jane stared at that terrible face in her dream, willing herself desperately to be somewhere else, anywhere else.

The man brought his face close to hers, their noses almost touching. She winced as his breath washed over her face.

She closed her eyes, trying to block it all out.

He tightened his already painful grip on her, shaking her so that her head banged hard against the floor, making her involuntarily open her eyes while he raged and yelled words that made no sense to her.

78

Her eyes locked with his, were drawn hypnotically into the deep soul-less brown wells.

Mesmerized by the madness she saw there, the room began to spin.

She felt like she was falling as vertigo gripped her.

Michael wondered what nightmarish images so tortured the woman lying in the hospital bed. Was she reliving that terrible night in her mind, over and over?

He spent most of his shift sitting there with her.

There were two things he didn't know.

That the nurse, Molly, saw him there; and that Jane was about to wake up.

Molly watched the orderly, unseen. She still felt a nagging suspicion of the man, even though his sitting with the young woman and comforting her softened her opinion of him.

Maybe he wasn't so bad after all. But she just couldn't shake that feeling that he was bad, very bad. She was sure he was hiding something and that inflamed her suspicions.

She was about to slip out of her hiding spot where she was watching him from when the orderly got up and left the room.

Molly watched him go before she went into Jane Doe's room herself.

The medication keeping her in a coma-like state should be wearing off now.

The young woman could be waking up at any time.

She hoped it wouldn't be like the other times.

The doctor had tried letting her wake up a few times before, but she became so hysterical that they were forced to drug her back to sleep again.

19

Kathy sat there, waiting. Her pale blue dress clung elegantly to her tiny frame. Her dirty blond hair was drawn up on top of her head, a few long strands hung down in soft curls in contrast. Her blue eyes were almost a match for the dress. Her features were dainty, pretty, except for the ugly bruise surrounding one eye and a still healing cracked lip, compliments of her boyfriend Ronnie.

She hated him at the moment.

Perched beside her on the low concrete ledge edging a small strip of indoor garden near the mall entrance is an array of bags from various stores. A few more stood sentry on the floor at her feet.

Kathy could feel the cold concrete of the ledge soaking through her thin dress and into her buttocks.

A man stared at her with obvious interest as he walked by her, making her feel uneasy. After all, she'd heard all about the murders.

Her friend works at the coffee shop just outside the police station and she hears some the details that don't make it to the public, even if a lot of it is mere rumour and turns out to not be true.

Kathy glanced at her watch again.

"Where is he? The store's closing!"

She thought about the fight she had with her boyfriend after she told him about what she had heard from her friend.

He was adamant that she not go anywhere alone, insisting that he would be lost if anything had ever happened to her.

She insisted that nothing would happen.

His concern burned ugly and sour in her stomach.

If he was so concerned for her, then why did Ronnie hit her all the time?

"Go to hell!" she had screamed defiantly at the end of the fight.

His body had stiffened as he whirled on her, striking her with a loud smack.

The force of the blow sent her staggering backwards.

Kathy's eyes locked with his, burning with resentment and hatred, a red mark from his hand across her cheek.

"I had to do it to make you listen," was all he had said, looking with resentful guilt at her bruised eye and cracked lip from punching her in an angry fit only a few days before.

It was supposed to be an apology.

And then he was out the door, slamming it behind him so hard that dishes in the cupboards rattled and a glass that was sitting precariously tilted on a folded open magazine on the coffee table tipped over and rolled onto the floor with a thud.

Kathy had stood there staring at the closed door. It blurred and swam before her eyes as they filled with tears.

His car engine roared to life and the tires squealed as he tore out of the driveway.

"Go to hell," she had croaked almost inaudibly.

She knew he'd be back after he had a few beers and cooled off.

After repairing her make-up to cover the angry red mark on her cheek, she wrote a note and left it on the kitchen table.

"Gone to the mall. Pick me up at 8," the note said.

She had grabbed her purse and ran out the door.

As she did this she knew she was just asking for trouble. Ronnie would be furious with her for disobeying him. But she was angry and feeling defiant. If it caused another fight, then so what?!

Now Kathy regretted it. She was not looking forward to the coming confrontation anymore. She dreaded going home.

Well, she'd give him just a little more time and then take the bus home. If he did show up and she was already gone on the bus he'd be even angrier for wasting his time coming to pick her up for nothing.

Pushing the memory of the fight from her mind, she glanced at her watch again. Eight-thirty. The mall locks its doors in half an hour.

Impatiently, she got up and went to the doors to see if she could see Ronnie's car anywhere. Nothing.

She knew Ronnie well enough to know that he'd have

returned home by now, probably a few hours ago. That was his style. He'd take off in a huff, toss back a few drinks quickly at the bar down the street and be home in an hour a little more drunk than he'd left.

Kathy wandered back over to her parcels and sat down again, waiting.

The same man who had stared at her with so much interest earlier came back. He ambled up to her and sat down beside her.

"Waiting for someone?"

"Yes."

"Maybe I'm who you're waiting for."

She rolled her eyes heavenward.

"Not likely," she thought.

The obviousness of his bad line following her response made answering unnecessary.

He toed one of her parcels on the floor, looking at it with a studied expression.

"You have a lot of packages. You must be looking for a ride."

"He'll be here any minute."

"He already is." He edged his hand closer to her along the concrete ledge as though he were having trouble not touching her.

"I could give you a ride," he said quietly. A real nice ride, he thought to himself. "My car is just outside."

"No thanks," she said coldly, turning away from him to show that he was dismissed from her mind and her company.

"I won't hurt you. Just let me give you a ride home," he insisted.

"Go away," she said firmly. She glanced at her watch. Nine o'clock.

Standing up, she began gathering her parcels.

He started gathering them up too.

"Those are mine," she said flatly, a hint of fear in her voice, reaching to snatch the parcels away from him.

"You can't carry all these by yourself," he teased, pulling them out of her reach.

She gave him a nervous exasperated look, saying nothing.

"Look," he continued, pointing to a red Mustang sitting at the curb not far from the door. "My car is right outside the door. I'll just help you put these in my car and drive you home. You've read the papers, heard the news, it's not safe for a pretty lady like you to be on the streets alone."

She looked around, getting worried, fear growing from this man's persistence, and soon spotted a security guard walking towards them.

Relief flooded through her.

"We're locking up now," the guard announced as he approached.

She suddenly lashed out, snatching her parcels away from the strange man, catching him off guard.

The security guard stopped in front of them.

Trying unsuccessfully to look tough, he informed them, "You'll have to leave now."

"I can't," Kathy said quickly, giving the guard a pleading look. "I mean, this man is bothering me. He's trying to pick me up and won't let me leave by myself."

The guard looked at the man with the expression of someone who is bored to irritation with a young child's mischief.

"She's not interested buddy," he said. "How 'bout if you just leave her be and try to do your picking up somewhere else."

"This is none of your business," the man retaliated, challenging the guard.

"The lady is in this mall and she complained about you bothering her," the guard said flatly. "That makes it my job to make it my business."

"Thank you," Kathy said to the guard before she turned and fled out of the mall and into the growing darkness.

Giving the guard a baleful glare, the man started to follow her out the door.

The guard put a restraining hand on the man's shoulder.

"Let's just wait until she's had a chance to get far away," he ordered.

The man watched her disappear into the night beyond the door with regret.

20

Struggling off the bus with all her packages, Kathy strode angrily down the street. This wouldn't have happened if Ronnie had picked her up. She was focused on the man at the mall and how scared she had been. Kathy knew it was her own fault, that she shouldn't have gone and Ronnie would not have picked her up. But it felt better to deflect the blame onto someone else.

Kathy tossed her head irately as she crossed the street, her heels clicking on the pavement.

She felt the first drops of rain.

"Oh just great," Kathy muttered at the sky. "Now it's starting to rain."

The sky had turned dark quickly with the fast moving storm clouds that gathered during her ride.

She sped up, hoping to get home before the rain began to really come down.

Kathy was just passing a narrow darkened back alley when, from out of the shadows, a hand reached out and grabbed her arm, quickly letting go.

She stopped dead in her tracks, trembling violently.

Terrified, she began slowly turning to see who's there.

"Hey," a gruff male voice crooned in her ear.

She could suddenly feel the man's presence, almost touching her, a dangerous entity she could physically feel despite there being no contact beyond the brief touch on her arm.

Her first thought was that the man from the mall had followed her. Her face flamed with annoyance that burned her cheeks and pushed down her fear enough to confront him.

"That creep!" she thought, ready to whirl around on him and tell him off.

The thought was cut off quickly and replaced by panic as the man grabbed her again, pulling her backwards roughly into the alley.

Her scream was silenced by his other hand that cupped over her mouth just as she opened it to scream. She was dragged deeper into the alley.

84

Her parcels were left scattered where she dropped them on the road just inside the alley entrance.

In the darkness of the alley, the man forced her into a dark blue car.

The rain started to come now, a light pattering of raindrops falling from the sky.

Shoving her roughly to the floor of the passenger side in the front, she was wedged tightly in the small space, restricting her movements so she could not fight or be seen by passersby.

Too scared to make a sound, she looked up at him, thinking with surprising rationality.

"This is not the mall man."

"I'm going to die," she thought to herself, surprising herself with the lack of hysteria. She studied him. "He doesn't look like a killer. He looks like a nice man."

"But," she considered, "Ronnie doesn't look like a jerk and he hurts me all the time."

The man started the car, keeping a restraining hand on her, and drove out of the alley, crushing one of the parcels under a tire.

The moment the car cleared the alley he accelerated, barrelling down the road only to suddenly find two young men, possibly in their teens, crossing in front of his car without looking.

His foot instinctively found the brake, pressing hard.

The tires screeched in protest and Kathy was thrown forward against the glove box as the car suddenly lurched to a near stop, narrowly missing mowing the two young men down.

The boys jumped out of the way with a yelp, one of them spinning back around to kick the car's side and give the driver the finger while yelling some very rude profanities at him.

The man glared at the boys with a look that made them both visibly flinch back.

He gunned the gas again, speeding down the street, the stench of burned rubber hanging heavily in the air behind him, black tire marks marring the pavement.

"Damn it!" the man cursed, hitting the steering wheel in frustration.

Kathy flinched as she cowered on the floor beside him.

"How careless," the man muttered, "stupid and completely careless.

He wasn't concerned about running over the young men and injuring them. They meant nothing to him.

He was angry at himself that they had seen him. They were possible witnesses.

And worse, if he had hit them that would have caused a scene he didn't want. He would have had to flee the scene, leaving the broken bodies lying in the street and the authorities looking for the culprit in a double hit-and-run that may have resulted in serious injuries or fatality to the two young men.

This was attention that he didn't want, risky.

"Oh well," he muttered, "at least it wouldn't be any big loss. They didn't exactly look like upstanding citizens."

It was quite the opposite actually.

If there were ever a pair he could peg as petty criminals on sight, these two were it.

The rain pattered lightly against the cement, leaving little puddles for the cars to whoosh through.

Whoops and laughter echoed down the street.

Running feet slapped wetly.

The two skinny young men, barely more than boys, who had just narrowly avoided being run over ran up the street and raced around the corner, ducking into a narrow alley between two buildings that was barely wide enough for a car to squeeze down.

"That was a good one," Toad exclaimed breathlessly, casually hoofing a bag from some store that lay on the ground, sending its contents falling out as it skittered away across the ground.

They both felt exhilarated from the rush of facing down the driver of the car.

In their minds the confrontation was much bigger and more dramatic than reality, and they came out victorious and proud.

Toad stomped on another bag that lay not far away, taking pleasure in the sound of something being crushed inside.

Short and scrawny like a pre-pubescent teen; Toad looked much younger than he really was. His wide face and large mouth made him appear much like a bad cartoon drawing of a toad's head grafted onto the body of a stick person.

Equipped with no sense and little intelligence, he was not considered desirable as a member by the street gangs and gang wannabe's populating the city. His light brown curly hair hung like a frizzy mop on his head.

By far, his best feature was his leather jacket. Torn and scarred, it was the proof behind all his tales of knife fights, shootings, and narrow escapes.

Only he himself, anyone who knows him, and anyone possessing the little intelligence required to see through his lies knew the truth. The tears, cuts, and holes were really made by scaling fences, the occasional ferocious Pekinese, and a few cuts he made with his own knife to make himself look tougher.

"Yeah, that geek didn't see it coming," Spider crooned.

His long bony arms stuck out from the armholes of his jean jacket like his namesake, the rough edges showing that the sleeves had been torn off. His name was tattooed on his arm, perhaps in the midst of an overwhelming identity crisis, crowning a jumble of lines and blobs that may have been meant to depict a spider resting on its web. His torn jacket showed no gang colours. He simply hadn't graduated to a high enough status of street life for any gang to want him, which didn't say much for him since gangs tended to recruit just about any dregs wallowing at the bottom of the societal cesspool. His long greasy hair hung limply, often covering his equally oily pimple-strewn face.

"So, where we gonn'a hit next?" Toad asked.

"Let's rest first," Spider panted. "Got'ta catch my breath."

"Hey! Toad! What'cha doin' back there?" he called out to his buddy who had disappeared into the darkened shadows of the alley.

"Takin' a piss," Toad laughed crudely. "Why? You wan'na hold it?" They both guffawed at this joke.

Lighting a thin marijuana cigarette, Spider looked up to see Toad approaching slowly, studying something he held in his hand.

"What'cha got there?"

"A purse."

"Lem'me see it. Already picked clean I bet."

Toad reached to hand it over, but Spider snatched it away rudely anyway.

Rifling through it, Spider found the wallet and threw away the purse. He opened it, examining the contents.

"Thirty-eight bucks," he spat. "A lousy thirty-eight bucks!"

"Any credit cards?"

"Yeah." He pulled out the cash and credit cards and stuffed them into his pocket.

Pulling out the driver's license, he held up his lighter and flicked it to give some light. He studied the photo with an approving leer.

"Lemme see," Toad whined.

Handing it over, Spider grabbed his crotch, gesticulating and thrusting.

"Oh, hot mama! I've got something for you!" They both giggled like demented children.

"Hey," he shouted suddenly, "let's go see if we can use these credit cards."

Handing the driver license back to Spider, who stuffed it into his pocket with the credit cards and cash, Toad ran for the alley entrance.

Spider followed.

Whooping and screeching like baboons with recent lobotomies, they ran out the other end of the alley and vanished into the darkness up the street.

21

All through the long drive Kathy was wedged into the tight space on the floor in front of the seat beside her abductor.

She tried craning her neck a few times during the drive to look out the window and see where they were going.

This was quickly rebuked each time with a powerful open handed slap to her head that left her dazed and smarting.

Mostly she obediently kept her head down. Her legs became more and more painful from cramping until they finally became numb and lost all feeling.

She surreptitiously studied every inch she could of her captor on that long drive, memorizing him. Not that she could see much with her head down.

I wonder where he's taking me, she thought.

She had moved beyond irrational tears and pleading into a saner and clear thinking terror.

She was going to die. She knew that. There was no point in being hysterical about it. It wasn't the first time she'd felt this way. She had been close many times when Ronnie got into one of his moods, angry or feeling sorry for himself, and was drunk to the point of mindless rage.

Sometimes Ronnie got too carried away and went too far.

She was scared of him, hated him, often wishing he would just kill her and get it over with. She was scared of death too of course.

In a sick and self-destructive way she was even scared of losing Ronnie and being all alone. But more than anything else she was terrified of what Ronnie would do to her if she ever tried to leave him.

She looked up at the man in the driver's seat and almost smiled, thankful.

In a way she was glad he chose her, that he would kill her. It meant she was finally escaping from Ronnie. She simply didn't have the courage to kill herself and now someone else was going to do it for her.

At last she would be free of the beatings, of Ronnie's

temper, of fear. She didn't have to be afraid anymore.

During the drive in silence, the man's mind had little to do but wander as his eyes watched the road ahead.

He was attuned to the woman crouching beside him, feeling her every movement without having to see it.

Now and then she'd try to look out the window, no doubt trying to get an idea of where they were or where they were going. Each time he reached out and cuffed her smartly.

He couldn't have her knowing their location or the path they travelled, just in case she did escape.

He had acted rashly when he took her, not planning it ahead as he normally did. He didn't have the ropes or blindfold.

He didn't really know why he'd rushed to snatch her.

Anger, maybe?

He thought that was the most likely reason.

He was sitting outside her house watching it and had heard the fighting inside and felt his cheeks burn with rage. He watched the boyfriend take off and then a little while later she came out. He had followed her to the mall, watched through the windows as that guy talked to her, probably trying to pick her up.

He followed her to the bus in his car, tailing the bus and then rushing ahead to beat her to her stop. He knew where she'd get off. She always got off at the same bus stop.

He thought as he drove, and with his senses focused on the woman beside him his mind went in that direction.

Before the other one, the one who survived and now lay in the hospital, the one they called Jane Doe because they didn't know her identity, before that he'd seen her in all their faces.

He saw her in each and every one of them from the first time he spotted them, every time he watched them, and even more clearly at the moment he took them.

And after he took them, he still saw her in them all.

Only they all turned out to be wrong. None of them were her. None of them were his sister.

But nothing felt the same after taking that one, the one they're calling Jane Doe in the news.

He had seen her in this one too; the one crouched beside him in the car, when he'd first spotted her. And every time he watched her after that, until now.

Something changed with Jane Doe. His conviction that Jane Doe was her had been so strong, that he had found her at last.

Even as he followed the woman now huddled beside him when she got off the bus, as he approached her and talked to her, he didn't see her in this one's face anymore.

He didn't feel the certainty as he grabbed her and took her into the car. He only felt confusion and doubt.

He had been sure before that this woman was her. But now he wasn't sure at all.

Ever since Jane Doe the image has been confused, he wasn't sure who this woman was anymore. The image of her is there before him in each of the women he's watching, and then it's gone, replaced by a resemblance that doesn't quite fit, a part of him knowing that it isn't her even as he stalks them and stakes out each woman.

And that feeling came on him even stronger as he took this one. In fact, while taking her he knew this woman was not his sister.

When he pictured her face as he looked at this woman, he didn't see his sister at all. Instead he saw Jane Doe, her pale face against the flat hospital pillow. He couldn't see her at all in this woman anymore.

He took this one anyway, despite the doubt, thinking the whole time that he should just walk away and leave her alone.

The blind rage was starting to close in, drawn out by the jumble of confused thoughts in his head.

He had to check it, to push it away and keep control.

He could feel the empty coldness creeping on, and behind it unreal calmness behind a bubbling pool of violence.

He didn't want that to happen again.

He knew that if it did, when he opened his eyes again, the woman would be dead and he would be full of remorse and confusion again.

He pushed it away, forcing the thoughts out of his head, and focused on the road.

He turned on the radio, hoping it would help, and drove on.

After what seemed like an eternity, the car turned onto a gravel road. The stones crunched under the tires and clunked against the undercarriage.

Kathy had begun to doze some time before.

With a lurching dip like a ship falling back to the water after coming off a cresting swell, the car bounced off the gravel road onto a dirt road.

Kathy banged her head painfully on the glove compartment, rousing her. They bumped and jogged along the dirt road for a while before turning off onto a badly overgrown driveway that stretched a long way, curving around to put trees between it and the road.

Kathy knew the road had changed only because of the change to slow rolling dips, the car no longer vibrating roughly from the gravel road. Now, as the car slowed to turn into the driveway, she could hear the whoosh of long grass brushing against the undercarriage and sides of the car, feeling the relative smoothness of the mud tracks beneath the tires.

When the car finally stopped the man just sat there for a long time, staring down at her.

She looked down, not daring to move or raise her head to look at him, trembling uncontrollably.

He patted her head tenderly.

She almost vomited.

Getting out of the car, he closed his door and walked around to the other side.

"What's taking him so long?" her mind screamed, waiting an eternity for him to open the door, her heart thudding so fast it dragged out her sense of time. Seconds seemed like long drawn-out minutes that would never end.

With a squeal of hinges the door opened.

The suddenness of it made her jump, almost squealing in fright.

The man grabbed her by the hair and roughly pulled her out. He held her up for a moment by a fistful of hair, the hair spilling across his fingers. He let go and she dropped to the ground, her legs too weak and numb to hold her.

"Get up," he commanded quietly.

She tried and couldn't.

Massaging her leg muscles, she flexed them, straitening and bending her legs. Painful needles began tingling through her legs as the circulation started to flow again.

He grabbed her by the wrist and started dragging her.

She squirmed and kicked, trying to get up, but he didn't give her the chance.

Kathy was scraped and cut from being dragged across the ground. He roughly hauled her up the steps and inside an old farmhouse, little more than a run-down old shack, adding bruises and a painful splinter to her injuries.

Slamming and locking the only door, he finally released her.

She slumped to the floor in a limp heap.

The man turned on a lamp. It burned dimly with muted yellow light. It was old, outdated and ugly, the kind of thing you'd expect to see in an old poor farmer's house and probably passed down a generation or two.

Trembling uncontrollably, her teeth chattered loudly like a steady drum roll introducing a new performance, the performance of her life, or her death.

Raising her head cautiously, she looked around.

The inside of the shack was as run down looking as the outside.

This old farmhouse was truly an old fashioned building. The inside walls were the same as the outer walls. Horizontally laid planks with mortar stuffed in the cracks between the boards. The last rays of sunlight peeped shyly between a few boards where pieces of mortar had crumbled and fallen out.

Studying the locked door, she felt helpless. The bolt looked solid and strong, a double-keyed lock requiring a key to open it from both sides.

Desperately she searched the walls.

"No windows," she thought wildly. "No windows, no escape."

The bare walls contained only the remnants of windows that had been crudely boarded up on the outside, their ragged curtains hanging uselessly in front of the glass panes.

There was nothing to brighten the shack with sunshine, or the promise of escape.

High on one wall a large crack teased with a narrow bar of sunset tinted light that slanted down to spotlight a piece of the worn floor.

She followed the bar of light with her eyes, hoping for a good sign. Her heart sank when she saw the rusty brown stain spotlighted on the floor. It was an old puddle soaked into the wooden floorboards.

She blanched.

Kathy inhaled deeply, trying to calm herself, and couldn't help trying to identify the odors invading her nostrils. A stale earthy smell, but not of mud, mingled with the dulled ammonia smell of urine.

"It smells old," she thought. There were also faint undercurrents of sweat, liquor, cigarettes, and something frighteningly unidentifiable. "The scent of fear," she thought.

The stifling gloom of the dark and dirty little shack weighed heavily on her.

She was startled out of her reveries by the sudden intrusion of the voice of her captor.

"Get up," he ordered.

She shook her head, silently mouthing the word, "no."

"Move!" he commanded, reaching to grab her.

She scuttled backward.

Her fingers trembled and fumbled so much that she had no control over them, she felt behind herself for something to support her weight, doubtful that her legs could.

He reached forward and grabbed her roughly by the wrist, pulling her to her feet.

"This is it," she thought to herself. "He's going to rape and kill you."

She braced herself mentally for what was about to come.

Only it never did.

She thought of Ronnie, what response he would expect. What would appease Ronnie and make him hurt her less. She nodded, a tear rolling down her cheek.

The man still held her arm, squeezing too hard.

She bit her lip, stifling a cry.

He squeezed harder, harder, until the pain was too much for her.

She cried out.

The man didn't know why he'd done that. He felt bad about it. He'd had the urge to put his hands around her throat and choke her, shaking her the way a dog shakes a rabbit in its mouth.

He didn't really want to hurt her and he didn't know what to do about it now. Apologize? No, you don't apologize to a woman you just forcibly kidnapped. If she lost her fear of him, he'd lose his control. Better to do nothing.

He put one hand on her delicate throat, holding firmly.

Just one little squeeze, he thought, and she wouldn't be able to breathe.

The rage was taking control of him. He was being pushed aside, becoming a spectator inside his own body with no control over what was happening.

He grabbed her, picking her up.

He was fighting with himself, trying to push the rage away, to control his own actions.

It was like some other being had invaded his body and pushed him out of the way.

He carried her to a back room. He stood her up beside the wall.

Bending over and opening a trap door in the floor, he pointed to the darkness below.

"Get in," he ordered gruffly.

22

The door to McNelly's office crashed open with a loud bang, shattering the silence.

Detective Jim McNelly leapt out of his chair, startled. His movements were ungainly, made awkward by his excessive bulk.

The other detective, Michael Underwood, stood in the doorway looking out of breath and excited. He started laughing at McNelly's reaction.

Breathlessly, Michael gasped, speaking too quickly, the words coming out disjointed between puffs of air.

"A little jumpy today, are we Jim?" Michael smirked.

McNelly didn't know why he felt so jumpy. Something was eating away at him, a vibe. He wasn't sleeping, was watching too many old cop shows on late night television, and had spent too many hours mulling over who could possibly be killing women and why.

"What's up?" McNelly growled.

"The same! They're the same!" All of a sudden Michael realized the ridiculous position the fat detective had taken and laughed.

Unimpressed, McNelly glared at him reproachfully, sitting back in his chair.

"What the hell are you talking about?"

"The women," Michael said, looking at him as though he should already know.

"What woman?" Jim reached for his cigarette in the ashtray.

"Not wo-MAN, wo-MEN! The women that are turning up dead, the little girl, the Jane Doe in the hospital." Michael blinked expectantly, waiting for it to click in McNelly's head.

McNelly turned to the desk to see why his fingers couldn't locate the cigarette burning in the ashtray. It was gone!

"Shit!" He started searching the papers scattered on the desk.

"The files," Michael asked excitedly, "where's the files?"

"Here on my desk, if they don't catch fire," McNelly muttered.

He was getting worried now.

Feathery curls of smoke drifted up to tease his nostrils.

Michael grabbed the files from the desk, rifling through them for the photos. He pulled some coloured stick-pins from a drawer in the other desk. One by one, he carefully pinned the photos to the empty corkboard, labelling each one with a name and a number coinciding with their order of discovery.

Jim ignored him, throwing papers and files to the floor in his haste to find the still burning cigarette.

The wisps of smoke grew fuller, thicker.

"Here's the thing," Michael explained urgently, "number one, Jane Doe. She was found in a downtown back alley, alive but presumably left for dead. Two, the little girl Mandy." He pointed to a nametag without a photo, "she got away."

Jim continued his bumbling search, crawling on hands and knees on the floor now.

"Three," Detective Underwood continued, "another Jane Doe, this one dead. The only lead to identify her is a small gold bracelet."

Jim's chair fell over with a crash.

"Four, Rebecca Shadway, dead, found buried in a sandbox at the school where she teaches."

Jim threw papers into the air, searching desperately.

The smoke grew heavier in the air, a curl of it dancing up provocatively from its hiding place.

"What do they have in common?" Underwood asked rhetorically.

Jim ignored him.

"Here's the thing, the general appearances are the same," Michael explained, "the injuries, details of the MO It's all the same! Ok, not completely. The little girl doesn't quite add up, but she still fits."

Jim bumped his head loudly underneath his desk and swore.

"Did you hear anything I said?" Michael asked, exasperated.

"Huh," Jim grunted.

Michael walked over and stepped on the smouldering cigarette, extinguishing it just as a flame leapt from the carpet, dancing merrily for a brief moment with a smell like burning hair before the life was crushed from it.

97

Heaving a sigh of relief, Jim crawled out from under the desk and stood up.

"What did you say?" McNelly asked.

"They add up, both Jane Doe's, the little girl, the teacher ..." McNelly interrupted Michael.

"They don't fit. Two were buried, dug up, and planted where they'd be found. The woman in the hospital was tossed out with the trash. The girl doesn't fit either," McNelly said. "I don't think this perp goes for kids. Usually it's one or the other, not both. He wants women."

"It's the mother," Michael explained. "The mother fits. I think she was the intended target. Something must have gone wrong."

McNelly looked at him curiously. Michael seemed to be agitated, like there was something very important he wanted to say but couldn't. Something seemed to be eating away at the younger man.

"I—he," Michael said, catching himself quickly and changing what he was about to say, "I think he wants to get caught. I think he wants to be stopped as much as someone else, I mean us, as much as we want him stopped."

"The man can't keep straight who he's talking about," McNelly thought. He wondered about that as he listened to Michael excitedly retell his story.

23

A bird chirped merrily, the sound muffled and far away.

Kathy slowly opened her eyes.

She was cold. Lying motionless, she took stock.

The room was dark and musty smelling, the only illumination a few bars of light slicing down between cracks in the ceiling. The dirt floor beneath her was only slightly damp, but that could just be the coolness that made it feel that way.

She sat up, her head ringing with pain.

Shivering violently, she looked around the little room for something to cover her chilled body. Her dress still damp with the rain from when she was kidnapped, the cold felt like it had seeped into her bones.

Nothing, the room was completely bare.

"Well, I'm alive," she whispered, "at least for now."

Poking and prodding, she carefully examined the extent of her injuries.

Still too weak with fear tremors to stand, she curled up into a foetal ball for warmth, wrapping her arms around her icy legs. A cold draught caressed her, as though to comfort her with the memory of freedom beyond these aged walls.

For a long time she lay there shivering, crying, listening and waiting.

Eventually sleep overcame fear and she dozed off, sending her mind into another world full of terrifying images and pursuing monsters.

24

Michael looked at McNelly in stunned silence.

"Yes," McNelly continued. "While you've been undercover watching the girl, I've been following leads and studying the evidence. I've pieced it all together days ago. Everything you just told me ... I already know."

"The only thing you have wrong," McNelly said, "that doesn't add up, is the little girl. By all accounts this perp targets women, not children. He didn't try to take the mother, he took the child. It just doesn't fit."

McNelly studied Michael. He noticed the clenching jaw, the twitch of a muscle in his neck, the pulse of a vein in his forehead.

"The man is too deep into this," McNelly thought.

Michael was studying McNelly in return. He seemed to be looking for a response, an answer to the question "why is he so convinced the girl is connected?"

Michael thought. He knew the girl was connected, an important piece of the puzzle. He just couldn't say why.

25

The hushed hospital corridors were pierced by a blood curdling scream. It was followed by scream after scream, a frenzied flow of frantic shrieks.

Nurses, doctors, and orderlies dropped their tasks and scurried about like frenzied ants, trying to determine the source of the continuing cries.

Molly nearly jumped out of her skin at the sudden desperate shrieks. It took her a moment to recover before she ran for Jane Doe's room where the screams were coming from, almost missing the doorway in her rush.

A shock-cart was produced and a team descended on room 214B where the frantic screams were coming from, like a SWAT team prepared for the worst attacking a terrorist encampment.

They all converged on the room within heartbeats of each other.

There, in the bed, Jane Doe sat up, her eyes wild with terror, mouth open, while an endless stream of screams poured out.

She stared at them wildly, not recognizing them, almost seeming to not even see them, as though another scene that was completely foreign to the hospital room filled her eyes.

She began tearing at the sheets covering her, ripping out her intravenous tube in the process as if she didn't even see it, trying to get up.

Her weakened body would not cooperate.

She fell out of the bed more than crawling out of it.

Nurses and orderlies were on her almost instantly, grabbing her and trying to pin her flailing arms even as she tried frantically to scratch their eyes out, to bite and kick them, as though fighting for her very life.

A needle was jabbed quickly into her arm, her struggles making it difficult. The plunger was pressed home.

Within moments the sedative took effect.

The cries stopped and the commotion began to dissipate as she slumped weakly in their arms, becoming little more than a rag doll.

The large number of mostly unneeded personnel resumed their unfinished tasks, leaving only a few nurses in the room to settle the patient back in.

One of them was Molly.

With a little effort, they lifted the unconscious woman back into bed, rolling her prone on her back and arranging her legs and arms straight before covering her with the sheets again.

Gently, Molly reinserted an intravenous line and checked the needle taped down to hold it in her hand.

A pair of orderlies returned with padded cuffs. Raising the side rails on the bed, they dexterously attached the cuffs to be bed and then to the patient, restraining her to the bed in case she woke up again. They were done in seconds and gone from the room without a word.

Confident her charge was settled back in and safe, Molly returned to the nurses' desk to page Doctor Greenburg.

From the nurses' desk, Molly suspiciously scrutinized the orderly who spent so much time watching that room and its occupant.

He was working nearby, tidying supplies on a cart that didn't look to her like they needed tidying.

Of all the people who rushed to Jane's room, he had kept steadily at his work, barely even glancing up. Although, she had noticed that his entire body had tightened up at the sound of Jane's frantic screams.

"He looks distressed", she thought, "more like a worried lover than an attendant."

But that wasn't the vibe she got from the man. She sensed a darkness in him, an ulterior purpose. Molly was certain he wasn't who he seemed to be.

Convinced he's hiding something and up to no good, she was more determined than ever to expose him.

Still, the mysterious orderly hovered nearby.

Dr. Greenburg arrived, rushing into Jane Doe's room.

Walking briskly past the orderly to follow the doctor into Jane's room, Molly snapped at him as she passed by.

"Don't you have some work to do?"

Her heart raced and her knees almost buckled beneath her by

the time she was standing safely beside the doctor next to Jane's bed.

She blinked in surprise as the realization hit her at last that, for the first time since being brought in, Jane Doe woke up. Until they sedated her Jane was groggy, probably hallucinating, and not very alert, but fully conscious.

Doctor Greenburg was busy checking the unconscious woman's responses.

Jane's wrist flopped limply, her eyes rolling in her head.

She wouldn't stay out long. The sedative given her to calm her frantic screams was fast acting, putting her to sleep quickly but would also wear off fast.

"We'll have to keep her sedated for a while longer," Dr. Greenburg said. "We don't want her waking up again like this and hurting herself. I'm putting in an order for a sedative to be administered regularly to keep her asleep. We'll pause it when we need her to wake up for tests, but she'll have to be monitored closely. We don't want her waking up alone again. Schedule the psychologist too. It doesn't look like she's ready to face the world just yet."

They've tried letting Jane wake up before, to the same effect.

Molly glanced at the doorway where she could just see the orderly's elbow sometimes coming into view as he sorted and stacked the supplies on the cart.

She wondered about the orderly being outside Jane's door when she started screaming. Coincidence? Or had something about him, something he was doing maybe, spooked her? Did something remind her of what happened, and if so, what?

Her extra sense was screaming at her that something was wrong, that something about the orderly was off.

"I am going to find out what you are hiding and expose you," she whispered, watching him out of the corner of her eye while pretending to be occupied with another task.

26

Stumbling unsteadily on the steps to the front door of the house, Ronnie braced himself against the door to steady himself and inserted his key into the lock.

Opening the door with exaggerated care, he sauntered into the house and closed the door behind him, swaying drunkenly as he turned away from the door.

"Kathy," he called in a loud whisper, thinking she might be asleep.

Crossing the living room to the kitchen, he called again, a note of danger entering his voice. "Kathy, where are you?"

Heading straight for the fridge, he retrieved a beer and leaned heavily against the fridge door. Twisting the cap off the bottle, he downed a third of the beer.

Glancing around the kitchen past the bottle held to his lips, his gaze came to rest on the piece of paper lying on the table. He lowered the bottle and pushed himself off the fridge.

Tossing the bottle cap at the sink, Ronnie advanced on the table. He Sank clumsily into a chair, and put down the bottle and slid the piece of paper closer.

Ronnie studied the note for a moment with a frown.

"Gone to the Mall. Pick me up at 8," the note read.

His expression hardened.

"Kathy!" he roared. "Kathy, come in here now!"

Silence answered him.

He slammed his fist down on the table, making the bottle jump with a rattle.

Getting up, he quickly went through their small home.

Slamming doors open and closed with increasing violence, he smashed the bedroom door open against the wall so hard the knob pierced the drywall with a shuddering thump, pinning the door to the wall.

"Kathy, you little whore, where are you," he hissed with deadly anger.

Returning to the kitchen, he snatched the beer bottle off the table and took a hard swig.

In a fit of rage, he hurled the bottle against the wall, shattering it. Beer and glass erupted in a foamy explosion, showering the room with amber rain and brown glass.

Ronnie roamed the house again, raging, insanely furious. The crash and tinkle of destruction followed him like a pet dog, marking his trail.

Finally he stormed out the door, slamming it so hard in his wake that the china trembled and clinked merrily on its shelves. The door shuddered loudly in its frame.

The car roared to life, tires screaming down the street.

Ronnie's black Firebird lurched to a stop at the curb outside the darkened mall, the motor idling.

Through the locked doors, he could see a few security lights dimly illuminating the insides of each store within his limited scope of sight.

"Shit!" He pounded the steering wheel with his fist.

Straining to see his watch in the darkened car, he cursed, "mother-fucking twelve o'clock. When I find out where you've been since the mall closed, you're going to be one very sorry little girl. What the hell have you been doing all night?!"

Putting the car into gear, he rushed out of the parking lot, cutting off a small white car as he turned onto the street.

Arriving home again, Ronnie stormed into the house, demanding, "Kathy, where are you?! Show yourself, now!"

A quick search showed that she hadn't arrived home yet.

"She's left me, that's it," he decided. "She's left me. I'll fucking kill her!"

Rushing into the living room, he grabbed the phone and dialled.

One ring, two.

He paced restlessly, clutching the phone so hard the skin covering his knuckles turned white.

Finally on the fifth ring a woman's voice answered groggily.

"Where is she?" Ronnie barked into the phone.

Surprised, Kathy's mother stammered, "What? Who is this?" She knew who it was almost immediately, but couldn't respond appropriately with the shock of this sudden angry phone call in the middle of the night.

"You know damn well who! You tell that little bitch if she doesn't get her ass back here in half an hour, I'll come get her!" Drops of spit flew from Ronnie's mouth in his rage. "And if I have to go over there and drag her back home, Kathy is going to be very sorry she pulled this little stunt of hers."

Recovered somewhat but still rattled, the older woman tried to reason with him.

"Kathy's not here Ronnie," she said. "What are you talking about?"

Her mind raced with the thought, her heart lurching with joy, "she left him. At last she left that terrible man." A faint smile tickled at the corners of her mouth.

"Don't lie to me," Ronnie screamed into the phone. "She's there! I know she is!"

"Ronnie, calm down." She was getting angry now, defensive. "Kathy isn't here. And even if she was, I wouldn't send her home with you in this kind of mood."

"Fuck you! Put her on the phone!"

"She's not here."

"You can't lie to me," he insisted. "I know she's there. She left me and she has no place else to go." A hint of panic had crept into his voice now as he finally realized there might be a possibility he had lost Kathy.

Kathy's mother smiled and countered, "Good for her. I knew someday she would get her senses back."

Seething with rage, Ronnie demanded, "You tell her she has half an hour. If she's not here when I get back, I'm coming for her! She'll regret that! You both will!" He slammed the phone down.

The brief silence followed by the buzz of a disconnected phone line rang with deadly intensity in the woman's ear.

"Oh, do be careful my little Katherine, wherever you are," she whispered.

Ronnie was furious. He shook with the rage like a person in shock. He let out an unintelligible shriek and punched his fist through the wall.

Pulling his scraped knuckles out of the hole, he kicked the

wall, putting his foot through it.

He stormed around the house, tearing up magazines and books, tossing things, and knocking things over in a violent temper tantrum.

A lamp crashed against the window, exploding on impact in a plume of orange ceramic. Amazingly the window did not crack.

He walked over broken shards and debris, mashing them into the floor as he stormed around the house destroying anything within reach.

Finally he stormed out, slamming the door behind him, not bothering to lock it.

Once again Ronnie was in his car, the tires screaming down the street, headed for the bar.

Part Six:
Don't Go Home With Strangers

27

Raising his pale putty-like face, the police officer standing at the reception counter of the police station looked up from the forms he was filling out to see what was causing the approaching commotion.

With a lot of scuffling, grunting, and cursing, two grimy looking teenagers were being dragged by two burly officers in uniform through the doorway into the station.

"What'd they do?" the man behind the desk asked, not really expecting an answer. Most of the other officers, and anyone else who has worked with him, don't like this sorrowful red-beaked man and try to avoid contact with him, or just ignored him when they can't.

"These punks were trying to use stolen credit cards," one of the officers replied as they pushed the boys past him into the inner general office area.

"Knock it off and sit down," one of them ordered as they pushed the two boys down on chairs crammed in the little space between their two desks, the officers sat in their own chairs. They exchanged meaningful looks for the benefit of the two nervous boys seated between them, then stared down at them with impenetrable expressions. This ploy had the desired effect.

The younger looking of the two teens began trembling. Puckering his large mouth, he turned his wide face back and forth between the two officers as though watching a tennis match.

His partner began sweating, his face paling behind the mask of long greasy hair hanging limply in front of his face.

"Okay, let's start at the top," the officer on the left said. "What are your names?"

"I'm Spider, he's Toad," the older of the two responded, the words spilling out in a fast tumble. He looked with nervous defiance at each officer.

"No," the officer reprimanded, "your REAL names."

"I—I'm Trev—," Toad began.

In a panic, Spider cut him off mid-name.

"No, don't tell them your real name," he whispered conspiratorially. His hair swung in long arcs as he shook his head.

"We can't tell them our real names." His voice broke as he continued urgently. "It's just Spider and Toad, and that's all the names we got." He stared at Toad, nearly in a panic over this blunder, trying to get the urgency of his message across.

"But why not," Toad whispered, glancing nervously at the waiting officer. "Why can't we tell them our names?"

"It's the code, dummy," Spider hissed.

"What code?" Toad asked, perplexed.

Leaning over to whisper in Toad's ear, Spider insisted, "the gang code! We wanna join a gang, so we gotta follow their codes. That means no names, just nicknames."

"We can hear you, you know," one of the officers said as if talking to a four year old.

The other officer leaned heavily over the desk, talking sternly right in their faces, hammering a large fist onto the desk with a loud thump.

"I don't give a rat's ass about gang codes, or street rules, or your tree-house club laws, or any of that crap! If you don't tell us your names we're all going to be here for a very long time."

The two teens jumped with a squeal and looked around with surprised fright.

"What are your names?" the officer repeated angrily.

"Trevor," Toad squawked.

"Trevor what?"

"Um," he lowered his eyes in embarrassment, shoulders slumped, head hanging, "T-Trevor Finklestein." His voice trailed off into a whisper.

The two officers' eyes shone with suppressed mirth, the corners of their mouths twitching briefly. One of them had to turn his head away as he tried to regain control. His face was once more grim and angry as he turned back to the youth.

"And yours?" the officer glared down at Spider, intimidating.

"James," he said, his voice quiet and defeated.

"James ...," the officer prompted.

"Collegen." He gave the officer a shifty-eyed glare, scared enough to try to be discrete, yet too accustomed to meeting every situation he didn't want to be in with resentment and moody defiance.

Standing up and towering over the two scrawny boys, the officer gave them a satisfied grin, much like a tiger who just found a nice helpless tender little snack trembling with fear caught between his mighty paws.

"Well boys," now that the introductions are over, where did you get the credit cards?"

"Found 'em," Spider mumbled, studying his hands clasped in his lap.

Turning and pacing a few steps away, the officer turned back to them, thrust his hands in the air in exclamation, and loudly announced.

"YOU FOUND THEM! And where did you find them? In someone's home? Their car? In some little old lady's purse as she walked down the street?"

Heads turned as many of the people scattered through the large room looked to see what the commotion was.

One little old lady tut-tutted as she glared at them especially hard with disgust.

Unnerved by this unwanted attention, the two teens glanced around, trying to shrink into themselves.

The other officer, who had been sitting silently at his desk and almost forgotten, got up and stalked around to the other side of the space between the two desks.

All their attention focused on their antagonizer, the two teens were oblivious to the second officer moving into position behind them.

Leaning over them, he barked loudly.

"Where did you get the cards?!"

Crying out in unison, the two teens jumped nearly out of

their chairs. Trembling, they both turned to face him.

"In the alley," Spider gushed, an edge of hysteria creeping into his voice, making it crack. "We found the purse in the alley."

"What alley?"

"Just some alley." The teen shrugged.

"And what about the woman?"

"W-what woman?" Toad whined.

"The woman you two little creeps mugged," the officer glared down at him.

"That's another thing," Spider thrust in timidly.

"What is?" the officer asked, almost cowing him into silence.

Gathering his courage, Spider rubbed his eyes and swallowed dryly before continuing.

"That crack about the little old lady." He stared at the officer, waiting for a response, looking as though he fully expected it to come in the form of a sharp cuff in the side of the head.

The officer's silence spoke louder than words.

Shifting nervously, Spider went on.

"You know there's no old lady. You got the driver licence. You know it's some young chick and no old lady. We don't rob no old ladies." His voice trailed off nervously.

Ignoring this, the officer continued to grill them.

"So what did you do to the woman? Hit her? Knock her down? Cut her?"

"There's no woman," Toad squeaked. "We just found the purse, that's all."

"Right," the other office cut in. The teens whirled around to face him. He continued.

"So what? This woman just happened to detour down some alley, drop her purse, and leave without noticing she lost it? Is that what I'm supposed to believe?" His smirk said that he didn't believe a word these two punks were saying.

"There was other stuff too," Toad mumbled.

"What stuff?"

"Bags, just lying about, junk from stores like at the mall."

L.V. Gaudet

"And what did you do with those bags?"

"Nothing" Toad mumbled.

"We kicked and stomped them," Spider cut in, his face full of smartass attitude the officers wanted to wipe off of it.

The two officers exchanged a quick glance.

"And did you see anyone else around? Any witnesses we might find that might have seen you?"

"No," Spider was petulant like a little boy.

"Convenient, no witnesses to your non-mugging of the woman whose credit card you tried to use."

The teens shook their heads, "No".

"So, we have no reason to believe you didn't hurt the woman when you mugged her. How bad did you hurt her? Is she in the hospital?"

The cops didn't think so, there had been no calls about assault victims, but they were getting tired of this game and wanted to get to the bottom of these punk kids and the stolen wallet. Fear would make them talk pretty fast. It wasn't worth wasting any more of their time on than they had to.

The teens were getting more scared. This was getting more serious than they'd thought when they found the purse.

"Th—there was someone," Toad piped in hopefully, "maybe."

The cops looked at him expectantly.

Spider looked at him in confusion.

"That guy," Toad went on, "the one that almost ran us over. He came peeling out of the alley where we found the wallet. He'd have seen there was no woman. He saw us and there was no woman when we got to the stuff."

The cops exchanged looks again.

Toad had no idea what he had just said, or what it might mean.

They had to get as much information from these kids as they could now. This case just possibly got a whole lot bigger than a simple purse-snatching and attempted credit card fraud.

This questioning continued for the next two hours before the officers finally locked the two teens in a holding cell to sit and think about it for a while.

112

"Let's break for dinner, then swing by that alley before we go to this lady's house," one of the officers suggested.

Rubbing his stomach hungrily in answer, the other officer grabbed his jacket and followed his partner out.

28

Ronnie sat in a chair in the living room staring dejectedly ahead of him. He was slumped down in the seat with his legs stretched out in front of him like a long ramp.

He lifted the beer to his mouth mechanically, took a long swallow, brought it down again, and finally rested in on the chair's arm with his hand firmly fastened to the bottle. He sat there for a while in the darkness, not bothering to turn on a light.

The doorbell rang hollowly through the house.

Grumbling, Ronnie swallowed the rest of his beer and dropped the empty bottle to the floor.

The doorbell rang again.

"I'm coming," he snarled under his breath, pushing himself out of the chair.

Broken glass crunched under his boots as he walked to the door with a bit of a stagger.

Opening the door, Ronnie sullenly studied the two uniformed police officers standing on his steps.

Mr. Kingslow?" one of the officers asked.

"No," he eyed them warily.

"Does a Miss Katherine Kingslow live here?"

"Yeah, what of it?"

"What is your name, Sir?" the first officer asked.

"Ronnie. Ronnie Crowley."

Mr. Crowley, we would like to talk to Miss Kingslow if she's home."

She's not here," Ronnie grumbled, shifting his weight threateningly as anger flared in his beer-fuzzy brain.

He was thinking about Kathy having the gall to leave him, almost forgetting about the two men standing in front of him.

The second officer saw past Ronnie's frame blocking the doorway when he moved.

He quickly took in the overturned small end table, its broken lamp laying a foot and a half away, scattered coloured glass and ceramic trinkets, some cracked into large pieces, others shattered into deadly confetti.

He shifted his stance and his gaze, trying to see more.

He spied a kitchen chair overturned in a doorway, the corner of a large bookcase, or maybe a china cabinet, he couldn't quite tell which, lying face down amid the rubble.

The place looked like it had been tossed in an especially destructive robbery.

His suspicions were instantly turned from the two punk kids who claimed to have found a lost purse to the man standing before him. However that purse came to be separated from the currently absent Katherine Kingslow, there was definitely more to the story than the two punk kids. But they had already suspected that back at the station.

Nudging his partner with an elbow, he gestured toward the open door with a movement of his head.

Taking his partner's cue and having noticed the mess too, the first officer asked, "Have you had a break in Mr. Crowley?"

"No," Ronnie said roughly, not bothering to elaborate. He knew damned well the officers were referring to the mess behind him. He was getting more edgy.

"Is everything alright Mr. Crowley?"

"Yeah, fine."

"Are you sure now?" The officer craned his head, obviously trying to see past Ronnie and get a better look at the inside of the house.

"This place looks like someone tossed it over pretty good."

"I'm fine," Ronnie said firmly, intending to be dismissive, but sounding more defensive. "The girlfriend's just a lousy housekeeper."

It was obvious that Ronnie knew the officers were not buying the poor housekeeping excuse.

"Where is Miss Kingslow, Mr. Crowley?" He kept his face passive, showing no emotion or intent.

"How the hell do I know?"

"Where is she?" He repeated with more authority. "Inside?"

"She's gone." Ronnie said, almost a whine, his eyes watering with self-pity. He was getting more nervous, the mess behind him growing heavier on his conscious. He was starting to feel like an idiot for trashing the house in an angry tantrum.

115

Worse was the nagging thought in the back of his head that if anything did happen to Kathy, trashing the house only made him look guilty. They'd be sure to try to pin it on him.

He moved to block either officer from seeing more of the mess behind him than they already have.

"What do you want Kathy for?" he asked, breaking into a nervous sweat.

"We just want to talk to her, Ronnie," the first officer responded amiably.

"What about?" He thrust out his chin defiantly.

"We found a couple of boys trying to use her credit cards, that's all. We assumed they were lost or stolen and came to get a statement from her." He was being condescending now, sensing how volatile the drunken man in front of him could be.

"Is that okay Mr. Crowley?"

"Yeah sure, I suppose," Ronnie gave in sulkily.

"So, where's Kathy?" the second officer repeated the question.

"I don't know," Ronnie admitted with a slow shake of his head.

"Sure you don't," the first officer sympathized. "We'd like to come in and take a little look around if you don't mind."

Ronnie's eyes hardened with an edge of wildness like a cornered beast. His breath quickened, turning to shallow breaths.

Raising a trembling hand, he poked the officer in the chest with his finger.

"There's nothing to see, so get out a my face," he slurred.

"I'm sure there isn't," the officer placated. "But still, we'd like to take a look around Mr. Crowley."

Ronnie was really starting to panic now. He had assumed Kathy was at her mother's and that she'd left him, but he really didn't know for sure. He knew what the trashed house would look like to the police, what they'd think.

What if Kathy wasn't at her mother's? What if she was hiding from him? What if her mother really didn't know where she was? How did these kids the cops mentioned get her credit cards? What if something bad happened to her? He'd get blamed!

He knew now that he never should have wrecked the place, no matter how mad Kathy made him. He should have controlled his anger, but he'd been so damned mad. It was her fault, not his! Kathy made him do it. She always does things to make him so angry.

Now it's going to look like he'd done something to her, killed her or made her disappear maybe. But he didn't, at least he doesn't think he did ... did he? Sometimes he gets so angry and drunk that he blacks out. But this time he's sure he didn't do anything but trash the place when she didn't come home. He hoped.

Oh, shit! His heart sank. He was in very big trouble.

His mind turned to paranoia as it sometimes did when he was drunk.

Ronnie started to wonder if maybe Kathy had set him up. She had planned all this! What if she had played him for a fool so he would trash the place? Then she'd hide until he was put away in jail for doing something to her. Something he didn't do.

Fury began to grow in Ronnie as he thought about Kathy trying to frame him, trying to make the police think he did something to her.

"You got a warrant?" Ronnie demanded.

"Well, no we don't," the officer soothed. "Come on Mr. Crowley, make it easier on us won't you? It would sure make it easier on yourself."

"I didn't do anything."

"No, of course you didn't. We'd just like to take a look around, ask you a few questions, that's all. You know, about Kathy losing her purse."

"You don't have a warrant, you can't come in," Ronnie spat. "And I've nothing to say to you."

Taking a step back, he grabbed the door, slamming it shut in the officers' faces.

The door never made it.

Bracing his shoulder against the moving door, the first officer wedged himself between the door and its frame.

"What did you do with her Ronnie?" he asked sternly.

"GET OUT!" Ronnie roared, pushing against the door. He

seemed to grow physically in size with his explosion of rage, but that was a trick of stance as he leaned forward on the balls of his feet, standing straighter and taller. It was more of a base animal reaction, trying to look bigger, and was not something he did consciously.

"We saw the alley Ronnie," the second officer bluffed. We know something happened. Those boys didn't mug her." He paused dramatically. "Someone beat them to her."

"GET OUT, GET OUT, GET OUT!" Ronnie bellowed.

With a nod to each other both officers threw their weight at the door in unison. It crashed inward, slamming against the wall with a loud bang and knocking Ronnie backwards.

Recovering before he hit the floor, Ronnie charged them blindly with a drunken brawler's snarl.

Each grabbing him on one side, the officers spun him around and threw him face down on the floor. One officer went down with him, twisting his arm at an unnatural angle and thrusting a knee painfully into his back to make sure he didn't get up. They landed hard, knocking some of the wind, and the fight, out of Ronnie. He held Ronnie down like that; balancing most of his weight on the knee digging into Ronnie's back while his partner wrestled Ronnie's other arm into place and cuffed him.

Dragging their captive out to the car, they read him his rights and radioed the station. Soon the squad car pulled away from the curb and drove away.

The man sitting in the dark car from a shadowy driveway across the street watched Ronnie being hauled away.

"Another time, bastard," he muttered.

The man waited until the cruiser car was out of sight before starting his engine.

The dark blue paint of the car was illuminated by the light of a streetlamp as it slid by beneath the light.

It drove to the end of the street and turned the corner, vanishing from sight behind the houses.

Soon after another squad car pulled up, parking outside to guard the house. It was now a potential crime scene, all depending on Kathy's whereabouts and condition.

This was no longer a case of a lost or stolen purse; there was now a possible domestic assault or missing person involved.

Two hours and forty minutes later a crime scene unit pulled up in front of the house. The men climbed out of their vehicle and went into the house.

29

At the police station, Ronnie had been left in a small cell-like interrogation room to sleep it off.

The room had only one small window in the door with reinforced wire mesh embedded in the glass, the only furniture a small metal table and two uncomfortable metal folding chairs.

Unkempt, hung over, and his shirt torn from struggling with the two police officers, Ronnie sat on one of the chairs looking morose.

His head pounded at every sound from outside the room, spun with dizziness and felt detached from the rest of him. His mouth felt pasty dry as though it had been stuffed with wads of cotton all night long and tasted as if that cotton had been first used to clean up week old vomit. His whole body hurt and exhaustion hung heavily on him. His stomach felt a sourness that even a churning stomach would have improved.

The hours sitting at the police station had allowed the intoxicating poisons of the alcohol to leach out of his body, leaving him suffering from an immense hangover.

The smell of vomit in the room didn't help.

Neither did passing out on the hard cold floor in a drunken stupor for a while or vomiting into a waste can until he wished someone would just reach inside his mouth and rip his stomach out already.

Ronnie groaned in pain and self-pity, his eyes red more from the alcohol poisoning than from the drunken tears.

They had left him there for hours, as though they had forgotten he was there.

At one point, after yet again pacing the small room in agitation, Ronnie had banged on the door for twenty minutes straight, yelling for attention.

He felt as though the whole world was torturing him. His voice was hoarse from his dry throat and the yelling. He desperately needed something to drink, to urinate, and to lie down and rest his alcohol-swollen brain.

Finally, one of the two officers who had brought him in

came to escort him to the washroom. He was ready to pee himself by this time and half ran for the bathroom.

"What took so long?" Ronnie whined, "I'm gonna piss myself! You guys trying to kill me or something?"

Once returned to the room the officer allowed Ronnie to have a can of soda pop, but ignored his demands of a phone call.

Ronnie guzzled the drink, wishing he had a case of them, his body so dehydrated from drinking that the one soda made his thirst even worse.

He gagged, almost vomiting the drink.

"More?" he asked the officer hopefully.

Without a word, the officer took the empty can and left the interrogation room.

They left him alone once again to wait for another forty-five minutes.

The two officers entered the small room, repositioned Ronnie so that he sat in one chair, one officer leaning against the table out of sight behind him, and the other sitting in the second chair in front of him.

They began grilling him brutally, playing different versions of bad cop-good cop, bad cop-bad cop, and two good guys just trying to help a pal in trouble. When they finally stopped to take a break, all three were exhausted and frustrated.

Finally admitting they have to release Ronnie, they warned him against leaving the city, cautioning him with the threat of constant surveillance.

They were angry over not getting what they wanted, and for their wasted time.

Ronnie had only told the truth as he knew it, a story they didn't believe.

After talking to the couple's neighbors and the young woman's mother while Ronnie cooled his heals in the interrogation room, they were more than ever convinced that if something had happened to his missing girlfriend Kathy, Ronnie had something to do with it.

They would be watching Ronnie. He was their number one suspect in Kathy's disappearance. But they wouldn't be watching him that closely.

Both officers felt that most likely the woman had simply had enough of this jerk and left. She was probably holed up somewhere, at a friend's perhaps, waiting for his rage to die down.

The things that bothered them, giving them enough suspicion to doubt this, was the mother's genuine concern and the ruined state of the small house.

Women escaping violent partners don't always go home to mama, and it could very well be that the man did have a drunken tantrum and wreck the place after finding her gone. But the wallet and parcels abandoned at the alley entrance made the situation suspicious and Ronnie look very guilty of something.

But their prisoner was sticking too well to his story for it to be made up. He just didn't seem that smart.

They had enough doubt to question their belief she simply ran away, but nothing more.

This kind of case was tiresome, generally a waste of their time, and irked them with the knowledge that once found she would most likely just go back to the man.

As they escorted him to the door of the building, Ronnie paused.

"Why'd you come?" he asked. "Who called you? That nosy old Mrs. Krampton?"

"Your girlfriend's mother called," one of the officers answered dryly. "After you called her and threatened her, she called us. Funny, she thinks you did something to your girlfriend." He exchanged an amused look with his partner just to get under Ronnie's skin.

"No, no," Ronnie whined. "We just went over all that. I had nothing to do with anything. She's probably left me." He had the nerve to pout like a little boy.

"Get out of here before we change our minds and lock you back up," one of the officers said, opening the door for Ronnie.

The following day the two officers went to the mall Ronnie told them Kathy frequents.

They doubted very much they would find anything there.

They got nowhere with a random questioning of the staff in

various shops. They didn't expect anything would come of it.

The officers unexpectedly hit the jackpot when they started on the mall security guards.

One in particular remembered in lewd descriptive language the pretty lady he rescued from the clutches of what he seemed to view more as competition than a man harassing a woman.

The man's description did not match the boyfriend.

Acting more full of bravado and authority than his position warranted, the mall guard expressed his desire for her to come back and thank him properly by fulfilling his most wicked fantasies, obviously in hopes they would relay his frank message to the woman once they found her.

Shaking their heads in disgust, the officers left the ignorant guard to his useless puffed-up display to begin their search for the mysterious man with the red mustang.

When they finally received them, the video surveillance tapes from the mall would prove to be of too poor quality to be useful.

They now had a second suspect in Kathy's disappearance, although they were still betting on the boyfriend as a sure thing.

Part Seven: Budding Romances, Wistful Wishes & Pamela Makes 7

30

The early evening wind howled against the run-down little farmhouse. With no windows and the lamps unlit, the only light illuminating the inside of the century old building were beams of weak sunlight shining through the cracks in the walls.

The floorboards creak and groan loudly in protest as the man paces restlessly in the small house.

Nervous energy raged beneath his veneer of control and he tried to calm himself, to think. He has to think hard; hard about Jane and about how to rescue her from the hospital.

"I knew she knew me. I was sure she was dead when I left her in that alley. But she's alive. She's waiting there for me in the hospital, surrounded by police, doctors, so many people. I've found her this time! She seems untouchable, almost.

She needs to be rescued, taken from that place and brought home. Stupid, stupid me! Thought for sure she was dead, just like the others. Damn, I was sure of it."

He smiled briefly at the memory of her, his face falling back to its original sullen look as his thoughts rolled on.

"I left her in a dirty alley that night, buried under a trash heap, left her for dead..."

These were the thoughts racing through his mind over and over again as he tried hard to concentrate on solving this problem, getting Jane out of the hospital without being caught.

He continued pacing restlessly in the gloomy room.

The sound of pacing and the creaking and groaning floorboards above were amplified in the empty root cellar.

Empty except for bugs, the occasional mouse peeking out, and the terrified woman huddled in a corner.

Kathy shivered violently from cold as much as fear.

She shifted, stiff with the chill seeping into her joints from the damp earth floor and rough cement walls she crouched against. She was exhausted but too afraid of the mice and large bugs to lie down.

"I must be nuts," she thought to herself, "scared of rodents and bugs down here with the real monster up there."

Glancing furtively at the two mice sniffing about in a dark corner, moving slowly but steadily closer to her in their quest for something to eat, she mostly stared up, transfixed by the wooden boards making up the ceiling of her prison.

HE is on the other side of those boards.

She could see him through the cracks, or rather the suggestion of him, his shadow. Pacing, endlessly pacing.

She wanted to scream at him to stop it, to stop that endless pacing. It was wearing on her already frayed nerves.

The only light penetrating the blackness of the cold damp cellar are a few stray beams of weak light filtering through cracks in the ceiling above, cutting across her dirt streaked face and body and part of the dirt floor. It made an impotent spotlight that gave her just enough light that she wasn't in utter and complete blackness. It was a small reminder that the world still exists beyond her prison.

Kathy didn't realize at first that the endless pacing had stopped, such was the hypnotic embrace of her fear.

For some endless minutes the silence was broken only by her ragged breathing.

With an ominous scrape, the trap door in the ceiling above was pulled up, creating a square of blinding light in comparison to the darkness below.

The man above let down the frayed rope ladder. It was the only way of climbing out of the root cellar, especially for someone too numb and weak from cold, hunger, and exhaustion to pull herself up, even if they could manage to grasp the opening in the floor above.

"Get up here," the man ordered gruffly.

She trembled violently, unable to move.

He waited less than two minutes, although it felt like an

eternity to the woman huddled in the cellar, and then barked loudly.

"NOW!"

She jumped spasmodically.

Forcing herself painfully to her feet, Kathy approached the ladder, tight with nervousness, trying to stretch some of the aches and stiffness out of her joints.

She stopped immediately beneath the trap door and looked up, squinting to see into the relative brightness of the dimly lit room beyond.

"Come on." He motioned for her to come up.

Swallowing the bile rising in her throat, she grasped the ladder, raised her left foot up to the first sagging rung, and heaved herself up with a grunt. The rope step dipped with her weight and dug painfully into her tender foot.

Forcing herself to go on, she put her other foot up into the next step and pulled herself up again. Sliding in her grip, the coarse rope scraped against her hands and feet.

She forced herself up another step, trembling with weakness and fear, the rope swaying perilously with each effort, threatening to dump her to the floor below.

Sweat broke out on her skin from the effort, chilling her further while at the same time the heat of exertion flamed her skin with a rush of heat. She grunted, forcing herself up another step. Her hands growing sticky from sweat made the ordeal a little easier. At least she didn't have to grip the rope so tightly in her fists to keep her grip from sliding painfully. Burning pain shot through all her muscles, the strain too great for her in this weakened state.

Kathy had no idea how many days she had been held captive with little food or water. The man had tossed down water bottles and wrapped sandwiches with the deli tag stripped off, but those seemed to come too far apart and the hunger and thirst gnawed at her in between.

This was the first time he allowed her out of the cold damp root cellar since he first put her down there. She was forced to defecate and urinate in a corner of her prison and was unable to wash this whole time.

The stench of urine, feces, and body odors in the root cellar grew stronger and more putrid each day, adding to the musty stench of mildew and other unidentifiable odors.

Those were the worst, the smells she couldn't identify. They frightened her the most.

The whole house must have reeked with the smell. She was sure of it.

Trembling with exhaustion, Kathy finally reached the top rung. Grasping weakly at the wooden floor above for a grip she couldn't find, fingers slipping on the rough wood, she tried to pull herself up the wide gap between the top ladder rung and the floor above.

Just as her strength gave out and she began to fall, her captor reached down and grabbed her wrist, stopping her fall with a painful jerk.

She cried out from the sudden pain and surprise.

Dangling there, Kathy whimpered piteously, nothing more than a reflex action now and idly studied the rope brushing against her face.

Her mind drifted, briefly wondering how something that appears to be so badly rotting could hold her weight, as though the matter were inconsequential.

Her reverie was broken when she was roughly pulled up and her nightmare received a fresh dose of horror.

She collapsed on the floor when he released her arm, exhausted beyond belief. The floorboards popped and groaned with the man's weight as he turned and left the room.

She lay there unmoving and just listening.

When the man didn't come back Kathy sat up tentatively. She looked around, her whole body trembling, her mind focused entirely on the doorway.

Kathy didn't know how long she stayed like that. It could have been minutes but felt like hours.

At last she got up, hunched low, and half crawled half walked to the doorway.

She peered around it carefully and didn't see the man.

She moved off down the short hallway to the living room entrance.

127

She saw a chair. Her eyes stared at it, her mind clinging to that chair, and she darted out to scurry and hide behind it.

The small living room grew steadily darker inside as dusk descended. The wind whistling through the cracks in the walls where the mud had fallen out from between the rough cut wooden slats gave the only reprieve from the growing stench inside. It also gave an idea of just how old this house was. The place needed repair as badly as it needed a deep and very thorough cleaning.

Little more than a shack, the house leaned a little more with each winter's burden of snow.

It was only a matter of time before the ancient house would finally collapse.

Kathy didn't know how long she huddled behind the chair. Time had little meaning here. Anxiety made the world feel like it was rushing against her at breakneck speed, yet every breath seemed to take forever.

With the growing darkness, the light squeezing through cracks between the boards of the walls changed direction, the warm yellow glow now escaping into the darkness outside.

Kathy waited for the man to come for her, to attack her and beat her, and to do whatever else he planned.

Instead, he walked calmly into the room, ignoring her at first, and then gave her an almost shy look.

The man saw things very differently from his captive's view. He saw her as a willing guest in a way, although a reluctant one, slowly warming up to being there.

But for Kathy, who was accustomed to the brutal treatment of an abusive man, his out of place behavior was worse than being toyed with like a cat playing with the mouse it's about to kill.

It absolutely terrified her.

The man also decided it was time to put her to work cleaning the farmhouse.

The place stunk.

"Let's get this place cleaned up," the man said gently. He held out a hand to help her out from behind the chair.

Kathy huddled further back in the corner.

The man withdrew his hand.

"Ok, go slow," he reminded himself.

"The smell must be bothering you as much as me," he said. "Here, I'll help. Together we'll get this place cleaned up."

Frightened, Kathy crawled out of the corner behind the chair and used the chair to help her stand up.

"Let's start with the cellar," the man said.

He led her back to the cellar.

Kathy trembled even harder at the thought of going back down there.

She just couldn't possibly go down there again.

He made her go down before him and watched her warily as he climbed down himself, awkwardly bringing a bucket and shovel.

He knew better than to let her be on the floor above where she could slam the trap door closed and trap him below.

"He's going to kill me and bury me in the basement," Kathy thought desperately.

Instead, he dug a hole and shovelled the excrement inside, burying it as he filled the hole in. She'd had no place to relieve herself except the floor of the cellar.

He kept a close eye on her the whole time, gesturing any time he thought she might be inching towards the rope ladder.

"There," he said, "that will take care of the smell."

He plopped the pail down, pointing at it.

"For," he paused seeming embarrassed to say it, "you know." The man nodded towards the freshly buried excrement.

He then had her follow him back up the rope ladder.

Upstairs, he put her to work cleaning.

The already weak and exhausted Kathy grew steadily weaker. While she worked he sat in a chair watching the woman labour, his eyes dreamy.

The man talked as he sat watching her work, half to himself and half to Kathy.

"We're going to have company soon," he said wistfully.

"She's alive and she's coming back to us. I just have to figure out how I'm going to pick her up. So many people, so many people. They don't want her to come home, but she needs to. It won't be easy, but it can be done."

Already in knots, Kathy's stomach clenched and churned nauseatingly with the need to vomit.

He was going to kidnap another woman. She wasn't sure what terrified her more. The thought that he would soon be putting another through this horror, or wondering what happened to the last one that came before her, what will happen to her when the new one comes?

Why was there no one here when she came? She knew he was the one who had kidnapped those other missing women. At least, she was sure of it anyway. She had a feeling that the woman he was talking about was the Jane Doe in the hospital that she had heard about.

Did this mean he was about to kill her to make room for the new woman?

Trembling, weak and sick as much from fear and disgust as from exhaustion, hunger, and dehydration, Kathy barely managed to finish the job.

Moving slowly around the room, her slouched movements were more like she was dragging herself around the room rather than walking.

Done, she sank slowly to the floor, half-collapsing. Kathy tried feebly to get up; afraid she wouldn't be able to get back up again.

Her eyes fluttered closed as darkness descended on her mind. She was unable to raise herself off the floor.

Sitting in the armchair, the man stared at the unconscious woman sprawled on the floor a few feet away.

"I know now that you're not her," he whispered softly to the unconscious woman.

31

Plates clinking, the clattering of cutlery and the usual sounds of a busy kitchen competed with the light music in the diner to give it a comfortable homey feeling.

The two police officers were off shift now after releasing Ronnie and decided to stop for a meal before going home.

Sitting together at a table, they were discussing the case of the missing woman Kathy Kingslow, the possible lead with the man from the mall they have yet to locate, and the boyfriend being a strong suspect.

"We might have to pass this case over to Detective McNelly," the first officer said.

The other nodded.

The case was falling into McNelly's jurisdiction. If their groundwork came up empty in attempting to locate Kathy, they would have to hand it over.

"Yeah," he said. "This is definitely looking like it's probably going to end up being a missing person or homicide."

32

The man was sitting in his chair in the old farmhouse. The two ancient lamps burned dimly, filling the shack with a muted depressing glow with pockets of deep shadows.

Shadows clung to the wall behind his chair like dark shrouds.

The vision of the woman in the hospital filled his head. The memory of her was so strong that he could smell her as though she were still there with him at the farmhouse.

Her face seemed to float before him, constantly changing, fluctuating between that of the real woman and what he has always imagined his sister would look like today, finally settling on an image that was neither and both combined.

His mind brought him back to that day that he took her, the bruises she left on him as she kicked and fought and screamed while he dragged her forcibly to his car.

Her face that day was entirely that of his sister, almost a mingling of his sister then, his child sister, and the woman he imagined she'd grown into.

He hadn't seen her in years, not since that terrible day so long ago when he'd failed her.

Sadness crept in over his failure to protect his little sister. She had been all that he'd had left in the world besides Father.

Memories of his mother and life before Father were mere ghosts hovering at the edge of his conscious mind, untouchable, there but just out of sight.

A part of him always tried to tell him his sister was gone forever, dead, and that he had seen it, that he had been there to witness the terrible accident.

It was his fault she was gone. As her older brother it was his job to protect her.

But he was just a boy. How could a mere child protect anyone? Asking himself this never made him feel any better.

Another part of him, a more hopeful part, tried to push the memory of that accident away and tell him that he was wrong, that his sister could be alive somewhere, that she was alive somewhere and he just had to find her.

Then the urge to find her would come over him with a powerful force that could not be denied, the need to protect her and keep her safe and redeem himself for failing her so many years ago.

He had felt so sure that day he took Jane Doe that at last this one was the one; that he had finally found his sister.

Of course she put up a fight. He hadn't seen her since she was a small child.

She didn't recognize him.

But once he had her safe she would learn to recognize him. They could make up for those lost years, he could make up for failing her so terribly so many years ago.

Urges stirred within him as he thought about her, the time he spent with her, her angelic face as she lay sleeping in the hospital bed. Oh, how he longed for her, to have his sister home and safe where he could protect her.

He knew she wanted to be with him too, where she could feel safe, although a part of him tried to say she didn't. They were family. He was all she had too.

A small part of him, a part he pushed down deep inside, called out to him, telling him that this wasn't right. She wasn't who he thought she was. He was wrong and should just leave her alone. But he knew better. She WAS her, the one he'd been looking for all these years. She was his sister.

She was so strong, hanging in there, hanging on just for him. He had been certain she was dead.

When he heard she was still alive his first reaction was fear. It filled him, bursting through his chest in a panicked tightness that froze his lungs and made him unable to breath.

Sure he was afraid of getting caught; after the things he'd done who wouldn't be?

But more than that was that fear of knowing you did something so terrible that nothing could ever make it up.

He felt the self-loathing turn in his gut, the fist of her rightful anger squeezing his heart, the fear of confrontation with his victim that turns every man into a little boy facing the wrath of a furious parent.

He had sat there staring at her in the farmhouse that day, the grown woman she had become cowering and hiding behind the chair just as she did as a little girl hiding from Father.

But then her face changed.

It wasn't his sister staring back at him anymore. There would be no glimmer of recognition if they just stared at each other long enough.

The woman staring back at him with terror-filled eyes was a stranger.

Then the rage came over him as it always did.

When he came back to himself again the woman lay on the floor broken and covered with blood.

Remorse washed through him like a tidal wave, almost knocking him over.

He stared at his bloodied hands.

He stared at the broken woman on the floor, her face swimming before him, changing, becoming his sister and then a stranger again, and finally settling on a combination of the two.

This one was different somehow.

He didn't know why.

Instead of his usual care in making certain she was dead and then carefully disposing of her in the woods where she would not be found, he felt pulled by panic.

It felt the same as the panic he remembered the day his sister had the terrible accident, one of the very few things about that day he could remember.

Without thought he picked her up and carried her to the car, not even bothering to check the body or wrap it to hide it from the sight of possible witnesses. He grabbed a shovel from the shed, tossing it in the back with the body.

He drove to the woods. Parking, he gently took the body from the car and grabbed the shovel, walking the rest of the way.

He set her down as gently as he could, first dropping the shovel on the ground so he could use both arms.

He dug the hole and gently laid her inside.

He began filling in the dirt over her.

Then suddenly he stopped and tossed the shovel away with a cry of sorrow.

On hands and knees now he dug frantically at the soil, unburying the partially covered woman.

He pulled her from the ground, sobbing, checking her for breath, wiping away the dirt with loving hands.

"I'm so sorry, sis, I'm sorry," he sobbed.

He almost dropped her when a faint groan escaped her lips.

He looked around frantically as if he half-expected help to materialize, his heart pounded in his chest.

It was his little sister in his arms once again, her frail little body limp and lifeless. It was his little sister, a small child, who had moaned and not the woman.

He tried to wipe away the dirt and blood with his tears. She seemed so tiny in his man-sized hands.

He looked at his hands in confusion.

How did they get so big, like a man's?

He looked down at himself.

He was a boy again with boy's hands, holding his sister's body that he had frantically dug up after Father had buried her in the woods.

Father was at the barn now, cleaning up the blood.

A noise interrupted his thoughts.

Just like that the woods retreated into the past, taking the child that was his sister with them.

The boy was gone now and he was a man again, standing in the old farmhouse.

He turned his head and looked at the body lying motionlessly on the floor in an uncomfortable position, like a rag doll tossed carelessly to the floor.

This wasn't his sister, the one in the hospital they called Jane Doe.

This was a different woman completely.

He was even more confused. How did she get here? He thought it had been his sister, Jane Doe, here and not this woman.

This one had called herself Pamela.

Was this the moan he heard?

The woman was slender, her clothing torn and dishevelled and her hair a tangled mess that didn't quite hide her face.

135

She was covered in drying blood, turning sticky as it thickened and congealed, drying into a crust, its odor filling the room so that he could taste it when he inhaled. It turned his stomach with a metallic queasiness and exhilarated him at the same time.

He thought for a moment about Kathy huddled in the cool darkness of the root cellar beneath his feet. He felt a pang of remorse that he may have upset or scared her with this new girl.

He didn't know why he did it.

He'd known before he took her this time that this was not his sister. His sister was in the hospital. This was not his sister he was rescuing.

Since he'd found his sister none of them were the same anymore. At first he'd see his sister. He'd follow her, making sure it was safe before taking her away to safety. Then he would learn he was wrong and it wasn't her.

Ever since Jane Doe, as they called her in the papers, he's seen them all for who they really were before he even took them.

And yet he took them anyway, only to be filled with the rage when they were not her.

Loneliness? He wondered.

His thoughts turned to Kathy sleeping in the root cellar. A softness came over him, a feeling he could not describe yet it felt good.

He had come to feel closer to her than he had any girl in his life, save for his sister.

And he would soon be reunited with her.

He didn't even remember taking this woman.

When did he leave? He didn't even remember that.

After Kathy had collapsed on the floor earlier, he'd gently picked her up and carried her to the root cellar. He'd even covered her with a blanket and left extra water bottles, a sandwich, and even some apples, a banana and cookies next to her.

He'd felt bad over how exhausted she was and realized he'd been neglecting her and not giving her enough food and water.

He felt terrible about it. So terrible that he wanted to punish himself somehow. He deserved it.

Giving her that extra care just felt right. It made him feel a little better that he could make up the neglect a little bit, although it still didn't seem like enough. Later he would do more, after she'd had a good sleep.

After that he remembered sitting in the chair again.

He'd needed fresh air.

Now he remembered.

He had gone out for a drive and then, still feeling claustrophobic in the car and a need to escape, he parked and went for a long walk.

He didn't even know where he was. It was an area unfamiliar after an unknown amount of time driving on autopilot.

He remembered seeing the woman, but he also remembered the streets and buildings of the city and thought it strange to have somehow gotten there. He didn't recognize the woman beyond the general familiarity of sharing an appearance similar to the other women. Although he now remembers that he had been watching her for weeks.

Then he was back in the farmhouse standing over the body, brought out of his thoughts by the faint moaning sound from the woman on the floor with no memory at all of what happened between.

He staggered backwards, swooning with the confusion of it all and let himself fall backwards into the chair. The old springs creaked in protest.

Another low moan came from the motionless form.

He just stared at her for a moment then got up from the chair, walked over, and nudged her with his boot.

No response.

He nudged again, harder.

A soft groan.

He knelt down over her, rolling her onto her back, leaning in close.

Her eyes fluttered open, looking dazed and unfocused, and then they cleared and focused on him.

They widened in fear, welling with tears.

He gently placed his hand over her mouth, cupping his palm

snugly over her mouth and pinching her nostrils closed. His other hand came up to firmly grip her head, holding it still.

Pamela tried to struggle, but her efforts were useless against the much stronger man in her dazed and weakened state.

She stared at him hard, trying to communicate with her eyes, begging, pleading, and promising.

Her eyes asked a million questions. Why? Why me? They told him of her terror, begged him to just let her go, promised not to tell, and gave him all the reasons she had to live.

She thought about Roger, seeing him frantically pacing the apartment in worry, imagining him barging through the door to save her.

The man held firm, looking into her terror filled eyes. His eyes were cold, sterile, and emotionless.

The strain showed in her eyes, the terror, and the pain.

Desperation coursed through her. She didn't want to die. She so desperately did not want to die. She was terrified of dying, more than she was of what this man had done to her and might yet do.

She was scared dying would hurt. She hurt so badly already, but dying was the ultimate hurt.

She tried to fight him, but she was too weak and he was too strong.

Then the pain started. Her lungs ached for air, they screamed with the agony of their hunger for life giving oxygen. Her jaw muscles ached to open her mouth wide and breathe in big gasps of air. Her lungs began to feel as though they'd burst, the pain spread throughout her entire body, drawing her fear out in increasing waves of desperation, giving her strength to fight back.

It wasn't enough strength.

He continued to stare into the woman's eyes, reading the terror and pleading in them. He had to hold more firmly as she struggled, shifting to use his legs to pin her down when the woman found a reserve of strength. He could see the pain in her eyes as she struggled desperately for air, the pain pushing away even the fear. Her eyes seemed to bulge from her head as her lungs must have felt as though they were exploding in her chest.

Pamela's heart ached for Roger, poor dear Roger.

And then she was no more.

Pamela stopped struggling with a suddenness that was anticlimactic.

He loosened his grip and got to his feet.

The silence after the violence above seemed deafening in the dark root cellar.

Then after moments that felt like eternity came the soft muffled sounds, scrapes against the floor above, and the drumming of something that sounded like someone's heels thudding in a spasm against the floor above.

Then the silence returned and drowned out those muted sounds.

The floor creaked above Kathy's head. She was huddled in a corner, her knees folded up near her chin, holding herself tightly and trembling uncontrollably. A faint light from a crack between the floorboards above sliced across her face in the darkness. Her face was wet with tears and dirt streaks. Her eyes looked almost on the verge of madness with the wild fear in them.

Terror trembles wracked through her body in wave after wave.

With a scrape and a whine of the hinges, the hatch was pulled open and the dim light from above blazed into the blackness of her prison.

There was nothing but silence above.

She stared at the opening, trembling and afraid.

A lot of time passed. She had no idea how much.

At last she unwound herself and crawled forward cautiously, stopping beneath the opening and looking up.

The man stood there staring down at her through the opening, his face awash with tears, eyes rimmed red, and his features contorted with the pain of sorrow.

He dropped the ladder down.

Moving as though the weight of the world sagged on his shoulders, he turned and stepped away out of sight.

Kathy stared up at the opening.

Cautiously she moved, standing up in the square of light

splashing down into the root cellar and reaching for the rope. She climbed, pausing as she breached the opening to look for the man's location, judging the danger, and then climbing out of the hole to crawl out onto the rough wooden floor.

She crouched there a moment, trembling so hard she thought she would fall over, frozen with fear like a deer caught in the headlights as she looked for the man. There was no sign of him.

At last she ventured further, moving cautiously through the house and freezing with a jolt of shock at the living room doorway the moment she spotted him standing in the room there.

She stared at the man, trying to judge his mood.

He walked to his chair and sat heavily, the chair creaking with his weight.

He looked at her. His eyes were haunted; troubled by something that filled him with remorse.

She cringed as his arm snapped out towards her, expecting violence or some kind of attack.

He held a rag in his hand, his fingers releasing it as his arm snapped towards her, tossing it to her.

Reflexively, she lashed out to block a blow, catching the rag instead.

He nodded towards the motionless form sprawled on the floor.

She swallowed hard, nausea almost making her swoon.

Steeling herself, she got up and approached the woman on the floor.

She knew what he wanted.

She started cleaning up the blood.

As she worked, Kathy snuck glances at the man.

His face was contorted in pain, the sorrow evident in every part of him as he sat there weeping for the woman lying dead on the floor.

Something in her stirred. Sympathy.

She hated herself for it, but she couldn't help but feel for his pain. Inside, a part of her felt a need to comfort this monster that had the nerve to sit there weeping for the death of a woman he had brutally murdered.

In her prison below, she had heard every sound from the brutal attack.

As the man sat in the chair silently, his prisoner working to clean up the blood, his mind drifted on a tide of memories.

He thought about the woman he'd just killed, the one he was currently keeping in the dirt floored root cellar beneath the old farmhouse, and about the woman he had mistakenly left for dead.

He thought about the other victims that have not yet been discovered and the ones that have come before.

Also the victims that came before he had even begun to look for his sister.

He knew he should stop. He had to stop.

The pieces were starting to come together for the police and it would only be a matter of time before they were put in the right order and the puzzle solved to reveal who is behind the killings.

It was time to lay low for a while, perhaps to move on. He had to be more careful. He had begun to be careless, leaving his victims where they were sure to be found instead of making them vanish altogether.

Does a part of me want to be caught? To be stopped? He wondered. Why else have I been leaving them to be found in places that make big headlines?

The problem is that he couldn't remember leaving the women in those places, except for Jane Doe. That memory was vivid in his mind.

He would have sworn he'd disposed of them properly, every one of them. He had memories of it, but now he was completely confused about what was real and what wasn't.

Nobody else knew. Nobody but him could have left those women there; in the parking garage and the playground.

Nobody but him.

It was impulsive and stupid. He knew that, he was no dummy. He knew that is exactly the sort of behavior that puts you away for life.

In his case a life sentence would be short.

You don't do the things he's done and survive life in a jail cell. Even in protective custody someone like him would never be safe. And the thought of spending the rest of his life in the darkness of a solitary cell while his mind rots into madness was terrifying.

"I deserve it," he thought, self-loathing and morality eating away at his insides and making him feel as if he were being torn into pieces.

He thought about the little girl he'd almost kidnapped. Why? What was he thinking?

He was there for the girl's mother, just to watch that day. It wasn't time to take the woman yet.

He vaguely remembered thinking about how the little girl looked like his lost little sister, who was about that same age when the accident happened. He remembered a wave of protectiveness over the little girl washing over him, coursing through him, filling him with a need that could never be fulfilled.

His sister was dead, and has been for many years. She's beyond protecting.

He didn't remember what happened after that, just a confusing jumble of partial memories until he found himself puking until he thought he'd ruptured something inside.

And then all at once the old farmhouse vanished.

In its place was a different farmhouse.

It was the same house, but in a different time. It looked the same, same old floor, same size and layout. But it all looked so different. The furniture, decor, the stove ... all were suddenly from another era. The odor of burning logs filled his nose, coming from the old wood stove in the kitchen that was an old electric range moments before.

He was confused. The old wood stove had been replaced decades ago with an aging electric one.

He could hear the squeal of a little girl playing outside, the barking of a dog at play, both suddenly cut off by the surprised yelp of the dog.

He could hear the dog's feet padding on the ground as it scampered away crying, a sharp slap against skin followed by the girl's hiccupping sobs, and a man's angry voice.

He watched the door swing open, the little girl's dress scuffed with dust seemed to dance merrily on her as she ran into the house. Her face sported a red mark where she had been slapped and tears streamed down her cheeks. She looked hurt.

Not on the outside where her face certainly smarted from the hard slap. She looked hurt on the inside, where scars showed only on the soul.

The little girl scurried into the corner, huddling behind the old chair. She stared at him with sad eyes, her soft brown hair framing her delicate face.

"Why?" her eyes asked. She was shivering with fear.

The man's heavy footsteps thumped against the wooden step outside the farmhouse door. It wasn't really a step, more a wooden platform lying on the ground so less mud was tracked in. His hand grasped the edge of the partially open door, swinging it open all the way as he entered the farmhouse.

He was a bulky man, not in a fat way, but in the way of a man used to working a hard day's honest work every day of his life. He wore worn coveralls that were smeared with the grime of the day's hard labour. His face was lined from many hours spent working in the sun and wind.

This was Father.

Father glared at him as he sat in the chair staring back.

He felt an urge to run, but knew it was pointless.

Father stepped forward swiftly. One, two, three steps. He paused and raised one open palm, a threat.

He cowered in his chair before Father.

"Papa, please, no," he begged. "I did all my chores." Father wasn't really his father. He really wasn't clear on how they were related. He just knew this man had raised him and his sister for as long as he could remember and he called him Papa and Father.

A soft whimper came from the corner behind the chair.

Father's attention turned to the little girl huddled there, trying so hard to disappear.

It was useless. You couldn't disappear no matter how hard you wished for it.

He knew. He wished for it with all his might every day for his little sister and himself.

Father's anger grew at the sight of the little girl, his eyes blazing with a violent rage.

143

He didn't know what she'd done to make Father so angry, probably nothing. Protectiveness filled him. He needed to protect his little sister.

He risked a smack in the back of the head, turning to look at the little girl cowering behind the chair.

"Run," he mouthed, careful not to let out so much as a silent breath.

He stumbled getting out of the chair.

"Papa, I forgot the wood for the stove," he said, staring up at Father in fear.

Father paused, sighing deeply. It was a sound of frustration.

Father turned his angry glare on him, making him feel like he was shrinking into himself, growing smaller with every nervous breath.

The little girl scampered from the corner, just a flash of hair and dress in the corner of his eye as she bolted for the still open door and out into the waning sunshine.

He breathed a sigh of relief.

Father would hit him over the wood, but his little sister would go hide someplace and come back later ... after Father calmed down from whatever had made him so angry.

Part Eight:
Strange Hospital Visitor & The Woods are Grave Indeed

33

Detective Jim McNelly groaned, vacantly staring ahead as he sat at his desk. A dwindling cigarette smouldered between his yellow-stained fingers, a tendril of smoke lazily winding upwards to fill the room with its stink.

Michael Underwood entered the small office with his usual jaunty step. His smile faltered when the saw the grave look on the older detective's face.

"What happened?"

"Found another body," McNelly said without looking at him.

Michael shook his head with frustration.

"This has to end. We can't keep turning up bodies like this."

McNelly grunted in agreement.

Beth came swiftly into the office, looking like she was on a mission.

"We identified the new body," she said briskly.

Both men turned to her expectantly.

"This one is hitting closer to home," she said.

"How's that?" McNelly asked.

"The perp came back to revisit a prior scene," she said. "The guy that found the body in the parking garage," she indicated a woman's picture on one of the bulletin boards on the wall, "the vic is his girlfriend. Her name is Pamela Watson."

"Damn!" McNelly thudded his fist against the desk top. "I don't know if we're getting closer to this guy, or if he's getting closer to us."

Michael looked suddenly pale. How could this be? He thought wildly.

He was clearly shaken up by this news.

"Where did you say the body was found?" he asked.

145

They were interrupted by the sudden appearance at the door of another officer, Jerry LaCroix, a general duty officer who dealt with a lot of domestic disputes and assaults. He was currently investigating the attempted abduction of a child, the perpetrator assumed to be the father although the mother was not cooperating and insisted it was a stranger who tried to take her kid.

"Jerr," McNelly called, using the familiar shortened name that often rankled the man.

Jim didn't like LaCroix.

LaCroix's eyes narrowed slightly at this use of his name.

"Looks like our cases are overlapping," LaCroix said.

"How so?" McNelly raised one bushy eyebrow in question.

His gut suddenly churned, pushing acid up into his throat and giving him heartburn. He had a feeling akin to déjà-vu. Only not that something was happening again, but that something was about to happen that he was so strongly expecting that he might as well have already lived through it.

"The attempted child abduction," LaCroix said curtly. He didn't say it that way to be rude. He just normally talked like that when something struck a deep cord, and this case was hitting home hard. Any case involving a child always did. But the habit made him seem short and irritated, making people dislike him instantly.

"Remember it?" he asked.

"Yeah, I remember," McNelly said. Everyone in the force has heard about it.

Michael and Beth both watched the exchange, waiting to see how it would play out.

Beth felt a flutter in her stomach, like butterflies flitting around.

Michael suddenly felt tenser. What had this man learned about their cases that his own team didn't already know?

"Well," LaCroix went on, "I've been doing some digging in some unrelated cases, because I've hit a brick wall you know."

He paused. LaCroix knew some officers took offence to someone else digging into their cases. Although he also knew that Jim McNelly was the sort of cop who welcomed information no matter how it came about, it was still always a good idea to broach case jumping diplomatically. Unfortunately, diplomacy was not one of LaCroix's strong points.

McNelly's expression was unreadable. He waited for the other detective to continue.

LaCroix decided to just jump right to the point.

"I noticed that witness descriptions of the car the abductor in my case was driving matches witness accounts on your suspicious car seen in the area of your case."

"Which case?" Jim asked. "We have multiple abductions."

He was sceptical. He'd already dismissed any link between their cases and the child when Michael had brought up the possibility of the attempted child abduction being related.

"Actually, it's more than one," LaCroix said.

Michael's breath came faster. Jim wouldn't listen when he tried to tell him they were linked, and now LaCroix was doing the same thing and Jim was finally listening and maybe even considering the possibility.

"Ok, this isn't so bad," Michael thought. His team had already picked up on the repeated presence of the dark blue car at more than one of their scenes. It was a fairly nondescript car in a fairly common color. Most people wouldn't put a name to it and those that would were more likely to get it wrong than to get it right. That was a common problem with witnesses. He had also already brought up the child's mother having a strong resemblance to the type their perp seems to prefer, making her a possible target. At least he had tried to tell McNelly she fit, but McNelly had dismissed it immediately since the perp had targeted the kid instead of the mother, breaking from the character they had already pegged him as.

"A lot of cars match the same general description," Michael said. "It's a pretty common color and body type."

But McNelly's interest was piqued now. His heartburn and roiling stomach told him this mattered, that there was sure to be some connection here. His gut told him it was more than just coincidence.

"Which cases?" he asked.

"The apartment garage, the school yard, and a car matching

the description almost ran over a couple teens near the most recent disappearance, that woman, Pamela Watson."

LaCroix fairly hummed with smug pride over this last name. He knew McNelly's team had just been handed that file this morning. He watched their reactions gleefully.

Beth's eyes blazed with barely concealed anger.

Michael looked a little bit sick.

McNelly puffed out his moustache with a heavy sigh signalling annoyance but otherwise seemed unaffected.

"Looks like our perps like the same kind of car," McNelly admitted grudgingly.

"More than that," LaCroix continued, "the child's mother fits the general description of your victims."

"Yeah," McNelly said, "but a lot of women fit the general description."

"I think the guy's been staking out the house," LaCroix said. "I have neighbors that think they've seen the car in the area for weeks; usually in the same block and always with the driver just sitting there and not getting out. After a while the car just drives away."

Michael's heart sped up. So, witnesses have seen the man in the car, possibly may even be able to identify him.

"Do we have a description of the driver?" Michael asked.

"That's the odd part," LaCroix said. "Although neighbors have noticed the car a number of times, nobody seems to have paid enough attention to know what the driver looks like except that they think it might be a man."

"What about the girl and her mother? They must have gotten a good look at the man."

Michael was having a hard time trying to hide his tension. This was very important. He had wondered over this before, but hadn't had the chance to pursue it and find out.

LaCroix looked at Michael. His expression was mostly unreadable, but a wary curiosity showed in his eyes and in the set of his mouth.

"Oh yeah, they got a pretty good look at him all right," he said guardedly.

Michael wondered now if LaCroix was worrying about

protecting his own case from the prying attention of his team after digging through their case files himself, or if there was something else he had pieced together that he hadn't told them yet.

"This guy has to know they got a good enough look at him for a line-up or even a sketch artist," McNelly said.

Michael nodded, his expression grim.

"We're watching the house," LaCroix said.

Does he really have people watching the house? Michael didn't think so. It would be a big use of manpower to have a car sitting outside the woman's house, an expense that wasn't approved lightly.

"So," McNelly said thoughtfully, "you're pretty sure then that the real intended target was the mother and that it's our perp? Why?"

"Yeah," LaCroix said. "I didn't think so until I started looking at the similarities, but then it hit me that he could have been using the kid to get to the mom, maybe to draw her out of the house."

This was a tactic he'd seen before, but in the domestic cases he usually dealt with. It was a rare leap to assume in a kidnapping or attempted kidnapping of a stranger.

Beth cringed inside. LaCroix had been trying for some time now to join their team. This could potentially be his way in. She despised the man and couldn't possibly work with him. She'd made a mistake dating him briefly and it ended badly. If he joined their team, she'd have to put in for a transfer. That sucked. As stressful as her job was, as hard as the cases hit her in the heart like a physical blow to the stomach, she loved her job. There were none like it in this small force.

"Well," McNelly shrugged, "you didn't really bring us anything we didn't already know. Michael here had already brought this possibility to the table."

LaCroix looked disappointed. Annoyed and possibly a little insulted, yet disappointed like a boy who didn't make the little league hockey team.

"Thanks Jerr," McNelly said. "Let us know if you happen to come up with anything we can use." It was clearly a dismissal.

LaCroix turned and stalked out of the office.

A smile lurked at the corner of Beth's mouth.

Michael tried not to let out a noticeable breath of air.

Going for the kid was a dumb move for any perp, Michael thought. A very dumb move that might just get him caught. It was a rash act and one that had not been thought out at all.

He looked at the clock. It was time to get going. His shift at the hospital would be starting soon.

34

At the hospital later, when evening visiting hours were at their peak, the hospital bustled with activity. Hospital staff moved about their business, patients who were mobile were up and about stretching their legs, and visitors milled around looking uncomfortable and awkward, wishing they were anywhere but here.

The pollens and perfume of flowers hung in the air of certain hallways and rooms, an invisible trail showing which guests had received fresh flowers from friends and family.

To Michael the smell was like a bad woman's perfume, cloying, insistent, and invasive.

He was dressed in his orderly costume and keeping himself looking busy near room 214B where Jane Doe lay sleeping.

That nurse, Molly, was on tonight, always giving him those distrustful looks when she saw him. She seemed to hover around that room.

"Well, good for her," he thought. "That poor girl in there needs someone to watch out for her when I can't."

But, he also found the nurse to be an unpleasant nuisance, one that he tolerated for Jane Doe's sake.

The rooms were crammed closely together with often up to four patients stacked in a room, their beds separated by a thin curtain and a single chair that visitors couldn't help but continually bump into the next bed every time they got in or out of it, much to their neighbors annoyance.

It was not only the busiest time for the residential floor of the hospital. This was also the time Michael's job got harder. There were many more people to watch, and with the increase in people also came the increased chance of someone who can recognize him being in the crowd of visitors.

He left his position to go use the washroom and then slipped into a supply closet to make a phone call to the precinct to see if there were any updates on the case.

When he came back to room 214B a nervous looking man was hovering outside the door.

The man looked like he had once been big and bulky in a muscular way, wore a heavy overcoat, and had dishevelled hair. His age-worn face looked as though he was old enough to be the woman's father. There was no family resemblance. He had the ageless look of a man who looked older than his years from too much time spent working outdoors.

Something about the man unnerved Michael. He had a familiarity about him that he just couldn't place. An unexplained coldness seeped through Michael's veins and he felt the sudden urge to pee.

He took mental note of every detail of the man.

He couldn't start questioning the man, not without blowing his cover, but he might just have to play the helpful hospital orderly to try to get some information about the man.

The nurse, Molly, was eying the man warily.

Molly had been feeling unusually on edge all day today, getting a disconcerting feeling she couldn't place her finger on.

It was like something was out of place, but try as she might she just couldn't figure out what it was.

This man hovering awkwardly around Jane Doe's door jangled her nerves even more, adding to her anxiety. She knew he had to just be a visitor, but she couldn't shake the nervous feeling he gave her.

Taking her attention away from the visitor, she glanced up and saw the orderly.

For just a brief moment she felt relief at the sight of him, the emotion reflecting in her expression.

Her face flamed with an embarrassed flush as she immediately remembered her suspicions about him.

She was confused by her own reaction.

She admonished herself.

How could she feel relief at seeing a man she couldn't stop feeling distrustful of, even though he had never given her a reason for those feelings?

She felt a tinge of resentment, as if she had just been tricked.

She's been distrustful of the orderly since the first day he started, something about him making her uncomfortable. Whenever the orderly was around she felt like the mouse who can feel the cat's eyes glued to it, taking in every whisker twitch, feeling every hair on its tongue, and tasting the fresh warm blood before it even prepares to pounce on its victim.

She can't turn to him with relief and hopes for rescue from the threat of a new visitor to the unfortunate girl in room 214B. That is, assuming the man isn't here to see someone else entirely. He could just be lost or wasting time while waiting, perhaps for someone being released. There was a lot of both daily.

She turned her attention back to the stranger lurking around room 214B.

She'd had enough of watching this man hovering and, feeling a sudden rush of courage from the presence of an unlikely ally, came out from behind the nurses' desk to confront him.

"Can I help you?"

"I-um," the man stammered, broke off, and then looked down at his hands.

They trembled a little.

He clearly was there for a reason and seemed a nervous wreck about it.

She sensed his nervousness. Picking up on his mannerisms, the shaking hands, haunted eyes, and jerky motions, perhaps on a deeper and more psychic level.

She liked to think it was the latter.

"Are you looking for someone?"

He looked at her.

Something about his sheepish nervousness played on her. Molly felt for him, wondering if some loved one of his had some terrible accident or illness, or maybe he really was there looking for Jane Doe because he seemed somehow stuck at that doorway, undecided and unable to go in or move on.

Maybe his nervous behavior was founded on self-recrimination, guilt over not coming to find her sooner.

Maybe he knew her! Maybe someone had finally come to find her!

Her heart skipped a beat with a hope that showed in her tired eyes.

153

At the same time her nerves jangled a stern warning at her.

Hope and dread; empathy and a vague feeling that screamed, "No! Don't trust him!" The feelings tugged her in different directions.

Molly felt dizzy with confusion for a moment. Her senses were rarely wrong and this time she was getting opposite signals at once. The man was a helpless victim of his need to find a lost loved one or some other tragedy, in need of help and support, but her senses also said he was far more dangerous than the hunting cat is to the mouse.

Watching discretely, Michael also sensed that this man was dangerous and that he was here for Jane Doe. There was no reason for this assumption, just a gut feeling.

It was time to act.

"Hey there," Michael said as he approached the man and nurse, trying to be both casual and authoritative.

The man turned to look at him.

Confusion etched the man's face, and then he paled noticeably as a look of struggled recognition came over him.

The man turned and ran.

"Damn, he must have recognized me," Michael thought. "He knows I'm a cop!"

Michael ran after him, his soft-soled shoes making a softer whisking throb on the waxed floor than the man's clopping shoes.

The other man made it to the elevator first, instinctively slipping in sideways through the narrowing gap just as the doors started to close behind the passengers that just finished disembarking.

He turned and watched the orderly running towards him as the doors whispered in their tracks, narrowing the space between them with a speed that seemed to be stuck in slow motion.

And then the doors paused just before they squeezed completely shut and began to open.

The man stared at them in mute shock.

He couldn't understand it.

He turned his head and saw the other passenger who he hadn't noticed before.

The passenger was giving him a good-natured smile, his arm extended, and his finger pressing the open button.

Seeing the orderly running for the elevator behind the other man, the entirely clueless Good Samaritan inside the small car had pressed the open door button, keeping the door open for Michael those few precious seconds too long for the strange visitor to make his escape.

The visitor ran from the elevator as the doors whisked back open, turned and darted down another corridor, passing only inches from Michael's clutching fingers. He raced past people, almost bowling an old man over, and knocked objects into the path behind him to slow down his pursuer before he finally crashed into a stairwell door with a loud bang of the push-handle.

The heavy door swung open and his footsteps pounded down the stairs, echoing off the walls in pursuit of his hurried descent.

By the time Michael entered the stairwell, the man had already left it through a lower level door.

Michael leaned out over the railing. He had no way of knowing by which floor the man may have left the stairwell.

He slammed his hand on the railing in frustration. If he picks the wrong floor he's lost the man. The options at least were few, but alone he still had little or no chance of catching him.

Not enough to risk blowing his cover for.

Defeated, he exited the stairwell to return to his post guarding Jane Doe's door.

But first he had to find a quiet place to make a phone call. The reception in the stairwell would be patchy at best. He'd have to call this in. With some luck, if they kept a low profile, the stranger might return and he might manage to follow him next time.

Meanwhile, he would get McNelly to request the hospital video footage so he could review it later.

Michael couldn't get through to McNelly. Reluctantly, he decided he would have to try again later and left a quick message. He needed to keep an eye on their Jane Doe in case the strange visitor returned.

155

When Michael returned to his cart outside room 214B Molly was already on the phone talking to the police. She impatiently tapped the corner of Detective McNelly's card on the desk as she stopped talking to listen.

Michael couldn't be sure if she was talking to McNelly or someone else, but he had a pretty good hunch it was McNelly.

Minutes later the distant wail of sirens approached.

Within minutes the area was cordoned off and police were searching the hospital grounds.

Michael looked up at the sound of the sirens, his eyes flashing with lethal anger. So much for a low profile. He stalked off; knowing it was better that no one saw his reaction.

He would have to find a discrete place to talk to McNelly. No doubt the detective would be there shortly and he'd have to try to pull him aside without risking his cover.

Molly saw the look of rage in the orderly's eyes as he suddenly stiffened and stalked off like a stiff legged dog with its hackles raised. The look in his eyes scared her.

Why was he so angry all of a sudden?

Was it something to do with that strange man? And why did he chase him? Did he think that man might be the one who had kidnapped Jane before? Or was there something going on between him and the strange man?

She was pretty sure she'd seen recognition on the man's face when he saw the orderly right before he ran away.

Maybe she was right all along and the orderly was up to no good. Maybe this man coming here and recognizing him interfered with whatever he was up to.

"Well, good," she thought, "it serves him right."

The man was angry. She was his. His! Today was the day he was going to take her back, take her out of the hospital. It was impossible now.

He had to get her out soon. Someone else had too much interest in her. That other man was hanging around and watching until he fled.

What did he want with her?

The place was crawling with cops now, and after this they

would be watching her even more closely.

He'd have to be even more careful when he made his move.

That damned nurse would probably be the most trouble too.

His stomach sank into a bottomless pit of loss as he watched her talk on the phone with the police.

He would have to dispose of the nurse, later.

Lawrence Hawkworth had been hanging around the hospital, buttering up patients and staff and asking questions conversationally; digging for information.

Lawrence felt strongly that this predator who left her for dead would return for Jane Doe.

It had been announced to the world days ago that she was still alive. It was only a matter of time before he struck.

It would be risky to come to the hospital, but he didn't think that would stop the man.

Lawrence also wondered how it was that, despite the publicity this unidentified patient has received in light of the new revelation there may be a serial killer on the loose, the photo he surreptitiously took splashed across the news, and the police's attempts to identify her, no one has come forward yet saying they recognize her.

No family, no friends, and no neighbors or co-workers.

He had even made sure this mystery hit the wire so that it would be picked up and spread by other media services across the country.

This had made national headlines, splashing her face across billions of screens and newspapers.

The mystery of an unidentified woman who is the sole survivor of a possible serial killer is just too juicy for any media group to ignore.

Lawrence was convinced her kidnapper has been to the hospital and that someone had seen him.

He just had to find out who.

Lawrence was milling around the hallway down from the elevators by Jane Doe's room.

He stood facing an old man who was wearing the telltale nightgown of a patient, a second gown hanging open in front, worn as a bathrobe to cover the opening in the back that tended to gape open when you moved. A good thing too, since there were few people who would want to see an old man's bare ass peeking out the back of his hospital blue nighty.

Lawrence was listening to the old man ramble, only half listening, yet his mind still sorting and compartmentalizing the man's story, picking up on what was important, who he has seen, while discarding the rest.

Movement behind the man caught Lawrence's attention, drawing it away from the old man. His ears had already picked up the peculiar sound of running footsteps.

"Must be some kind of emergency," he thought.

Beyond the old man's shoulder, a man raced into the elevator.

Seconds later an orderly appeared, also racing for the elevator.

Lawrence only half listened to the old man, his attention drawn to the scene at the elevator.

The first man jumped from the elevator car, spinning in a sudden turn even as the orderly reached out to grab him.

Barely missing the man's clutching hand, the first man bolted down the hallway towards Lawrence and the old man, past a woman in the hallway, his feet slapping against the floor.

The old man turned towards the commotion, taking a step towards the center of the hallway as he did, and was almost bowled over by the running man.

Lawrence stared at the man curiously as he raced past.

The second man, who Lawrence now saw was the orderly, Michael, ran towards them in pursuit of the racing man.

Lawrence turned to watch the chase, automatically putting out a steadying hand for the old man who was left off balance.

"Curious," he said.

The man burst through a stairwell doorway, followed by the orderly who stopped short at the open door looking in.

Footsteps could be heard echoing down the stairwell.

Moments later, Michael returned looking quite agitated.

He walked past Lawrence and the old man without even seeing them.

Discretely, Lawrence slipped down the hall to the elevator, taking the elevator down after a short wait.

The stairs would have been faster, but he couldn't have the strange man getting suspicious he was following him.

Lawrence stepped out of the elevator on the main floor, pausing to look around for only a second.

He quickly headed in the direction of the stairwell the man had taken.

Lawrence did not open the stairwell door. Instead he listened for the clatter of feet running on the metal stairs, although the man must have cleared them by now.

What he heard was the sound of a door closing.

The man must have gone to be the level below, to the underground parking.

Lawrence hastily followed suit, entering the stairwell and taking the stairs down three at a time, careful to make his feet land on the edge of each step and on the extreme side, to minimize the noise.

When he left the stairwell through the door below, he made a point of not looking rushed, opening the door casually and letting it close behind him as anyone else would who was simply heading for their car.

Lawrence ambled along through the lines of cars, his pace faster than the average man because of his long legs, making his pace causal but purposeful.

He spotted movement a few rows over.

Whoever it was had ducked behind a support pillar, vanishing from sight.

"Ok, so we're playing this game then," Lawrence thought.

He continued on to his car as though nothing unusual was going on, his senses keen to any movement in the garage.

A woman got off the elevator with two children in tow. The boy tried to race ahead only to be deftly grabbed by the collar by the woman, pulling him up short mid-sprint.

"She's obviously experienced at dealing with the little traffic darter," Lawrence thought.

The little boy glared up at the woman sulkily, tugging away from her grasp.

"Now you know better than to race out like that in a parking lot," she admonished.

The little girl followed along holding the woman's other hand, seeming oblivious to everything around her.

The little girl's dazed look suggested she was the reason they were at the hospital today.

Lawrence got into his car, started the engine, and made his way slowly to the exit.

The trio were stopped now next to a car that had seen better days. The little boy stuck his tongue out at Lawrence as he passed by them. The woman was rummaging in her purse, probably for her car keys, while the little girl leaned against the dirty car looking too tired to stand.

Exiting the underground garage, Lawrence swung the car around, hoping he'd found a discrete enough spot and parked.

He waited, watching the parking garage entrance.

He hoped the man would come out this way, that he hadn't just made a side-trip to the garage in an attempt to put the pursuing orderly and anyone else sent to chase him off his trail.

After what seemed like forever, the old car finally emerged with the woman and kids inside.

Lawrence waited.

From where he parked he could see both the garage entrance and the exit, as well as the main doors and one side door.

If the man chose any of the other exits, he'd lose him.

Lawrence glanced at his watch. If he gave up too soon he might lose his chance, but if he waited too long he might miss the man emerging from another door.

He waited a long while more that seemed to rush by so fast that he was certain the minutes were clicking by just as quickly.

The man did not materialize.

"Damn!"

He put the car into gear.

Lawrence followed the road around, swinging around the hospital, scouting for any sign of the man on foot. He may have parked his car somewhere else, if he had even come in one.

His foot itched to press the gas harder, to hurry before he lost his quarry.

With great effort he kept his speed slow and even, driving around the corner of the building and then finally around the next corner.

He had just swung around the final corner of the hospital, bringing the underground parking garage exit into view in the distance, when he spotted a car emerging from the garage.

Could it be?

Had the man waited this long to leave? Risky, unless he suspected Lawrence was following him, or that someone was watching for him to leave.

His heart sped up, anxiety pumping adrenaline through him.

Pursuing a possible witness who may have reason to not want to be witnessed always scared the crap out of Lawrence. You never knew what might happen at the end of the pursuit when they realize you've been following them. He's had run-ins before that ended badly, though that never stopped him from scooping the story.

Lawrence kept moving slowly towards the intersection.

As luck had it, the car turned in that direction, passing by him at the intersection ahead instead of going the other way.

The car might be black, he thought. But Lawrence couldn't be sure. At a moment like this living in a world of greys from white to black was frustrating. He silently cursed his color blindness.

What he was certain of is that the driver was the same man the orderly had chased from the direction of Jane Doe's room.

He turned at the intersection and followed the car.

35

The wind blew through the trees, making them sound as though they were whispering to each other.

It was in that early part of the evening when everything seems just a little bit muffled as the sunlight begins to fade before the blazing colors of sunset stretch across the sky.

Only the occasional warble of a bird could be heard as the birds prepared to go to roost for the night.

The sounds of night insects were beginning to multiply despite the coolness of the waning day.

A shout echoes through the trees.

Laughter.

The bark of a dog.

"Hurry up slowpoke," a man's voice calls, "it will be dark soon and I don't want to still be on the trail then."

"Scared of the dark?" a woman calls back, joking.

"Funny," the man replies.

The dog comes running up the trail and pauses to sniff the air. The scent of something has caught the dog's attention.

Tail wagging, the dog snuffles around and then bounds off the trail into the woods.

"Corky!" a woman's voice called in the distance.

Moments later a man and woman come jogging up the trail.

"CORKY!" she called again.

The dog barked somewhere off in the woods.

"Here we go again," the man said, annoyed. He would have preferred to leave the dog at home. He would have preferred to not have a dog at all.

They struck out together through the brush in the direction of the bark, branches cracking beneath their feet as they pushed their way away from the path.

The couple found the dog in a little clearing where he was digging furiously at the ground.

It wasn't much of a clearing, with trees standing tall and proudly reaching for the sky. But for some reason there was very little undergrowth here. A network of water trenches flowing downhill showed how the lack of growth to stop corrosion had been allowing the rains to wash away the top layers of the soil.

The woman tried to pull the dog away from whatever he was digging at.

He strained against her, whining eagerly.

She managed to pull the squirming animal back a few paces, trying to get him under control.

"What 'cha got there?" the man asked the dog. He was getting more annoyed with the dog.

The dog looked at him eagerly, tail wagging.

The man went to investigate what the dog wanted so badly.

"Probably some dead animal," he said, approaching the spot, assuming that's what it had to be.

"Eew, that's gross Corky," the woman said.

With a sudden lunge the dog pulled from her grasp and went back to furiously digging, spraying the man with mud, digging his muzzle hard into the dirt with a muffled puff of air.

The man was clearly not impressed.

Angry, he grabbed the dog's collar and pulled him away roughly.

The dog turned to his master, tail wagging, and a big dog grin around a large yellowed object covered in dirt. The object bulged out around his lower jaw like a deflated volleyball.

The woman let out a little yelp, her face turning pale.

The man stared in disbelief, his jaw hanging open and slack.

The dog proudly held up his prize for all to see.

It was a human skull with bits of shrivelled skin and hair still clinging to it in places.

The lower jawbone dropped off, landing in the disturbed dirt with a soft plop, looking, the woman thought briefly, like a set of discarded dentures.

Her face flushed and her head spun dizzily. A wave of cold sweat washed over her with an overpowering weakness in every fibre of her being. She almost fainted even as she told herself it had to be fake.

Her husband's stomach turned queasily.

Corky happily dropped his treasure on the ground and started to gnaw on it.

It took a moment to break the spell shock had put on him.

He jumped forward and pulled the dog away too quickly.

The dog yelped in surprise, straining towards the bone, whimpering and staring after it in disappointment as the man dragged him away and back to the trail.

The woman numbly followed.

Not a word was spoken. None were needed.

Police swarmed the woods, yellow police tape wrapped around the trees to mark off a large area fluttered in the wind. Men and women wearing gloves, coveralls, and heavy boots carefully excavated the site in the sickening glow of battery-powered lights, POLICE in bold letters stamped on their backs.

The surrounding woods were filled with people combing them for the tiniest of anything that didn't belong or the slightest sign of anything that had been disturbed.

More vehicles full of officers borrowed from surrounding areas were showing up to help, their roof lights adding to the strobes already flashing in the growing darkness on the side of the highway where they had to park and hike in.

They had a lot of ground to cover and the very nature of it, woods with years' worth of fallen leaves, twigs, branches, and old trees, only served to make the task more difficult.

They had come searching for the rest of the human remains to go with the skull found by a pair of hikers.

They didn't find those remains, but what they did find was much more disturbing.

The first thing they found was what appeared to be an open grave that could have been dug weeks ago, possibly months or longer, from the condition of the already crumbling edges and erosion washed into the hole by rain. It could have even been dug years ago. Then again, with the recent rains it could have been dug only a few days earlier. At this point the age of the dig site was pure speculation.

Their first guess was that the grave went with the skull. Probably whoever had buried the body felt some need to return and dig it up, likely to move it to what the individual thought would be a safer place. Although it didn't seem there could be any place safer than this. The area was remote and not easily accessible.

The narrow trails were little more than deer trails, used occasionally by the odd die-hard hunter who wanted to get further away from civilization and the rare intrepid hiker who was at greater risk of getting lost here than in the endless parking lot of seemingly endless rows of identical cars outside a sprawling mega mall.

It didn't get more secluded and safe than this if one were looking for a place to bury a victim.

Something must have spooked this perpetrator, making them risk moving the body.

Apparently they lost their head along the way.

It's likely the remains never would have been discovered if it weren't for the coincidence of this couple that just happened to come all the way out here to hike, their disobedient dog with a good nose, and the skull partially exposed at the surface of the ground where the animal might get a whiff of the almost non-existent scent of desiccated flesh still clinging to the bone.

The investigators were ready to call this search over.

But then the search for any more scattered remains turned up something they were not looking for.

This secluded grave was not so secluded after all. Not beneath the earth anyway.

First one grave was discovered with the help of a cadaver dog, the remains not having been buried very deep and the actions of the elements eroding away the topmost layers of earth to bring its grisly contents closer to the sky above.

Now they had two graves instead of one.

They'd have to conduct a more thorough search.

When they found the third grave, things looked a lot more sinister, and obviously bigger than their small force could handle. They started calling the neighboring departments for help.

Who knows how many more graves would be uncovered.

They hoped none.

Jim McNelly waddled around the woods unhappily, puffing

on a cigarette as if his life depended on it.

"How many graves so far?" he asked one of the men watching the excavation.

"Five more and counting, and that doesn't include the second open grave we found."

McNelly raised his eyebrows.

"Second open grave?" he asked.

The other officer nodded.

"This one is much more recent, definitely dug only a matter of days ago maybe, maybe yesterday or today.

McNelly's stomach soured.

This grave might have been meant for Jane Doe, or for another victim.

But it just didn't quite add up. Why would the perp dig a grave only to leave his victims lying around where they'd be found? What changed? It had to be something significant enough to make the perp risk getting caught.

Of course, they didn't know these graves belonged to the same man who was leaving bodies lying around. The odds of having more than one serial killer in the area were slim, making the likelihood they belonged to the same man strong.

Chances were good that out here nobody would have ever discovered the graves.

Also why would he go from hiding them to publicly displaying them?

He thought hard, his mind ticking away, rolling everything around inside and reorganizing all the information.

Same perp, different MO? Different perp? Did he suddenly want to get caught? Did something change in the woods? Did something change in the perp? Was he just being reckless, perhaps thinking that if he hasn't been caught yet he can't be caught at all?

"Got another one here," someone called out.

"Here too," another person called.

"Here," a third called.

McNelly paled, looking as though he'd aged a great many years, obviously affected by the sudden discovery of so many more graves all at once.

It should have taken days or weeks to find this many graves and they've discovered eight in only a matter of hours.

He rubbed a rough hand through his hair and over his face as though to rub those years away.

"This is going to be a long night," the other officer said.

McNelly nodded.

The fact that they were finding so many graves so fast meant something. And when he found out what, McNelly was sure he wouldn't like it.

Part Nine:
Jane Doe Walking

36

Molly was in a panic as she bustled about, turning this way and that and not knowing which way to go or what to do. Her calm nurse's training had abandoned her, leaving her at a loss.

Jane Doe was missing!

Molly had just started her shift and it had been a normal day from the moment she woke up.

She had gone about her routine very routinely and caught the bus as usual. She noted which of the regular passengers got on and off at their usual stops and which didn't. The passenger she thought of as Lady Lavender because she always wore that lavender scarf and matching purse must still be sick since she was not on the bus again. Lavender had looked pale and was congested the last time she'd seen her three days before.

Molly hadn't had any feelings of anything being out of place or any negative vibes.

As she entered the hospital, the usual people were all in their usual spots.

Everyone except the elderly custodian, that is. He wasn't where he should be, giving her the usual morning nod as she passed by.

Molly had wondered only briefly at that and shrugged it off. There could be almost any reason for the friendly old man to be somewhere else in the hospital at that moment.

It was the first and only hint that something might be wrong.

The missing custodian jangled her nerves a little bit, but no more than usual when something was out of place.

Molly didn't like things to be out of place, out or order, or in any way out of the ordinary.

On her floor everything seemed to be as it should, until she started her rounds.

Her pen was where she left it at the nurses' desk. The other nurses knew to never touch it. The desk was orderly; the files where they should be, even the chairs were in their usual places.

Brusquely she set about her duties, beginning with making her rounds of the patients under her care.

The first room she visited was 214B.

Molly had walked into the room, talking to Jane Doe as though the woman might be awake and hear her, just because you never knew if she might really be able to hear even when unconscious.

She had stopped dead in her tracks at the doorway and almost dropped her clip board.

The tidy sheets that normally curved up and over the mound of the motionless body had been casually tossed aside as many people would do when getting out of bed.

The mattress sheet lay slightly wrinkled and empty.

It was as though Jane Doe had just gotten up out of bed.

At first Molly's heart had leapt with joy.

Jane Doe was awake!

It didn't register on her that both side rails were in the raised position.

She immediately rushed to the usual spots she might expect to find a patient who had just woken from a drug induced stupor.

No Jane Doe.

She checked the woman's chart to see if she was scheduled for any tests or treatments, or if there were any notes that might lead to her whereabouts.

There was nothing more than the quick jots of the night nurse checking the sleeping woman's vitals.

She checked with the other nurses, the lab, and anywhere else the young woman may have been taken.

No Jane Doe.

Could she have awakened, alone and confused, and wandered off?

To leave the hospital by the main door, Jane Doe would have had to pass by the security desk. The desk was manned at night.

The patient had also been kept in restraints since her last waking that resulted in a violent fit.

169

She called the security desk to see if they had seen any patients wandering or trying to leave.

Nothing.

Her heart beat wildly in her chest even as a cold hand seemed to crush and squeeze the breath out of her.

Panic was starting to build. She looked around wildly for help to magically materialize, wandering a little way up the hallway in hope of seeing someone, praying that someone would be Jane Doe.

There was not another soul outside of the patients in their rooms.

She stopped herself, took some deep calming breaths, and rushed to the nurses' desk where she grabbed the phone with a trembling hand.

Within seconds of hanging up the phone again the intercom burst to life with news of the missing patient. A bored sounding voice droned off the information, detailing Jane Doe down to the hospital gown she wore and what department she had wandered off from.

The announcement was repeated verbatim immediately and would continue to be repeated every ten minutes until the missing patient was either located or deemed to have left the hospital.

Doctor Greenburg had just stepped into the elevator, pressed the parking garage level button, and watched the elevator doors whisk closed when the first announcement played.

His first reaction was to ignore it.

He had just finished working a double shift, including an eight hour surgery. He was exhausted and sore. He felt beyond bone weary. He was going home for some much needed sleep.

Misplaced patients were nothing unusual. They wandered off fairly often.

When they announced the department it got his attention, but only partially.

He only half listened to the replay of the announcement.

Suddenly it hit him. Jane Doe!

He had just seen her not more than an hour ago and she

could not possibly have woken up. She was medicated and would not be able to wake up on her own.

He was stuck in the elevator as it slowly descended.

He could press the next floor button and take another elevator back up, but that might take even longer.

He watched impatiently as the numbers above the door counted the floors down. They seemed to be moving slower than normal.

When the elevator finally reached his intended destination he jabbed the button for the floor he needed to go back up to. He impatiently jabbed at the close button as if it would help, urging the doors to close again quickly.

After an interminable pause, the doors finally began to slide closed just as a dark car drove slowly past the elevator, making its way to the parking exit.

He sighed and watched as the numbers slowly counted their way back up to the second floor.

The doors slid open and he rushed out of the elevator and down the corridor to join the fray already outside room 214B.

Molly was in a tizzy. She had never lost a patient before. And of all the patients to lose, perhaps the only thing that would have been worse for her would be if it were a child or a baby.

During her brief lapses of consciousness, Jane Doe had been groggy and disoriented. She'd seemed to be suffering from loss of memory.

Molly was surrounded by nurses and other staff, animatedly telling her story to a pair of security guards who were still sweating and breathing heavy from their run to room 214B.

In her mind she couldn't stress enough just how urgent the situation was, that the missing woman was the victim of one abduction already and possibly for the second time now, how traumatized the woman would be, and her lack of memory.

One of them called on his walkie-talkie, passing along the caution to try not to frighten her.

Michael had just entered the hospital when the announcement of the missing patient had begun to replay again.

It was just more intercom noise to him in a place where the

intercom never stopped chatting its barely understandable garbled warbling, and he wasn't paying attention to the announcement.

He had missed the part of the announcement that the message was about a missing patient.

Michael headed for the cafeteria to grab a coffee and a bite to eat before starting his shift watching Jane Doe.

At the cafeteria he perused the stations of available food choices, read the options on the menu board, and got into line behind a pair of elderly women.

The blue haired woman ahead of him was tut-tutting at the white haired woman next to her.

"Really," the blue haired woman said, "you would think it wouldn't be so difficult to keep track of people."

"Mmm-hmm," the white haired lady nodded.

"What if it was someone with Alzheimer's?" Blue Hair said disapprovingly.

"Oh, but the age was much too young," White Hair disagreed.

"But what if?" Blue Hair insisted.

"Oh yes, what if?" White Hair agreed now with a nod.

"To lose a patient," Blue Hair tut-tutted, "disgraceful. How can you trust a hospital that loses people?"

"I heard that they have a patient here with amnesia," White Hair said conspiratorially.

Blue Hair gasped.

"What if they lost her?" Blue Hair was horrified.

"Mmm-hmm," White Hair agreed, self-satisfied.

Michael watched the women, curious and only a little bit alarmed by the talk of missing patients. He pictured Jane Doe in his mind, peacefully sleeping in her hospital bed.

Noticing his interest in them, the two women turned to him with a look that said, 'Mind your own business.'

Something about the situation was bothering Michael. He knew that a patient wandering off was nothing new. In his first days undercover at the hospital he panicked every time one was announced, but he soon learned to ignore them beyond a general curiosity.

"Well, it doesn't hurt to find out a little more," he thought.

Instead of sheepishly turning away as the women expected him to, he looked at them with interest.

"Did you say someone was missing?" Michael asked.

"Oh yes," White Hair piped up, now being sociable and smiling at him warmly, charmed by the attention of a younger man.

"They lost a patient," Blue Hair added, obviously a little put out at letting him into their conversation uninvited, like a surprise visit for tea by that annoying neighbor you really don't like.

At that moment, the message began to replay again.

Blue Hair pointed at the intercom speaker on the wall, her finger stabbing out accusingly at it.

Michael's face fell as he listened, his expression becoming one of concern.

He turned and raced out of the cafeteria, leaving the two old women staring after him in surprise. Blue Hair looked indignant.

"Oh the poor man," White Hair said, "she must be his wife."

"Oh yes," Blue Hair tut-tutted.

Michael arrived in the hallway outside of room 214B and had his fears immediately brought to reality by the commotion that made it plain that Jane Doe really was missing.

A few staff members offered him only a cursory glance. A few others looked curious about his sudden hurried appearance at the scene.

Nurse Molly offered a look full of suspicion that clearly said he was not welcome here.

Molly was watching Doctor Greenburg, who stood in front of her talking to the security guards, when the sudden appearance of the orderly caught her attention.

The orderly looked agitated, stopping in his tracks from a dead run just beyond the outskirts of the group huddled in the hallway outside room 214B.

"What is HE doing here?" she wondered, fear for the missing woman turning to instant suspicion.

173

Her gut instincts had told her all along that the orderly was up to no good, and now they screamed that he had taken poor Jane Doe or otherwise done something to cause this, although it didn't seem possible or likely.

"Go away, just go away," she thought, glaring at him, hoping her thoughts alone would be strong enough command to make him obey.

He didn't go away, but he did seem to be trying to look invisible beyond the edge of the group.

Molly couldn't help but wonder at the look of stunned shock on the orderly's face. He looked like he was trying to act calm, like none of this mattered, but he couldn't hide his feelings.

He looked like a man who had just suffered a traumatic loss and hadn't yet come to terms with it. As a nurse, Molly had seen that look many times over the years.

The look was unmistakable.

Molly started to doubt herself.

The orderly looked just as shocked as she had felt over finding Jane Doe missing.

He looked scared.

Why would he look scared, unless he was either worried he would get caught or was worried for Jane Doe?

He had spent so much time hanging around Jane Doe. She had even seen him sitting by her bed holding Jane's hand on occasion.

Could she be wrong about the intentions of the man who made her so nervous?

Had he in fact come to have the same concerns for Jane Doe that she herself had?

Could his feelings for the woman run deeper?

She shook her head as if that would clear her confused thoughts and put them into order.

It just didn't feel right.

The man watched discretely as he had so many times.

In all the commotion heads had turned in his direction as they had with each person who arrived outside of room 214B.

The nurse's suspicion laced look lingered the longest, as it did for each person who arrived as though she might solve this mystery if she just memorized the faces of each person.

He didn't like her looking at him for so long. Her suspicious look unnerved him.

The moment he arrived to find the commotion he knew something was very wrong.

His heart had skipped a beat when he heard the announcement of a missing patient over the intercom and knew it was her.

He had planned to be much more discrete about approaching the room today. Today was going to be special. Today Jane Doe was going to come home with him.

But the fear of what the message might mean brought him to her room in a hurry.

Instead of relief to find Jane safe as he'd hoped, he was dropped into panic.

She's gone!

Where could she have gone?!

That man! The strange visitor who had been hanging around outside her room! He had seen him. He had seen his reaction when the nurse confronted him, his guilty look that said he was up to something he didn't want found out.

He had tried to follow when the visitor fled from the hospital but lost him before the visitor even made it out of the hospital.

Looking at the visitor had given him an odd sense of déjà vu. He looked familiar, though he couldn't place him.

Something about him made his pulse quicken and his stomach sour. It made him feel afraid, though he didn't know why.

Why was he here? Why at this room? Why did he seem to be studying the woman through the open door? Why had he fled?

Suspicion was born from these unanswered questions.

Did that visitor take Jane Doe? Did he come back and take her from her room?

He suddenly felt hollow inside, his guts a vast chasm of emptiness spanning the world between himself and wherever she was.

"Cassie, my sister," he thought numbly

He was going to take her home today, take her where he could look after her and keep her safe.

He was too late.

But what did this man want with her?

Who was he?

Was he someone he'd seen without realizing when he was watching her before he took her the first time?

That could be why the man seemed so familiar despite not being able to remember ever seeing or meeting him.

Was he someone from her life? Then why didn't he come forward before this when her picture was first in the paper?

If he had taken her, he obviously hadn't checked her out under normal circumstances.

He'd taken her without witnesses. He'd kidnapped her.

Dr. Greenburg looked around the group for someone who could help him. He spotted an orderly hovering just beyond the pack of people chatting too much in their excitement, looking like he was busy with other tasks although that seemed odd in the circumstances.

He waved at the orderly, catching his attention quickly. Obviously the man wasn't as disinterested in what was going on as he seemed. He could see the man's strained look.

He motioned the orderly to come over.

"Help me with this," Greenburg said, motioning to the bed inside the room.

Michael nodded, squeezing his way through the group and into room 214B.

The doctor pointed to indicate what he wanted and Michael went around to the far side of the bed, unlocking the wheel locks that prevented the bed from rolling.

He looked at the restraints still on the bed. Both side rails were in the up position.

Somebody had removed them from Jane's wrists, allowing her to be moved from the bed.

They checked the restraints, and the side rails, checking through the bedding.

He knew he shouldn't be doing this, should in fact be

leaving it for when the police arrived in uniform to search the room. He should be discouraging the doctor too. This was not his scene. His job was to guard Jane Doe.

Refusing might blow his cover though.

A part of him also wanted to tear the room apart himself instead of waiting for others to do it, waiting to be debriefed after. If there were any clues he wanted to find them now.

He wanted to find Jane Doe now, not later.

Who knew what kind of danger she was in.

Even if she had woken up and gotten up on her own, which was unlikely in her drugged state, someone had to have at least loosened one of the wrist restraints so she could get out of it to undo the other.

As he worked his mind turned again to the strange visitor he had chased away from this room.

He was the top suspect in Jane's disappearance.

He couldn't stop thinking about the man and wondering if he had taken her. Was she alright? Had he hurt her?

Fear sat low and heavy in his stomach, the hollowness it left building and expanding.

Dr. Greenburg made a noise of unpleasant surprise.

"What's this?" he demanded, turning and looking around as if there might be someone in the room with the answer.

The crowd at the door had not moved, continued to chat excitedly, and not a single one even noticed the doctor searching the bed and equipment.

Michael looked at him quizzically.

"Nurse!" the doctor called, "nurse!"

He turned to Michael.

"Check the chart. Who was on last shift?"

Michael turned to get the chart. Nurse Molly had left it on the table not far from the bed after discovering the patient missing.

Just then Molly pushed through the crowd into the room.

"Doctor?" she asked.

"Did you touch this?" Greenburg demanded.

"Touch what?" Molly asked. She suspected he meant the intravenous tube he held in his hand but wasn't sure.

177

"The IV. Did you touch it?"

"No," she said, confused. "I came in, Jane wasn't in her bed, and I-I," she had to stop and think a moment.

"The chart," Molly continued, turning slowly and looking about the room, "I left it-."

"Here," Michael said, picking it up from the table.

She wanted to snatch it from him but didn't want to risk touching the man. He still gave her the heebie-jeebies.

"Who was on last shift?" Greenburg repeated.

"Uh, Crawford I think," Molly blurted out. "Sally Crawford."

"Where is she? Gone home?"

"I don't know. Why?"

"Somebody," Greenburg held out the intravenous tube accusingly, "tampered with this IV"

He reached under the thin mattress.

"The tube from here was not going to her arm." He indicated the intravenous bag hanging from the pole next to the bed.

"The IV is going into this instead."

He pulled out another intravenous bag that had been hanging from the bed under the mattress, showing the line going straight from one to the other.

"But, the tube in her arm?" Molly asked, dumbfounded. She had been certain she noticed fluid in the tube running to the needle in Jane's hand.

Greenburg shrugged. Without the patient's arm to check they had no way of knowing what was going on with the tube in her hand.

Molly gasped, realizing the implications.

"She's not getting fluids, she could dehydrate!"

"She's not getting the medications," Greenburg corrected, "she could have woken up and gotten up herself."

"Or been taken!" Molly gasped. "What if she's been taken by-by that monster?! She'd be easier to take out walking."

Greenburg nodded.

"Call security again, let them know, and find me that night nurse. I want to know if she saw anything."

"Someone taking her would explain the restraints. She

couldn't have gotten up on her own with those wrist restraints."

The night nurse came into the room. She had just been heading out of the hospital for home when she heard the announcements and returned, knowing that she might very well be in a lot of trouble.

She had been standing just outside the door listening and heard just enough of the conversation to know what was going on.

"Uh, Dr. Greenburg," Sally Crawford said nervously.

The three turned to look at her, surprised by her sudden appearance.

"Dr. Greenburg, I loosened one restraint and undid the other because I thought the patient looked too uncomfortable. And besides, she was drugged anyway. I didn't think anything would happen." She was on the verge of tears.

"I didn't touch the IV except to change the bag and administer the medication."

"Did you see anything?" Michael and Greenburg asked simultaneously.

The two men looked at each other for a moment, and then turned back to the nurse.

"I didn't see anything odd about the bag. It dripped like normal. The tube going to the patient was still filled with fluid as it should be."

Sally broke down sobbing, afraid for her job.

"Of course it dripped normally," Greenburg said more to the room than the people in it, "it was flowing into another bag just the same as it would the patient's arm, the tube clipped to control the flow."

Shaking his head in what could only be a mix of wonder, shock, and concern, he put the IV bag down on the bed.

"Call that detective, McNelly," he said, turning to Molly.

"No, better yet," he hesitated, changing his mind, "get me the number. I'll call him myself."

Molly nodded and scrambled out of the room.

"Sally, you go to the staff room and get a hold of yourself," Greenburg said.

Turning to the orderly, he finished giving his orders.

"Make sure security watches the room. Nothing gets touched. And tell them to do a thorough sweep of the hospital."

Just as they all left the room sirens became audible outside, and not the usual ambulance wails common to hospitals.

Jane Doe wandered the corridors of the hospital.

She didn't look much different from any other patient wandering aimlessly, looking lost and groggy in the strange surroundings, blue hospital gown tied in the back.

The only thing unusual was the rubber tube trailing along with her, a tube without its companion intravenous bag on a rolling coat rack stand.

It was shift change for most of the hospital staff, that time when the people coming off shift are tidying up last-minute stuff or giving patient updates to the people coming on, and the people coming on are getting ready for their shift and receiving patient updates.

The halls of the hospital were largely empty, except for the occasional patient stumbling or shuffling about, going for a walk.

One more patient stumbling around didn't seem unusual to anyone who saw her.

Jane had woken up alone, feeling groggy and disoriented.

The sterile whiteness of the room, the open curtain in a ceiling track that went around the bed, the antiseptic smell, and the distant sounds all spelled out "hospital."

"Ohhh, I'm still here," she moaned desperately, feeling like a prisoner being kept without any explanation why she was imprisoned.

"Is this a hospital or a mental hospital?" she wondered. "I don't think I'm hurt or anything."

She tried to focus on the signals coming from her body through the fog filling her mind. There was some vague numb achiness, but it was the sort of feeling she got if she was so overtired that she slept without moving or turning over all night long.

"I don't think I had surgery."

Her nose was terribly itchy, one of the less pleasant side

effects of the medication that has been pumped into her to keep her sedated and easy to manage, only being stopped for brief periods when they needed her to be a little bit lucid to run tests or for the hospital psychiatrist to assess her.

She had tried to scratch her nose only to find her arm held down.

She looked down at her arm in surprise, immediately frightened to see that her arm was in fact bound by a padded cuff fastened to the bed rail.

In a dazed panic she tried to pull her tethered arms away from the bed rails, only to almost smack herself in the face with her other hand.

Jane looked in surprise at her free-flailing arm and then to the rail on that side of the bed.

Someone had removed the cuff off that hand.

"Why am I here? Why am I cuffed to a bed?"

Jane tried to remember how she got there, but she couldn't.

Her memory had glimpses of a man in a lab coat, different women and men who were probably nurses or something. There were snatches of conversations, people talking as if she wasn't there in the room, tinny garbled announcements echoing as if coming through bad speakers, but little else.

The heavy fuzziness of her head and the confusion that filled it like thick cotton only made her more uneasy.

"I don't like this," Jane mumbled.

She wanted to call out, to see if anyone was out there.

The place felt deserted.

Jane was just about to call out, but then thought better of it.

The memory started coming to her of waking up feeling just like this, struggling to sit up and then to stand, getting out of bed on weakened wobbly legs.

And then someone was grabbing her, pushing her, trying to force her back into the bed without explanation.

She remembered her mind exploding with images, they flashed back at her, images of a man whose face seemed to be just a blur, being kidnapped, being taken to a place that seemed very old, the man hurting her. They were mixed with other, more sterile, images, endless faces in lab coats, men and women, their faces swimming and changing all becoming him, the painful jab of a needle, endless mumbling, and the squeak of cart wheels.

She remembered the terror that filled her, fighting back, trying to escape the man, and the painful pinch in her arm right before she lost all feeling to her body, losing all control over her limbs, falling limply into his grasp. She remembered her head lolling about, being lifted. She didn't feel the bed, but knew she was being put back in the bed.

And suddenly it wasn't the man anymore, but other people, people in nurse uniforms.

And then the world dimmed and closed in as she dropped back into the dark void of unconsciousness without dreams.

The memory agitated her even more, filling her with a sense of urgency, desperation.

Had I been kidnapped? Brought here against my will? What is this place?

She needed to get out of here, whatever here is.

Jane fumbled with the one restraint that still tethered a wrist.

In her dazed state she just couldn't manage to undo it.

She struggled with it, tearing at the cuff with her fingers, trying to unfasten it and finally giving up and just trying to squeeze her hand through it.

She looked like an animal caught in a trap, ready to gnaw its own foot off in terror and desperation for freedom.

And suddenly she was free.

The cuff was loose enough that she could slip her hand through it, but tight enough to make it difficult.

She stared at her hand in surprise.

It took a moment to get her wits enough to try to pull herself into a sitting position.

Both bed rails were in the up position and she used them to pull herself up.

Jane paused, exhausted, and looked around the room, her fuzzy head empty of all thought.

Then she remembered.

"I need to get out of here."

She looked around blankly, at the foot of the bed, at the bed rails trapping her within a steel two-sided cage.

The foot of the bed was open. A small rolling table was up against the foot of the bed, providing a barrier in her vision that seemed like an impenetrable wall to her drug addled mind.

But she just knew somehow that there lay the path to escape.

With difficulty, she crawled over the blankets, her legs tangling up in them, making her way clumsily to the foot of the bed.

Once there, she tested the immovable rails, and then pushed on the wall, almost falling off the bed when the table suddenly moved from the pressure of her push.

She scrabbled frantically, trying to save herself from falling. Suddenly, in that moment of lost balance, the floor felt like it was many feet away.

Even more disoriented by the sudden movement of the wall that was a wheeled table and from her near fall from what seemed an impossible height, it took Jane long moments to get her bearings and feel like it was safe enough to dare leaning over the side to look down.

She needed to know just how far a drop she had to get off of this thing.

She no longer saw the bed as simply a bed. Now it was a platform way up high, though she had no idea why she was there or how she got up there.

Her head swooned with dizziness and the room went out of focus as she looked over the foot of the bed.

"That's so far," she whispered.

But she had to do it. She had to get out of this place before he came back.

"No," she reminded herself, "before they come back."

Turning herself around, she went over the edge feet first, clinging to the railings on either side for dear life, feeling tentatively with her toes for anything to support them as she began her long climb down.

And quite abruptly her feet were on the floor.

She was so surprised by this that she had to twist around to look, while holding tight to the rails just in case.

Yep, there her feet were, on the floor.

She stood up carefully, using the bed to steady herself.

183

On wobbly legs, Jane staggered to the door of the room.

She paused in the doorway, looking up the hallway first one way and then the other.

The hall was deserted.

She had no idea which way to go. Nearby there was a long desk. There was no one at the desk.

She went up the hall the other way, shuffling along against the wall, keeping one hand on the wall to steady herself, her drugged legs not wanting to cooperate.

By the time she reached the junction where another hall joined this one, Jane forgot where she was going and even why she was in this strange place, walking, feeling groggy and dazed.

So she just kept on going.

When Jim McNelly got the call about Jane Doe being missing, he immediately sent in the troops to lock down the hospital grounds to find the girl.

He wanted to find her as much as he wanted to find the bastard responsible.

Guilt already gnawed at his ulcer. If anything happened to her, well, he felt like it was his fault.

He should have done more to protect this one, especially since he failed to protect the others.

He knew these thoughts were impossible. He couldn't possibly protect everyone all the time.

But that didn't stop the guilt from eating away at his gut.

McNelly waddled off the elevator with a grunt, his bulk making its impossible passage down the crowded hallway.

"What the hell are you all doing standing around here?" he demanded to no one in particular and to everyone in general.

"Lock down and go find them!"

As if waiting for his words to release them like hounds at a foxhunt, the crowd of junior officers, security guards, and hospital staff scattered.

They should have already been locking down the hospital grounds, screening everyone coming and going, and searching the place.

Most of his searchers were hospital staff and security guards.

They had plenty of experience in watching for wandering patients while doing their duties, but were not what he wanted with a complete lockdown and search with a dangerous criminal who might be on the grounds.

"Damn," McNelly swore.

People seemed to be coming out of the woodwork; hospital staff, guards, and a handful of police officers.

Reporters were starting to show up too.

Michael needed to get out of here.

With more people showing up to search for Jane Doe, the chances of someone recognizing him and blowing his cover was rising.

It burned him that he had to leave. He wanted to stay and search for Jane himself. He needed to find her.

The hollowness inside him was only getting bigger, the worry over what happened to her building.

He gave McNelly a curt nod as he passed him by.

McNelly acknowledged.

Michael made his way stealthily out of the hospital.

Seeing him go, Molly had an idea. She would try to follow him, to see what he was up to once and for all.

She lost him on the next floor, but continued on, determined to catch up to him and follow the orderly.

She caught site of the other man, the visitor who had run from the orderly, blanched, and ducked through a seldom used door, hoping he hadn't seen her.

The strange visitor who Nurse Molly had earlier confronted, and who then fled the hospital after seeing Michael, had returned to the hospital.

He had also returned hours earlier.

On his first return trip, the visitor had timed it for the busiest time of day, when the halls were filled with visitors and the staff with distractions. With the commotion came the opportunity to move about unquestioned and unnoticed.

He made his way to Jane Doe's room, careful that no one paid him extra attention.

185

Once there, he stopped and stared at her as she lay in a drug induced sleep. Sleeping like the dead, motionless, expressionless, without even the slightest hint of the faintest curve of her mouth in a smile or the creases in her forehead that went with the slight downward curve of a frown on her lips.

He had watched her sleep before this too; before she was left for dead in a pile of trash in an alley. It was a long time ago. She had been a child then.

She mostly frowned in her sleep then too.

While the newspapers had dubbed her "Jane Doe—The Mystery Woman", he knew who she really was.

The first time he came to the hospital, when that nurse confronted him outside her door, it was a rash move committed without thought or planning. It was reckless.

After seeing her picture in the paper, reading that she was alive and where she was, he felt the need to see her.

The nurse was overbearing and protective, suspicious of this strange visitor hovering uncertainly around Jane's door, and with good reason.

And he had been quite uncertain.

Should he go in and risk being noticed?

He wanted to see her, but it wasn't worth the risk.

He knew they would be watching her room.

He also knew all too well who Detective McNelly and his team were; all of them.

He had spent most of his life on the wrong side of the law.

He knew who most of the cops on the force were. He made it his business to know before he came here.

It was only a matter of time before McNelly cracked this case, but that was the crux of it.

Time.

The closer McNelly got, the more urgently Jane Doe needed to be dealt with. Before the other one came back for her, the man who had hurt her.

As McNelly closed in on the case, so did his small window of time to get the girl.

He almost tried to take her then and there, even with the nurse as a witness, as risky and stupid as it would have been.

Then the orderly showed up.

He recognized the orderly immediately, blanching at coming face to face with the younger man.

He desperately hoped the man in the orderly's uniform, the man of many uniforms, did not recognize him.

The confused look of recognition on the orderly's face terrified him.

At once he was certain he'd been recognized, that the orderly knew him. But he quickly realized that the confused expression really meant that he'd only seemed familiar, that he didn't place his face—yet.

He turned and ran.

The orderly's footsteps pursued him.

Relief had washed over him after he lost the younger man.

This time he planned ahead.

This time he knew exactly what he needed to do and how to do it. Before coming he had to change cars again. It was easy to find one that would not be noticed missing for hours if you were smart about it. He left the other one where he'd taken it from, the owner left completely unaware someone had taken it.

Alone in Jane's room hours ago, he had gently brushed his fingers across her cheek.

It felt cool to the touch.

Only the quiet monitor hooked up to her suggested this was not a mere lifeless corpse laying there.

He pulled an empty IV bag out of his pocket, its long flexible tube trailing after it. He had pilfered it from a supply drawer before coming to her room.

He laid the empty bag on the bed.

Carefully, he took the tube going from the full bag hanging from a stand and steadily feeding fluids into Jane's arm.

He squeezed the clip on the thin flexible tube, closing the drip.

He needed the tube to look normal, fluid filled.

He carefully switched the tubes and bags around. The bag on the stand was now feeding down the tube and going into the empty bag, the clamp just below the fluid filled bag controlling the slow drip. He squeezed the clip on the thin flexible tube going into the empty bag, setting its pinch just right.

He checked to make sure the flow stayed at the same steady drip.

He brought the tube that was supposed to be going to Jane's hand so it ran under the blankets out of sight and tucked the empty bag up below the bed so that gravity would continue to feed the liquid out of the full bag hanging from the pole as normal.

He then tucked the now loose tube still going to the needle in Jane's hand under the blankets as well. The tube was knotted to make sure it remained fluid filled at her hand.

He left her bare arm exposed, with the tube running under the blankets, looking quite normal.

No one would notice the switch unless they pulled the blankets away to check.

He didn't think anyone would.

He was counting on it.

His second re-visit was planned for shift change, the other busiest time of day.

With the hours in between, the medications had time to work their way out of Jane's body.

She would be groggy and would have trouble walking, and probably would be too dazed to even know what was going on, but she would be able to walk out under her own power.

There was no way he could take her out unnoticed carrying her.

Now he was back and biding his time, waiting for the right moment, when the announcement started calling out the details of a missing patient.

He didn't connect the two at first.

Then he did.

"Damn it!" he swore.

The whole world seemed to swirl and spin continuously for Jane.

She continued wandering halls aimlessly, the loose IV tube dangling uselessly from her arm, using the walls to steady herself, her weak legs threatening to give out.

188

She wanted to just slump to the floor and go to sleep.

Even the effort of that seemed too much.

Mostly she didn't know where she was, or even think of it.

Every now and again, Jane got a glimpse of someone in a bland uniform, the generic sort that could belong to anyone working in a hospital, though she was too groggy to make that thought, and she would feel the urge to hide from them, the need to get out of this strange place.

As her sightings of these people increased, so did her confusion and vague feeling of urgency.

She didn't really know why she needed to escape at this point. She only knew she had to get out of here.

Her mind was too fuzzy to focus on anything.

Call it accident or coincidence, but Jane somehow managed to avoid the searchers un-methodically searching the hospital.

Twice a frantic employee had even tried to usher her into the nearest residential room "for her safety".

Walking seemed to be helping the medication wear off a little more.

Jane's legs felt a little less wobbly, her arms less like limp boneless rubber.

She tried doors as she passed, most leading to entrapment in tiny rooms.

An orange-red light caught her attention, drawing her to it mindlessly like a moth that can't help but flutter around the light of a flame.

She tried the door and found herself faced with the cold confines of a tiny bare concrete room.

Only this room had stairs.

Jane slipped inside, letting the door close behind her.

She looked up. That path seemed impossibly hard. Down would be easier.

Wavering and almost falling at the first step, Jane cautiously made her way down the stairs.

They seemed to go on forever.

She passed the first door without even seeing it; so intent was her focus on finding that next step.

She paused at the second door, confused.

189

"Was I going down?"

She looked down the stairs, then up.

"Was I going up?"

Jane spotted the door again and the stairs evaporated. The only thing that existed in her world now was the door.

She pushed on the door and it was unmovable.

Jane sighed heavily. She was just so tired.

She leaned against the door, unwittingly depressing the bar lever, unlatching the door. It moved a fraction with a whining groan.

Surprised, Jane straightened up, staring at the door.

She pressed on it again. Nothing. She lowered her hands, bracing herself, and pushed the bar lever.

The door swung open and she staggered through, turning, and found herself confronted by another door. Jane concentrated on that bar and pushed, staggering forward as the door opened. She squinted, her eyes burning her with the brightness of the daylight outside.

Jane stumbled blindly through the door, letting it close behind her.

The fresh air seemed unreal after the stink of sterility of the hospital.

Her vision returning after the shock of bright light, Jane started wandering along the outside wall.

She didn't even notice the screech of tires not far away, the sound of an approaching vehicle, or the car door opening.

Suddenly, a man stood before her, his face washed with relief.

"There you are!" he cried out happily.

"Come," he said softly, putting his hands on each of her arms, "I have to get you out of here, get you someplace safe."

She nodded mutely.

Safe.

Safe sounded good.

Jane's foggy mind wasn't able to put the thought together that she probably should wonder who this man is.

All she knew was that she wanted to sleep.

Sleep and be safe.

The man felt like he would burst as he left the hospital.

She was gone! Where was she? Did someone take her, or did she just wander off? What if that other man hanging around took her? Who is he and what does he want with his sister?

He had to find her before anyone else did, but how? He couldn't stay and search for her. He would be recognized sooner or later.

Getting in his car, he stared back at his own eyes reflecting at him in the rear-view mirror.

The eyes of a monster.

He hated those eyes and the secrets they held.

Grimly, he started the car, backed out of the parking spot, and roared through the parking lot.

He was just approaching the exit when a lone figure standing against the wall of the hospital caught his attention.

He had almost missed the figure, partially obscured and standing in a delivery ramp that went down below the level of the ground around. The large delivery door was closed and at the base of the ramp a little distance from it was an exit door where staff probably hid to smoke without leaving the hospital grounds.

His pulse leapt and his heart skipped a beat.

He slammed on the brakes, reversed, and changed course, rushing to pull up beside the woman.

Her hair was dishevelled and she wore nothing but a hospital gown tied in the back. A useless IV tube trailed from her arm.

She looked terrible.

She looked wonderful. Jane Doe. Cassie.

In the trunk, a bound and gagged woman was tossed about by the sudden movements of the car as it skidded to a stop.

She was beyond feeling the bruising jolt of her body slamming into the side of the trunk from the car's sudden breaking and accelerating.

Her nurse uniform was rumpled and soiled.

The bloodied nametag said "Molly".

Her sightless eyes stared into the darkness accusingly.

Happiness burst through the man even before he could leap from the car, almost missing putting it in park in his urgency.

He jumped in front of Jane Doe, excited and filled with relief.

"There you are!" he cried out happily.

"Come," he said softly, putting his hands on each of her arms, "I have to get you out of here, get you someplace safe."

She only nodded mutely.

Gently, he drew her towards the car.

"You look so tired. I bet you just want to sleep."

She nodded, the motion barely discernable.

He opened the back door of the car for her.

"Here, lie down here and just go to sleep. When you wake up you will be safe."

Jane could barely crawl into the car; she was so weak from the drugs that had barely begun to wear off.

He helped her gently.

Lying down across the bench seat, she closed her eyes.

Closing the door softly, he rushed back to his seat, closing the driver's door that he'd left open.

"Sleep now, sleep," he said softly.

Jane was asleep before the car made it out of the parking lot.

The man's mind swirled with happiness.

I found her!

She's safe!

"Kathy will be so happy," he said softly, not wanting to wake up his passenger.

He sped off for the old farmhouse, careful not to go so fast as to risk being pulled over.

Part Ten:
New Friends & Escape Attempt

37

The man's excitement only mounted as he drove on towards the old farmhouse.

By the time he started down the long driveway, he was ready to jump out of the car before it could even make it to the house.

As soon as he put the car into park and shut it off, he scrambled out, rushing for the house only to stop mid-stride.

Oh yeah, he thought, turning around and heading back to the car.

Opening the back door, he gently shook Jane's shoulder.

"We're here. We're home."

She groaned groggily, her eyes fluttering to life.

He helped her sit up and get out of the car.

Jane wobbled a moment before she got her balance. Her legs were still rubbery and her head was very fuzzy.

"Just take it slow," he said, helping her to take the first few steps towards the shack.

Once in the house, he helped her sit down in the chair before rushing off.

Jane barely saw anything of the yard outside, her fuzzy mind was so focused on just standing and taking that first step, and then the next and so on.

She didn't see anything of her surroundings until she was finally seated and left alone.

She was glad the man left the room.

The commotion of his excitement was too much for her confused mind. It made it impossible to concentrate on even the most basic thing like walking.

The quiet of the small house enveloped her, making her feel better, less confused.

She looked around at the walls, plank and mortar with cracks of light where the mortar had fallen away.

"This place must be pretty cold and draughty," she thought. "I could peek out those cracks and see outside."

She didn't know why she had that last thought, but someone peeking out cracks seemed right, even if it felt like something a child would do.

The place was shabby in the way that a very old place gets despite the simple acts of maintenance.

The furniture and lamps were very old and well used.

The place had a musty odor to it, distinctive to old buildings.

When the man rushed off after leaving Jane in the chair, he went to quickly put a few things together.

He had a special surprise planned for Jane's homecoming.

Done, he went to the trap door to the root cellar, unbarred it, and pulled the door up and over on its hinges.

"Kathy," he called to the darkness below.

His breath hitched in his throat when there was no sound from below.

Worry suddenly tarnished his joy.

"Kathy," he called again. He waited. Nothing. He frowned.

He tossed down the rope ladder, about to climb down to take a look.

She had to still be there. There was no way out except the trap door, which was too high for her to reach and barred from the outside.

Just then her pale moon face appeared in the darkness below the opening.

The face was sallow and thin, eyes red rimmed and edged with dark circles from much more than the long shed tears.

The face looked unreal, ghostly, a mere phantom of the woman.

The man smiled in relief.

"Kathy, come up," he said, his excitement returned. "I have something special to show you."

Still weak despite the extra food, water, and blankets he had been giving her, Kathy reached for the rope ladder and made the slow awkward climb up.

When she got to the top he helped her out.

She stood motionlessly beside the dark hole to the root cellar, waiting silently, not looking at him.

The man just stared at her for a moment, taking in her dirty dress, the smudges on her face, arms, and legs, and her dirty tangled hair.

Did she really look like this? So thin? So—so neglected?

Once again his excitement was pushed aside by other feelings.

This time it was guilt. Guilt, remorse, and sadness that he wasn't taking better care of her.

He cupped her chin in his hand, lifting it to make her look at him.

She suffered it, turning her eyes away, avoiding meeting his.

"It's ok, Kathy," he whispered. "I already told you that I made a mistake, that I know you're not her."

Kathy didn't know if she should feel some small form of relief or fear, so she settled on feeling nothing at all.

If she wasn't the one, then he didn't need her. He had no reason to keep her.

She was sure he also would never let her go.

But why hasn't he killed her already then, like he did with the others that he kidnapped and were not *her*?

He moved around to catch her eyes, making her look into his.

"I found her Kathy," he said. "This time I really did, I know it. I found her."

She just stared at him expressionlessly.

Just when he thought she didn't hear, she responded.

"So, I guess that means you're going to kill me now," Kathy said emotionlessly.

He had to think about that for a moment.

Killing her would be the natural course of events. It was what he had to do.

But the thought seemed utterly foreign to him.

Forced by her words to think about it, he felt torn apart by a sudden overwhelming loss.

"We'll deal with that later," he said, his voice catching with emotion.

195

He swallowed, trying to wet his suddenly dry throat and get control of his voice.

"Come," he said, "come meet her."

The man led Kathy to the tiny living room where Jane still sat looking around the shack in confusion.

Jane turned to look, her attention caught by the sound of their approach.

It was the man who picked her up outside that place, promising to bring her to safety. She didn't recognise the man beyond that moment, although even through the fuzz cocooning her mind she felt like she should.

Beside him stood a petite woman who looked very sick and drawn, her hair a tangled mess that hadn't been washed or brushed in days, her dress and visible skin smudged and dirty.

Jane stared at the woman who stared back at her with eyes hollowed by trauma.

The terrible state of the other woman didn't even register with Jane at first.

Jane's eyes were focusing better now, but much of what she saw didn't really register in her brain.

Kathy just stood there motionlessly, looking at the woman in the chair. She looked in part because she knew it was expected of her, in part hopeful that somehow this woman will save her, and in part out of curiosity.

Was this really her?

Could this really be the woman that the man had kidnapped her and others for, thinking they were her?

She knew she couldn't blame the woman, but she resented her.

If not for this woman, she would be at home safe right now.

Ronnie flashed into her mind.

Ok, maybe not that safe, but she wouldn't be here, a prisoner kept locked in a cold, damp, and dark root cellar with bugs and mice and who knows what else either. She wouldn't be waiting to die at the hands of this man, even if she always felt that sooner or later Ronnie would kill her in one of his drunken rages.

"Oh, just kill me and get it over with," she pleaded mentally with the man standing beside her. "You don't need me now that you have her. She's the one you want anyway, not me."

Looking at the woman in the chair, Kathy took in her blue hospital gown, bare feet, dishevelled hair, and the IV tube still trailing from her hand. The confusion and exhaustion were plain on the other woman's face.

The man stood nervously beside Kathy.

This was it, the moment he had longed for.

He had finally found her. For real this time, he was sure of it.

But now things were different. He was anxious that the two woman like each other. He didn't know why it mattered so much when a part of him knew he had to get rid of Kathy, but it did.

He needed Kathy to accept her. He needed her to like Kathy.

"Kathy, this is her," he said, the mix of emotions threatening to make his voice crack. "They called her Jane Doe in the paper because they didn't know who she is, you must have seen that."

In his excitement it didn't even occur to him that Kathy didn't know who the woman was, didn't know her name.

He had never even given her a name to call him by, even though it would have to be a fake name. But that was a conscious precaution. Names were dangerous. If she had his identity and escaped, he'd be caught.

He addressed Jane.

"This is Kathy," he said simply, not offering any explanation.

Jane looked to him and back at Kathy again.

She saw Kathy's terrible condition this time.

"What's wrong with her?" Jane asked.

"What? Nothing," he said, clearly taken off balance by the question. He knew what she meant but didn't want to admit to his neglect.

"She looks sick and dirty," Jane said.

The man looked at Kathy, really seeing for the first time since he got home just how terrible she looked.

"Oh, Kathy," he groaned, "I'm so sorry."

He hung his head, feeling awful for neglecting her.

"Come, we need to get you cleaned up."

He started leading Kathy away to the bathroom.

197

"You should take out the tube and find her some clothes," Kathy said emotionlessly.

He looked back at Jane, seeing the tube dangling from her hand and the hospital gown. He had forgotten about them.

"Oh, yeah," he said. "You first," he said, turning to Kathy.

He led Kathy to the bathroom.

"Shower, get cleaned up. While you do that I'll see if I can find something for her to wear."

He looked at Kathy's filthy dress.

"And something else for you too."

He gently pushed her into the bathroom, closing the door behind her.

Rushing to Jane's side, he knelt down.

"I have to take this out, it might hurt at little," he said apologetically.

Jane looked down in confusion at the tube taped to her hand.

Carefully he started to peel away the layers of tape, trying his best to hold the needle so it wouldn't move and cause her any discomfort. He slid the needle out, a bead of blood following it.

He looked around.

"You're supposed to put something on it, cotton or something, to stop the blood," he thought.

He didn't have anything.

He put his thumb on it, thought better, then brought her other hand to it and placed her thumb over the oozing hole.

"Here, keep your thumb here, put pressure on it."

He went in search of cotton and a small bandage or anything that would serve the same purpose.

Kathy stripped nervously, getting into the shower only reluctantly.

The steam was already filling the bathroom.

The heat felt so good after the damp chill of the root cellar.

Once under the cascade of hot water, Kathy thought she'd melt from the sheer pleasure of it.

The water fell like a downpour of soft rain, warming her even more than the steamy air, washing away the dirt as much as the desperation and fear.

She lathered herself slowly, taking pleasure in the mundane simplicity of the act.

Kathy couldn't help but think while she was in there.

She thought about the woman in the other room.

Could she really be the one? Could she really be the woman he had been looking for?

She had never seen him so happy, so excited.

Maybe that meant he had found her at last?

She felt happy for him, sending her mind immediately into turmoil. She frowned.

She almost laughed. It wasn't a humorous laugh, but one bordering on self-mockery.

"Of course you haven't seen him so happy before," she chided herself, "how long have you even known the man? How many days, weeks? Has it been Months?" She really didn't know how long. Time had ceased to have any meaning.

"And how can you feel anything but hatred for this man? Happy for him? Because he found some woman? He KIDNAPPED you!"

"Now he's going to kill me, now that he has her," she whispered sadly.

Strangely, the sadness didn't seem to be about the loss of her own life, but of something else.

It wasn't about Ronnie either. In fact, despite the fear, loneliness, and sorrow, she'd actually come to feel relieved that she didn't have to be always afraid of what mood Ronnie would be in today.

Even though she knew it was certain her kidnapper would kill her sooner or later, he hasn't actually hurt her.

She'd always thought Ronnie would kill her sooner or later too, but he did hurt her; often.

The other woman didn't seem upset or scared. She didn't seem at all like you would expect of someone who was kidnapped.

Did she go with him willingly? Does she know who he is, what he is? Kathy wasn't sure. The woman also seemed dazed, like she had been drugged. Maybe she was drugged and did not know what was happening.

Resentment towards the other woman flared in her chest.

It was quickly replaced by pity.

She doesn't know what he is, does she? She doesn't know what she's in for, how much danger she's in.

Kathy's thoughts were interrupted by a soft knock at the bathroom door.

The man opened it just a little.

"Uh, sorry," he said sheepishly, turning his gaze away like a proper gentleman, seeming embarrassed to be intruding on the privacy of the bathroom.

"I found you another dress."

He reached around, hung the garment on the door knob and closed the door softly behind him.

Kathy clutched the shower curtain to herself the moment she heard the click of the door latch opening.

She stood frozen as he spoke, listening to the latch as the door closed again.

She hadn't dared to look during the intrusion.

She was afraid to look now, afraid he'd still be there, standing outside the shower.

At last she looked. The bathroom was filled only with steam. Steam, and the dress hanging by the scruff of the neck off the doorknob.

She finished up quickly and barely dried off in her rush to put the imagined safety of clothes between her and her kidnapper, struggling to pull the dress on fast, the fabric clung to her damp skin as if reluctant to cover her.

The dress didn't quite fit, sagging in places and a little too big. It also had an odor to it, the kind you get when you've packed clothes away for years without so much as a mothball or anything else for the dampness and smell.

She wiped off the mirror with a corner of the towel, leaving streaks of water droplets and steam on the glass but clearing it enough to see her reflection.

This was the first time Kathy had seen herself since she'd been kidnapped.

She blanched at the sight of herself.

"Do I really look this bad?"

She took in her sunken hollow eyes, her sallow skin, and her cheeks that seemed to want to cave in.

"I look like I'm dying," she thought miserably.

Taking her eyes off her own face reluctantly, she focused on the dress in the mirror.

It looked old. Not in a worn out way, but in a sitting in the closet a long time way. The dress was well out-dated, gone out of fashion decades ago.

Just how old is this dress?

Cautiously, she opened the door.

He was standing right there, so close his face must have been almost touching the door.

Fear flashed through her, the sudden constriction of her throat the only thing that stopped her from letting out a yelp.

She stared up at him, looking down only because he was shoving something into her hands.

She almost dropped it; her fingers seemed numb and unable to respond.

Kathy looked down at what he'd handed her.

It was a toothbrush and a hairbrush.

"There's toothpaste in the cabinet," he said, pointing to the mirror.

Kathy stepped back dumbly, turning to stare at the bathroom mirror in confusion.

When she turned back to the doorway he was gone.

While Kathy was in the shower, the man went on a scavenger hunt.

The shack had a small crawlspace above the ceiling, its ancient insulation looking like a blanket of sawdust.

He stood on a ladder, the trap door to the crawlspace open, his head and shoulders sticking through the hole in the ceiling, and rummaged through old boxes and suitcases that had been shoved up there. Some looked just old and worn; others look like they'd been stuck up there brand new decades ago.

He studied the suitcases, tossing aside any that looked water damaged or chewed by rodents.

Finally finding one that looked good, he popped the latches

with difficulty, breaking one to open it.

He quickly rummaged through the fabric, pulling out a dress and then a second, carefully dropping them to the floor at the bottom of the ladder.

He brought one dress to Kathy in the bathroom, suddenly becoming as awkward as a little boy when coming face to face with the closed bathroom door with the sound of the shower hissing on the other side.

After feeling around while avoiding looking and hanging the dress on the inside door knob, he closed the door quietly behind him and brought the other dress to Jane, who still sat in the small living room.

Jane just sat there after the man led the other woman away, floating on a cloud of haze. She stared at the room before her, not really seeing it.

She felt a vague sense of familiarity. It could be the look of the place, the smell, anything. But the drugs that had kept her in a coma-like state and still pulsed through her veins in weakened strength didn't let her dwell on anything.

Jane's mind had been clearing since she woke up in the hospital, slowly but steadily. But it was still easier just to not think at all.

An undercurrent of unease darkened the soft cloud she floated on.

The sound of the man rummaging somewhere in the small house played in the background as unnoticed as the song of a distant bird outside.

And then he was before her, kneeling down to face her on her own level.

She blinked slowly. It took time for her to focus on the man before her. He didn't look familiar and yet he did.

"I brought you something," he said, pushing a pile of fabric into her lap.

"It's a dress."

She just looked at him blankly.

"To replace," he looked down at her blue hospital gown, "you know."

Taking her hand gently, he led her to her feet, drawing her forward to a short hallway. He ushered her into a small bedroom.

He helped her by untying the strings on the back of the hospital gown. The gown fell open at the back.

Avoiding looking at her bare backside, he left the room, closing the door behind him.

Jane looked around the room passively.

It was a very small room. Two single beds were pressed against the walls of the room with just enough space between to cram a small dresser between them.

The beds were neatly made with very old looking quilts. A soft rag doll lay on the pillow of one bed, its dress showing where it had been clumsily repaired, and the stringy tangled brown yarn hair was stained and frazzled. It looked like someone had tried to brush it with a hairbrush at some point, fraying and frizzing the yarn.

Jane looked down at the dress she still clutched in one hand and dropped it onto the bed.

She tugged on the front of the hospital gown, letting it slide off, and then clumsily put the dress on.

Her limbs were still uncooperative, feeling like numb rubbery branches instead of arms and legs.

The man came back to the bathroom, standing in the doorway watching Kathy.

She had finished brushing her teeth and was just finishing working the tangles out of her hair.

He nodded appreciatively. He realized with a touch of guilt that he should have thought of this sooner.

He cleared his throat to get her attention, startling her.

He instantly looked sheepish when she jumped and turned to him with a look of fear.

"Sorry, I didn't mean to scare you," he said.

Kathy just stared at him, her mind working, waiting to find out what he wants of her now.

She looked beautiful to him.

"I need you to go back down," he said. "Just for a little while. I want to spend some time alone with her."

Kathy's eyes narrowed accusingly, a look almost hinting on jealousy. The idea of going back down into the cellar both relieved and terrified her.

"It's not like that," he said, "I swear. You know who she is to me."

"You didn't answer my question," Kathy said softly, forcing her face to go expressionless again.

"What was that?" he asked.

"Are you going to kill me now? Now that you have her? Now that you don't need me?"

His eyes softened.

"No," he said quietly, "I'm not going to kill you."

Kathy knew she shouldn't push it any further; that she should just accept what was offered and let him lead her back to the root cellar without another word.

But she was torn inside. He had found a replacement, and not just any replacement but HER. Her life was in more jeopardy now than it ever was.

She wanted to know.

She needed to know.

How much longer did she have to live?

"When?" she asked. "Are you going to kill me later? Tomorrow?"

"I'm not going to kill you," he said it again.

"Why not?" she asked.

"I-I need you," he said, whispering the words as if they were a secret no one could know but him.

Kathy's head swirled in confusion.

She stared into his face, his gentle eyes, the eyes and face of a monster capable of committing unspeakable acts.

Her heart ached with the tumult of emotions that tore through it.

She'd wished for death many times over during the time she spent trapped here, just wanting him to kill her so she could be free, so this could all be over. She felt cheated out of that wish.

But she was also afraid to die. His words made her heart soar—he wasn't going to kill her. He needed her! Could this be true?

Her eyes reddened with the tears that were suddenly brought to them.

The man misunderstood her tears.

"It's ok," he whispered gently. "It's ok. I won't make you stay down there long. Just for a little while. Ok?"

He led her to the trap door, helping her down until she was dangling on the rope ladder.

To her surprise he had changed the knotted length of rotting homemade rope ladder with an actual rope ladder, with two strong looking sides and flat hard rungs for steps. It was like one she'd seen in movies, thrown over the side of a boat to let people climb up and board it.

"To make it easier for you," he smiled.

Gingerly, Kathy climbed down.

Once her feet were on the solid dirt floor below, the man closed the hatch above, locking out the light. She listened to the thunk as he barred it closed from above, preventing any possible escape.

But the root cellar was not as dark as usual.

Kathy turned around, not sure what to expect.

The blankets piled in the corner had been transformed.

An old mattress now lay on the dirt floor, neatly made with blankets and a pillow.

Not far away was another makeshift bed, and between them sat an oil lamp, its yellow flame licking the air inside the glass shield.

Salvation.

She could burn the place down, escaping in death if not life.

38

Sitting at his desk in the shared office, Jim McNelly chewed on the butt of his unlit cigarette, staring moodily at the foul coffee in his cup.

Not only did the coffee from the machine taste even worse than usual today, it also wasn't sitting well in his stomach.

McNelly wished the cigarette butt and coffee were jerky and a pitcher of draft beer.

His stomach roiled again, the acid eating at his ulcer like a kid on a lollipop.

On the desk before him lay piles of documents compiled on the case he was studying.

The mass graveyard in the woods had taken precedence over all other cases, although McNelly felt it in his gut that the graveyard, Jane Doe, and the other bodies found were all one and the same case.

He couldn't say why he felt that way. The differences in disposing of the bodies publicly vs. burying them deep in the woods didn't add up.

They were still missing a lot of documents. The graves were still being carefully excavated, samples tested, and autopsies performed on the remains uncovered within them.

McNelly glared at the next desk where Michael Underwood should be sitting going through these files with him.

Where the hell is he? He can't be involved in the search for Jane Doe; he'd blow his bloody cover.

If they do find her, she'll be back at the hospital and they'll need to keep Underwood undercover watching her even more closely now that she's disappeared once already and its clear someone tampered with her IV. If the perp hasn't gotten her, that is. Then she'll just be going to the morgue.

Despite the senselessness of it, McNelly was sure Underwood was somehow involved in the search for Jane Doe.

With a regretful sigh McNelly took a swig of his now cold coffee, winced at the taste of the nasty brew, and returned to studying the documents before him.

He studied picture after picture of ground with numbered tags, excavated holes, skeletal remains, even generic shots of the area, taken to give an idea on the scope and location of the graves.

He poured over reports about the depth and locations of graves, the amount of wear estimated by weather, and the makeup of the layers of earth cut through to dig them and mixed together to bury the bodies.

McNelly took greater care in studying the autopsy reports themselves, specifically the results of tests done to estimate the ages of the victims when they died and how long they likely lay interred in the ground.

Despite the large volume of reports that still haven't come in, McNelly was seeing a very clear picture of the makeshift graveyard.

With a grunt, he got up, scooped up a handful of photographs, walked around the desk, and started tossing them face up on the floor before the bulletin board one by one in a seemingly random fashion.

It wasn't random at all. The back of each photo was labelled with a grave plot number and other reference numbers, the front corner of each color labelled to indicate an age range for the grave.

On the bulletin board was a map of the site of the graves, marking each grave discovered to date with a plot number that corresponded with the number on each document for that grave plot.

As the photos accumulated, a pattern began to appear. There was orderliness to the graves; they were clustered by color code.

At last McNelly stopped and just stared down at his handiwork, the floor carpeted with photographs of open graves, their victims staring accusingly back at him with their sightless empty bone sockets or decomposing sagging faces.

"Damn," McNelly swore, "this looks like an old city cemetery."

The oldest graves were grouped together with other color-coded photo's shifting colors spreading out like a cemetery adding new sections over the years.

Then it struck him. The graves themselves span a long period of time, just like that old city cemetery they resembled.

Beth walked into the office.

She stopped in her tracks, staring at the mess on the floor.

She looked at the photographs spread across the floor, the pile of files on McNelly's desk, then at McNelly.

Her first thought was that he was pissed that his partner. Michael was nowhere to be found and wasn't responding to attempts to contact him.

She was about to say something smart about McNelly tossing evidence all over the floor, but then the pattern of the photographs caught her eye.

Beth stared down at the photo spread, and then studied the board.

"That's a lot of graves. How long of a time span do they cover?" she asked.

McNelly grabbed a stack of papers off his desk, scanning them quickly as he flipped pages.

"Too long," he sighed.

"How long is too long?" Beth asked.

"Has to be generations of perps." He levelled his stare at Beth. "They've started working in the oldest section now. We don't even know yet how far back the graves go."

"But that means..."

"There's more than one perp burying bodies here. Apparently we found a local popular spot for dumping bodies."

Beth shook her head.

"But, that's impossible," she said. I mean, the odds are impossible. Multiple serial killers alone are extremely unlikely. But for them to pick the same place to bury the bodies..." She didn't need to finish.

"Unless they're working together," McNelly suggested. "The ages of the graves suggest it could be a multi-generations father-son team. Daddy taught his boy the family trade and he continued with it even after the old man was too old to keep doing it, teaching it to his son and so on."

"Do you think so?" she asked.

"So far only the one grave shows evidence of being dug up.

208

That's the body that's still missing. We have the skull hikers found and nothing else. As best could be determined, the rest of the graves have never been tampered with.

Whoever is burying these bodies has to know where the other graves are. There is no way more than one person could have buried bodies here without ever accidentally digging up one of the other graves, unless they know where they all are.

Even if it was only one perp, it would be almost impossible to keep track of all those bodies unless they had a map of some sort, like cemeteries use to keep track of their burial plots."

"Holy crap!" Beth breathed.

Beth studied the map again, noting the orderliness of the graveyard.

"And by the sheer numbers of them I'd say it's more likely to be at least three if not more perps killing them. If it was only two, they were pretty damned busy," McNelly said.

This was entirely unbelievable.

"So, these guys, these perps, keep an actual map of some sort showing where all the bodies are? A map they would have to communicate with each other and share? That's a whole lot of trust to put in each other. Is this some kind of murder club? A special club for local serial killers? That's the sort of thing that happens only in movies and books."

Beth was shaken. Never in her career could she ever imagine she'd come across something so crazy, so impossible.

"But how? How would they share, advertise, find members? How could they have collected so many bodies without anyone ever noticing?"

"That's what I'd like to know," McNelly growled. "They'd have to have been taking people from a pretty wide area and transporting them here. And it's not only women either. The types of victims are all over the place. As far as I know we haven't had any missing persons reports for decades. The last case I can remember was a woman who disappeared with her two kids. I remember studying that case as a recruit. The detectives in charge figured she had taken the kids and ran to keep them away from their father."

"Abusive?" Beth asked.

209

"No," McNelly shook his head. "As I remember the case, the husband was leaving the wife for another woman. The detectives figured it was punishment, a cheated wife's revenge. He broke her heart, so she broke his by taking away the kids."

"There must have been other missing persons, from the neighboring jurisdictions. Those wouldn't be in our files unless they had contacted us."

"We'll have to investigate that," McNelly said. "With the numbers involved you would think we'd have heard something anyway, even if just in the news."

"I'll start checking into it," Beth said, "and I'll check over a wide area."

"A very wide area," McNelly added.

39

The man brought in a kitchen chair and set it down in front of the living room chair Jane sat in. He sat down on it, leaning forward intently, his words rushed and excited.

Everything seemed to be moving so fast. His pulse was racing, his mind was racing, and the events of the day seemed to be moving at breakneck speed, giving him the feeling that he had to rush to keep up.

Jane Doe sat there, her foggy mind ever so slowly clearing. Her vision was still having trouble focusing even as her mind still struggled to focus.

Her memory was still lost in a swirl of drug-induced fog that let only confused images pass through.

But the drugs weren't the only thing affecting Jane's memory. In an act of self-preservation, her subconscious had shut down much of her memory, the events hiding there much too traumatic for Jane's shaky mental state to deal with, especially with her weakened body still recovering from the brutal assault committed against it.

The man sitting before her was leaning forward towards her, staring at her hard as if his very gaze was the only thing keeping her there in existence. As if he thought if his stare wavered even a fraction she would suddenly "poof" cease to exist. He was talking quickly, his voice as intense and excited as his stare.

Jane couldn't focus on what he was saying. Staying focused was just too hard still.

It was something about this place. She knew that much; that he was talking about this place and years past. Things they saw together, things they did.

He talked as if she should know him, as if she should know this place and remember a shared past.

But she doesn't know who he is. She tried listening to his voice, studying his face, paying attention to what he said.

The man was a stranger to her. This place was strange to her. The memories he shared were not her memories.

Jane tried to look into her own mind, her own memories,

searching for even a hint of these things.

The memories simply weren't there and that scared her.

It wasn't that these particular memories were missing that bothered Jane, it was that her mind seemed to be completely empty of all memories save for a few confusing and frightening jumbled images of what felt like only the past few days.

She remembered waking up in a strange place that she knew had to be some sort of hospital.

She remembered glimpses of people in her room, ignoring her, sometimes talking as if she wasn't there.

She remembered them repeating the name Jane, and so thought that might be her name, though she wasn't sure.

She remembered getting out of bed and being grabbed, attacked. She remembered fighting back, terror, the need to escape, and more people attacking her, a sharp pinch in her arm, and losing control of her weak body while her mind cried and screamed in frustration and anger and fear.

She remembered people passing by outside her door, a man hovering who looked like a big ugly skinny buzzard bird, and another older middle-aged man who seemed to want to talk to her. The hospital people made him go away, but he came back. They didn't know it, but he came back.

But mostly she remembered hushed whispers she couldn't understand and the name Jane repeated again and again.

She also began remembering this man now as the drugs waned, who she didn't know, sitting by her bed and always hovering around her room.

The man reached forward, touching her knee, bringing her attention back to him as he had each time her mind wandered off.

Jane turned back to look at him, her stare blank.

He stared at her expectantly; his endless talking paused as if waiting for something, maybe waiting for a reply from her.

Jane swallowed. It was an automatic response to the dryness in her throat and the nervousness that gripped her.

Something about this man unnerved her. A vague sense of danger, the urge to get up and run, nagged at the edges of her nerves.

Jane didn't think she could run if she had to. But why would she have to? This man wasn't threatening her. She didn't even know who he is. She didn't even know why she was here. It was just so confusing.

How did I get here? The thought touched the edge of her mind, fleeting.

The man's steady stare and the pressure of his hand on her knee drew her eyes back to his.

She should say something. She didn't know what.

So she said the only thing she could think of, her name.

"Jane," she croaked, her voice still hoarse.

He blinked in surprise.

Apparently this wasn't what he was expecting.

Jane had no idea what he wanted. She'd missed most of what he said.

"What?" he asked.

"My name," she asked, "is it Jane?"

The man's face fell.

His eager look suddenly turned crestfallen.

"I've disappointed him," Jane thought.

The man's expression changed again.

He stared at her in confusion, his mind working, his eyes narrowing in thought.

And then the rage came over him.

He felt so much excitement he could barely contain it. He wanted to scoop her up out of the chair and hug her, yelling to the world that she was home, that she was safe.

He could barely think what to say even as the words poured out, stories and memories of the time they spent together, his feelings of helplessness and loss after he lost her, his dreams of finding her again.

He thought that if he talked enough about their time together, and of this place, that she would have to remember. The memories would come flooding back and she would know him.

But she just sat there, seeming to go between confusion and disinterest.

Whenever her attention wandered, he reached forward and

213

touched her knee, bringing her attention back to him.

He was hopeful.

He knew he could make her remember.

But then she asked the question that brought all those hopes crashing down.

Her name.

She didn't even know her name.

His heart sank.

She has to know him. She has to remember him.

If she didn't...

He didn't even want to think of that.

But he had to.

If she couldn't remember, then maybe he'd made a mistake. Maybe it wasn't her after all.

He looked at Jane, his heart ready to burst, the confusion on her face filling his heart with confusion.

Her face is right. It's her.

But her confused expression made him doubt.

If this really was her then why can't she remember? Why doesn't she remember him? This place?

It's the drugs, he told himself. They made her forget, made her confused. Once they wear off she'll remember.

But he could see that the drugs were wearing off.

She seemed more stable, less shaky and wobbly. She'd seemed as if drunk when he found her outside the hospital. Her speech was slurred, her movements wobbly and uncertain, staggering with each step, and her eyes were that very intoxicated kind of delirium.

Her gaze, though still unfocused, was much clearer now. You could see it in her eyes that her mind was working, thinking, measuring.

She should remember me.

She doesn't remember me.

It's her.

What if it isn't her?

It is.

It can't be her. She'd remember.

He felt the burning rage washing over him.

214

Suddenly his hands were around her throat.

Jane froze in shock.

The man's mind was beyond all thought, all reason. The rage had come over him.

His hands tightened, choking off her air, painfully crushing Jane's windpipe.

Frantically, she clawed at him, thrashing about, kicking at him, her still drug groggy body too weak and uncoordinated to fight back effectively.

He dragged her roughly from the chair, into a standing position, spurred by the violent urge to tear the woman in front of him apart.

"YOU ARE NOT HER!" he yelled. "NOT HER NOT HER NOT HER NOTHERNOTHERNOTHER!"

Kathy sat alone in the cool damp root cellar, watching a mouse search around in a darkened corner. Sometimes she could barely make out the rodent's movements, and others she couldn't see it at all.

The occasional squeak told her it was still there.

At the beginning of her captivity Kathy had trembled at the thought of sharing her quarters with rodents, her mind imagining large ugly rats waiting in the darkness for her to go to sleep, coming to gnaw at her face as she slept.

Now they came as almost a relief. She imagined they were trapped down here too; sharing her prison, even though she knew they probably had their own way to get in and out of the cellar.

When they were nowhere to be seen, and their endless sounds of chattering at each other and chewing were silent, Kathy imagined they had made a daring escape and were fleeing to safety, eager to tell the world of the woman trapped in a cellar.

Help would come.

Of course, she knew it wasn't true. More likely they were outside basking in the sunlight, finding new wonderful things to eat, visiting their rodent friends. She imagined them sitting in the grass and sharing a picnic as the little dressed up mice in children's stories did.

L.V. Gaudet

But these mice couldn't talk. Help would not come.

Suddenly the mouse scurried off in a hurry, vanishing in the darkness of the root cellar.

Alone. Again.

The sudden thump and yelling above startled Kathy.

She looked at the ceiling above as if she might see through it, see what was happening.

Kathy glanced at the dark corner, knowing the mouse was no longer there.

Did he sense something before it began?

And it had begun. Kathy knew it.

Just like before, with the other woman.

He had thought maybe that one was *her* too.

Only she wasn't, just like Kathy wasn't *her* before that. None of them would be his sister.

Then the rage came over him and he killed the other woman. Violently and ugly, the sounds had been terrifying. He killed her just like he killed the others before them.

Kathy didn't know why he didn't kill her. She wasn't sure he knew.

She stared at the ceiling above, listening, afraid.

Thumping, the woman screaming, the man yelling, words garbled by the floor they had to pass through to come into her refuge.

Kathy had a sudden urge to put out the lamp, leaving the root cellar in darkness.

If he came down to take her, it would make it harder to see her, giving her those extra seconds before he took her upstairs.

She sat on the mattress, knees to chin, huddled small and holding herself, rocking back and forth, and wishing the sounds from above would just go away.

They didn't go away.

The thumps continued, the screams, the rage-filled bellowing. Minutes felt like hours.

Kathy trembled in terror.

He was going to kill Jane Doe. She knew it.

But it wasn't just fear of the man killing the other woman that made Kathy afraid.

216

It wasn't even the thought that he might kill her after, just as she'd been certain he would after killing the other woman before.

What also frightened Kathy is that something about this woman felt different.

Maybe it had been his certainty that she was the one he'd been looking for, the one that she and all the others had failed to be.

Kathy thought that maybe this time he was right, that maybe this time he'd finally found his sister.

A part of her felt it was certain, a feeling she picked up from his certainty that could not be denied.

A part of Kathy was also afraid because of her own feelings.

A part of her wanted him to kill Jane Doe, to be rid of the other woman no matter how it happened.

The other woman frightened her.

If Jane Doe was his sister, then he didn't need her, and the only sensible thing would be to kill her.

Kathy didn't want to die.

She wasn't afraid of the pain of dying. Many times she'd wished for death as she sat alone in the root cellar, just as she'd sometimes wished Ronnie would just kill her and get it over with while he was beating her.

But Kathy was afraid to die.

She was afraid of what might be there, waiting for her beyond this life. She was afraid there might be an afterlife. She was afraid there might simply be nothing and that she would just cease to exist.

That she would wish death on another, an innocent woman, made Kathy feel sick.

What kind of monster am I?

Kathy was also afraid because she felt jealousy.

Why should I be jealous of this woman?

So what if she replaced me? Haven't I hoped for that? Haven't I hoped that he would find somebody to replace me, making him let me go even if escape would only be through death?

But Kathy couldn't help it. She felt jealous. The thought of him up there with Jane Doe filled her with it.

Kathy felt the jealous pangs of a woman who was watching another woman getting the attentions of a man she wanted for herself. She felt jealously that the other woman might go on; continue to live, while she would be killed for not being the right woman.

But that was ridiculous. She didn't want this man. She was his prisoner. She feared and hated him.

She also feared and hated her boyfriend, Ronnie.

But these feelings were different. She despised Ronnie to the depths of his rotten core. Her feelings towards her captor were shrouded in confusion and the unknown. Other than when he kidnapped her, and when the rage had come over him on realizing she was not the one he was looking for, he hadn't actually hurt her. In the time he kept her down here he never turned his anger on her or spoke cruelly to her.

All these thoughts tore at Kathy.

She was afraid for herself, her life and of what kind of a person all this was turning her into.

She was afraid of the jealousy that burned at her and her desire for the other woman to die.

Kathy felt overwhelmed with guilt over wishing a violent death on another, an innocent woman no less.

And yet, her instincts for self-preservation also cried out that if he did kill Jane Doe, maybe he would keep her around longer instead of killing her because he found his replacement.

She also felt pity for the man upstairs. If Jane Doe really was his sister and he killed her, he would hate himself.

"Stop it! Stop feeling pity for that man, that-that monster!" she chastised herself.

Finally fear that the man would kill that innocent woman pushed all other thoughts aside.

Kathy started screaming for him to stop.

She cried and begged and screamed, pleading with him as loud as she could.

The thumping, the screaming, the man's furious yelling continued above.

Kathy tried to scream louder.

"STOP! STOP! JUST STOP IT! PLEASE, DON'T HURT HER! PLEASE STOP! STOP!"

She screamed until her throat felt torn, her cries becoming shrill senseless shrieks venting all the fear and anger and frustration that filled her since he kidnapped her.

Her voice choked with sobs.

She kept on screaming, screaming until everything that she was, everything that mattered, became the scream.

Her voice grew rougher; her throat feeling like it was tearing with the frantic screams, her lungs aching.

Kathy was so lost in her screams that she didn't hear the silence above. Nor did she hear the creak of footsteps approaching the trap door, the bolt sliding, or the creak of the hinges.

She screamed and screamed.

Jane fought frantically, the man's grip on her throat making it hard to breathe, her weakened body refusing to listen.

He dragged her across the room, throwing her down on the floor, screaming at her, his voice a frothing rage.

The blind fury in his eyes terrified her.

He grabbed her again, shaking her, raging, yelling.

She kicked at him, scrambling across the floor, trying to escape.

Frantic screaming began below.

It was the other woman, her screams and cries unintelligible through the floor except for the odd word.

Stop.

Please.

Don't.

The voice was choked with tears, desperate, pleading.

The man didn't hear Kathy's frantic screams at first.

He continued his violent attack unabated.

But then the desperate cries from below began to break through his rage. They began to sink in.

He faltered.

His attack slowed down.

He stopped.

His face became a twisted mask of misery.

Kathy.

His heart ached, her tormented shrieks tearing at him.

The rage still filled him. His fists clenched and unclenched with the need to tear something apart.

His breath continued to come in ragged breaths, his chest heaving with the exertion, his muscles tense with violence.

Kathy.

His eyes burned.

He felt like his soul was being torn apart.

On one side was the rage, and the other sorrow.

His rage was hurting Kathy, terrifying her.

The thought of Kathy below, frightened and alone, filled with pain, pulled at him.

He didn't want to hurt her.

He looked at the trembling woman on the floor, her eyes, and her face. She was filled with terror and defiance.

Why?

He was confused.

Why is Kathy screaming? Why does she sound so desperate, so afraid?

He stared at the floor, imagining what the woman below looked like right now, screaming, her voice hoarse, sobs wracking her body, her face twisted and reddened.

He looked at the woman on the floor, staring at him as if expecting him to attack her at any moment.

But why would I attack you? Why would I hurt you? Did I?

He was so confused.

You shouldn't be afraid of me. You should never be afraid of me.

He stared at her.

It was her, Cassie, but she was so afraid.

Does she not remember me?

It's not her. She would remember me.

It's her.

It's not.

He was torn. He couldn't think. Kathy's screams tore at him, confusing him.

He looked at Jane without seeing her, seeing instead a trembling little girl, tears streaming down her cheeks.

He stepped forward and she cringed away.

She was the woman again, Jane Doe.

Was I attacking her? Why?

Suddenly he had to act. He had to get his sister away from him before he hurt her more than he may have already.

He had to make the desperate screams below stop.

He needed silence, to be alone, to be able to think.

He stepped forward swiftly, grabbing Jane and pulling her roughly to her feet.

It was the roughness of quick action, like a father yanking a child out of the path of a car, not one of violence.

He led her down the hall, unable to look at her.

She stared after him in confusion, unable to grasp the sudden change that came over him, the sudden violence, and now the sudden stiff business-like manner.

Without a word he brought her to the trap door to the root cellar.

He pulled back the bolt, drawing the trap door up, wincing as the screams below grew suddenly louder with the opening of the door.

He hooked the rope ladder on and dropped it down the dark hole, indicating that Jane should go down.

She swallowed hard, trembling so violently she could barely control her limbs.

She approached the yawning opening cautiously, the frantic screams from below making her even more afraid to go down.

He motioned again and she hesitantly got down on all fours, grasping the rope ladder and swinging a leg over the edge, feeling for the first rung.

Ever so slowly Jane climbed down the rope ladder into the darkness below.

He wanted to push her, to hurry her along, to slam the door on her head to make her go away faster.

He didn't want to hurt her.

He just wanted the moment to stop, to close the door on the screams below that tore at him, to stop the confusion.

221

He wanted to put her away, safe, before he has a chance to hurt her for real.

Kathy screamed like she'd never screamed before. She screamed as though help lay beyond the walls, would hear and come to their rescue.

She screamed as if he would hear, would stop.

She screamed as if it would matter.

She continued to scream, her throat feeling as though it were raked by barbed knives, the pain terrible.

Kathy jumped with a sudden yelp at a light touch.

She whirled around, silent at last, so filled with fear that her throat constricted, unable to make a sound.

In the darkness broken only by the lamp burning dimly, she stared at Jane Doe.

40

"We have to get out of here," Jane whispered.

Kathy just continued to stare at her, her body still trembling and her breath coming in ragged pants from the stress of the past moments.

Even through the fog of her drug induced confusion, the effects of the toxins clearing more quickly now though leaving her with the nauseating after effects, Jane knew this was a bad place.

"We have to find a way out and escape," Jane whispered again, wondering if the other woman was even listening or if she was too traumatized to hear what she was saying.

Giving up for now, Jane wandered off into the darkness of the root cellar, exploring its size, looking for any exit, a window or door.

Trance-like, Kathy wandered over and sat on the mattress, next to the lamp.

She seemed startled when she looked up as Jane reappeared, stepping from out of the darkness into the lamp's glow.

Jane sat on the mattress beside Kathy.

She still felt shaky and weak.

Jane looked around, studying what she could see within the lamp's light, the meagre accommodation.

She turned and looked Kathy up and down, taking in her emaciated condition, her hollow haunted eyes that stared ahead sightlessly, perhaps staring at horrors within her own mind. She noted the blank expression. She also noted the lack of bruises and other marks, the paleness of the other woman's skin.

At last she broke the silence.

"How long have you been here?" Jane asked.

It took so long for Kathy to respond that Jane didn't think she would, or maybe even could.

Kathy just shrugged.

"You don't know how long?" Jane asked.

Kathy shook her head mutely.

Jane suspected she'd been here for some time.

L.V. Gaudet

"Do you know where we are"?"

Again, Kathy shook her head in the negative, just staring ahead at nothing.

"Is there any way out of here?" Jane asked. "A window? Crawl space? Anything but the trap door?"

Again, Kathy shook her head.

"Does he ever let you out? Upstairs? Outside?"

"Not outside," Kathy said quietly, her voice hoarse from the strain her screams had put on her vocal cords.

Jane was hesitant to ask her next question.

As her mind cleared, so did her ability to think. And what she thought the woman would say was an answer she didn't want to hear. She didn't want to hear about the terrible things he's done to this woman. Terrible things he will probably do to her too.

"Did- has he done anything?" Jane asked. "...to you? I mean, has he hurt you? Done things to you? When he lets you out, what does he do?"

Kathy finally turned her gaze to look at Jane.

"I clean," she said quietly.

"Clean?"

"He lets me up to clean, sometimes just to talk to me."

Jane couldn't hide her surprise. She didn't really believe it, either. The other woman must not be telling her everything.

She had to ask.

"Just to clean and to talk to you?"

Kathy nodded.

"That's all? He doesn't do anything else?"

Kathy shook her head.

"He hasn't done anything to hurt you? At all?" She paused, and then added, "I mean, other than kidnapping you?"

Kathy shook her head.

Jane had to think, to take this in for a moment.

"He did kidnap you, right? You're not like his girlfriend or something? His wife?"

"No," Kathy said softly. "He kidnapped me. I'm not his girlfriend or wife."

Jane's mind still had to work harder, was still groggy, but

224

her thinking was coming clearer by the moment. Only her memory had not returned yet. Everything but snatches of memory from the hospital and the hazy time she's spent here was a blank.

This place was wrong.

It had a familiar feel she just couldn't place. It was a very strange familiarity. There was a feeling like home, but also a sense of danger, a vague feeling of urgency.

Something about this place was very wrong.

She looked around again, her eyes able to see into the hazy darkness of the cellar further now that her eyes have adjusted to the dim light.

She turned to Kathy again.

"Have you tried to escape?"

"At first," Kathy said. "I tried to find a way out."

She lowered her head, shaking it slowly.

"There is no way out," Kathy's voice was even quieter. "No way except the trap door and that's always barred from the other side."

"What about when he lets you upstairs?" Jane was feeling more urgency now.

She didn't like this feeling of being trapped, completely at the whim of another person.

Kathy shook her head again.

"No," she said sadly. "I never tried."

"Never? Why? Did he never give you the chance?"

Kathy looked at her, staring into her eyes.

"Where would I go?" Kathy whispered.

This answer stunned Jane. Where would she go? Home, anywhere, somewhere, somewhere that's not here. She thought Kathy must have meant simply that they were in the middle of nowhere, perhaps with no shelter to hide and no place to go for help.

But she had a feeling there was more to the answer than that; that maybe Kathy really did mean that once away from here and free she simply had no place else to go, or maybe just no place better than this.

Jane shuddered inside.

"We will find a way out," Jane said to reassure Kathy as much as she needed to reassure herself. "We will find a way out." The second time she said it entirely for her own benefit, to convince herself.

"He won't let us," Kathy said. "At least, he won't let you, now that he finally found you."

Suddenly Jane remembered the man's comments. How she was the one, how he had finally found her, how she belonged here. It made her feel gritty inside.

"Who is he?" Jane asked. "Who am I? I mean, who am I to him?" Jane didn't know who she was to herself even, but figuring out who she was to this man was a start.

"Her, you are her," was all Kathy said.

"Who is he?" Jane asked again.

"I don't know," Kathy shrugged. "He's just—him."

"What do you think he's going to do to us?" Jane asked. She already knew the obvious answer, what any man who kidnaps women eventually does to them.

"He's going to kill us, isn't he?" she said, answering her own question.

"Not you," Kathy said softly, emotionlessly, "just me."

"Why just you?" Jane needed to know.

"Because you're her and I'm not you. He doesn't need me now that you're here," Kathy said, though a part of her wasn't sure of that anymore. The man's comments upstairs had her so confused. Maybe he did need her after all. Just in a different way than he needed Jane.

"But why? Jane asked again, "why am I so important to him?"

Kathy just shook her head. Whether it was to mean that she didn't know or wouldn't say Jane couldn't be sure, but this questioning was getting them nowhere.

Jane looked around at the darkness beyond the dim lamp's glow in despair.

"We have to make a plan to escape," Jane said. "There has to be a way to escape."

"No," Kathy said with surprising conviction. "We can't! We can't escape."

"I know you are scared," Jane tried to sooth the other woman. "So am I. I'm terrified. But we have to try."

Kathy just shook her head mutely, her face still blank of expression as would be expected with someone who is in shock.

They both started at sudden sounds upstairs.

It had been quiet up there in the hours since their kidnapper put Jane in the cellar.

A door creaked open, footsteps and the creak of the floorboards, a muffled sound, the thud of something heavy being dropped on the floor, and a door slamming shut.

They both stared at the ceiling above their heads, waiting in silence, holding their breaths, hearts beating faster.

41

Trapped within the confines of the rough burlap, Connie tried to hold her breath in controlled shallow breaths as if the man would not know she was there if he couldn't hear her breathe. The perfume of decay came from somewhere in the confines of the vehicle.

She was bound tightly and unable to move beyond a squirming of her body and legs. Her legs were tied together, her arms pulled painfully behind her back. She was blindfolded and gagged beneath the burlap.

She could hear what was going on around her, but couldn't see anything.

The car had driven for what felt like forever, lulling her to feel the urge to doze off although Connie didn't dare let herself fall asleep.

She was tired, oh so tired.

At last, the ground beneath the tires changed sound. The car slowed and rocked as it drove over rough ground before coming to a stop.

Connie blanched in terror when she heard the car door open. She lay on the floor of the back of the car.

She fought with everything she had when she felt the man's strong hands grabbing at her and pulling her roughly from the car.

Ignoring her efforts as though they were the mewling of a weak little kitten, the man manhandled her, swinging her up and pushing the car door closed.

Her stomach lurched with the movement.

She was being carried somewhere.

She heard a door and struggled again, squirming against her tight bindings and the restricting burlap wrapped about her.

The man had to shoulder the door open after struggling with the latch, the burlap wrapped woman draped over his shoulder in fireman fashion making working the door difficult.

The floorboards creaked under his weight as he stepped into the small farmhouse.

His burden squirmed and made muffled sounds of protest as he shifted the weight off his shoulder.

Connie's stomach lurched again from the motion as she felt herself suddenly swung and dropping.

He dropped her thoughtlessly on the floor with a thud as he kicked the door, the door slamming closed.

Pain exploded in her shoulder as she hit the floor hard, her arms bound behind her causing her shoulder to wrench as it hit the floor.

She cried out behind the gag, her cries muffled almost into oblivion.

He took the time to latch the door, even that simple act showing the anger and violence that filled him.

He turned blindly for a moment, avoiding looking at the wrapped body on the floor, his eyes haunted with anger and confusion. His stance cried out with his turmoil, the tense muscles and hunched shoulders of a man ready for a fight, yet his movements were jerky and uncertain.

He paced first one way, then another, as if unsure which way to go.

Connie whimpered and squirmed on the floor, desperate to roll off the agony in her arm, before becoming fearfully still.

She listened to the sounds of the man moving around, trying to control her breathing and her muffled sobs, waiting for what was to come next. Her heart fluttered in terror, tears streaming from her eyes to soak the blindfold. She felt unbearably hot and sweaty trapped inside the burlap.

"Oh my god, I'm going to die," she thought. "I'm not ready to die. Oh please, I don't want to die."

Her soundless pleas went unanswered.

"Aaugh," the man groaned roughly, running his fingers through his hair, anguish deepening his feelings of anger and confusion.

At last he sat heavily in the armchair, sinking into its well-worn depths, resting his elbows on knees and cradling his head in his hands as if suffering from an immense hangover.

He sighed heavily, enough weariness to fill a lifetime in that single exhale of air.

229

Rubbing his scalp roughly with both hands as if to rub away all the nastiness inside; he finally looked up and stared at the motionless bundle on the floor.

She heard the man groan roughly, a sound of despair and desperation, more movements, and finally the creak of what might be the springs of a bed or chair.

Connie became even more terrified, imagining what the man would do to her before he killed her, imagining the worst possible things he could do to her.

The pain in her shoulder was terrible, but so was her fear.

Connie fought the urge to squirm and cry, lying as still and quiet as possible, begging her god that the man would not notice her; that he would forget she was there at least for a while.

He just sat there, staring at the woman bound and wrapped in burlap on the floor before him.

He wasn't sure if time was speeding up or slowing down. It had that strange feel to it, like he was speeding through time into an uncertain future he did not want to see, and yet it seemed as if time virtually stood still.

"Why? Why did I take this woman?" he thought to himself miserably. "What did I do?"

He had no idea what spurred him to take the woman.

He had found Cassie at last, although her failure to remember and recognize him had made him doubt. But still, he was sure Jane Doe was her.

It might just be the drugs that kept her from remembering; or maybe the terrible events of so long ago.

He knew that the mind tended to block out very bad experiences, a defensive mechanism to keep the person sane.

But shouldn't there have been some hint of recognition? Of memory? Something?

The woman on the floor before him was just one of the women he had been watching, one of the possibilities.

Each time he had thought he found Cassie only to be filled with doubts. The doubts brought on the rage when they didn't know him and he'd suddenly find himself faced with another battered corpse and little if any memory of how she came to be that way.

Each time as he disposed of the body his thoughts would turn to the other possibilities, the ones he still watched. He'd be full of hope that one of them would be his sister at last.

He had also always been so careful. Watching them for months sometimes, taking them only when the time was perfect, and always disposing of them so they'd never be found.

Until Jane.

Jane was different. Right from the start everything about her felt different.

And after the rage came over him and he found her lying lifeless on the floor, he just couldn't bring himself to bury her with the rest.

He didn't know why he put her with the trash. The thought of her being tossed out with the trash disgusted him. She deserved better, much better.

He had acted rashly.

In a way he did it to punish himself. If he would treat her like trash, letting the rage take over, letting her become yet another battered victim, then he deserved to suffer.

He didn't deserve to have a grave to visit her at.

He didn't deserve the decency of a proper resting place, the decorum and honour of a proper burial.

He deserved to be tossed out with the trash.

The one thing he did not consider, however, was that maybe the real reason was that he wanted her to be found, to be caught, to be stopped.

After Jane he watched the other women only half-heartedly. They resembled her, but they weren't her.

The rage came over him much faster after Jane. He acted more rashly each time, more recklessly.

He found himself tossing cautions to the wind, even leaving the bodies in places they were certain to be found.

Places that would give the authorities greater reason to come after him.

That confused him even more. He didn't remember doing those things. He thought he had buried them, putting them safely beyond the reach of ever being discovered.

He felt reckless and out of control.

Still, the doubt was always there. What if Jane wasn't Cassie? What if he hadn't found her yet? What if she was still out there waiting to be found, to be reunited?

Once he learned she was still alive, his heart soared with the possibilities, and with the certainty that this had to be her after all.

He'd wanted to laugh at the name they gave her.

Jane Doe.

So plain, so simple. So unlike her real name and unlike her.

He had to get rid of this woman; this new one who he knew was not Cassie.

He tried to make himself get out of the chair, to go and pick her up and carry her out to the barn, to do what had to be done.

He couldn't.

He couldn't make himself budge.

The anger that had drawn him to take the woman, that fuelled his actions all the way back to the farmhouse, was gone.

The anger and confusion had soured into despair, rotting away inside him.

He just couldn't bring himself to do it.

He tried to bring on the rage.

But the rage simply wasn't there now.

"Shit," he groaned. "What am I going to do?"

"I'll just have to put her with the others for now," he decided, "just to give me time to think."

It seemed a mammoth task, but he forced himself out of the chair, to take those few steps forward.

Grabbing a folding survival knife from his pocket, he began cutting away the bindings wrapping the woman tight inside the burlap.

In the root cellar Kathy and Jane listened to the sounds from above with baited breath.

Jane didn't know what to expect, what to wait for.

Kathy had her suspicions, and as the moments of silence above dragged on her uncertainty grew.

"What's he doing?" Jane whispered.

"I don't know," Kathy whispered back

"Do you think—" Jane swallowed hard, the words sticking in her throat. "Do you think he's getting ready to kill us, or one of us?"

Kathy shrugged. She didn't know, but she couldn't shake her suspicion. It hung heavy in her stomach, a tight knot of feelings she didn't want to feel, or to admit to.

"What are you thinking?" Jane asked, looking at Kathy, seeing the look on the other woman's face. "I know you have an idea of what he's up to. What is it?"

Kathy turned to her.

"I think he brought another one home," she said.

"Another what?" Jane asked to confirm what she suspected the other woman meant.

"Us," Kathy said.

"But why?" Jane asked. "Wasn't this all to find me, whoever or whatever I'm supposed to be? If I'm whatever he's looking for, then why did he kidnap another woman?"

Kathy looked at Jane hard, her eyes accusing, though the look was not directed at Jane.

"I don't know," she whispered a little harshly. "He doesn't need anybody else."

"I must not be what he was looking for," Jane said sadly, thinking of the woman who was probably upstairs, and of their own certain fates.

She didn't want to be who the man was looking for, whoever that was. But she also didn't want anyone else to be either.

"You're the one," Kathy said.

She turned back to staring at the ceiling, listening for sounds from above, her eyes hard and cold.

Jane studied her profile for a moment, wondering, before joining her in staring at the ceiling.

They stared for a long time.

"Why is it taking so long?" Kathy thought. "It never took this long. We should already be hearing the sounds of violence above."

The sound of the bolt latching the trap door sliding back startled them both.

They jumped and turned as one, staring at the trap door.

233

The trap door swung open, splashing a square of light down into the root cellar.

The rope ladder dropped down the hole, dancing merrily for a moment as it fell and unfurled from where it was attached at the top.

"Come up," the man said gruffly, his voice choked with emotions he couldn't quite get under control, "both of you."

Reluctantly, Kathy and Jane approached the square of light.

Jane moved ahead to go first, instinctively putting herself before the other woman who seemed so fragile, both physically and emotionally.

Kathy laid a hand on Jane's arm, stopping her before she reached the square of light.

"No," she whispered so softly Jane could barely hear her. "Let me go first."

Jane hesitated uncertainly then nodded in the darkness, letting the other woman go ahead.

Kathy stepped into the square of light and looked up to the opening above, the light washing her face with a sickly paleness that had more to do with her ashen complexion than with the warm yellow light from above.

The man stared down at her for only the briefest moment.

It was long enough for her to see the torment in his eyes and the roughness of his face as he fought to keep his emotions in check.

He turned away quickly as if not wanting her to see him.

Cautiously, she grasped the rope ladder and began her slow climb, her limbs weak and shaky.

Just as Kathy reached the top and started trying to clamber onto the floor above, the man grabbed her and hauled her up out of the hole with a suddenness that startled Jane as she watched from below.

Frightened, Jane approached the ladder. It was her turn.

Still feeling sick and shaky from the medications, and weak with fear, Jane began her slow ascent too.

Just like with Kathy, the moment she reached the top and started trying to pull herself onto the floor above, rough hands grabbed her suddenly, yanking her up out of the hole.

She yelped in surprise, although she'd expected it after watching the same thing happen to Kathy.

Jane struggled in the man's grasp, trying to pull free, to hit him.

He pulled her to a standing position, dragging her away from the hole, and steadied her, ignoring her attempts to fight him off.

"Don't fall in the hole," he said, nodding towards the opening as he released her and stepped away, turning his back to her.

Jane felt the urge to run at the man, screaming and flailing, to jump on him and try to pound him into the floor, to bite and kick and scratch.

And she almost did too.

But Kathy put her hand on Jane's arm, drawing her attention towards her, shaking her head and mouthing the word "No".

Jane trembled with the need to attack this man, visibly struggling to calm down and control herself.

"Come," he said, walking away and down the hall towards the tiny living room.

They obeyed nervously.

Scrabbling and scratching noises were coming from the living room.

There they found a dishevelled and frantic woman desperately trying to unlatch the door to escape.

Terrified and confused after the man untied her and left her lying prone on the floor while he left the room, Connie had gotten shakily to her feet.

The pain in her shoulder throbbed. She could move her arm, but it was painful.

She looked around frantically, immediately rushing for the door as soon as she saw it.

She tried to pull it open, fighting with the door.

It was locked with a double-keyed lock and no key.

She heard sounds from another room, the man talking to someone and what sounded like someone struggling with something.

She tried the window, the boards covering it from outside leaving slats of light between them to splash across her, and couldn't budge it. Even the latch locking the window wouldn't move, possibly rusted closed with age.

Connie went back to the door, trying again, desperately wishing it would somehow open.

The people suddenly appearing in the doorway startled her.

She froze as they entered the room, staring at them in mute terror, trembling so hard her fingers could barely grasp the latch.

The women looked shocked. One was skinny and pale and sickly looking. The other woman looked shaken but in better health.

The man stood just behind them, watching the two women, turning to her as she stared at them.

Frantically she attacked the door again, her trembling fingers not cooperating.

"It won't work," the man said softly.

She stumbled to the small window, pawing at the window and its frame even though it was boarded up from outside, missing and grabbing at its latch, trying to open it while frantically looking back and forth between the other people in the room and her desperate task.

Jane and Kathy stopped at the doorway, just watching the frantic woman, their faces showing very different emotions.

Jane's face was filled with sadness, sympathy, and fear.

Kathy watched the new woman with a look of suspicion and anger, although it was impossible to tell if the woman was the direct source of those feelings, or just the presence in the farmhouse of another woman.

Connie heard movement behind her, turning just in time to see the man approaching.

A guttural sound of fear escaped her and she jumped sideways, trying to dodge around the man, certain he would grab her.

The man moved forward towards the terrified woman who was still trying to escape.

She tried to dodge him with a frightened grunt.

The little room didn't allow much room for escape. He could

have grabbed her easily, but instead let her run past him.

The only door to the outside was locked and all the windows nailed closed and boarded over. She could run anywhere in the little farmhouse she wanted. There was nowhere to go, no way out.

She raced past him to another room, searching frantically for an escape, trying the window that was nailed and boarded too.

Desperate, her heart feeling like it would burst with the fear that tore at it, Connie ran from that room to another, looking for a way out, trying every window, but not finding another outside door.

Connie couldn't bring herself to try dodging the people in the living room and couldn't search any more rooms without cutting through the living room.

She raced back to the farther room, crouching down in the farthest corner, trembling and crying.

"What is this place?" she sobbed desperately. "Who are these people?"

Seeing the two women who seemed to be there without a fight even if not by choice had really shocked her.

Visions of stories she's heard of religious cults basing their religion around providing the leaders with multiple wives in a bigamy lifestyle, sister-wives, and child brides flashed through her mind. She remembered the story a few years before of a man who kidnapped women for his wives. But, was that real or a movie? She wasn't sure.

Her thoughts moved in that direction. When she was first taken she thought she'd been kidnapped to be raped and murdered. But now she wondered, was she to be some perverted bugger's spare wife?

Or, she thought, was this some kind slave ring? Was she kidnapped to be sold as a prostitute? Would they hold her down and inject drugs into her to make her an addict to keep her too stoned to escape and dependent on them for more drugs?

She didn't want to think anymore. She didn't want to be here.

She screamed and cried in anguish and fear, pleading for escape, for rescue.

They stood in the small living room, all three of them feeling awkward for their own reasons, listening to the frantic scrambling and cries of the terrified woman as she searched for an escape.

They watched silently as she peeked around a corner only to retreat away from the living room again.

Jane felt the urge to go to the woman, to help her calm down, to try to help her. Her panic would not help her or them to escape.

She took one step in that direction, stopping herself self-consciously, remembering that their captor stood silently only a few paces away.

Seeing the look on Jane's face, her step towards the terrified woman, and reading her intentions, filled the man's heart with hope.

Hope that she was coming around. Hope that she was remembering at last.

"Go," he urged silently, not daring to say what he thought. "Go to her, help her. I know it's what's in you to do. You always wanted to help others, to make them feel safe, to make them be ok. It's who you are."

He turned to look at Kathy, hanging his head sheepishly at her look.

Kathy glared at him accusingly, her eyes burning with anger.

"Why?" she asked softly, her voice trembling but controlled.

"I'm sorry," was all he could manage, coming out in a soft half-choked whisper.

Kathy took a step towards him, shocked at her own reaction, terrified by her own feelings and angry bravado.

Jane stared at Kathy in surprise, her mouth open in a little o.

"What are you doing?!" Jane wanted to scream at her.

She could only watch in mute shock.

The man flinched, almost taking a step back when Kathy stepped towards him, closing the gap between them by that small step.

The anger built in Kathy despite her fear, perhaps even fed by her fear. All the anger, the dread, and the anguish of the years spent being the victim, being Ronnie's victim and now this man's, it all built and boiled up inside her, suddenly lashing out at her nearest tormentor.

"Are we not enough for you?!" Kathy demanded angrily, taking another step forward.

He held his ground, staring at her with a shocked expression that matched Jane's.

"You have two of us already! Is that not enough?! Do you need more?!" Kathy's voice rose with the tide of anger boiling over.

"Do you have to keep taking more?! More women to hurt?! To kill?!"

She stepped forward again as she spoke, closing the quickly dwindling gap between them, staring up at the man with hate filled eyes.

"Are we not good enough?! Will we never be good enough? How many more do you need?! HOW MANY?!"

She was almost touching him now; she was standing so close, glaring up at him.

He stared down at her, motionless except the flinch that came with the start of each angry sentence.

He looked peevish, like a man who had just been caught cheating on his girlfriend.

"I-I," he stammered, "I'm sorry."

"Why?!" she demanded.

"I don't know!" he finally spit out. "I just don't know. I don't know why, and I don't know how to stop!"

He looked distraught and lost.

During the confrontation, Jane took advantage of the man's distraction to move towards the small window. She peeked out through the crack between the boards. This was the first chance she'd had to see outside since she was brought here in a drugged state.

She was relieved to see the sky and trees, fields beyond an unkempt yard of tall grass, the dirt tracks of the driveway that widened out into a parking area of mixed dirt and gravel overgrown with grass and weeds.

She stared out the window mesmerised, welcoming the sight

of freedom just beyond the prison of the barrier.

And then something caught her eye.

Something absolutely wonderful.

She almost squealed with delight, catching herself just in time, holding her breath.

Down the overgrown track that was a driveway that seemed more a road with its endless length that vanished beyond the trees was movement.

A pickup truck was coming slowly up the track, approaching the old farmhouse.

The man had just burst out his confession to Kathy, feeling utterly wretched, when he noticed Jane standing at the window staring out fixatedly at something.

He wondered what had caught her attention.

Was it memories flooding back at the sight of the yard?

He walked past Kathy, ignoring her angry glare, not seeing the sudden mix of confusion and pity that furrowed her brow, intent only on Jane and the window.

He moved to stand behind Jane, looking out the window at what she saw, picturing the two of them in the yard, his own memories teasing at him with a happy scene that made him feel the danger that always lurked beneath every happy moment.

Something about the scene wasn't right, but he couldn't see what it was as the scene played out in the yard, fed by his imagination.

Then he saw it.

The truck coming up the driveway.

The truck didn't fit. It wasn't right.

He snapped out of it, stepping back quickly and turning, anxious.

"Someone's coming," he said.

He was panicked.

No one ever came here. Not in the years he has used this place as his secret place, and almost never in the years he grew up here as a child.

The place was not on any route anyone would take to anywhere, the road dead-ending just beyond the road that came into the property. The driveway was basically a long overgrown road, barely recognizable as a road where it branched off the other road, which was also very rarely maintained and little more than a single vehicle dirt road running between farmers' fields.

Even the farmers that tended these tracks of land rarely came down that road, having developed more convenient access points to their fields over the years as small family farms became larger farms with the growth of the machinery into huge lumbering beasts that could cover much larger areas.

The old farm property itself was rundown and looked long abandoned. The barn and other buildings leaned heavily as though the weight of their years bore forever down on them, roofs sagging, and walls marred by scattered broken boards. Some windows were boarded up, some featured glass that was cracked or partially broken out, shards sticking up like crooked teeth.

The old farmhouse itself was a tiny old building, more a shack than a house, like the old houses farmers built with their own bare hands using a hammer and hand saw years before they had access to electricity, plumbing, and power tools.

He even generally took care to park his car in the barn out of sight so that if anyone did happen by they would have no reason to suspect the place was in use.

For all intents and purposes, it was an entirely forgotten place.

Who could possibly be coming here? Why?

He had to get the women put away out of sight before the intruder reached the old farmhouse.

Jane stood glued to the window, watching the pickup truck slowly grow bigger as it approached.

Kathy's expression closed up tight, her face becoming an unreadable mask.

"Was someone really coming?" Kathy thought. She barely dared to believe it.

"Someone's coming," the man said again, louder, more urgently.

"Hurry," he urged the women, "to the cellar; quickly!"

Neither woman moved.

His panic grew when they failed to move immediately.

241

L.V. Gaudet

Why are they not going? What are they waiting for?

He wouldn't consider the implications of what went through his mind until later, but it didn't even occur to him that Kathy and Jane might not cooperate.

They belonged here just as he himself did, partners in this life, family. They would be just as eager to not be found out as he is.

The thought they might feel otherwise simply did not occur to him.

He was worried about the other one, though; the new one. He was terrified she would make a scene and bring the strange visitor's attention on herself.

He wanted to scream, to grab the women and run them all to the root cellar. They had to move faster.

As time raced through his mind at warp speed and the vehicle crawled closer to the house, he grabbed Jane, pulling her along towards the doorway, pushing Kathy towards it too when he got close enough.

"Go!" he ordered. "Move! Into the cellar! Now!"

Unable to do anything but comply, the women moved as ordered.

Jane looked back wistfully at the window.

Kathy stared blindly ahead at nothing, lost in her own thoughts.

"Shit!" The man remembered the other woman cowering in another room.

Leaving Kathy and Jane to climb down, he raced across the house to grab the other woman.

He stooped down over the woman huddled on the floor, grabbing her roughly and pulling her up even as she screeched and fought against him, her smaller size no match for his strength.

"Stop it!" he demanded, dragging her along, her attempts to fight him off futile.

The last head was just vanishing down the hole to the cellar as he dragged her into sight of it.

Her eyes widened in terror at the sight of the hole in the floor and the other woman vanishing down inside it.

242

"Go!" he ordered. "Down into the cellar. Now!"

She shook her head, her eyes rolling in fear, her limbs turning weak and watery with dread. Her face paled and washed in a sudden sheen of fear sweat, looking like she was about to swoon into a faint.

"Now!" he said roughly. "Climb down now or I'll throw you down there."

Reluctantly she approached the yawning hole, got down on her knees, and began the careful climb down.

The climb was difficult, the pain in her arm and shoulder flaring bright and hot, blinding.

She barely made it to the floor below before he leaned over to look down into the darkness below.

"Make a sound and I'll kill you," he threatened the three women below.

He was terrified the new woman would scream for help and that the visitor might hear.

He swung the hatch over, slamming it closed with a loud bang, closing off the light and leaving her blinking in the darkness.

In his rush he did not pull up the rope ladder.

He fumbled with the latch, finally forcing it home, locking the hatch.

He rushed to the living room, taking a quick look out the window.

He spotted his own car in the drive.

"Damn!"

He couldn't just not answer the door; not with his car out there in sight.

Whoever was here would wonder how a car came to be left here with no one around.

He unlocked the door and rushed out, locking the door behind him. He dashed around the house to the dilapidated barn, hiding out there in the relative darkness with baited breath, his heart threatening to pound right out of his chest with its hammering beats.

He waited for the unwanted visitor.

243

42

The truck came slowly up the rough track that acted as a driveway, bouncing along.

At last it came to a stop beside the dark blue car parked outside the abandoned farmhouse.

The driver got out, closing the truck door behind him with a squeal of its rusted hinges.

It was the same man from the hospital, who had been looking around indecisively outside Jane Doe's room only to flee when confronted by Michael while he was acting undercover as an orderly.

Rust mottled the two-tone paint job of the truck. It was an older model that had definitely seen better days.

The visitor headed first for the edge of the yard, looking over the high grass around the edge of the woods as if looking for something in particular.

After an ambling search of that area he headed back to the farmhouse yard.

The visitor wandered over, looking into the windows of the car. He tried a door. It was unlocked.

Opening the car door, he gave its interior only a cursory look over, not expecting to find anything.

He sniffed at the air, his nose picking up a decidedly foul smell from the car. It was an unpleasant sweetish stink he was all too familiar with. The rot of death.

Closing the door, he walked around, sniffing the air.

The smell was stronger near the trunk.

He went back, opening the driver's door again, and pulled at the trunk latch to pop the trunk.

Nothing happened.

He tried a few times before giving up. Apparently the latch was seized or disconnected.

Closing the door he went to the trunk, giving it a tug up just in case.

The lid was locked.

The visitor wandered over to the farmhouse, looking in the

window through the crack between boards covering it.

What he saw looked fairly bare, empty of inhabitants, the old furniture sitting as it probably was left when the place was abandoned years ago.

But it didn't have the feel of a place that has been completely abandoned.

He had a sense someone was watching him.

He walked around, looking in another boarded up window.

Just a tidy kitchen, the old table and chairs endlessly waiting for that next meal, and nothing in view to suggest anyone was occupying the place.

He went back around to the front and tried the door.

Locked.

He wandered across the yard, opening the door to a small shed, the door creaked loudly on hinges so rotten that he had to lift and support the door to keep it from falling right off.

The shed had ancient odds and ends, covered with dust and cobwebs that probably spanned at least a decade.

He turned around and headed for the leaning barn, staring at its sagging roof with a little trepidation.

The visitor was half-way between the vehicles and the barn when a man suddenly stepped from the darkness within.

The man from the barn stopped, looking surprised, and just watched him. He recognized the visitor from the hospital.

The visitor stopped in his tracks, momentarily startled by the sudden appearance of the other man even though he fully expected to find him somewhere on the property.

Recovering quickly from his surprise, the man from the barn stepped forward, hand outstretched in the universal sign of greeting and friendly intentions.

"Hello there," the man started introducing himself, "I'm-"

The visitor cut him off.

"I know who you are," the visitor said.

"Well, I guess you have me at a disadvantage then," the man said. "And you are?" he asked.

The visitor was really putting him on edge. He had a familiarity about him. He had the strong sense that he should know who this man is, that he knew him from somewhere. Not knowing jangled his nerves, but not as badly as the sense of unease he was getting just from confronting the visitor. There was just something about the man that made him feel very edgy.

The visitor ignored the question. He fully intended to tell the man who he is, just not yet. He needed to learn something first.

"I know who you are all right," the visitor repeated, "and I know this farm too."

He looked around casually, the way a sightseer or curious neighbor might.

"What were you looking for out there?" the man asked, indicating the woods.

"Oh nothing really," the visitor said. "Actually, I thought I might find you over there, when I saw the car in the yard and didn't see anyone around."

"What do you want? Why are you here?" the man asked.

The visitor looked him up and down, studying him.

"Probably the same thing as you," the visitor said.

"What exactly is that?" the man asked.

The visitor shrugged noncommittally.

"Just checking the old place out."

"What business do you have here?" the man asked.

"Oh just visiting old memories," the visitor said casually, carefully reading the other man's reactions, "and looking for something I lost."

The visitor's behavior and vagueness was making him even more uncomfortable.

Who is this man? Why does he look so familiar? Of all the places to come to, why here?

"How do you know me?" he asked suddenly, demanding the answer outright.

"I've known you for some time now," the visitor said. "I know who you are, I know what you are, and I know what you do."

He winked at the man conspiratorially.

"I've been watching you."

Rage filled him. He wanted to grab the visitor, tear him apart, pummel him with his fists, and rip the answers right out of him.

The rage was visible in his eyes, in the flinch of his hands and in the tightening of his muscles and the shift of his stance.

But he carefully kept his face as passive as possible. He didn't want to reveal anything to this stranger.

"What do you mean you've been watching me?" he demanded.

"Just that I've seen you around," the visitor said amiably.

"I remember you from the hospital," the man said, trying to calm himself down, to think clearly.

He had to figure out who this was and what he was up to.

"Why were you at the hospital?" he asked.

The visitor shrugged as if to say the answer didn't matter.

"Oh," the visitor said, dragging out the word to show just how unimportant his answer was, "just there to see a patient."

"So why did you run away?" he sneered, thinking he must be on the right track to put this visitor on the defensive.

"That nurse was scary," the visitor said with a humorous twinkle in his eye. He wasn't going on the defensive.

"It's funny about those missing women," the visitor said, changing the subject.

"It doesn't seem so funny to me," the man said sourly.

"I wonder how many women are still missing?" the visitor went on conversationally. "And another one who just went missing," he paused as if thinking about it.

He didn't look like he needed to think about it. He looked like he already knew exactly what he was about to say.

"That Jane Doe," the visitor continued," I heard that she's disappeared from the hospital."

The man didn't like the way this was going. Instead of making the visitor uneasy, he was feeling the pressure himself.

This man knew more than he should. Who is he?

"That's who you were there to see, wasn't it?" the man asked accusingly.

The visitor ignored this.

He looked around the yard knowingly.

"Lots of places around a place like this to hide something," he said it as if he were changing the subject.

The man tensed, taking a threatening step forward.

What was this man implying? Was he implying he knew? Did he know? How could this man know he had women hidden on the property?

"What are you suggesting?" he asked, his voice low and deadly.

"Nothing at all," the visitor said, raising his hands in an open palmed appeasing gesture that implied he had nothing to hide and no ill intentions.

"I'm just saying is all," the visitor added.

"Saying what?" he growled.

"That a place like this could be a good place to hide something, say a missing woman."

The man barely stopped himself from lunging at the visitor and grabbing him, the rage almost overwhelming his shaky control.

Who is this man? Damn it, who is he? Is he a cop? A fed? Why did he seem to know so much, to imply things?

He took a threatening step forward towards the visitor.

"Get off my property!" the man ordered.

Connie stood at the base of the rope ladder, trembling, tears streaming down her face, still shaking from the final shock of the hatch above slamming shut so loudly and closing out the light from above.

Kathy stood near the mattresses, her anger now seeped away and her mind a twisted knot of confusing thoughts and emotions.

Jane could not stop thinking about the truck driving up the track towards them, the visitor.

They could be saved right now.

She moved to the ladder, staring up at the closed hatch with trepidation.

Connie took a step away, not wanting to be near anyone, as frightened of these other two women as she was of this place and the man above.

Her mind was in turmoil too.

Were these women victims too? Had they been kidnapped just like her? Or were they here to hide, or maybe to trick her?

Jane started slowly climbing the rope ladder.

When she got to the top she braced herself as best she could against the flimsy ladder, holding tight with one hand.

She reached up with the other, testing the trap door above.

Kathy turned to Jane.

"What are you doing?" Kathy whispered.

"It's locked," Jane whispered back in answer.

Jane tried again, pushing harder on the trap door, almost making herself fall off the rope ladder as it swung in protest to her efforts.

She tried craning around, looking up at the edges, studying the barest line of light filtering through along the edges.

"I don't think we could unlatch it from this side, even if we had anything to use," she said.

Jane climbed back down and looked at the two other women in turn.

"The visitor must be outside the house by now, maybe even out of their truck," she said.

Connie just blinked at her.

Kathy shook her head "no", knowing what Jane meant to do.

"If we make enough noise they might hear us," Jane said.

"No, we can't," Kathy warned. "Remember what he said, that he'll kill us."

"It's our only chance," Jane insisted. "If we can make the person hear us, maybe they can bring back help. We could be saved!"

"No," Kathy insisted. "We can't. He will be angry. And they might not even hear us anyway. And if they do-," she gulped. "If they do hear us, we might just be putting them in danger. He might kill them or lock them down here too."

"We have to," Jane insisted. "It's our best chance, our only chance right now. We have to."

She turned to Connie, looking at her pleadingly, knowing it was useless to try any more with Kathy.

Kathy had been here too long.

"Please," Jane urged Connie. "Help me. Yell with me. Call to the visitor for help."

Connie nodded.

Jane started yelling, cupping her hands to her mouth in an

effort to make it louder, trying to yell as loud as she could.

Connie joined in after a brief pause, the two women yelling together, their words garbled and clashing as they repeated the same words but not saying them together.

"HELP! HEY, DOWN HERE! WHE'RE HERE, WE'RE DOWN HERE! HELP! GET HELP! HELP US!"

"Oh please, please hear us," Jane thought desperately. "Please help us." The desperation hung heavily on her very soul. It all felt so useless, so helpless.

In the yard outside, the muffled sound of garbled yelling could just barely be heard.

The man blanched.

Did the visitor hear it?

Shit! Damn those women!

"Get off my property!" the man demanded again, taking another threatening step forward, raising his voice both to be more intimidating and to drown out the women.

"Get in your truck and go! Now! Get out of here!"

The visitor heard the women's cries for help, as muffled as they were.

He couldn't make out the words, but he didn't have to.

He didn't react to the faint garbled yelling.

He was pretty sure he would not make it off this property alive if the other man suspected he heard the cries for help. He was playing with fire as it is.

He put his arms out, placating, taking a step back.

"I'm going, I'm going," the visitor said amicably. "Sorry to have bothered you."

He retreated quickly to his truck, giving the man an apologetic smile.

He hopped in and closed the door without a word, turning the truck around in the yard and making his slow way back down the bumpy track.

"Shit! Crap! Damn!" the man swore, clenching and shaking his fists angrily.

Did the visitor hear? He didn't act like he did. He couldn't be sure.

He was torn. He didn't know what to do.

He didn't know who might have known the visitor was coming. If he killed him he might be putting them all in jeopardy of being discovered.

He would lose everything. Cassie, Kathy-.

But letting the visitor go was too much of a risk too. He knew things, possibly everything. He might be a cop, maybe a federal agent. At the very least he was probably going to report him the moment it was safe to do so.

The man was furious with the women. He was also terrified by the possible repercussions if the man had heard the women yelling and realized their situation.

He raced to the house, fumbling with the lock, and ran to the trap door to the root cellar.

He was shaking with rage.

He fumbled with the latch, pulling the door open, suddenly barraged by the frantic calls for help from below.

The women stopped screaming instantly, frozen with fear, hoping desperately the person opening the hatch would be the visitor, their saviour, and not the man who had put them down there.

The man got right down on all fours at the hatch, sticking his head down the hole and craning to look down into the root cellar at the three women standing in mute shock looking like deer trapped in the headlights of an approaching truck and certain brutal death.

His face was a twisted mask of fury and violence.

"GODDAMMIT I TOLD YOU TO KEEP FUCKING QUIET!" he raged at them. "IF HE HEARD YOU, IF HE HEARD...!"

The man let out a gruff sound of pure rage and frustration.

He slammed the trap door closed so hard the wood made a cracking noise as it banged down with a deep shudder. He stomped off.

He ran from the house and jumped into the car, fumbling with the keys.

The car kicked up dirt from its tires as it leapt forward, spinning around and tearing out of the yard.

He couldn't believe it; the truck was already nowhere to be seen down the long track to the road.

That visitor must have left in a pretty big hurry to move that fast down that rough path.

He had to catch up. He had to follow the visitor, find out who he is and what business he had at the old farm property.

Most importantly, he had to find out if the visitor was a threat. If he had heard the women's cries for help, he would have to get rid of him.

He thought hard, forcing himself to slow down as he approached the road. He couldn't just tear out onto the road. Not just for the risk of losing control of his car turning at such a high speed, but he knew he had to follow the truck discretely if he hoped to not alert the visitor that he was being chased.

Approaching the road, he slowed almost to a stop, looking both ways.

"What the hell?"

There was not a single vehicle in sight.

His heart tightened into a knot. He could barely breathe.

He had to make a quick decision.

He turned onto the road heading towards town. It was the most likely way the visitor might have gone.

He sped up, racing off in pursuit.

43

The man's face was a twisted mask of fury and violence, glaring down the hole in the ceiling above, even more frightening than the vicious fury in his voice.

"GODDAMMIT I TOLD YOU TO KEEP FUCKING QUIET!" he raged at them. "IF HE HEARD YOU, IF HE HEARD...!"

He seemed to sputter then, too furious to make words.

He let out a gruff sound of pure rage and frustration.

He slammed the trap door closed hard and stomped off. The wood made a cracking noise when it banged and trembled. The sound echoed briefly in the dark root cellar despite the dampening effect of the concrete walls and dirt floor.

Or maybe it was just their ears ringing from the loud assault on the women's ear drums.

They stared, stricken, listening in anxious fear as the man's feet stomped heavily across the floor above.

They heard the door slam shut above, followed not long after by the faint sound of the car's tires tearing up the yard as it drove away with all of the violence that raged inside the man himself.

Kathy was on the verge of tears.

"You see?" she moaned, her voice rough with the tears that clenched her throat nearly closed.

"You see?" she said it again. "You shouldn't have yelled. You should have been quiet."

Connie looked ill, her face pale and her body trembling.

"We're dead," she cried. "Our chance for help, and the person never even heard!"

"We're not dead," Jane said, her own voice catching with the fear that filled her. She knew, if *he* heard them the other person must have too.

She was staring up towards the closed hatch.

"We are," Connie sobbed. "You heard him; you saw how mad he was. He's going to kill us for sure now."

"No he's not," Jane said shakily. "We're going to escape before he comes back."

253

L.V. Gaudet

"H—how?" Connie asked, not believing it could even be possible.

"I don't know," Jane said. "But if we don't, we will be dead."

She couldn't take her attention off the trap door, thinking. She didn't think she heard the latch being closed. And with the cracking of wood, maybe, just maybe...

Kathy stood apart from them, her face twisted with sorrow and fear.

She shook her head, talking to herself although out loud.

"He won't kill us," she said. And truly a part of her believed it, although another part agreed with the other women that they needed to escape, that the man was furious enough to come back and kill them all.

Jane moved to the rope ladder that still dangled beneath the trap door.

She stopped at its base, grasping one side, staring up at the door above.

"What are you doing?" Connie asked, moving closer.

"Trying it again," Jane said, starting her climb up the ladder.

"It's hopeless," Connie whimpered. "We can't open it."

"I have to try again," Jane said. "Maybe he was too angry and forgot to lock it. Maybe the latch loosened from slamming it so hard. Maybe he didn't quite latch it all the way. He left in a pretty big hurry."

When she reached the top of the ladder, she pushed up on the door.

It didn't budge.

"No," she whispered, helpless.

She tried it again, pushing harder, pounding the door with her fist.

And suddenly it moved, just a bit.

"Help me," she called.

Connie climbed up the rope ladder beside her, the rope swinging precariously, both of them half hanging off the narrow ladder.

They both strained against the door above, pushing and stopping, pounding on it, and pushing again. The strain on

Connie's injured shoulder almost made her give up. Desperation kept her going.

And then the latch gave, its weakened wood giving up on the screws that had been pulled loose by the man's violent forceful closing of the door, the latch catching on its other half and forcing it to tear partway out of the wood.

He had forgotten to latch it. But in the violence of the act of slamming the door down the two halves of the latch had gotten wedged together in a way they weren't meant to be.

Jane and Connie sucked their breath in almost simultaneously in surprise, Connie almost falling off the rope ladder and pawing frantically at the swinging rope to steady herself.

They stared at each other in a mix of hope and disbelief.

Jane reached up cautiously, pushing up on the door, the ladder swaying precariously.

She climbed up another rung as she pushed up and then moved up another step.

Connie just held on, not daring to move or breath, her heart beating a fast tattoo of excitement and panic. She was afraid of somehow jeopardizing their escape as much as she was afraid the man's face would suddenly appear in the widening opening above.

Finally Jane was high enough to push the door up and over the apex on its hinges. It fell to the other side with a loud bang that made all three women jump and cringe, certain the sound would bring him running.

Below, Kathy stared up at the ceiling, trembling and waiting for the sound of the man's heavy tread on the floor above.

Connie started half climbing down, staring at the ceiling above, waiting for the sound of the man's footsteps and his snarling voice, ready to drop down the rest of the way to scurry off to hide in a dark corner of the root cellar.

Jane held her breath, not moving, listening, her head above the opening in the floor, looking around for any signs of their captor.

She was suddenly almost certain he had snuck back into the old farmhouse without them hearing, that at any moment he would come racing in, grab her roughly by the hair, and drag her out of the opening to kill her.

When at last Jane dared to move, she was trembling so much she almost fell back into the root cellar as she scrabbled out of the hole.

"No," Kathy whispered below. "Don't. We should stay here. He'll be mad. He'll come after us."

Connie turned and looked at her with disgust.

"I'm getting the hell out of here before he comes back," she whispered harshly. "You can either come or stay."

Connie scrambled up rope ladder as quickly as she could with her injured shoulder.

Jane helped her climb off the ladder onto the solid wood of the floor above.

Jane looked down the hole expectantly.

"Kathy," she whispered. "Kathy, come on. We have to go now. It may be our only chance."

In the dim light of the lantern, Kathy's face twisted into an expression of doubt, regret, and fear.

Not far away lay the path to possible freedom.

Freedom to go where? Back to Ronnie?

She didn't want to go back to Ronnie.

The man killing her in a furious rage would even be better than that. Being kept in this dark and chilly root cellar was better than going back to Ronnie.

At least the man who kidnapped her didn't hurt her all the time like Ronnie did.

Her eyes welled with tears that ran freely down her cheeks.

"I—I can't," she whimpered.

"Please Kathy," Jane begged. "Please come with us. I can't just leave you here with that monster. Come with us."

Kathy shook her head, a motion Jane could not possibly see.

Jane understood what the silence from below meant well enough.

"Come on," Connie urged, getting more frightened the longer they waited. "He's going to come back."

Jane waited, staring into the blackness below, waiting for Kathy to change her mind.

Finally, with a last desperate look at the dark abyss they had just crawled out of, Jane got up and went cautiously to the living room and the only exit from the old house.

Connie followed closely behind, both women listening and watching for any signs of their abductor, ready to run, terrified of what he would do if he caught them.

They were almost too terrified to try the door.

If it was locked, they may not be able to escape. Could they get the door open somehow? Or maybe a window in time before the man came back?

Jane's breath sagged out in a rough burst of air when she tried the door and it unexpectedly opened.

She jumped back instinctively, seeing the man's furious face on the other side, coming at her, filled with rage and violence.

Connie caught her breath, almost squealing from the shock of the door opening, seeing the door slam open with a loud bang and the man springing forward to grab them both in a vicious attack.

They were greeted by the mellow light of early dusk, the wind blowing softly, the sighing of the leaves on the branches of the trees.

There was no one there.

Jane poked her head out the doorway, looking around. There was no sign of a vehicle, their captor, or the visitor.

"Come on," she urged. "Let's go."

She bounded from the house and sprinted for the closest cover, the dangerously leaning barn.

Connie followed on her heels.

Connie was running straight for the barn, intent on racing into its darkness.

Jane grabbed her just before they reached the large open door.

"What?" Connie gasped.

"Wait," Jane whispered. "He could be in there."

Connie blanched at the thought, stopping in her tracks, looking like all her hopes and dreams had just been dashed, her will broken and trampled into the dirt.

Jane moved ahead cautiously, peering into the darkened

interior of the barn, searching for any signs of movement.

All was silent and still.

"Ok, come," she urged.

Connie paused before following her uncertainly into the unknown inside.

Once in the relative safety of the cover the barn gave them, Jane cautiously peered out, surveying the area to make sure it was safe.

"Ok, let's go," she whispered.

Jane raced from the barn, heading for the old dilapidated shed closer to the woods, stopping and leaning against its side and trying to hold her breath even as it came out in ragged fear-filled gasps.

Connie followed after, clinging to the other woman's arm as she too stopped to lean against the shed.

The shed was between them and the farmhouse, blocking them from the view of anyone who might be in the house, in the yard, or driving up the long path from the road.

Jane took a moment to collect herself, to control her breathing and her trembling limbs.

Beside her Connie wasn't doing so well, trembling so hard that she was barely able to keep herself standing.

Jane peeked around the shed, desperately hoping the man wasn't there.

The coast was clear.

She patted Connie's arm to get her attention, motioning to her to come.

They bolted the rest of the distance to the woods not far away, racing into the shelter of the trees, running and dodging, branches slapping at them painfully as they tore desperately through the woods.

They made it!

They had escaped but they couldn't stop running yet. They had to get as far away from there as possible.

Maybe they would find another house or a car on the road.

But first, they had to get far enough away that they might be able to avoid him finding them.

They weren't out of the woods yet.

In the dim light of the little lantern, Kathy sunk down on the mattress in despair.

Her heart felt empty, soulless.

"I should go after them," she murmured. "And do what? Go with them? Beg them to come back?"

She hung her head, holding it in her arms as though in terrible pain and sobbed.

The man felt sick; sick at heart and sick in his stomach.

He didn't find the visitor's truck.

Who was he? What did he want? And, most importantly, had he heard the women's cries for help?

His car bounced as he drove slowly down the trail back to the farmhouse.

At last he pulled up into the yard, shut the engine off, and let out a heavy sigh expressing how the weight of the world hung on his shoulders, dragging him down to the earth.

He got out of the car and headed for the house, and stopped dead in his tracks.

His jaw fell, his expression turning slack like a stroke victim's.

The door was open.

"No," he moaned.

His legs turned suddenly weak. He felt like he couldn't possibly walk.

He had to force himself to take a step forward, and another, and by the time he reached the open door he was running.

He raced frantically through the house, skidding to a stop before the gaping darkness of the open trap door.

Despair gripped him. He grabbed at his hair as though to pull it out.

"Augh," he groaned; a sound of desolation and pain.

His heart stopped beating, stuck motionless and heavy in his chest. His stomach churned and flopped, a brick of misery sagging heavy inside his gut.

"No," he moaned.

He didn't want to look. He had to. He made himself climb

down the wobbly rope ladder into the darkness of the root cellar.

His feet touched the safety of the dirt floor below, its firm stability lending his legs strength.

At first the root cellar was pitch black, the inky darkness surrounding him in its sightless cocoon.

The lamp was not lit. Its feeble light lent nothing to the dark root cellar.

The man looked around, trying to peer through the darkness, the light from the open hole above him the only thing illuminating the room beneath the house.

Its light didn't do enough to diffuse the darkness of the cellar, but in moments his eyes adjusted enough to the darkness to make out shadowy objects.

He moved to the mattresses, fumbling in the darkness and finding the book of matches.

He lit the lamp, its wick catching and flaring before it settled to let its warm yellow glow spread just a little in the dim cellar.

He turned the wick up, letting the lamp glow brighter and turned around, searching the darker corners of the cellar.

The cellar was empty.

He felt sick. Empty.

They were gone.

The light from above suddenly vanished with a loud bang that seemed to shake the very dirt of the floor.

He jumped, startled by the suddenness of it, and spun.

The trap door was closed.

He rushed to the bottom of the rope ladder, scrambling up the ladder with practiced speed.

Scraping sounds scratched loudly across the floor above, a clunk, a bang, and a loud thud.

He reached the top of the ladder, pushing up on the door.

It didn't budge.

He pushed harder, his muscles straining.

It was useless. It didn't even rattle in the latch. Something heavy had been dragged or pushed over the hatch. He had little chance of budging it from this awkward position.

He banged on the hatch futilely, pounding on it, punching it, the frustration twisting his features.

On the other side of the hatch Kathy shivered. Fear, bravado, and loss scrambled her emotions into a stew of confusion.

She sagged against the heavy cabinet she had dragged on top of the trap door. It was the kind of cabinet you would expect to find in an old farmhouse, where rooms were mostly empty shells and free standing cabinets were added for storage. The cabinet had been against the wall a few feet from the trap door.

She sweated from the effort.

There was no way he could push up the trap door against the weight of the heavy cabinet partially blocking it.

She had the blank look of shock.

The man started banging on the trap door from below, pounding harder and harder, the thudding echoing through the house and her mind.

She covered her ears, trying to block it out, sobbing.

She sank to the floor in a weak pile of limbs.

The bangs and thuds continued to echo through the house, vibrating the wood floor.

She felt the vibrations in the floor as though they went through her very soul

"Oh, just stop it," she whispered softly so only she could hear. "Please, just stop it."

The man started yelling.

He yelled to be let out, he cursed, he swore, he threatened and demanded, and finally he stopped pounding on the door and began to beg and plead.

"Who is up there?" he demanded.

All three? One? Two? Which? He couldn't guess.

"Let me out of here!" he yelled, pounding on the door. "Damn it let me out!"

He yelled, he cursed, he swore, he threatened, and demanded.

At last he began to beg and plead. He stopped pounding on the trap door.

"Who is up there?" he called through the trap door, tired from the endless pounding and yelling.

"It's you, isn't it? Kathy?"

She whimpered on the floor above, a tiny mewling sound.

"It is you," he called softly, careful to keep his voice gentle. "Where are the others? They left without you, didn't they? They left you here alone."

He was suddenly sure of it. Kathy was the one who trapped him. She was alone. The others had left her behind.

His heart leapt with joy that she was still there. Relief filled him. Kathy. She could have escaped with them and didn't.

For whatever reason, she stayed behind. But he still had to find Cassie fast before he lost her again.

"Kathy, please, let me out."

He looked up at the trap door, his muscles tense with the violence that boiled beneath the surface as he tried to control himself, forcing his voice to sound soft and friendly.

"Kathy, please. They left you here alone. Just let me out. I'm not angry, not at you. They did this. They left you behind."

He sighed heavily, his shoulders sagging in weary defeat.

If he couldn't convince her to let him out, he'd be trapped down there.

"Kathy, I'm sorry," he called up to her softly, but loud enough to be heard through the wooden barrier. I'm sorry for everything I've done; to you, to the others. I'm sorry I locked you in the root cellar. I'm sorry, it was wrong."

He paused, wondering if she was even still there, if she was listening.

"Kathy—" He hoped desperately she was still there, that she hadn't taken off, leaving him trapped in the root cellar. No one would come, no one would find him. He'd die down there, trapped like a rat in a cage.

"Please Kathy; if you let me out I won't put you back down here. I promise."

44

As the visitor drove slowly down the rough track away from the old farmhouse, he looked back through his rear view mirror. He saw the man run into the house.

He had heard the women's cries from inside. There was no doubt in his mind what the noise from the house was.

He knew they were there before he'd even heard them. He knew because he had been watching the man.

The moment he saw the headlines in the paper about the woman they called Jane Doe, her face looking pale and serene even in the harshness of the black and white photograph, he knew what was going on.

The man had come back to his roots.

He just didn't know when.

He came, driving the long distance to come here, to see for himself.

He watched the old farm property, abandoned decades ago.

He went to the hospital, needing to see the woman, to see that it really was her.

He didn't get the close look he wanted, but he got enough of a glimpse through the open doorway.

She had been a child the last time he'd seen her, but he knew immediately that it was her. Cassie.

And then he had to leave the hospital in a hurry, but he would be back. He had to come back for her, to take her before the man who'd left her for dead came back to take her.

The visitor had begun to implement his plan to take Jane Doe, Cassie, tampering with the intravenous tubes so she would no longer be drugged. He needed her to be able to walk out.

When he returned for the final step, to actually take her, she was already missing from the hospital and he knew immediately where to find her.

She would be here.

So he came to the old farm to get her, but the man was here.

He also knew this property very well.

Instead of continuing all the way up to the road, watching

behind him for the man to come out of the house, he turned off and drove across the ground where a mottled mess of gravel, rotting downed trees, and bare earth would leave little trace of the truck's passing.

He drove right into the trees, vanishing in what seemed like impossibly thick overgrowth.

The truck vanished just as the man came running out of the farmhouse.

He watched the man drive right past, the deep shadows of the branches above not allowing any rays of sunlight to filter down and give him away with a winking glint of light off metal.

He watched the house through the trees.

Should he go in? How far should he risk it right now? He had heard more than one voice yelling. He thought it was two voices.

That could be a problem.

It might take longer to release them if there were two. Were they bound? Chained?

Should he go in and find them and risk the man returning while he was still inside?

Maybe he should wait, watch, and come back later.

Movement at the house caught his attention.

Two women ran from the house to the old barn that looked to be on the verge of collapse.

They ran from the barn and vanished on the other side of the rickety little shed.

A brief moment later they ran for the woods, disappearing into their depths.

He pulled out of his hiding spot, driving down the path to the dirt road, his truck bouncing on the uneven surface, and turned to go in the opposite direction the man had gone, in the same direction the women were heading as they fled through the woods.

He had to find the two women. One of them would be the one the newspapers dubbed Jane Doe, the one he had come back to this town for. Cassie.

Jane and Connie raced blindly through the woods, their

lungs tearing with searing pain as their breath panted in ragged breaths from the effort.

Jane was lagging, falling behind and stumbling, still weak from her healing body and time spent being kept drugged and unconscious in the hospital.

"Come on," Connie urged, "we have to keep going. We can't stop."

She pulled on Jane's arm, pulling her along.

Darkness was closing in, the shadows in the woods growing deeper as the sky above still looked bright.

They slowed to a walk, gasping to catch their breath, sides hurting and lungs burning, dizzy from the effort.

"We can't go much further," Jane panted. "We have to rest."

She was hit with a violent burst of coughing. Her lungs felt like they would explode. Jane was doubled over, hands on her legs for support, trying both to keep her legs from buckling and the dizziness washing over her from making her fall.

Too exhausted to continue despite the urgent need to keep going, to put more distance between them and the old farm, Connie stopped pulling on Jane. She sank to the ground beside her, trying to catch her breath. Tears of desperation burned at her eyes.

"We'll rest for a little while," Connie managed between gulping mouthfuls of air.

Jane sank down gratefully beside her.

"Just for a little while," Jane gasped between fits of coughing.

They stared around, peering into the darkening woods. The underbrush was less dense here deeper into the woods than it was closer to the edge.

That they could see further was both a relief and a concern for both women. It meant they would see him coming from a further distance, but it also meant that he would have an easier time finding them.

"We should find someplace to hide," Jane suggested. "We can't continue much farther if we don't get some rest."

Connie nodded. She felt like she could sleep forever right now despite the fear that surely would make sleep impossible.

265

"We need to find some water too," Connie said. "I'm so thirsty."

Jane looked up at the darkening sky. The clouds were coming together, closing out the stars, making the world even darker as night closed in on them.

"It's getting too dark," Jane said. "We'll have to wait until the sun starts to come up."

Connie looked up at the sky too.

"I sure hope it doesn't rain," she said.

"At least we'll have water," Jane panted with a smirk.

They settled on a spot next to a fallen tree. The thick trunk offered both a barrier to prying eyes and a small sense of protection. The break in the branches above where the tree once stood let more light filter down there, allowing the undergrowth to grow thicker and taller in that spot. The rotting tree also nourished the plants around, encouraging them to grow in its place. Thicker bushes grew around it, adding to their cover.

The man could easily pass right by them without ever seeing them huddled down in that spot.

They lay down together, pushing at some of the branches, pinning one branch that tended to poke at them behind its neighbor, and huddled together for warmth.

"You sleep first," Jane offered. "I'll wake you in a while to switch."

Despite her fear, Connie was asleep in moments, her breath rattling in her chest.

Jane lay there looking around, listening to the sounds of the woods.

She didn't think she'd be able to sleep at all. She was too afraid.

After what felt like an eternity had passed, Jane gently shook Connie awake.

Connie woke with a startled jump, almost letting out a scream but managing to stifle it into a frightened yelp.

Jane quickly covered the other woman's mouth when she yelped.

If the man happened to be nearby, looking for them in the dark, he might hear.

Connie nodded at Jane and Jane lay down, staring into the darkness.

She eventually fell into a fitful sleep.

Connie fell back to sleep too.

The sky was starting to glow with the promise of the sun soon rising when Connie stirred, woken by the urgent pressure in her bladder.

She sat up, peering cautiously over the downed tree.

Stiff and aching from sleeping on the ground, her muscles tormented by the run through the woods, and her shoulder still painful, she got up slowly, moving her limbs gingerly, trying to work some of the pain and stiffness out.

The woods were silent of all sound but the rustle of leaves moving in the breeze and the warble of a bird.

A louder rustle in the undergrowth not far almost made her bolt in fear.

She almost laughed when a small grey rabbit appeared, nuzzling around for something worth chewing on.

The rabbit's head poked up, ears alert, and it scampered off the moment Connie moved.

She moved off a little way before pulling down her pants and squatting to pee, trying to balance with her legs spread far enough to not splatter herself.

Jane was suddenly torn from her sleep by frantic screams.

Her first instinct was to think it was a dream, but almost instantly she remembered where she was and recognized them as Connie's screams.

She looked over the downed tree fearfully, looking for Connie.

It wasn't until she stood up and moved to see around the bushes next to the tree that she spotted Connie a short distance away.

Connie was screaming frantically, fighting against the man holding her, her legs partially tethered by the restraining pants around her ankles.

He had come up on her as she squatted, grabbing her from behind in an unbreakable grip.

267

L.V. Gaudet

"Oh my god, he found us," Jane gasped.

Jane was terrified. She wanted to bolt, to run as fast and far away as she could while the man was busy with Connie.

Instead, she ran at him, putting her head down and shoulder forward and slamming into him with her entire body like a football player tackling another, trying to knock Connie out of his grip, hoping to knock the wind out of him.

The man didn't see her coming. He was focussed entirely on the fighting wildcat he was trying to hold on to, locking his arms around her, trying to pin her arms against her body. Her screams drowned out the sound of Jane's fast approach.

He roared with surprised anger when Jane suddenly slammed into him, almost losing his grip on Connie.

He pawed out instinctively, thrown off balance, grasping at anything that would steady him.

He got his balance quickly, spinning around with Connie still in his grip, glaring at Jane, his breath coming heavier from the effort of holding the woman.

"You left," he accused Jane. "You left after all I did for you, all I did to find you. You left!"

The rage was building in him now, blind rage that would take over his conscious thought. He tried to push it down, to stay in control.

"Run Jane, run!" Connie screamed.

"But—" Jane hesitated.

"Run!" Connie cried. "Or we're both dead!"

With a last sad look at Connie, Jane turned and ran, berating herself for her cowardice, for not staying and helping the other woman.

She stopped in her tracks only paces away.

"No," Jane said firmly. "I'm not leaving you."

She turned, looked for anything she could use as a weapon, saw nothing but useless thin sticks, and started approaching them, ready to strike him with her small fists, to kick and bite, whatever it takes. But she hesitated, uncertain and afraid.

Adrenalin pumped through the man's veins as the rage built.

He squeezed Connie in his arms, making her gag and gasp for breath as he crushed her ribs tighter. He grabbed her hair,

268

yanking hard, a sharp sudden movement, making her cry out.

It was a strangled cry.

It didn't last long.

In moments, his hands were around her throat, squeezing, shaking her like a dog with a rabbit in its mouth.

She beat helplessly at his arms, clawing at his hands, digging her nails into the flesh, her mouth gaping in desperate need to suck in life-giving air, her struggles desperate.

He still squeezed and shook her after she stopped fighting.

She was limp and lifeless, her arms flapping lifelessly, her weight held up only by his grip on her neck.

Jane realized almost too late that Connie was dead.

With a sob she turned and ran as if her very life depended on it, and it did.

Before long she could hear the sound of the man charging through the woods after her, ploughing through the branches and underbrush like a bull.

The visitor didn't find the two women, and with darkness closing in he knew he'd have little chance of finding them on foot in the woods.

Even in the daylight his odds of finding them in the woods on his own would be slim.

He also knew that it would only be a matter of time before the man who kidnapped them returned and discovered them gone. He would go after them. There was no doubt about that.

The only question, really, was what would the man do with them if he caught up with them?

The visitor had no choice but to wait the night out.

Most likely the women would try to make their way to the road. It was the most sensible thing to do out here where the next house might be a few miles away.

He drove slowly up and down the road for hours with his headlights off, watching for any sign of the women just in case they did make their way to the road.

Exhaustion getting the better of him, he had to just hope they had gone to ground for some sleep and get some himself.

He parked the truck and tried to sleep, mostly just dozing in and out without getting any real rest.

Haggard from the bad sleep, he got out of the truck as the first light of dawn began to spread across the sky.

He groaned as he stretched, his aging body finding this sort of thing much harder on it than it had decades ago. He tried bending his legs and arms, arching his back, working out the aches and stiffness.

He unzipped his pants, pulled himself out, and urinated next to the truck. There was no point in being discrete with no one around.

Putting himself back together, he got back in the truck, started the engine, and began driving back and forth along the road, expanding the distance with each pass by, watching for any signs of the women.

It was his best chance of spotting them if they made it to the road and hopefully picking them up before the man caught them.

Hours later, as dusk began to fall again and much further from the old farm property than he would have ever imagined, the visitor spotted a figure standing on the side of the road some distance ahead.

The figure was too far away to make out, but he was pretty sure it was a woman.

As he drew nearer, the figure grew clearer.

It was her. Jane Doe. Cassie.

She wasn't standing beside the road, but was slowly shuffling along, following the road as if moving on autopilot, a sleepwalker moving without any sense or knowledge.

Her hair was a mess, she was dirty, and her clothes were torn.

She looked even worse than she had in the hospital.

Her face was pale, deep circles of puffy skin beneath her eyes.

And her eyes, her eyes were empty and lifeless. Void of any sign of a conscious mind inside.

He pulled up beside her and stopped the truck, looking around for any sign of the other woman or the man he knew would be pursuing them.

He got out and stopped her with a restraining hand gently holding her arm.

"Hey," he said softly. "Are you ok?"

She turned and looked at him with her empty eyes.

Standing before her she saw a strange man, perhaps 30 years older than her, maybe more, haggard and rumpled looking.

She had not seen him when he came to see her in the hospital. Not the first time when he was confronted by the orderly and had to leave, and not the second time when he returned and came into her room unchallenged.

She had no reason to recognize him.

Even if she had seen him she'd have no reason to doubt it wasn't just coincidence that he happened to come along this road just now, or to think he might have been looking for her to rescue her either.

"Come," he said gently, "let me help you. You are a long way away from anything out here. How did you get out here? So far?"

Dazed, both physically and emotionally exhausted, and beyond the ability to form any real thought, Jane let him help her into the passenger seat of the truck, leaning back gratefully into the soft comfort of the seat.

He walked around the truck, watching for any sign of the other woman to appear or the man to come out of the woods in pursuit, and got in behind the wheel.

There was no sign of either.

Putting the truck in gear, he accelerated and drove away down the road, leaving the old farm property ever further behind.

Part Eleven:
It All Comes Together

45

Jim McNelly was sitting at his desk in his shared office staring at the photos plastering the corkboard across the room.

His expression was one of a man who was angry and determined.

The dark pictures told a gruesome story, photographs of grave after grave, the decomposing faces grinning out of them with their empty eye sockets, bones stained dark from the soil and rot, every one of them staring at him accusingly.

"Why didn't you help us, Jim?" they all asked. "Why didn't you save us?"

There were more pictures in a file on his desk.

The corkboard wasn't big enough for them all.

The photos on the board represented a cross-sampling, color coded by age and their location on the board matching the approximate location of the graves in relation to each other, showing the systematic spreading out of the makeshift graveyard as bodies were added to it.

A thick folder on his desk held the reports from the post-mortem reports.

Beth was out of the office right now following up possible identifications for some of the women.

The fact that a majority of the victims were believed to be women told a story itself.

A few of the women had been identified so far, but most of them were Jane Doe's.

The older cadavers would be the hardest to identify.

The ones that have been identified offered up a frightening surprise.

Except for the few most recent ones that had been left where they were sure to be found quickly, the victims were not local.

They also were from a wide geographic spread.

Two things have been made apparent from the post mortems and studying the graves.

The first that this was a popular burial spot for multiple killers, most of which travelled great distances from where they kidnapped their victims to bury them here, the distances varying greatly. The victims came from all over the continent.

This certainly made some sense of the lack of large numbers of unsolved disappearances in the area.

This was also frightening. It suggested a network of murderers, likely serial killers, communicating and working together for the safe disposal of their victims.

The proliferation of social media sites and online networking available in almost every household and growing numbers of coffee shops across the continent offering free internet access made this all the more likely in the last few decades.

But before that?

The ages of the graves spoke another story. This was the second thing.

There were graves spanning more than a century, spanning multiple generations of killers.

McNelly felt sick.

The acid in his gut churned and boiled, coming up to eat away at his ulcer, giving him heartburn.

Just then Lawrence Hawkworth's long beaked face poked through the doorway as he peeked in before entering the office.

McNelly looked up with a mixture of surprise and reluctant pleasure.

"How do you always manage to get them to let you in here?" McNelly grunted at his visitor.

Hawkworth grinned, a look that made his ugly face even more unpleasant to look at.

"I'm just that lovable," he said jovially.

He plunked himself down in a chair before McNelly's desk without waiting for the detective to invite him to sit.

"What brings you here?" McNelly asked.

Hawkworth's grin widened, predatory and pleased.

"I have something for you," he said around his wide grin.

"And you're going to love it."

McNelly looked him over.

"If it's not beer or a cigarette, then probably not," he said.

McNelly was extra grumpy today. The doctor had told him he had to stop smoking and drinking and, "for goodness sake stop eating anything you find in a jar sitting on a bar or store counter or you won't live another ten years."

He had managed to not have a smoke all day, but was pretty certain the moment he laid eyes on Hawkworth that he'd be having a beer very soon.

"No, no, nothing like that," Hawkworth shook his head, "even better."

Hawkworth grinned at McNelly, waiting for him to start begging for it.

"Just get to the point," McNelly muttered.

That was close enough to begging for Hawkworth.

"I've found you a killer," he said.

"Hmph," McNelly grunted.

"I saw the man hanging around Jane Doe's room at the hospital in the days just before she disappeared from there." Hawkworth waited eagerly for McNelly's assent. He knew the detective would have learned about the man the day it happened, probably within the hour.

"Go on," McNelly said, interested now but not willing to show it.

"Well, he high-tailed it out of there pretty fast when Detective Underwood approached him, even though he was dressed as an orderly. Looked like he'd seen a ghost, and not a friendly one either; almost knocked down an old man when he ran past me."

"Ok," McNelly prompted.

McNelly was really curious now. Michael hadn't said anything about it and this was definitely worth sharing with the detective heading your case. He had heard about the strange man when the nurse called it in of course, buy why hadn't Michael mentioned the man's reaction to him?

"Well, it seems your man tried to follow the visitor but lost him almost immediately," Hawkworth continued.

McNelly scowled.

"Sloppy, Michael, sloppy," McNelly thought.

Michael should have known not to abandon his post to chase down someone just because they may have recognized him. He should have stayed put and called in a description. Better to send more people to the area and increase their chances of laying their hands on the visitor to question him than one lone cop risking blowing his cover and leaving the package he's watching unguarded.

McNelly had his own ideas why Michael was in such a hurry to follow the visitor, but he wasn't ready to share them with anyone yet, let alone with a reporter, even one who is a friend and confidant.

Some secrets are best kept that way, until the right time to share them at least.

"So, he lost the man," McNelly said, prompting the reporter to continue. He knew the man had more to say, otherwise he wouldn't be here.

Hawkworth's grin got bigger, even though it seemed impossible to be any bigger than it already was. His eyes were triumphant.

"Well," Hawkworth finally gave up the gem he was bursting to tell, "I didn't lose him."

"You followed him?" McNelly asked despite having just been told that.

"Dumb, Hawkworth, dumb," McNelly said reproachfully. "If this man is the perp that would make him a very dangerous man and you a fool for following him."

"Ah," Hawkworth shrugged it off. He was by no means a brave man, but he did have a propensity for acting without thinking when his nose got the scent of a good story.

"So, was he driving? Walking? How did the man leave the hospital?" McNelly asked.

"He drove, but I was ahead of him. I was outside waiting for him. He got tied up in the parking garage."

Hawkworth winked.

"I think he spotted me and thought I was a cop or something. I'm pretty sure he waited until he thought I gave up and left."

L.V. Gaudet

He said this mainly for McNelly's benefit, knowing it would raise the detective's hackles.

It did.

"So, you followed the man, waited for him, and then took the risk of following him again," McNelly growled. "Are you just trying to do my job for me? Or are you trying to get yourself killed?"

McNelly sighed in frustration.

"Ok, so what was he driving?" he asked. He paused and thought, then partially answered for himself.

"I guess there's no point in asking you what color the car was," McNelly said. He knew the other man is colorblind. "Do you at least know what make it was?"

"Make?" Hawkworth asked confused. Then he realized. The detective wanted to know what kind of car it was.

He shrugged. "I didn't really pay attention to that."

"Some days," McNelly muttered, "I swear you are an idiot as well as an idiot savant."

He knew the reporter had an incredibly smart mind, that he could pick up on the most unimaginable things without even being aware, but he also was prone to attacks of tunnel vision, blocking out everything in the world around outside of that very narrow focus his mind was on.

"He's driving a pickup truck, older model," Hawkworth said. Even as he said the words, it clicked for him that the truck didn't match the description of a car that witnesses had seen in the area of some of the kidnappings and body dump locations.

"He changed vehicles after the hospital, probably using stolen cars, but looks like his own is the truck," he added quickly. "Two colors top and bottom," Hawkworth added quickly, "lighter and darker."

His face became serious.

"But never mind that," he went on. "I followed him. I don't think he knew he was being followed when he switched cars, but he was definitely taking precautions. I almost lost him a number of times.

He went to a place outside the city, somewhat secluded. It's the perfect spot to take victims."

276

It was more than the perfect spot. It was secluded, down a narrow dirt road that even a 4X4 truck wouldn't be able to drive over after a rain without getting stuck, surrounded by trees that made it invisible until you drove right up to it, and it lay just before where the road ended at an old single lane bridge that had washed out years before and was never repaired.

"It takes more than a location to decide someone is a serial killer," McNelly reminded him.

He wouldn't have used the term serial killer with anyone else. With Hawkworth there was no point in mincing words.

"I did some research afterwards," Hawkworth said. "I ran the truck's licence plate."

McNelly wanted to ask how the reporter managed that, but it was pointless. He probably wouldn't get an answer.

"The man's name is Jason Timothy McAllister," Hawkworth continued. "He grew up around here on an old farm property that's been in his family for generations. He still owns the deed to it."

"So, this farm property," McNelly asked, "that's where you followed him to?"

Hawkworth shook his head.

"No. He doesn't even own the property he's staying at. Looks like he's found another abandoned spot and is squatting there, probably lying low. Smart though, if anyone is looking they won't find him sleeping where the victims are, if he is taking them to the old McAllister farm. It doesn't look like he's been there at his camp very long. At least, if he has, he's the tidiest squatter I've ever seen.

There's almost no trace the man has been there."

Lawrence thought.

"You know, I'm not even sure he's squatting there. He could have just been checking the place out. But he was there for an awfully long time just to be checking a place out, seemed pretty cozy and comfortable there."

"Anything else you learned?" McNelly asked.

"His father, McAllister senior, was investigated for some murders way back. Nothing was ever found and he was never convicted of anything. He disappeared after that, the rest of the

277

family with him, Jason included.

It was only after Jason was an adult that he was seen around the area again.

A few people suspected it was the young McAllister boy, but they weren't sure.

I found his picture in a few old news clippings. Nothing about him really, he was just a face in the crowd. The face is a lot younger, at least by twenty years, but it's the same man from the hospital."

McNelly was really itching for that beer now.

"Why don't we call it a day and go down to Peabody's Pub?" McNelly said, groaning as he pulled his great size out of his chair.

Hawkworth got up, eying McNelly, undecided.

He made a decision.

"I found something else," Hawkworth said.

"Tell me on the way," McNelly grunted.

46

The man stumbled through the woods. The trees seemed to sway and swoon around him.

He was beyond exhausted.

The events of yesterday, the night spent searching the woods and surrounding fields for the missing women, and the early morning pursuit when he found them that lasted all day and which he didn't remember parts of, had all conspired to drain him physically and emotionally of all strength.

Dusk was beginning to close in again. It would be too dark to see and he didn't have the strength for another all-night search.

He needed sleep, desperately.

The trees thinned ahead, the brighter sky above glaring through the sparse branches.

He stumbled on towards the light, breaking through the edge of the woods just as the visitor's truck disappeared behind the trees as it moved along with a bend far in the distance.

Before him, an expanse of long grass stretched into the distance to either side, broken by the long ribbon of road that vanished into the distance with it.

He looked left and right. There was no sign of a living soul.

It was hopeless. He had to give up the search. He had lost her again.

"I'll find you again," he said.

His heart hung heavy in his chest, seeming barely able to move to pump the blood. His heavy lungs sighed dispiritedly.

Shoulders slumped in more than just exhaustion; he turned around to make the difficult way back through the woods.

It would have been easier to follow the road back, but it would have taken longer. He also had to find the body of the other woman he left in the woods.

The problem was that he wasn't sure where he left her.

He remembered the pure joy and elation when he spotted the woman through the branches, squatting to pee.

He remembered the rage coming over him, trying to push it

279

back, and the darkness winning as it washed across him, blinding him.

He remembered vague moments of clarity as he strangled and shook her, wanting to stop, wanting to not hurt her, worried that Cassie and Kathy would be very upset with him.

He wasn't planning on killing the woman. He didn't know what he was going to do with her, and obviously couldn't just let her go, but he hadn't planned on killing her. Not yet anyway, although he knew that was his only choice.

He remembered seeing her, his sister, the look of horror and anger as she stared at him with the other woman's throat in his hands, and the terror as she turned and ran from him.

He remembered parts of the chase through the woods, others were void of any memory, and long stretches were filled with mindless frantic searching.

He had to find the body. He had to dispose of it.

He didn't know where.

The place he buried the others was compromised. It had been found and the bodies were being exhumed. He couldn't go back there. He wasn't worried about being caught for those. There was nothing there to tie him to them. He was too careful for that.

He still had the body of the nurse in the trunk of the car to dispose of too.

He roamed the woods, zigzagging back and forth, thankful the sky was clear and the full moon gave him some light to see by as the darkness settled in.

It was full dark, the moon high in the sky, by the time he finally found the woman's body where he'd dropped her like a discarded rag doll.

He struggled, trying to pick her up, almost too exhausted to manage the feat.

Slinging the body over his shoulder in a fireman's carry, he trudged off slowly through the woods, heading for the farmhouse.

The moon had moved well past its zenith when the man came stumbling out of the woods with his gruesome prize slung over his shoulder.

Too exhausted to do anything else, he shuffled across the yard to the barn, dropping the body unceremoniously in a dark corner.

He sagged against the wall. The rotting wood groaned with the weight.

Forcing himself to keep going, he kicked some loose straw over the body, dust and mould from the grass dancing up into the air in a small cloud.

He rummaged around for some other items to toss over the body.

He didn't want any animals dragging it off, trying to eat the remains before sunrise.

Satisfied, he stumbled off to the house, barely making it through the door.

He collapsed into the chair in the small living room with a deep exhalation of air.

His head tilted and he nodded off to sleep almost instantly, his snores coming in ragged coughing gasps.

Sunlight poured through the open door of the old farmhouse, spilling across the floor to spread its warmth like a blanket over the man sleeping in the chair.

He woke up slowly, groggy, blinking from the bright light.

He got up unsteadily to his feet, his face weary with exhaustion.

He started stumbling to the kitchen, wanting coffee.

He stopped in his tracks, turned and stared at the open door in horror.

His pulse quickened and his heart sank as a hollow emptiness filled his soul.

He rushed from the room, going quickly from room to room in the small farmhouse.

He found her in the second bedroom.

"Kathy," he gasped.

His heart grew with the relief when he saw Kathy curled up on one of the narrow twin beds.

She must have lay down there to rest, fully clothed and on top of the blankets, and fallen asleep.

He approached the beds and snatched the cover off the other bed, gently draping it over the sleeping woman.

Her eyes fluttered open and she looked up at him, sleepy but expressionless.

"See," he said gently when he realized she had woken up," I told you I wouldn't put you back down in the root cellar."

He left the room, thinking that she would go back to sleep, and went to the kitchen to make coffee.

With the coffee brewing and Kathy safely in the other room, his mood perked up. He started bustling about the kitchen.

He was going to make her a great breakfast for when she woke up.

He had barely started when Kathy came into the kitchen, the tiny kitchen seeming filled to capacity with the two of them.

He turned, surprised, and recovered quickly.

"I'm making breakfast," he smiled at her, proud like a little boy showing his mother how he can do it all by himself.

He waved her out of the room.

"Go," he said, "sit while I make you breakfast."

Kathy shook her head.

"Let me help," she said softly, brushing against him by necessity as she squeezed past him to start cracking the eggs sitting on the counter.

His heart soared with joy while they worked together to make breakfast. It was a blissfully happy domestic moment, the sort he had always dreamed of having, even as a kid.

His brow furrowed and he frowned, the moment ruined by the sudden uprising of a memory from his childhood.

His mother was cooking breakfast in the kitchen while his sister, a pretty toddler in a booster seat, drew unrecognizable pictures at the table, the warm sunlight filling the kitchen.

It was a different kitchen, larger and brighter.

His father walking in, saying he had to go, that there was an emergency at the office he had to deal with. No, it couldn't wait.

The awkward goodbye and the look of guilt that flashed across his father's face as he lowered it heading out the door, thinking no one noticed the look.

His mother cracked the eggs angrily and scrambled them as

if she were trying to kill the very birds that gave birth to them.

His mother slapped filled breakfast plates on the table, two of them, one for each child, before she swept out of the room trying to hide the devastation on her face.

His sister was oblivious, but he saw.

It was strange having this memory of a mother and father he did not remember having. He wondered where it came from.

Then the scene changed suddenly and it wasn't his baby sister who was just learning to talk sitting in her booster chair chewing on crayons as much as she scribbled pictures with them.

It wasn't his mother or father from the scene before either.

His sister was older, but still very small and young, a pre-schooler. She didn't draw as she sat at the tiny table in a tiny kitchen, this kitchen, but sat there quietly, sullenly.

There was no mother in this memory.

A different man stood in the kitchen, recklessly scrambling eggs, hashed potatoes stinking up the kitchen as they burned in the pan, and he felt dread at the idea of entering that little kitchen. This was the father he remembered.

He pushed the memory away, not wanting it, not wanting to remember, especially right now.

But it was too late and the happy domestic moment was ruined for him and he continued with the task of making breakfast together with Kathy mechanically.

Kathy woke to the soft touch of the bed cover landing on her.

She opened her eyes; almost afraid of what she might see, carefully keeping her expression blank.

She looked up at the man standing over her.

So, he had come back at last.

She felt relieved more than anything.

After he ran off into the woods after Jane and Connie, she didn't know what to do.

It was her chance to escape, to run away and get far away and never come back.

But where would she go? She didn't want to go back to Ronnie. And she didn't want to go back and stay with her mother and deal with the woman clucking over her with her I told you so's and always watchful looks.

So she sat in the living room and waited.

And waited.

At last she ventured out. The sky was dark by then and deep shadows lurked everywhere.

She'd shivered more at the unknown lurking in those shadows than at the cool night air.

Some of the noises out there were identifiable, the wind, an owl. But some she couldn't identify and they made her nervous. Distant barking yips that she wasn't sure was a dog sent a shiver down her spine.

"Do they have wolves around here or coyotes?" she wondered. The idea of meeting either one in the dark was frightening.

Then she realized he didn't lock the door. She wasn't locked inside the little house. She really could just leave.

The car was parked in the yard.

She went to it and tried the driver's door.

It wasn't locked.

She searched the car but couldn't find the keys.

She had to hold her breath. The smell in the car was terrible. It was sweet and kind of fruity smelling and bad, like a bad perfume mixed with turpentine and something rotting.

Kathy went back into the house and searched for keys.

There were none to be found.

She was trapped after all. Where would she go? How would she get there?

She also felt so confused.

The man had begged and pleaded and finally broke down and cried while she had him locked in the root cellar, covering her ears and trying not to hear him.

When she finally let him out, he scared the crap out of her.

He climbed out looking shaky and helpless, but then suddenly lunged at her.

Except instead of grabbing her and throwing her down the open hole in the floor as she'd expected, he wrapped his arms around her and hugged her fiercely, then seemed to realize what he was doing and gently released her.

He didn't lock her in the root cellar again.

He left to find Jane and Connie, leaving her standing there filled with confusion, fear, and shock.

After giving up the search for keys, she sat and waited again. She waited for hours.

The day brightened and slipped by and she made herself something to eat. She wasn't hungry and really didn't feel like eating, but she made herself eat it anyway.

She had to eat something.

She waited as night began to fall again and eventually went to lie down on top of one of the narrow beds in the second bedroom, wondering who might have slept in these twin beds in years past.

She was afraid.

She was all alone and no one knew where she was.

What if he never came back?

The next thing she knew, she had been woken up by the gentle touch and soft breeze of the blanket settling on her and he was back.

Tentatively, she pulled the blanket off after he left the room and followed him down the hall.

She found him in the kitchen cooking.

She didn't want to be alone. She had just spent hours alone and afraid.

So when he tried to shoo her away she decided she would stay.

She pushed past him, putting him between her and the door, brushing against him to fit in the tight space as she did.

You couldn't move in the tiny kitchen without touching the other person to get past them.

She found her pulse quickening with anxiety and something more.

Her skin tingled at his touch when his hand accidentally brushed hers as they worked.

She was torn with confusion.

He seemed so happy, so gentle. But this was the man who had kidnapped her, who had murdered other women as she wept

285

and trembled in terror in her prison below.

Then he stiffened and his face changed.

Apprehension filled her. Was he about to become the killer again?

He seemed lost in thought, something unpleasant was going on there, and then he became distant and mechanical, ignoring her as if she weren't even there as they worked together to finish making breakfast.

Her heart ached.

She felt alone suddenly. As alone as she had been sitting there for all those hours waiting and not knowing if he would come back, if she would be left here to walk the miles of road in search of other people and help.

They ate in silence.

When he finished he got up quickly.

"I have things to do," he said curtly, leaving the room.

Kathy wondered if she had done something wrong.

He headed out to do his grim task alone.

He had two bodies to dispose of and no idea where he would do it.

47

Jim McNelly was really starting to hate his office at the moment.

He felt closed in, barricaded, though he couldn't say if he was barricaded in or the world was barricaded out.

It didn't really make much difference.

He itched to get out, to hit the streets, chase down leads and close this case.

This case was having a terrible effect on him.

Every file, every picture; each and every report, communication, and interview was a glaring accusation against him.

"Why didn't you save us?" the pictures said, the corpses glaring with their empty eye sockets.

"Why didn't you already know this?" every interview demanded.

"You let them down Jim," the reports accused, "just like you let your wife down."

He couldn't help it. Even before his wife he took every victim's pain personally, felt like a failure for not preventing them from suffering from their anguish before it could even happen. Since his wife he felt that all the more acutely.

He had let her down. He wasn't there.

There was nothing he could have done anyway. He had heard that said to him so many times. People die, it just happens. It was nobody's fault. It wasn't his fault. He couldn't have stopped it anyway.

That didn't stop the guilt then and it doesn't stop the guilt that he feels even more acutely now over every victim.

And there were so many, so very many victims here.

After leaving the pub McNelly talked to the people Hawkworth had talked to.

He had to interview them himself.

He looked up the newspaper clippings.

He visited the same places.

He went to the property Hawkworth had followed the hospital visitor to and sat there watching for a very long time.

The man never showed up. Nor was there any sign he had ever been there. It was as if Hawkworth had made it all up, but McNelly knew better. The reporter didn't make things up. He might stretch the truth a little in his stories, but never blatantly made it up.

He researched the names the reporter had given him, though it wasn't easy since things weren't widely recorded in the time frame he needed to research.

At last McNelly had retreated to his office to pour over all the notes and files, reports and communications.

More responses had come in from other precincts across the continent, linking bodies in the graves to missing men, women, and children from Canada, the United States, and Mexico.

The locality spread was incredible. It seemed impossible.

The range of ages of the graves themselves was even more staggering.

Beth was busy searching the web for any social network sites that could be the hub for serial killers to communicate.

That part wasn't entirely farfetched.

Pedophiles used the same system for sharing photos, video, and victims across the world, so why not serial killers too?

That thought struck McNelly hard, a blow to the ulcer burning in his gut.

"We need to spread our net wider," he grumbled, realizing this killing network might not be confined to the one continent.

This was one of the terrible things about the internet. Things that once were limited to a small area can now be committed on a global scale; bad things.

He mulled everything in his head, moving bits around, rearranging evidence.

He was sure now that McAllister senior was guilty of committing dozens if not more body disposals.

Was he the body guy for other killers? There were too many and their disappearances too wide spread for one man alone to be the killer. Could he have been the go-to guy for getting rid of human remains, thereby keeping the killers safe from prosecution for a murder that cannot be prosecuted without a body?

Or was he just one of many killers sharing the graveyard?

He suspected McAllister held the key somehow, that he was a caretaker of sorts for the improvised graveyard.

More telling was that there seemed to be gaps in the burials. There seemed to be no bodies buried in those blocks of time when no McAllisters were living at the farm, although forensics was a sketchy business and mistakes can be made.

He was also convinced that McAllister Senior was likely directly responsible for a number of the bodies residing there, at least when he was young enough. If the man was even still alive somewhere today he was probably in his eighties now. It only made sense if you were in the business of disposing of other killers' corpses to have your own too.

But he seemed smart about it, taking victims from somewhere else to dispose far from where they were kidnapped and killed.

He wasn't so sure of McAllister Junior.

Jason T. McAllister had vanished along with the rest of the family when Senior had apparently gotten cold feet and took off with his family in tow.

There are little records he could find to indicate that McAllister junior had returned, but that was indeed his face captured in the newspaper photos.

Apparently he was a very private man, just like his father.

The deed to the old family farm had transferred to him as a young man with no notation as to why.

McNelly had been able to get some anecdotal stories that suggested the young man had lived at the farm for some years, but could find nothing to suggest what he did for a living or even if he had ever married.

One old woman said she thought the man had children, but her husband said it was hogwash.

"Hogwash. What a word," he mused. He hadn't heard that term used in decades.

Jason McAllister was never known to have married or even dated. From the witnesses' stories, he was something of a reclusive man who tended to welcome visitors with hostility and open threats just like his father before him. Everyone in the area

289

knew to give both the McAllister men and their property a wide berth. And then nobody remembered seeing the man around, though none could say when they stopped seeing him.

McAllister Junior seemed to have just vanished without anyone even noticing if or when he did.

He still held the deed to the old abandoned farm.

Apparently Jason T. McAllister has now returned. Surveillance video from the hospital confirmed it.

The man in the video was older, by about twenty years or so which fit with the timeline, but he had no doubt it was the same man from the old newspaper photos.

Now what business would he have at the hospital? And around Jane Doe's room?

McNelly thought he knew. He felt it in his gut. This man was the new caretaker of the killer's club graveyard, taking over the family business from McAllister Senior and probably guilty of murdering a number of the bodies there.

He was also sure he was the one who kidnapped Jane Doe and left her for dead.

But the recent killings didn't add up, starting with Jane Doe.

The disposal was sloppy.

Maybe not sloppy in the sense of the word, but it seemed to be done with the intent of getting caught.

And it started before the makeshift graveyard was found, so that wasn't the cause.

Besides, the dumping spots seemed premeditated, planned. It was as if he was trying to get more bang for his buck when the bodies are found.

Even more curious was the one detail in the autopsies of the women found strategically dumped.

Traces of foreign matter had been found on the bodies, suggesting that they had been wrapped and buried before they were dumped. There was no indication they were buried alive.

The perp was suddenly burying them and then changing his mind and digging them up, making sure the bodies would be found and escalating the impact it would have in instilling fear and making headlines.

But why would he go to the effort of burying them and then

dig them up again to dump them in public locations?

This made it seem unlikely that these were his own victims, not unless he wanted to get caught. He was definitely trying to get somebody caught and charged with murder.

This change in the way he operates just didn't make sense.

McNelly just couldn't wrap his head around the why of it.

Maybe the man was tired of being in the disposal business.

Maybe it was a grudge against one or more clients.

Either way, he had to find Jason McAllister, and fast.

And then there was the other thing. Hawkworth's final revelation sat like a cold stone in his gut.

McNelly looked at the clock.

Neither Beth nor Michael has returned yet.

Hell, he hasn't seen Michael in a few days. He was tracking down anything he could find on that missing nurse, the one who was playing mother hen to their Jane Doe until the moment she disappeared.

Still, it was unusual for the man to not at least check in or drop by at the office at some point.

He knew the Jane Doe case has hit Michael hard. He was pretty sure the younger man had developed feelings for the victim, though he wasn't so sure they were romantic feelings.

"They'd better not be," he thought. "That would be a conflict of interest."

It was time to go visit the old McAllister farm, but McNelly knew better than to go alone.

He picked up the phone and dialled.

It rang again and again and finally went to voicemail.

"Michael," McNelly barked into the phone, "where are you? I have some new leads on the Jane Doe and graveyard cases. Well, actually they're the same case. I have to go visit a location and I want you there."

He gave directions and hung up the phone.

"Damn," he muttered. "Where the hell is he?"

McNelly dialled the phone again, an internal number this time. He needed to round up some backup.

Most likely the McAllister farm was abandoned, but there was always the chance the perpetrator might be there.

48

The man came out of the woods dirty, exhausted, and sweaty, a shovel slung over his shoulder.

He had just finished burying Connie's body.

He didn't like it, burying it so close. It was too risky.

But he had no choice.

The burial spot was compromised and everything was falling apart.

And more troubling, Jane was still missing after running away. He was worried. Was she lost in the woods? Hurt?

If she went in the wrong direction she would just travel deeper into the woods, further from humanity, and she would likely never be found.

If she made it to the road there was the chance one of the rare cars that pass this way might see her and pick her up. More than likely he would find her first.

"I will find her again," he said with a mixture of bitterness, determination and desperation. He couldn't help the uncertainty nagging at him. What if he didn't find her before someone else did? She could identify him. If she made it out of the woods, if she talked to the authorities, his identity would be compromised.

But before he could look for Jane again he had to dispose of Connie and the nurse and get out of there.

He would come back later and move them someplace safer when it was safe to do so.

He had already scoured the car and house of anything that might lead to him.

Fingerprints were his main concern.

The car was stolen from another district and wearing plates from another vehicle that he had conveniently spotted poking out of a box just inside a garage as he passed, one of many such licence plates left unused after a car has been sold and the plates no longer needed. They weren't even reported lost. The stickers were easier, peeled off another car and glued onto the plates.

He would abandon the car someplace where it likely wouldn't be found for years, setting it ablaze for good measure.

But what would he do with Kathy?

He didn't know.

He couldn't leave her behind, and can't take her with him. And he couldn't bring himself to harm her.

He had to stop thinking about that right now. He had work to do still. The nurse still had to be disposed of.

He dropped the shovel by the back of the car and took off the rough work gloves. They would hold nothing but sweat on the course surface inside. They would be burned later with the shovel and the car.

He wiped the sweat that was dripping down his brow and ran his fingers through his hair. A stretch to work some of the aches out of his muscles was only a temporary relief.

He looked up to see a truck approaching the rough trail to the old farmhouse.

Cupping a hand over his brow to block out the sun, he strained to see against the glare of the sun as the truck drew steadily closer.

It was the same truck from the other day.

The visitor had returned.

He glanced quickly at the farmhouse with a worried look.

What would Kathy do?

Running to the house would only bring attention to it, maybe make the visitor suspicious.

He stood there and waited as the truck approached.

It seemed to take forever.

At last the truck pulled up and the driver put it into park, killing the engine.

The visitor got out. It was the same man as before.

He strode towards the visitor, his stance aggressive.

"I kicked you off my property already," he said sternly. "What business do you have here?"

His jaw was set and his hands clenched into hard fists.

"I own the property," the visitor said flatly, levelling his gaze at the younger man and watching carefully for his reaction.

He couldn't hide his shock.

"H—How?" he stammered. "This is my property, how can you think you own it?"

293

"I hold the deed," the visitor said, a faint smirk tilting the corners of his mouth.

He was stunned.

This property had been in his family for generations, the deed passed down every generation. His own father had told him that.

He didn't remember the conversation any more than he remembered most of his childhood that hid behind a dark shroud inside his mind, revealing small bits and snatches.

He just knew it.

But now, suddenly, he wasn't so sure.

Did his father really tell him this? Without the memory to back him up, he couldn't be sure.

The visitor took a step forward, closing the gap between them a little.

"This farm has been in my family for generations," the visitor said.

He looked more closely at the visitor, the lines around his eyes and mouth, the skin worn from age and long hours spent working outside.

The sense of familiarity, the certainty that he had seen this man before, came on strong.

"I know you don't I?" he asked.

"Yes, you do, David" the visitor said.

He almost staggered backwards with shock.

He stared at the visitor, blinked.

He had to get his wits about him.

"Shit," he thought, "he is a fed. He has to be."

He started trembling, the quick shiver of someone in shock that would soon turn to a full-fledged shuddering case of the shakes.

He tried hard to control himself. His face flushed red with the effort and turmoil of emotions. He broke out in a sweat. His face hardened and his jaw clenched. He ground his teeth, trying to hold back the panic and the anger that was beginning to flare inside.

This was the wrong time to get angry.

"How do you know me?" David asked, the anger in his voice

barely controlled. "How do you know my name?"

"Oh, I've known you for a long time, David McAllister," the visitor said.

"In fact, I've known you since you were a boy." The visitor looked at him curiously, as if measuring just what kind of a man this boy had grown up to be.

The visitor would have been a young man in his twenties when David was a child.

"I don't remember you," David said. "Were you a neighbor? You weren't a teacher."

David hadn't had teachers that he could remember. He was home schooled of sorts.

He didn't remember learning to read, or print, or do simple math. But he had known, and taught himself more, and taught his younger sister what he knew too. He had been smart enough to mostly get by, lying about his lack of education when needed.

"You didn't have any neighbors," the visitor said, amused. "You know that."

David didn't know what to say, what to think.

He stared at the visitor, trying to place him.

Images started to take shape. The visitor's face transformed in his mind, becoming younger.

He knew this man.

He had known him for most of his childhood.

David hadn't seen this man in years, not since he ran away in his early teens.

"Father," his mind reeled, the name ringing hollow.

And suddenly a strange and unpleasant feeling washed over him, the same as it did in the car when he almost kidnapped the little girl.

David broke out in a cold sweat, felt woozy, and thought the world was about to spin wildly out of control.

His mind turned inward and the smoky shroud covering his childhood thinned just a little.

"I'm your father," the visitor said, his words muffled and echoing across a million miles, barely audible in the vast distance, carried to him on the wispy veils of blocked memories and mind shrouding fog.

295

David's proximity to the older man and their conversation stirred long repressed memories, causing them to come suddenly to the surface.

These were memories from even earlier than any of the other memories he has struggled with.

Memories from when he was a young boy.

It was a good day. It was a bad day.

David was a little boy again, younger even than in most of his other memories.

His little sister was so little sitting in a baby seat in the car, while he sat so big and proud in his big boy booster seat beside her.

They were driving, singing, all four of them.

His little sister Cassie, who hadn't stopped talking since she learned how, drowned the rest of them out with her pixie voice as she tried to follow along to a song on the radio that she didn't know the words to.

Dad smiled back at them in the car's rear-view mirror, giving him their special wink, before turning his attention back to the road ahead, keeping a steady grip on the steering wheel.

Mom was happier than she had been for weeks.

It was going to be the best day ever.

At last they arrived at the zoo. He skipped around the car while Dad got out the stroller for his sister and Mom strapped her safely into it.

David loved all the animals, ones that looked like strange cows with oddly turned horns, and deer that didn't really look like deer.

He stopped and peered hard into the lion's cage as though the beast would suddenly appear even though Dad said the cage was empty.

Dad said the girl lion had died of old age, and then the boy died too.

"Why?" David asked.

Dad didn't know, but Mom said it was probably from loneliness and a broken heart after the girl died.

Dad gave her one of 'those' looks.

His favourite animal was always the monkeys.

His little sister liked the bright pink birds the best.

It was the best day ever, just as he'd thought; the four of them at the zoo together.

Mom and Dad didn't fight even once, and they had been fighting a lot lately. But the tension was still there. The sadness at the corners of Mom's eyes that even her best attempt at smiling could not hide. Dad was distracted as ever, there but not really there, as if he'd rather be someplace else.

But they were together, and Mom wasn't yelling or crying, and Dad wasn't angry or yelling. Everything was going to be ok now.

They had hot dogs and ice cream, and sugar coated donuts that left a fistful of sugar behind in the bag; a little boy or girl's size fistful anyway.

And at the end of the day, tired and happy, they grabbed bags of cotton candy before heading for the car.

Only Mom got in the driver's seat and Dad didn't get into the car with them.

Why wasn't Dad coming?

He would come later, Mom had said.

David watched his dad through the window as Mom drove away.

He saw a woman driving a car that was approaching, going the opposite way. The car passed them, going to the zoo entrance as they left.

He remembered wondering why she had no kids with her. You took kids with you to go to the zoo, unless you were really old.

The car stopped and his dad got into the car.

Where is Dad going with that woman, Mom?

She didn't answer. At least David didn't think she did.

Her face reflected back at him in the mirror, her jaw clenched and her face stony. She didn't look at him. She only stared straight ahead as if she wanted to look at nothing.

At first he thought she was angry about something, but her eyes were wet.

She was trying hard not to cry again.

Cassie fell asleep first in the back of the car as they drove.

297

David remembered his own eyes getting heavy as he watched the sadness etched into his mother's face and in her eyes reflected back at him in the car's rear-view mirror while she drove home.

The next thing he remembered was his mother's startled cry.

Her car door was open and a strange man was coming in through her door.

Was the man going to drive now?

Why?

David remembered the fear on his mother's face, her hitting the strange man with her fists, scratching at him with her painted nails, kicking at him as he shoved her across the seat, an animal sound coming from her, frightened and desperate. That scared him more than anything ever had in his life, before or after.

The man showed her something and she suddenly grew quiet and still.

David had wanted to look over the seat to see what it was.

He remembered the desperation in his mother's eyes when they met his briefly before she quickly turned her eyes away.

Somehow he just knew what she wanted.

She wanted him to be quiet, for the man to not notice him and his sister in the back seat.

He remembered how his tummy suddenly felt sick from his own fear. He knew then that something was wrong. This was a very bad man.

David unbuckled his seat belt as quietly as he could and silently slid to the floor before the back seat.

Reaching up, he unbuckled his little sister.

Cassie looked down at him with a smile, suddenly awake.

He put one finger to his lips in a "Shh" sign, motioning Cassie to come down as he helped ease her from her seat.

Together they huddled on the floor, Cassie looking up at him with big trusting eyes, silent as if somehow sensing the seriousness of the situation.

They fell asleep after a while, huddled on the floor, first his sister and then himself, waking up to the car door slamming and their mother's cries.

Cassie's face scrunched up about to cry and he hugged her,

whispering in her ear to stay quiet and not cry.

The man dragged his mommy roughly from the car, dragging her across a dirt yard to an old barn.

Cassie stared at him with wide frightened eyes.

They heard her cries, her begging, screams, and then silence. The two children clung to each other, staring and listening.

A long time passed.

The man came to the car, got in, and started the car.

"Mama?" Cassie asked.

David froze in fear, mouthing the word, "No." But it was already too late.

The man froze and just sat there a moment.

He turned around; hitching himself up to look over the back of the seat, finding the two small children huddled there.

The man turned off the car and got out, walking away, pacing back and forth.

"SHIT!" he yelled.

He came back and looked at the kids through the window.

They stared back, wide eyed.

He turned away again, angry, muttering to himself.

He didn't want kids. What would he do with kids? Witnesses. Can't let them go, can't keep them.

David stared back at the man who ranted and walked back and forth, clutching his little sister's tiny hand.

Other memories followed, a crashing tidal wave that made David stagger, almost knocking him off his feet.

Years' worth of memories, all muddy and spotted with empty spots of unknown. They were partial memories, missing key pieces, but revealing enough. More than he wanted to know.

David turned to the older man, his face twisted in turmoil.

"Father," he whispered, filled with a great hollowness inside that seemed so vast it would swallow him up and the entire world with him.

He couldn't believe he had not recognized the man the moment he saw him that first time.

"How did I not recognize him?" he thought. "I guess it's true what they say about the mind blocking out bad memories."

He turned to the man, face ashen.

"You are not my father. You never were," David hissed.

It was a revelation that hit him hard. He was still in shock to discover this man was his father, and to have so many memories of those years growing up at the farmhouse come suddenly crashing back.

But it hit even harder to realize this man wasn't his father at all.

What happened to his real father?

"My mother," David said softly, "you never told me what happened to her did you? Where she went?"

He wasn't expecting an answer.

No answer was necessary.

This man had kidnapped his mother, just one of many victims, and killed her.

Only he had found a surprise in the back seat of her car, two small children.

"You couldn't let us go because I might have talked. It was all my fault you kept us."

"I never wanted you. I never wanted kids," Jason McAllister said.

"But you couldn't bring yourself to kill us either. So you kept us."

He looked up at the older man.

"But why keep her too? Why my little sister? She was too little to tell. Why did you keep her too?" David suddenly needed to know why this man kept his little sister too. His treatment of them made it plain he'd hated and resented them. Even little kids could see that. Maybe they could see it more clearly even than an adult could, despite their desperate need to please and be accepted by that very adult who despised them so much.

"I kept her for you," McAllister said softly.

"When you were here the other day," David asked, "you heard them didn't you? You heard the women."

McAllister nodded.

"When you left," David continued, "you didn't really leave, did you? You saw them."

He was starting to get angry again. But, he was also battling the fear he had of this man all those years he lived with him as a child. The man had terrified him. And after his sister's accident, after it was just him and this man alone and he had finally ran away, he lived on the streets, always watching over his shoulder and suspicious of every car that passed by, living in abject terror this man would find him.

"Did you let them out? Take them? Did you kill them?" David had to know.

McAllister shook his head.

"No," he said, "that was your own carelessness that let them escape."

"You saw, but you didn't try to stop them. Why?" David demanded, controlling his voice with difficulty, trying not to let either the fear or the anger crack his voice into something unintelligible. "You know the rules. You taught them to me."

McAllister shrugged it off.

"I wasn't concerned with the other one," he said simply. "Whatever happened to her was of no consequence to me."

David glared at him, his eyes hardening, and the anger beginning to win out against the fear.

"If I stopped them they would have wanted help," McAllister continued. "They would have begged me to go back and drag the other one out of the house, to rescue them all."

He paused, letting it sink in.

"I was only interested in her," McAllister said. "If the others saw me, I would have had to kill them. Now, how would that have looked to her?"

"I could always come back for the others," McAllister finished.

David blanched. His first thought was that it was as if the man actually cared what impression others might have, others who would never know.

But he quickly realized the truth. McAllister was only concerned about what Cassie would think, how she would feel about it. He would spare her watching him kill the others, spare her having to know he had done it.

Better to let her think the woods did it.

Or worse, to think that he, David, did it.

301

David looked at McAllister, his eyes full of questions he wouldn't ask.

There was one question he would ask, however.

"You took Cassie, didn't you?" David asked, "After she escaped."

"Yes," McAllister said.

David had to think this over, rolling the possibilities in his head.

If McAllister didn't believe she was his sister, he would have killed her already. If he did believe she was-.

He just didn't know what the other man would do. Would he have killed her? She's not a little girl anymore, and she hasn't seen either of them in many years. She may not even remember either of them.

Cassie might go to the police.

His face set and his expression grew stern as he pushed the fear further down, letting some of the anger come to the front to give him courage.

"Where is she? Where is Cassie?" David demanded softly, the threat clear in his voice.

"What have you done with her?" His tone grew a little more forceful. "Did you kill her? Is she alive? What have you done with my sister?"

McAllister just looked back at him with a knowing smirk, too confident, too calm.

"WHERE IS SHE?!" David screamed.

49

"Don't worry," McAllister said at last. "Cassie's fine. She's safe."

David was breathing heavily, his fists clenched in tight knots and his muscles taught with emotion.

"Where ... is ... she?" David demanded slowly in a low and dangerous voice.

"Give her to me!" he ordered.

McAllister shook his head.

"She's someplace safe where you won't find her," he said evenly.

David was taken aback.

"P-protect her? From me?!" he sputtered.

"You're the one who kidnapped us," David raged. "You're the one who murdered our mother, all those women!"

He was shaking with barely controlled fury, spittle flying with the force of his words.

"You're the one who destroyed our childhood! You're the one who turned me into this-this murderous monster!"

He was breathing heavy, panting with rage.

"You're the one who hurt her!"

McAllister shook his head, just a little bit sadly, mostly to say "no".

"You don't remember, do you?" McAllister asked.

David glared at him.

"I remember all right, I remember all too well," David growled.

"No," McAllister said softly, "you don't, do you?"

"You have to be stopped," McAllister said suddenly.

David's anger evaporated a bit. He looked at the older man.

He knew it was the truth. He had to be stopped. But he also had to find out where she was, to get her back, to get her away from this man before he could hurt her again. If he hasn't already killed her, that is.

"You can't stop," McAllister continued. "Somebody has to stop you."

"You didn't stop, did you?" David said defensively. It was also an accusation.

"No," McAllister admitted. "But I have control. You are out of control. You can't make yourself stop. You can't let yourself stop."

"I can," David insisted. "I can stop if I want. Now that I found her again I can stop, and I will."

"No you won't," McAllister said. "You never will. I know because you are right, I did make you. I made you into the monster you are, and that monster is not capable of stopping. It's a sick addiction for you. You are broken inside David, and nothing can fix you."

Realization suddenly dawned on David. His jaw went slack and his eyes widened, all the anger suddenly deflated as the shock hit him.

"The bodies," he whispered, staring at McAllister in wonder.

"That was you. I-I thought..." David couldn't finish the sentence.

McAllister nodded.

"You thought it was you," McAllister said. "You thought you were messing up, thinking you buried them when you really put them somewhere else. You even went to the graves to see if the graves were there, and you couldn't find them."

"How?" David asked, his mind reeling.

"I'm very good at what I do," McAllister said simply. "I moved them and hid the graves. You've been sloppy, not tracking where you buried them all. You weren't even sure exactly where their graves were so you missed looking in the right spots entirely."

"There are so many," David said softly, turning inward to himself, seeing the graveyard and its terrible guests spanning the distance before him deep in the woods.

"You moved the bodies," David accused, his voice becoming firm, staring the other man down.

"You moved the bodies so they would be found. You were trying to get me caught."

"I had to," McAllister said gently. It wasn't an apology. There would be none.

"Why?" David asked.

"To stop you," McAllister said.

David felt betrayed.

"You-you took us, kept us, hurt us, and you try to tell me that you have to stop me?! That you have to protect her from me?!" David was getting defiant, his anger coming back again.

"Why didn't you just kill me? If you had to come back to stop me, then why didn't you just kill me? Isn't that what you do? What you are supposed to do?" David stared him down, looking for the answer in his eyes, a muscle twitch, anything.

It was there. He had the answer.

Jason T. McAllister was a monster too, a murderous cold blooded killer. But he could not kill them as children, or let them go, raising them as his own instead.

And he couldn't kill him now. It would be murdering his own son.

David was torn with emotions.

"Where is she?!" David demanded. "Give her to me! So help me, if you've hurt her ..."

"I never hurt you," McAllister said, his voice still gentle as though talking with all the restraint and patience in the world to a troubled youth. "I never hurt either of you."

"YOU DID!" David yelled.

"You hurt us here!" He poked his own head hard with a rigid finger. "And here!" He pounded on his chest with his fist.

"And her accident ..." David trailed off.

McAllister cocked his head, looking at the younger man with a look that was mostly curious.

"You really don't remember, do you?" McAllister said.

"It was you," McAllister continued. "You're the one who hurt her. When I found her-."

McAllister choked a bit, his face showing the emotion that he'd been trying to keep under control.

"When I found her, I thought she was dead," McAllister said. "You thought you had killed her. You blamed me. As kids will do, you couldn't face taking the blame and blamed me for what you did."

McAllister ran his hand through his hair. He suddenly

looked very tired and much older.

"I had to help you get rid of the body."

David couldn't believe it. He didn't want to.

His mind reeled, his head spun and his knees turned weak as the curtains of fog parted a little more in his mind.

He was beginning to remember, but just little bits, scattered and confused.

The barn.

The blood.

Trees.

Walking through the woods carrying a heavy shovel.

Father walking beside him with something slung over one shoulder, carrying it easily as though it weighed little, though he walked as though carrying a terrible weight.

The graves. So many graves.

Digging.

Running through the woods, tears streaming down his face, blinded by them, his stomach tight and painful and his chest being torn from him with the pain that ripped through it inside.

David shook himself out of it and looked at McAllister, his face as twisted with emotions as he felt torn inside, the mixture of feelings pulling him apart to all the corners of the Earth.

"No," he shook his head, the words barely able to escape his lips. "No, it was you. It was you."

"Cassie didn't die, you know," McAllister said. "I found you hiding after what you did. You couldn't even put the words together to tell me what you had done. But you were covered with blood and the look on your face said it all.

I found her in the barn. I thought she was dead too at first. So I made you get the shovel to clean up your own mess.

I wrapped her up and carried her to the woods.

She was still so little.

When you couldn't bury her yourself I had to do it for you.

You ran away. You couldn't face what you did, so you blamed it on me, telling me to my face that I did it."

McAllister choked.

It was the first time he showed real emotion. He couldn't hold it back anymore. He was full of sorrow, regret, and anger, all vying to control his features.

David couldn't say anything at first; though it was obvious he was filled almost to bursting with unsaid things.

"You did it," David said in a low dangerous voice. "You did it. Whatever happened, it was you. You brought the women. You made me help clean up after you were done with them, digging the graves, tossing in the dirt to cover them up. They were people. People!

"You showed me the graves, took me to pick up the other bodies. You showed me how to hide the bodies and when their killers had to die too to protect your secret.

"Whatever I am, the monster I became is you. It's all you. I'm you."

"I know," McAllister said softly. "I'm sorry."

"What happened?" David asked. "When you killed Cassie, what happened?"

He still wasn't ready to admit the truth.

"You know better than I do," McAllister said. "You were there. I just cleaned up your mess."

"She was my sister!" David said, his voice rough with emotion.

"I was supposed to look after her and protect her!"

"Remember the barn," McAllister said, his voice levelling as he fought to control his emotions. "Remember the blood, her screams. You will remember. You're right, it is my fault. I turned you into the monster you are. But you weren't supposed to hurt her. Not Cassie. Not your own sister. And now you don't know how to stop."

The world was beginning to fade away for David as his mind turned inward and the memories swirled inside a black fog in his mind, turning his stomach with their terribleness, a terribleness he couldn't quite see but rather sensed.

And just like that he flashed to the past.

It was dark and shadowy, slats of light coming through rough plank walls. It stunk of ancient manure and stale hay. There were no animals kept there anymore. The manure odor was leached into the wood from decades before, a reminder of

307

what the building was originally built for. It was not meant for this.

Just a boy, David pressed himself harder against the rough planks making up the stall wall, desperately wishing he could disappear.

The smell of blood touched him. It filled his nose until he gagged on it and vomited into the musky stale hay. The blood. So much. So much blood.

He wanted to scream, but he didn't dare.

He stared at his bloodied hands.

Cassie had just had a terrible accident.

Only it wasn't an accident at all.

David peeked through the slats to see her lying there, covered in blood, unmoving, so small. Cassie was dead.

The bile came up into his throat again, burning.

He ran out of the barn, across the yard, and into the shed. Closing the door behind him and blocking out the light, he wedged himself in behind the clutter in there, crouching and hiding in the back.

He sat there for what felt like forever.

He dozed after a while, woken by the sound of a truck.

He shivered and felt cold although it wasn't cold at all. He was ice, his skin clammy and sweaty. He felt weak and nauseous.

Suddenly the shed door opened and the fading sunlight spilled into the dark shed.

His father towered in the doorway.

"Come out of there boy, now," his father commanded.

David couldn't make out his father's face in the shadows with the sun hanging low in the sky behind him, but his voice was cold as ice and dangerously even.

Only somewhere inside he knew this wasn't his father. Not his real father.

This man, this father, was Jason T. McAllister, a young man who seemed to be as old as the world inside.

Reluctantly, David crawled out, terrified of what the man would do.

McAllister looked at him, his face expressionless.

"Damn," he swore angrily, looking the blood covered pale and trembling boy over. "What have you done?!"

"B-b-b-rn," David stammered, not able to even get the whole word out.

McAllister walked away, heading for the barn.

The boy watched mutely, frozen in place. The whole world seemed to swoop and spin, taking him dizzyingly with it.

McAllister returned without a word, his face set hard.

"Get the shovel," McAllister said in a low voice that was seething with barely controlled rage.

David just stared at him mutely from the relative safety of the shed.

"Move!" McAllister barked.

David jumped, and scrabbled to his feet, racing for the barn.

He paused outside, not wanting to go in.

McAllister was behind him, startling him.

"Get in there and grab the shovel," he growled.

David went in, careful not to glance at where he'd left his sister laying in the filth on the floor.

He scurried across and grabbed the shovel.

When he turned around McAllister had the girl's small wrapped body draped over his shoulder like a sack of potatoes.

"Let's go," McAllister said.

Slinging the shovel over his shoulder, the boy followed the man, his shoulders slumped and his body numb with shock.

It was a very long walk through the woods.

When they reached the spot, McAllister set Cassie's body down as gently as he could

The boy dropped the shovel on the ground near her. It made a dull ringing noise as it hit the hard-packed ground despite the dry long grass that failed to cushion the blow.

"Pick up the shovel David," McAllister snapped at David.

David stared at the shovel reluctantly, his body stiffening with resistance.

"Pick it up," McAllister barked. "You will clean up your mess!"

David picked up the shovel angrily, glaring at McAllister with hatred even while his whole body shook with fear of him.

McAllister pointed to a spot on the ground.

"Dig!" he commanded. He watched the boy make half-hearted attempts with the shovel, the boy's frustration and anger visibly mounting.

And then the boy snapped.

He attacked the ground with the shovel, jabbing hard as if he might kill the very Earth; destroy the world by tearing it apart and with it everything that was his life.

McAllister nodded.

"That's it," he said, "let it out."

The boy attacked the hard ground again and again, the violence of the attack growing with his rage until he finally wore himself out.

He faltered, paused, and finally stopped, gasping for air.

He had made very little headway.

Without a word McAllister took the shovel from the boy.

He chopped down with the blade, stabbing the shovel blade strait down at the ground, his arm muscles tense with the effort.

The shovel bit deep, cutting a punishing gash into the ground.

He put his foot on the shovel, pressing down with his weight, leaning on the handle, forcing it deeper before tearing it loose with a shovel-full of clumps of dry hardened dirt.

He stabbed again at the ground with the shovel's blade.

He dug the hole and then gently picked up Cassie's small wrapped body and carefully laid her inside.

David just stood aside watching, sobbing.

McAllister straightened up, turning to the boy grimly.

"Fill it in," he said sternly.

David wavered on his feet, almost swooning at the thought.

"Fill it in, boy!" McAllister barked.

Sobbing harder, David began filling in the dirt over her.

Then suddenly he stopped and tossed the shovel away with a cry of sorrow.

David bolted, running blindly through the woods, screaming with all the torment that tore his soul apart.

McAllister quickly finished filling in the grave, spreading leaves across it to cover it. He would come back later to fix it up better.

He picked up the shovel and started for home.

David had stopped and collapsed by a tree, sobbing until he couldn't sob anymore, exhausted from the emotions and stress of the day.

He was still sitting there, not far from the burial spot, when McAllister strode by purposely with the shovel. He either ignored David or didn't see him.

David watched him pass, looking around frantically as if he might suddenly see before him an escape to another life, shaking even harder than before, his face twisted with anger and loss.

David got up and ran back towards the burial spot, skidding like a baseball player coming into the base just beneath the outstretched hand of an opponent trying to tag him with the ball, dropping down next to the grave.

On hands and knees now he dug frantically at the soil, heedless of the hard mud and stones tearing at his fingers, un-burying the small wrapped body of his sister.

He pulled her from the ground, sobbing, tearing the blanket away from her head, uncovering her face, checking her for breath, wiping away the dirt with loving hands.

"Cassie, Cassie, I'm so sorry sis, I'm sorry," he sobbed.

He looked around desperately as if for help to materialize, his heart pounded in his chest. It felt impossibly swollen with sorrow.

Cassie's small body hung frail and limp and lifeless in his arms. He tried to wipe away the dirt and blood with his tears. She seemed so tiny in his hands, the hands of a boy.

He looked desperately through the trees.

Father would be at the barn by now, cleaning up the blood.

He looked back down at the partially wrapped body.

He saw her as she was on the floor of the dim barn, broken and lifeless.

She was covered in wet blood, turning sticky as it thickened and congealed, drying into a crust, its odor filling the barn despite the wide open doors and draughty broken slats of the walls so that he could taste it when he inhaled. It turned his stomach with a metallic queasiness, exhilarating him at the same time.

311

Cassie was gone. Dead.

David wailed in sorrow and loss, filling the trees and the sky with his grief.

He hugged her lifeless body close, sobbing.

When he got up at last he staggered off, leaving her on the ground like a discarded rag doll. Then he jogged. Then he ran. He ran hard, not paying attention, hoping he would slam into a tree with enough force to kill him.

"I found Cassie when I went back later," McAllister said. "You dug her up and left her. I was going to wrap her up again and rebury her, but when I went to wrap the body I saw something, a flicker of life. She was alive. Barely, but she was still alive after all that.

I—I couldn't bring myself to just bury her alive. I had to get rid of her. I couldn't take her to the hospital obviously, and she was so badly hurt. I couldn't just leave her like that either.

I couldn't bring myself to finish her, to strangle her with my own hands."

McAllister looked down at his hands with disgust, as if they were dirtied beyond ever being clean again. He went on with his story.

"I went back to the barn. To get the shovel and something else to cover her with so I wouldn't have to look at the shape of her tiny body as I beat her to death.

When I returned Cassie was gone.

I was frantic. I raced around the woods searching nearby, I ran to the highway.

I got there just in time to see a couple putting her in their car and driving away.

Cassie was stronger than either of us thought. She must have woke up and wandered to the road."

David stared at him in shock.

"I tried to keep tabs on her, watching for any chance to take her. But I lost track of her after that, as if the child welfare system had just swallowed her up like she'd never even existed.

My only hope was that she'd blocked it all out, that she'd forgotten and had no memories of anything she'd seen, and that

I'd been careful enough to not let her see anything. I had always been careful of that, after all little girls should not be subjected to stuff like that."

Even in his cruel abuse of the women he killed, McAllister still in his own way tried to protect the children.

"We had to move on after that, just in case," McAllister continued. "I kept looking for her though. And then a few years later you ran away.

You were easy to find, and to keep tabs on, but I never found her until her face appeared in the newspaper."

He paused, letting it all sink in.

One thought stuck in David's mind with the heavy pall of dread. He found me! How soon after I ran?!

McAllister's next words barely registered.

"I'm going to stop you David," McAllister whispered, "even if I have to kill you to do it."

50

David couldn't believe what he just heard.

The revelation that it was he, not McAllister who had hurt his sister was hard enough to swallow.

He would not have believed it had the terrible memory not come crashing over him, a memory that left him as weak as if he were on his deathbed, his limbs shivering with the effort to keep him standing. He was bathed in a cold sweat that stunk of fear.

McAllister looked past David, his attention drawn by something in the distance.

David turned around to look.

A car was approaching.

An ancient brown Oldsmobile creaked and waddled along the trail towards the house, it's protesting springs audible even at this distance as it rumbled over the rough drive.

"Damn!" David muttered.

He was visible to the occupants of the car. He knew they had to have seen him, even though they were too far away to recognize him.

They may not have seen McAllister, however.

Apparently McAllister wasn't waiting around to find out.

McAllister bolted for the woods, running surprisingly fast for a man his age on his long legs.

"Shit!" David swore.

There was nothing to do for it but to wait. He tried to push back all the emotions, to calm his trembling limbs and make his face passive and expressionless.

McNelly thought his kidneys would be bumped out with the hard rocking of the car as he drove slowly towards the abandoned farmhouse.

"Where the hell are they?" he muttered. "Where's my backup? They're supposed to meet me here."

At last the Oldsmobile arrived and rocked to a stop. The engine cutting with what sounded like a death rattle.

McNelly looked around before opening the door. He thought

314

he'd seen two figures standing close together in the distance, but now there was only one man.

He must have been mistaken, a trick of the distance and long dry grass and the trees waving in the breeze behind the man.

The driver's door squealed and groaned as McNelly opened it and got out.

He looked at David in surprise.

"Michael!" McNelly exclaimed.

McNelly looked around.

"How'd you get here? Where's your car? You didn't come in this, did you?" McNelly indicated the dark blue car and two-toned truck parked nearby.

He looked again at the truck, recognizing it from the description.

"McAllister," McNelly muttered.

Michael's mind was working quickly.

"Uh, I uh, I parked down the road and hidden, just inside some bushes," Michael said quickly. "I wanted to come in unnoticed, check this place out. Just in case, you know."

McNelly turned to him.

"You got my message?" McNelly asked.

"Message?" Michael seemed dumbfounded.

Clearly he hadn't gotten any of McNelly's many messages or he would have known immediately what he was talking about.

McNelly studied Michael.

"What are you up to?" McNelly thought.

"I had a hunch about this place," Michael said, seeing the suspicion in the other man's eyes. "Well, not about this place exactly, but places like it. Abandoned, out of the way; I was checking them out. Guess I was mostly out of the service range for my phone."

"Anyone here?" McNelly asked.

"No, I don't think so," Michael said.

"Whose vehicles are these?" McNelly asked.

"Don't know," Michael said. "I was going to run the plates when I got back."

"Well, my backup was supposed to meet me here," McNelly said, clearly annoyed that they weren't there yet. "They aren't

315

here, but there's two of us. We should start looking around this place, at least get the place locked down."

McNelly pulled his gun and held it at the ready, pointing to the ground. Michael pulled his from a holster hidden beneath his clothes, following his lead. They started a cursory search around the open yard of the property, not seeing much of anything.

Every now and then McNelly glanced at Michael, his look curious and a little bit suspicious.

"I'll check the house," Michael said, "you check the barn."

McNelly shrugged and turned towards the barn, about to head in that direction.

Michael started anxiously for the house.

Just then the sound of vehicles rumbling over the rough path to the house could be heard.

Backup had arrived.

They were rocking and bobbing hard as they approached quickly over the rough trail.

It was only two cars.

McNelly had expected more than that.

Michael's heart sank. He had known McNelly wouldn't likely come alone. But when the man came on scene without backup he had hoped this would be the exception. Or, at least the backup would run late enough for him to deal with the situation, although he didn't know how yet.

He glanced quickly at the house.

How would he keep them out of there? This was serious. He could not let them in the house to find Kathy.

He jogged over to the vehicles as they pulled to a stop next to McNelly's Oldsmobile.

McNelly was slowly waddling over. He never seemed to do anything quickly.

"Hey guys," Michael said as the officers got out of their cars.

He looked about as if looking for something. In a way he was.

"This it?" Michael asked.

"Oh there's more," one of the officers said.

"Where the hell's the rest of them?" McNelly demanded angrily.

The officer turned to him.

"We thought we'd come in on all sides," the officer said.

McNelly gritted his teeth, annoyed.

"When you're done playing SWAT, we have a farm to search," McNelly growled.

They turned toward the woods that pressed against the edge of the farmyard, their attention drawn by the sound of dry branches crackling and breaking.

Two officers walked out of the trees, preceded by McAllister, their weapons trained on the square of his back as they followed him out. His hands were cuffed behind his back.

"Caught this guy making a run for it through the woods," one of them shouted.

The officer turned back to McNelly.

"Glad we're playing SWAT now?" he said. Clearly he was put out by McNelly's comment.

McNelly just gave him a look that said "shut up".

The officers from the woods approached the group with their prisoner.

At the same time other officers began to arrive from other directions. They did indeed have the farm surrounded.

McNelly glanced at Michael, wondering why he looked so agitated. He turned his gaze to McAllister, ready to say something.

McAllister glanced at Michael, his look an unreadable message.

McNelly caught the look and glanced quickly at Michael, curious, just in time to catch the look Michael gave the other man.

Was that a warning?

McNelly had the distinctly unpleasant feeling that something was going on here that he didn't know about.

"Alright," McNelly said, looking around to include everyone, "let's get this show on the road."

The two cops took McAllister and put him in the back of a squad car.

McNelly started directing the search efforts, sending the men in two's to search the barn, the shed, and the tall grass along the edge of the woods.

"I'll check the house," Michael offered again.

McNelly nodded.

"Go with him" McNelly said to two officers who had not yet been assigned a job.

Michael quickly jumped in.

"It's ok," he said. "This is a pretty big place. Maybe it would be better if they looked somewhere else. You know, spread out our resources."

"Now why is he so intent on that house?" McNelly wondered, though he didn't dwell on it. It didn't seem important at the moment. He chalked it up to Michael letting himself get too attached to the Jane Doe. He was probably anxious to find her, although he should know protocol enough. You never go alone into an unknown situation.

If they did ever find her McNelly was certain she wouldn't be alive. The thought made his gut burn.

He pulled Michael aside, waving the two officers to go get on with the search.

"Look," McNelly said, "you know the rules. You don't go in alone. We don't know what's in there. We'll do a cursory search for now. If there is anyone alive on this farm, we'll find her."

One of the officers who first arrived gave a quick call on his radio.

Minutes later the sound of more vehicles approaching would announce the arrival of more police vehicles, ones that had dropped the men off and then held back on approaching the farm.

Michael was very anxious now.

"Crap, shit, damn!" he swore silently in his head.

He couldn't hide the agitation now. It was plain as day.

McNelly put a hand on his shoulder, trying to comfort him.

"If Jane Doe is alive we'll find her," McNelly said.

Only it wasn't Jane Doe that Michael was freaked out about.

He started a few times, making himself stop, wanting to go racing into the house and throw the cops out before they could find her.

It didn't take long.

One of the officers appeared at the open doorway of the

house, grimacing as he stepped out into the sun.

Behind him the other officer helped a blanket wrapped figure out the door.

Michael's chest felt ready to burst. He felt sick and dizzy, his legs so weak he was sure they wouldn't be able to hold him up.

He thought he would implode at any moment. He seemed to be getting sucked into himself, the world around him spinning wildly out of control even as it pressed down on him, threatening to crush him in a giant invisible fist.

"Kathy—" he thought desperately, the rest of the thought never materializing.

He was scared. More scared than he had ever been in his life. What would she do?

Michael watched silently as the officers led Kathy past him and McNelly.

She clung to the blanket they had wrapped around her, an automatic quick fix for anyone who might be in a state of shock, and she certainly had every reason to be. She walked a little unsteadily, blinded by the sunlight she wasn't used to, her eyes watering and her vision blurred from the sudden change from the dim lighting inside to the world outside.

She kept her head held high, not looking at him but passing him by with a silent expression that he couldn't read.

She looked at the man in the back of a patrol car she was brought past, turning to stare straight ahead again, her face passive and expressionless.

They put her in the back of another car to wait while they radioed for an ambulance.

She never uttered a word, nor did she look directly at anyone except McAllister.

What she was thinking was known only to herself.

Michael's whole world was gone, like a bubble that suddenly popped.

51

Months had gone by since the taking of the McAllister farm.

Between Connie's body found buried hastily in the woods, the nurse in the car's trunk, and the discovery of Katherine inside the farmhouse, they had enough evidence to put Jason T. McAllister away for the rest of his life.

They had also found the hospital gown and intravenous linking him to the still missing Jane Doe.

A massive search was conducted of the woods adjacent to the farm property, as well as the ongoing search of the area of the woods where the secret graveyard was found.

Jim McNelly looked worse with every passing day, blaming himself for every victim, drinking and smoking more.

He knew without a doubt that McAllister was involved in murdering at least some of the women in the makeshift cemetery in the woods.

He knew with even more certainty that the man was somehow involved in burying many more victims of other killers in that graveyard.

But what he didn't know was how to prove it beyond a reasonable doubt.

They had no proof of anything.

Even his presence at the McAllister farm and the fact he owned the property was not absolute proof of guilt. The place had been abandoned for years, and he had been living elsewhere during that time, hundreds of miles away. The fact he drove his truck across country to get there planted a large seed of doubt against his guilt despite the circumstantial evidence against him.

That didn't stop McNelly from trying to get the man convicted on the circumstantial evidence they did have.

The trial took months of gruelling testimonies, thousands of exhibits, and a lot of strain on everyone.

The one living witness, the woman rescued from the farmhouse, had proven to be of no help.

It seemed that Kathy had been so traumatized by her experience that she could not even recognize her own abductor.

They had tried everything.

When faced with a police line-up, McAllister square in the middle seeming entirely unconcerned while the other men shifted uncomfortably, she silently shook her head, looking at the men behind the glass with a look of such confusion, as if she didn't understand why they were even there.

When sat down with books of photographs, she idly turned the pages over as if she were looking through a magazine she wasn't really interested in reading, casting questioning looks at detectives Michael Underwood and Jim McNelly, yet not saying a word.

It was unknown if even the psychiatrists were able to get her to talk at all. The first one, called in the day they found her to help her work through her terrible ordeal, had quit saying he couldn't help her and giving no further explanation. He seemed very agitated. The second one has been working with her ever since, but those conversations are protected and not available to the investigators.

The third psychiatrist, there to assess Kathy and testify in court on her condition resulting from her trauma of being kidnapped and held captive, said she was too traumatized by both her kidnapping and other events and couldn't seem to keep them straight.

He testified that she seemed to confuse the abuse she suffered at the hands of her boyfriend and being kidnapped, which she seemed to see almost as a rescue despite the fact they found her weakened from near starvation and discovered where she'd mostly been kept locked in deplorable conditions in a dirt floored root cellar with no windows and very little light, with no access to toilet or water to wash with.

And when she was finally rescued, to learn that her boyfriend had been brutally murdered in what was probably the most savage beating anyone on the force had ever seen seemed to have put her over the edge. She responded only with a soft sigh and hint of a smile at the corners of her mouth.

All of these things seemed to conspire to put the woman in a terrible state.

She was in shock, suffering from a severe case of post-traumatic stress disorder, which was entirely to be expected. However, she seemed unable to discuss what had happened, and the psychiatrist was adamant that talking about it and facing it was absolutely necessary for her to assimilate it and move on.

During the trial, on the days Kathy was in the courtroom, she sat passively listening to the prosecution describe a horrific tale of kidnappings and murder in all the appalling details of the brutal attacks against the victims.

She watched without reaction as hundreds of items were shown and described.

On the first day, when asked to stand up and point out her kidnapper, she looked at Jason McAllister in the prisoner's box in confusion. She turned and stared at the detectives, Michael Underwood and Jim McNelly who sat in the gallery as if looking to them for an answer as to what she was to do, and finally sat down staring straight ahead without a word or gesture, as if she didn't know what was being asked of her.

The defence argued that McAllister wasn't even present to commit the crimes, and that he had in fact abandoned the farm property, the property taxes paid by an old family trust fund he wasn't even aware of, and had moved some distance away.

Their entire defence was based on his absence and that someone else must have been using the abandoned property.

Finally, the trial of James T. McAllister came to a close and the jury was sequestered to make their decision.

The media was having a heyday with it and there was little choice but to lock the jury away from the influence of all those wild rumours and speculations.

It took them seven and a half weeks to come to a decision.

And then the verdict came in at last.

Guilty.

They didn't find him guilty on all counts. Hell, they didn't find him guilty on most of the counts. There simply wasn't the evidence available.

The question of whether McAllister was involved in operating a network of serial killers, helping them dispose of their corpses, was never resolved.

He was, however found guilty of the kidnapping and

imprisonment of Kathy and the kidnapping and murders of Connie and the Nurse, Molly.

They still haven't found the woman who's almost lifeless body was discovered dumped in the trash, seemingly beginning it all.

Jane Doe was still a big unanswered question.

Who was Jane Doe and what did McAllister do with her?

Without a body, McAllister was acquitted for the murder of Jane Doe.

However, he was found guilty of kidnapping Jane Doe, twice, although it was counted as only one count.

The guilty verdicts were small consolation for all the people involved in the case, people who had so much invested in bringing it to a close and seeing justice done.

McNelly sat at the table in Peabody's pub, the newspaper folded on the table in front of him. He stared at the headlines, his beer already turned piss warm.

His gut roiled and gurgled, the acid creeping up and burning.

The paper was two weeks old already, looking bedraggled, and circular rings stained into it from coffee and beer. A small hole, its edges darkened and charred, marked where a cigarette ash had fallen on the paper before being hastily swept off on the floor.

GUILTY: JAMES T. MCALLISTER FACING POSSIBLE DEATH PENALTY FOR KIDNAPPING AND MURDERS OF MULTIPLE WOMEN.

Today the judge was supposed to announce the sentencing date.

This was supposed to be the time for celebratory drinks, but he felt anything but celebratory.

Everyone was certain McAllister would get the death penalty, including the newspapers apparently.

McNelly wasn't so sure.

For Jim McNelly this case was not yet closed.

McNelly grabbed the newspaper, getting up and leaving without touching the beer. He left with the weight of unfinished business riding on his shoulders.

Doors clanged and echoed hollowly from somewhere inside the brick penitentiary. It seemed to be an incessant background noise.

The guard led Michael up the aisle of cells in their most secure wing.

This was the block where the prison kept the worst of the worst. They were kept alone, one man per cell, and seldom allowed out of their cells. When they were allowed out to use any of the prison's facilities, it was only when the rest of the prisoners were safely locked in their cells, and always well escorted by guards.

It was a question of safety for the prisoners. This was protective custody.

The man Detective Michael Underwood was coming to visit was in protective custody.

He followed a guard down the echoing hallway of cells in the protective custody ward.

When they arrived at the cell, it was empty.

The guard shrugged.

"They must've known you were coming," the guard said. "He must have already been put in an interview room. Follow me."

Michael wondered at that. He hadn't sent word ahead that he was coming. McNelly maybe? Maybe.

They retraced their steps, were let out back through the locked door at the end, and the guard led him up another hall towards the private interrogation rooms. These were used for visits that could not be held in the general visitor's rooms; usually meetings with lawyers and prison psychologists.

There, Michael was let into one of the rooms.

McAllister sat inside, his wrists and ankles shackled.

He was being kept in a maximum security prison while waiting for sentencing, a tribute to how dangerous he was considered to be.

The room held a single table bolted to the floor and two chairs. A small reinforced window in the door allowed the guard to look in to see that everything was alright, but could not hear the conversation inside if was kept at a reasonable talking volume.

McAllister was dozing in the chair. He woke up when the door opened.

He looked at Michael calmly as the guard allowed the younger man in, closing the heavy door behind him.

They were alone.

McAllister's shoulders shook as he let out a little chuckle.

"What's so funny?" Michael asked.

"They couldn't convict me of anything I did, but they got me on your crimes, David." McAllister seemed amused by this.

"They're your crimes as much as mine," Michael said. "You made me what I am.

"That I did, David, that I did," McAllister said a little regretfully.

He looked serious now.

"I never would have been caught you know, if I didn't try to get you busted."

"That's because I don't exist," Michael said. "I made up Michael Underwood, and the little boy you kidnapped was presumed dead a very long time ago. That leaves only you."

McAllister shook his head with a chuckle.

"You were sloppy, but not as sloppy as I thought," he said.

Michael's expression changed. He had questions, but the answers to some weren't that important. Others, the answers were very important.

"Why her?" Michael asked. "Why my mom?"

McAllister shrugged.

"She was pretty," McAllister said. "I liked her. I always liked women of a certain type. She was my type."

Michael nodded. He understood, but he still wanted nothing more than to tear this man apart and kill him in the most horrific way. He kept his face calm and curious, controlling the emotions inside him.

"My dad?" Michael asked. "What happened to him?"

McAllister shrugged again.

"Don't know," he said. "He wasn't around when I took her—took you."

McAllister studied Michael's face, seeing the boy he used to be hidden in that hard man's face.

"He was cheating on her, you know," McAllister said.

Michael gave him a questioning look.

"Your dad, he was having an affair," McAllister went on. "Do you remember how unhappy she always was? How much they fought every time he went out or came home late? How often she cried when she thought you wouldn't see? Maybe you were too young to remember. He was leaving her for another woman. I felt bad for her, being so sad and alone."

"So you killed her," Michael said softly, keeping his voice even.

"Yeah, I guess so," McAllister said softly.

"After all these years," McAllister changed the direction of the conversation, "they catch me for your crimes."

"You did enough of your own," Michael said. "It doesn't make much difference which ones they got you for."

"I guess not," McAllister agreed.

"You can't go on as Michael Underwood, you know," McAllister said.

"I know," Michael replied.

"She's ok with all this?" McAllister didn't believe the woman his son kept alive would be.

"She is," Michael said.

Michael had one more thing he needed to ask, an answer he needed.

"Where is she?" he asked. "Where is Cassie?"

"Safe," McAllister said.

"Tell me." Michael was getting more insistent. "Where's my sister? Is she alive or did you kill her? Did you leave her locked away somewhere to die while you were here?" He waved his arm wide to indicate the prison. "Is she safe and alive somewhere?"

His voice was getting loud enough for the guard outside to hear.

The guard's face appeared in the window, checking to make sure the prisoner was behaving himself.

McAllister gave the guard a benign wave.

Michael turned around, waving the man off.

Controlling his voice again, lowering his tone, he demanded harshly.

"Where is my sister?!" It was the low warning growl a dog might give.

McAllister's refusal to answer was making him angry.

McAllister shook his head.

"I'll never tell you," he said.

Michael knew it was useless. The man will never tell.

He had to stop his hands from shaking, control his anger.

He went to the door and pounded on it to get the guard's attention, glaring at McAllister.

Michael turned to the door just as the guard's face appeared in the window, signalling to the guard that the meeting was done.

"They'll give you the death sentence you know," Michael said.

McAllister smiled, it was a knowing smile, full of calm confidence.

"No, they won't," he said. "I know where the bodies are."

Just then there was a sound of metal on metal at the door, the guard unlocking it to let Michael out.

The guard opened the door, holding it open for him.

Michael paused in the doorway, looking back at the man who had pretended to be his father for so many years, the man who had taken everything away from him.

He turned away and walked out without saying goodbye.

"I'll show myself out," he said to the guard and headed off down the hall, vanishing around a corner as the guard radioed in that the prisoner was about to be moved.

McNelly walked past as the guard was getting ready to move McAllister back to his cell. The guard nodded at him and McNelly nodded back.

When he stepped out of the prison, Michael felt a sudden uplifting, a soaring freedom, as if he had just been released from the very prison he was walking away from.

A little distance away, standing alone beside a picnic table on the lawn, Kathy waited for him. The sunlight shone off her, turning her into an even more wonderful sight. The breeze playing with the skirt of her sundress, dancing her hair, somehow made the vision that much more beautiful.

He smiled and walked to her.

Kathy looked at him, her eyes full of questions and concern for him.

He turned his smile on her.

"Everything's fine," he said. "Let's go."

He took her hand in his, turned his head and looked down at the little girl standing on the other side of him, taking her hand too.

"Everything's going to be just fine Cassie," he smiled to the little girl, "you'll see."

Kathy looked around to see who was there, saw no one, and looked up at him, confused.

"Who are you talking to?" she asked.

He smiled at her.

"Nobody," he said softly as he walked forward, leading his two girls along to the parking lot.

68067362R00184

Made in the USA
Charleston, SC
06 March 2017